ALMS FOR OBLIVION

Other titles by the same author

Sleep of Death

Death of Kings

The Pale Companion

ALMS FOR OBLIVION

PHILIP GOODEN

Constable · London

Constable & Robinson Ltd
3 The Lanchesters
162 Fulham Palace Road
London W6 9ER
www.constablerobinson.com

First published in the UK by Constable,
an imprint of Constable & Robinson Ltd 2003

A copy of the British Library Cataloguing in
Publication Data is available from the British Library

ISBN 1-84119-382-8

Printed and bound in the EU

Time hath, my lord, a wallet at his back
Wherein he puts alms for oblivion,
A great-sized monster of ingratitude.

Troilus and Cressida, 3, iii

Vita Brevis

My boyhood friend Peter Agate arrived in London on a foggy morning in the autumn of 1602. Within a few days he was dead and it was the general belief that I had killed him.

There was a grim aptness to my address at the time: Dead Man's Place. This Southwark street was closer to the Globe playhouse where I worked than some of my other London lodgings had been. That was in its favour. Against it was the street name and the character of my landlord, Samuel Benwell.

I didn't care about Dead Man's Place, or not much anyway, but I struggled to show the same indifference towards my landlord as I did towards the name of his street. There was nothing absolutely wrong with Master Samuel Benwell except his prying interest in the private doings of my Company. He preferred his own sex, I knew, since he had once approached me in a very familiar fashion, with practised hands and averted eyes, and been rebuffed. He didn't seem to mind, as long as I continued to answer questions about what we players got up to – or what he hoped we got up to. I might have taken offence at Benwell's assumption that we spent most of our time pleasuring each other, but it would have been churlish. I owed him something for his easy acceptance of my rejection. Besides, it was true that the Chamberlain's Men had three or four who were that way inclined, even if we were no different in this respect from other playhouse companies.

Humouring Master Benwell was worth money to me. By some unspoken arrangement, we settled on a lowish rent in exchange for which I tantalized him with theatre gossip. In truth, Master Benwell provided most of the talking. Licking his lips and with a queer, glazed look coming into his eyes, he would ask me a long, complicated question that gave him more pleasure in the unravelling than any answer might provide. A question as to the lodging arrangements of our boy apprentices; or whether in our tire-house and elsewhere in the playhouse there were nooks and cupboards where conversations of an intimate nature might be conducted. Was it true, he asked, that young Martin Hancock, who had not so long ago played Viola in *Twelfth Night*, was a notorious catamite? Messrs Burbage and Shakespeare now, Dick and Will, were they privy bedfellows? This last item I indignantly denied but I assented to most of the rest, sometimes adding a flourish or two of my own while making it clear that my tastes were more orthodox.

As he listened to my answers, Master Benwell's mouth hung open and his tongue licked round his thin lips. His tooth-work and his lip-work were not sights to relish. This was tedious but – as I kept reminding myself – it was worth three whole pennies a week to me, the difference between the rent he'd initially proposed (one shilling and threepence) and the shilling we settled for. Benwell had no other tenants. His place was like his mind, pretty filthy. I don't know what he did. Hanging about seemed to be his principal occupation.

Hanging about was what he was doing on that mid-morning when I finally groped my way back to my lodgings. Fog had draped itself over Southwark like a greasy coat and I couldn't see more than a few yards. I was returning to Dead Man's Place because, in my hurried departure that morning, I'd forgotten the little bundle of scrolls containing my lines. I'd been about to enter the Globe when I realized this. It wouldn't have mattered if I'd been word-perfect, but I wasn't. Since this was our first rehearsal Richard Burbage would forgive me for not being word-perfect. What he wouldn't forgive was my coming to the playhouse without my lines, a fact he was bound to discover the moment I started stumbling over them. If he was in a bad mood, I might even be fined. So, in the bustling delay which always seems to attend a rehearsal in its early stages, I reckoned I'd have enough time to slip back to Dead Man's Place and pick up my lines.

Forgetting my part was something I'd never have done in my early days with the Chamberlain's. I suppose it was a sign of how much more easy I felt in the Company. Well, there's such a thing as being too comfortable. Certainly, this was not a comfortable morning to be abroad in. The fog seemed to have grown thicker and danker as well as nastier-smelling since I'd quit my warm bed that morning. (Reluctance to get up until the last moment was the reason for my hasty, scroll-forgetting departure.) If I hadn't been very familiar with the route between playhouse and lodging I might easily have taken the wrong turning.

I reached Master Benwell's front door by instinct and quickly opened and closed it, as if the fog could be excluded. A few wisps and tatters sneaked in all the same.

"Master Nicholas."

I was used by now to my landlord's silent presence. That is, you might think you were alone and turn round to see, oh yes, Master Benwell leaning against the wall or tucked into a corner. So I didn't start in surprise when he uttered my name but was already shaping in my mind a brisk excuse that I didn't have time to stop and talk – must get back to the playhouse – only returned for my part. No, not 'part' . . . Benwell would be quick to seize on the word and examine it for hidden filth . . . you had to watch your mouth around Benwell.

"You have a friend, Nicholas."

"I hope so," I said. "More than one on a good day."

"I mean a *visitor* and a friend," said Benwell, standing in the dimness of the little hallway. "At least he claimed he was your friend."

"What was his name, Master Benwell?"

"He didn't want to give it."

"Did he seem honest?"

"Do you have friends who aren't?" countered my landlord.

"Legions of them. Rogues and scoundrels all."

"You naughty players," he said.

"You know us," I said, moving towards the stairs.

"I showed him up," said Benwell.

I stopped in my tracks.

"Why, was he at fault?"

Oh, the sword-like flash of wit on a damp, foggy morning. At the same time, I puzzled over the real meaning of Benwell's words or rather over the identity of the person waiting for me in my first-floor room.

"What?" said Benwell. "Oh, I have you now . . . was he at fault? Ha. No, he said he was a friend. He seemed honest. I wouldn't have 'showed him up' otherwise. Oh, you *stage people*."

While my landlord was rattling on in the gloom, I went rapidly through some possibilities. No man likes to be surprised in the room where he makes his bed. So my visitor wouldn't give his name. Why not?

A creditor?

Well, yes, I had a couple of creditors. There was Martin Bly for example. But the few shillings which I owed to the landlord of the Goat & Monkey tavern for sack and ale – very little of it consumed by my abstemious self (I priggishly add) – would not justify a personal visit to my room. And then there was the more than few shillings for which I was in debt to Master Benjamin Nicholson, a bookseller in St Paul's Yard. A few pounds in fact. But *he* wouldn't bother to come calling for money owing to him.

It's a little sad if the only unexpected visitor you can expect is a creditor, so I speedily summoned up a more worthy alternative. A rival in love? But this didn't seem to fit the case either.

Who was my unknown visitor then?

And suddenly I had it.

It must be someone from another company of players, someone who'd come to offer me more money and bigger parts than the Chamberlain's provided. Hence the anonymity, the touch of mystery. A delicate mission, you understand.

Such is the odd way the human mind works – or the way mine works at any rate – that I'd no sooner got hold of this idea than I became convinced of its truth. Upstairs in my room was waiting an emissary from, say, Henslowe of the Admiral's Men, a rival group of players. I'd once worked briefly for Henslowe, which added a bit of backbone to this belief. Also there was the fact that an apparent agent of Henslowe's, a rather dislikeable man called Gally, had been hanging around the Chamberlain's haunts recently, maybe in the hope of enticing some of us away. These were competitive times in the London playhouses. Now I thought that Henslowe must have heard of my new eminence with Chamberlain's. Of course, I'd turn down any offer, however extravagant, however coaxing . . . but it is agreeable to be asked.

All of this went through my head in about a twentieth of the time it takes to tell it and a smile must have been sneaking about my lips.

"Pleasant thoughts of your gentleman friend upstairs?" said Benwell, whose eyes glimmered in the grey light of the lobby.

"I must go and see who it is," I said, but inwardly convinced of the situation I've just described. I bounded up the narrow flight of stairs two steps at a time, wishing to give to Master Henslowe's man an impression of energy and purpose even on a miserable morning like this one. I'd altogether forgotten about my playscript, the original purpose in returning to my lodgings.

I flung open the door of my room. The light was very poor – the window was pinched and dirty, and the fog seemed to have permeated my chamber too – but, after a moment's hesitation, I recognized the stooping figure standing uneasily near my bed. There wasn't much space to stand anywhere else and the lowness of the ceiling meant that anybody who was taller than average had to hunch up a bit. All the same this person was hunched up more than necessary. I knew that stance, that stoop.

It wasn't anybody from Philip Henslowe's company.

I wasn't about to be offered a new job.

There was nothing for me to turn down.

"Hello, Peter," I said.

"Nick. I knew it was you. I heard your voice downstairs."

Peter Agate gestured awkwardly at my meagre furnishings as if it was *his* room and he was apologizing for the inadequacy of our surroundings. Like the stooping posture, this tentative gesture was typical of him.

"You were the last person I expected," I said.

"I'm sorry to disappoint you – if you were expecting someone else."

"Not at all. I wasn't expecting anyone. I wouldn't usually be here at this time of day."

The absurdity of my earlier speculation – that my visitor was from another acting company, come to tempt me to greater things – rushed back on me. I was glad of the dimness of the room, since Peter couldn't witness the warmth that now spread across my face. It might have been embarrassment that caused me to repeat, "Not at all."

And I moved towards Peter Agate and wrapped him in my arms and he responded by wrapping his around me, with a sigh of relief, I think, at discovering that his old country friend Nick Revill was still his friend in the very different circumstances of the city.

After we'd released each other we stood back. Like true Englishmen, we were a little uncomfortable at renewed friendship.

"Your landlord was good enough to allow me to wait up here. I hope you don't mind."

"My dear fellow," I said in a magnanimous fashion and then, thinking better of this, modified it to, "Dear Peter . . . you've given him stuff to think on for weeks. He couldn't wait to tell me that I had a visitor."

"He asked if I was a – a player," said Peter. I thought I detected an odd catch in his voice and wondered whether he was insulted by my landlord's speculation.

"Oh, Master Benwell loves plays and players. He loves the *backstage* aspect of things. He will talk to you for hours about it. But you didn't give anything away? Not even your name?"

"Just being cautious, Nick."

I regarded the tall, shambling figure in front of me. He looked no different to my eyes, no different in outline anyway. I wondered whether I seemed different to him.

"What were you going to do? Wait for me until I came back?"

"I suppose so."

"I might have been hours."

"I'm sorry. I couldn't think of anything else to do."

"Don't say sorry," I said.

"Sorry," he said again.

"The same old Peter," I said. "Another apology and I shall kill you."

This rough speech was a way of trying to reassure him that everything between us was as it had always been – although we hadn't seen each other for, oh, more than three years.

He laughed, mildly.

"You're probably wondering why I'm here?"

"Not yet. Any question like that is swallowed up in the pleasure of seeing you once more."

True, I hadn't yet started to wonder at his presence in London, in Southwark, in Dead Man's Place, in my room – I was genuinely pleased to see my old Somerset friend again, no lie – but of course as soon as he mentioned it, I did start to wonder why he was here. There was a pause.

"You have a London gloss, Nick. You have acquired manners. Address."

"You'll find me the same country lad underneath," I said.

Another pause.

I sensed that Peter had something to say, probably a story to tell. At the same time I recalled the reason why I'd returned to my lodgings.

"I normally wouldn't be here, only I forgot my scroll – my part in the play we're practising."

I reached across to the rickety little table where my few possessions were piled and took the rolled-up papers.

"There's a rehearsal I must attend immediately," I said. "Otherwise Burbage will use my guts to tie his points."

"That would be Cuthbert?"

"No, it would be his brother Dick. But you're well informed."

"For a country lad."

"Town or country. Most Londoners know of Dick Burbage, but not so many could name Cuthbert. He's more behind the scenes. Which is where I ought to be now, if you'll forgive me. We shall talk later."

I made to go through the door then stopped and considered.

"If I were you, Peter, I wouldn't want to spend two or three hours shivering in an ill-lit room. There's an ale-house nearby. The Goat & Monkey. A players' place, if you don't object to that. Martin Bly's the landlord."

I said this, I must confess, not only because I was thinking of my friend's comfort but also because I wanted to show off my familiarity with the neighbourhood. I almost added, in reference to his drinking at the good old Goat, 'Put it on my slate,' before reflecting that patronage can go too far. (Also I was reflecting on that little debt of mine.)

"Thank you, Nick," said Peter. "I have no objection to a players' place, none at all. I'll try it."

I gave him a couple of directions, making them pretty precise on account of the weather, and said I'd join him in the tavern as soon as I could. As I paced speedily through the fog in the direction of the Globe, hoping that I wouldn't have been missed yet, part of my mind was occupied with the question of exactly why Peter Agate had quit his home in Somerset and suddenly appeared in London.

Like me, Peter came from the village of Miching. Or rather he came from outside that spot, a place once lovely, now blighted. He was lucky in being a little removed from the village – as I had been lucky. The memory of that early spring morning returned, its terrible flavours and colours hardly diminished. That bright morning when I had run down towards my birthplace, fear taking tighter and tighter hold of my guts.

I saw myself, as if from the outside, leaping over stones, skidding on the downhill path, rounding blind corners, the dead silence of the village masked by my panting breath and the blood thudding in my ears. I'd been absent, trying to get a position with a troupe of players, a hopeless excursion, nothing came of it (except that my absence saved my life). While I was away the plague struck. My father and mother, the parson of the village and his wife, died. So did most of the rest of the village. I don't know how many exactly. I didn't stop to find out. After I witnessed my neighbours' bodies being forked into a common pit, after I saw the red cross splashed on my parents' door, I ran and ran. I spent that night shivering and weeping on some open high ground above the Bristol Channel. I almost caught my death of cold.

But I wasn't the only survivor from our hamlet. The Agates were the wealthiest family in Miching, living in a residence that maintained a proper distance from the village folk. Their manor – called Quint House – was set apart, on a place where the ground rose. The parson and the squire and the schoolmaster stand out even in a modest village, by reason of their education or their rank and riches. It could be said that they cling together, having no true equals among the other inhabitants. In particular the parson may well cling to the lord of the manor when the parish is in the gift of the latter. Peter's grandfather, also called Peter, had been the patron of Miching parish. Many years before, he had bestowed the living on my father. In turn my father often bestowed compliments on old Peter Agate. In my hearing he many times called him a good man, a pious man. My father meant what he said. For one thing, old Agate was dead by then and there was no advantage in flattering him. And for another, my father despised the idea of flattering. So, if he said grandfather Agate was pious, it was the simple truth. I never knew old Agate but I formed a mind-picture from my father's description, of someone with a stern, unyielding face and a manner to match. A bit like my father, I suppose.

And, just as in most villages the parson, the squire and the schoolmaster consort with each other, so their offspring are expected to play together. In Miching we had no schoolmaster – though my father occasionally took that part – so squire and parson made an elevated society of two (although everybody knew who occupied the higher rung on the ladder). Peter and I were thrown together from early on. He was the sole boy in a family of girls while I had no living brothers or sisters. We even looked a little alike, I suppose. We stayed friends as we grew up, although never so close as in those boyhood years. On countless summer evenings I had made the journey down the slope from Quint House, never thinking that the world needed to be any bigger than the few dozens of acres which separated church and manor.

The Agates' distance from the village was life-preserving, as it turned out. The plague's a funny thing. Its dragon's-breath will strike down everybody in one dwelling and leave a neighbouring one unscathed. So it was with the Agate place and its occupants.

It wasn't until a month or so after I'd fled from Miching that I discovered that the family of my friend had survived. It was perhaps remiss on my part, even cowardly, not to have enquired after them but I'd assumed they were dead. The end of my own parents seemed like the closing of the book of my past life, one which I had no wish to open again.

I was in Bristol but ready to depart for London, there to make my fortune. And like every young man off to make his fortune in a capital city, I was sure I'd soon be rich and famous and, the next moment, just as certain I'd soon be dying – of hunger and poverty, or after a violent attack by robbers – in a ditch in the city suburbs. It was in one of these gloomy moods that I encountered Peter Agate in a tavern by Bristol docks. We met like ghosts, each thinking the other dead.

After we'd recovered from the shock of seeing one another we exchanged stories, speaking in quiet and hesitant tones as if imparting secrets. Unlike me, Peter had been at home when the plague came calling. He had no idea how he and his family had escaped the common fate of the common folk a small way down the hill. True, a handful of the villagers hadn't been affected either but the Agate household was preserved whole and entire, down to the humblest servant. They'd lost some of the field-workers, though, and this was the reason why Peter was in Bristol, hiring hands on his father's behalf. He told me something which I didn't know and which shook me a little. It was that my father had, like me, been absent from the parish when the plague struck. Unlike me, though, he had not been abroad on a frivolous errand but staying at a remote farm, tending to a dying man. While he was away the pestilence took possession of Miching. Hearing this, he could have chosen not to return. But he did return. My mother was still there, of course. So were all his parishioners. When they died, so did he.

After Peter finished his story, I sat in silence for a time. Then I ran swiftly through my own narrative. Perhaps I was a little ashamed at my flight from Miching, compared with the way Peter had continued to stay on there, compared with my father's courage in returning.

Still, all that village life was behind me now. I was going forward not back, forward to a new life in London. To be a player, I told him. Going to fortune or to ruin. (Strange that I never considered a middle course, involving neither.)

We stood for an instant that spring evening outside the waterside tavern, saying farewell. The air was cold but there were still some gleams in the sky. My earlier gloom had lifted. I'd felt my spirits rise as I described to Peter my planned pilgrimage to London and its playhouses. I had already fallen in with a gaggle of Bristolian carters who were setting off eastwards at first light. I might accompany them as far as Trowbridge. After that I was ready to take whatever travelling companionship fortune threw in my way. As for Peter, since he had concluded his father's hiring business he might have returned to Miching straightaway but I think he meant to try what Bristol had to offer by way of diversion for a day or two. He seemed fired up by drink to try his chances in a big town. Me, I had my ambitions set on an even greater town. We clasped arms about one another, briefly, awkwardly, as if we were going to tussle like boys. I don't think we ever expected to see each other again.

And now here was my childhood friend come to London. Come, it seemed, to see Revill. Naturally I couldn't help wondering why.

These speculations occupied my mind as I threaded the foggy thoroughfares to my work-place. Few people were abroad on this unhealthy morning. The fog was so dense that the white flank of the Globe loomed up in front of me quite unexpectedly. But I brightened up to see it, like a sailor sighting the cliffs of home. I made my way quickly inside to the tire-house, which was the costume-room and the only indoor area large enough to hold the whole company of players, if in rather crushed conditions. We were there not for a full-scale rehearsal (that would have taken place outside on the stage) but for what Dick Burbage called a chamber practice, an early run-through of unfamiliar material. In any event, we were not performing this piece in the Globe playhouse at all but in a different venue, perhaps a more select one, as I shall shortly explain.

As soon as I walked into the smoky, damp-smelling room my good cheer evaporated. There was a hush.

"Oh, Master Nicholas," said Dick Burbage. He was standing like a schoolmaster on a little dais to one side of the room. This was his customary position when he supervised a rehearsal.

"Dick?"

"In your own good time."

"I am ready," I said, brandishing the scroll which contained my part.

"You may be ready, but are you sorry?"

"Sorry . . .? Oh yes, sorry for being late."

"Did you get lost in the fog?"

There was some laughter at this from a few of my fellows, a combination of pleasure at my discomfiture and relief that they weren't dancing on the end of Burbage's tongue.

"In the fog? Why, was I *missed*?" I said, laying a little stress on the last word. Oh, the sword-like flash of wit on a damp, foggy morning (and for the second time too). There were a few belated groans and jeers as the joke penetrated. Personally I considered that it was worthy of taking its place beside one of Master Shakespeare's lesser puns, almost worthy.

Burbage looked slightly put out and I could see him debating inwardly whether to tear me off a strip or whether to pay me back in kind. Fortunately he chose the latter.

"Beware, Nicholas, otherwise it will be a *fine* morning for you despite the fog – or the mist."

By his half-smiling he seemed to say that, on this occasion at least, he wouldn't be levying the shilling which was often imposed for lateness at rehearsal. This fine, this tax on tardiness, was not fine; it was a whole day's pay, whose loss one could resent. Nevertheless you had to respect Dick Burbage's public display of good humour. He and the other shareholders in the Chamberlain's, and the rest of us, had reason to feel apprehensive at the moment.

"Now," said Burbage briskly. "To work. Your cue from the Prologue, Nicholas, is:

. . . do as your pleasures are:
Now good or bad, 'tis but the chance of war."

So I began, assuming the appearance and pose of love-sickness:

"Call here my varlet; I'll unarm again:
Why should I war without the walls of Troy
That find such cruel battle here within?"

Et cetera.

Afterwards Burbage told me I looked liverish rather than love-sick. But I think that it was his way of having the final word.

When we'd finished our chamber practice Dick Burbage gave the time for our afternoon rehearsal, which was to be on the other side over the water. He coupled this with a warning about lateness (directed at N. Revill, I felt). Then he left us to our own devices for a couple of hours. So I hastened to meet my old friend, sure that he would inform me of his reasons for coming to London. Peter Agate had done as I'd suggested and searched out the Goat & Monkey ale-house to drink away the remaining hours of that fog-bound morning. In between nervous gulps of ale, he told me why he had left home and come to London. He intended to find his fortune on the stage. Why this disturbed me I don't know, but it did.

"You want to be a player!"

"Is there anything so surprising in that?"

"Well, no."

"After all, Nick, I have only to look at *you*."

"Don't take me as an example."

"Why not?"

If my tone was dubious, Peter's showed an uncharacteristic sharpness. He was normally gentle and conciliatory. Either the drink was getting to him or this project of becoming a player was very close to his heart. I picked my next words carefully.

"First of all . . . "

"Yes?"

"You realize how . . . difficult it is to turn player?"

"For a country dweller?"

"For anyone, it doesn't matter where they're from."

"So, difficult for everyone – except you, perhaps."

I was divided between the desire to suggest how smooth my progress had been since coming to London (although it hadn't all been smooth) and the contrary wish to play up difficulties and obstacles (although it hadn't been *that* difficult either). In the end I split the difference and made do with a shrug.

"All right," I said, "let's suppose that you eventually do join a company of players . . . "

"Yes, let us suppose that," said Peter. "Eventually."

"But the story's not over. Even when you are secure as a member of a company, you're still at the mercy of that company's fortunes. You may be the finest troupe in the world but that doesn't exempt you from a run of bad luck – and bad luck's bound to come sooner or later, when your seniors choose the wrong plays, when the plague comes calling, when the Council decides to close you down, when you lose your patron . . . "

This was an oblique reference to our current situation in the Chamberlain's but I didn't want to say too much to Peter and checked myself. However, the comment seemed to go over his head.

"If and when, if and when," said Peter. "These are just the chances of life, Nick. You're sounding like a worried old man. If you're talking chances now, look at us. We've both survived the plague while those around us have fallen."

I shifted uncomfortably on the bench in the Goat & Monkey. The place was almost empty, apart from four boatmen playing primero at a distant table and a couple of men talking earnestly together in a corner. One of them had a lined, chalky-white countenance. The other I recognized. It was Thomas Gally, Philip Henslowe's agent, though largely self-appointed to that position. Gally had taken to hanging about on the fringes of gatherings of the Chamberlain's Company at taverns and elsewhere. He was playing the part either of a spy or a tempter, we supposed. (This was the reason I'd jumped to the conclusion that my unknown visitor that morning had come with an offer.) There was rivalry of a friendly sort between us and the Admiral's but it was rivalry on a knife's edge and might turn hostile at any moment. In Tom Gally's case, this sense of threat was enhanced by a strange mannerism he had of holding his index finger close to his right eye and squinting down it from time to time in the direction of the person he was talking to, as if taking aim with a pistol. At the moment his finger-gun was pointing at the white-faced old man opposite him.

I looked back at Peter Agate's eager, almost pleading face and realized with alarm that he wanted my approval for his plans to become an actor. It wasn't enough that I didn't object; he wanted my active agreement. While he was waiting for it he clutched at his tankard. Perhaps it was Martin Bly's ale that was fuelling this itch to play.

"Our cases are not the same, I think," I said, struggling to find words to put my reasons into. "I had neither mother nor father remaining in our village, and no brothers or sisters in the first place, nor anyone I truly cared about – apart from you, Peter. There was nothing and nobody left for me there. You have a mother and a father and a gaggle of sisters."

"My mother died last year."

"I am sorry to hear it."

This was no mere form of words. I was sorry. I remembered Margaret Agate, not least because she'd often bestowed more kind words and smiles on me in a day than my mother provided in a twelvemonth.

"Your father though?" I said.

"Is still living."

"That's well."

"Is it? To tell the truth, my father and I had a bad falling out over precisely this, my intention to become a player."

"I fell out with mine too. But I still say our cases are different, Peter. I had nothing . . . to look forward to. You have that . . . gaggle of sisters only."

"What you mean to say is that there are no males in my family apart from me and so it's in my own interest to stay put in Somerset and wait for my father's property to fall into my hands. That's what you mean to say."

"I would not put it so nakedly but, yes, I suppose so. You have no need to trouble about the future. You have property and land stored up for you."

"And that should be enough?"

I suddenly saw how feeble a position I was trying to argue him into. Was I suggesting that my boyhood friend ought to remain rusting in the village of his birth for the rest of his life? That no dream or ambition was required of him except to step into his father's shoes at the moment of God's choosing? I asked myself how I would have reacted to such advice. The answer was, badly.

"I'm sorry, Peter. You're seeking advice from the last person who should be trying to persuade you against something you've set your heart on. I spoke from honest friendship when what I should have done is wished you luck. I hope it's not too late to do that."

For the first time since I'd joined him on the ale-house bench Peter's expression relaxed. He placed his tankard on the table and put a reassuring hand on my arm. I noticed that both the men in the corner, Tom Gally and the chalky-faced one, had stopped their conversation and were now looking attentively in our direction.

"That is what I hoped you'd say."

"It's not exactly strong encouragement."

"It's not strong discouragement either, like my father's."

"He disapproved, eh?"

"When I said we'd had a falling-out, I was understating things. You remember my father?"

"Both your mother and father I have affectionate memories of."

Though I didn't remember him as clearly or fondly as I did his wife, Anthony Agate had always appeared to my young eyes as an easy-going fellow, the sort who'd fall in with a son's plans – or at least not oppose them too vehemently.

"Something happened after my mother's death," said Peter. "Until then my father had been tolerant enough. His good temper even survived the pestilence. He could not thank God often enough for preserving our household. But when my mother died it was as if his old self went underground with her. He was like a gloomy, raging ghost in the house. My young sisters were afraid to be in his presence and visibly shook if he spoke to them. Not that he wanted anything to do with them. Me, he threatened with words and even struck on occasion if I went counter to his wishes."

"As when you said you wished to be a player?"

"Only to hint of that caused a storm. He said players were scum and the devil's droppings and worse. I saw that I could never win him round, any more than I could uproot an oak. And there were other things besides which were wrong in our house. So I decided that there was no other path except . . . evasion, escape."

"What about your sisters? I can remember them although they were all quite small when . . . Anne and young Margaret and . . ."

"And Katherine. Katie. Believe me, Nicholas, I often think of them."

Peter bit his underlip. He picked up his tankard and put it down again uncertainly.

"You think I should have stayed behind to care for them?"

I said nothing because I could think of nothing to say. I suppose I did think that Peter Agate ought to have stayed in Miching and protected his young sisters against an overbearing father. Having no sisters myself I perhaps had a rather overdeveloped, even knightly sense of what was due to them. But what right had I to say anything to Peter concerning a situation which I'd never been in? I'd already done enough damage to our friendship. So I changed the subject, or part changed it.

"Why should you want to become a player now anyway?"

"*Vita brevis*," said Peter.

"Eh?"

"*Vita brevis, ars longa*, Nick, you know."

"Life is short while art is long."

"Yes, well, it's more the *vita brevis* bit I'm thinking of. What we want to do we ought to do when we can, because who knows . . ."

Peter had no chance to say any more because the chalky-faced individual who'd been sitting in the corner suddenly sprang towards our bench. He left Gally sitting at their table.

"Do not, sir, do not! Oh, preserve yourself!"

He had an earnest, resonant voice. Crumpled ears stuck out from under his cap. Close to, he looked older, more lined.

"Are you addressing us?" I said.

"Not you, master. You are already lost. No, this is the gentleman I would warn."

He looked at Peter, who in turn looked even more uncomfortable. Now, you run across madmen in the streets of London and occasionally in indoor places like taverns too. They're not usually dangerous but you can never be sure.

"Warn? Me?" said Peter. "Warn me?"

If my old friend was going to spend time in London he'd soon learn that the best way to deal with these unfortunates was not to respond.

"Beware the playhouse, young man," intoned this pale old person. "Do not join them, master. I was once as you are but I saw the light."

The moment he started in on the playhouse I recognized him, or rather his type, one that you might find out on the streets more often than in the tavern. Abstinence and playhouse-hating usually go together. Perhaps he was merely pretending to drink and waiting for the chance to rant at unwary players. The Goat & Monkey was well known as a theatrical haunt. The only puzzle was why he was keeping company with Tom Gally, Henslowe's agent.

By now the little crew of boatmen were sufficiently interested in the scene to lay down their cards and turn towards us. Gally meantime regarded the scene with detachment, squinting down his finger towards us.

"Tell me," said the pale person, shifting in my direction and fixing me with his protuberant eyes, "what is the playhouse? What is its character?"

Pretending to think, I said eventually, "It is a den of delight."

"You are wrong!" he said. "A playhouse is like the sink in a town for all the filth and folly to flow into."

"It is a place where pleasure and instruction go hand in hand," I said.

"It is like a great boil on the body that draws all the bad vapours and humours into it."

"I can see we're never going to agree," I said.

"*You* are already sunk into the perilous pit, master, you

are damned. I can tell by your clothing and your manner that you are one of that unclean generation."

I bowed my head slightly in acknowledgement. Of course he was able to identify me as a player. Perhaps Tom Gally had pointed me out as one. My first instinct, on sensing where this lunatic was heading with his questions (to which he already had all the answers), had been to make a rapid exit from the Goat & Monkey. But something held me back. Peter Agate wished to become a player, didn't he? Well then, let him see that not everyone approved of the trade, that not everyone would applaud his choice. In his inexperience he probably believed that his father's hostility was unusual. It wasn't. Plenty of people hated the theatre and here was one of them.

"This is the gentleman I wish to save." Chalk-face's bulging gaze shifted back towards my companion. "He is not yet part of your foul fraternity. He is not yet lost."

I left it to Peter to reply to this, if he chose to. When he did reply I was impressed by the steadiness of his tone.

"Sir, you were not invited to join us from your corner. This is not polite. You were not privy to our conversation. It can only be that your ears are like tennis rackets, ready to snaffle other men's balls."

By luck or instinct, Peter had hit on a sensitive spot. The pale-faced individual's ears were indeed prominent even though he'd done his best to shroud them with a cap, which he now pulled further down. His ears did look a bit like tennis rackets, I suppose.

After that stroke of wit from Peter I didn't think we could improve on things. There was no arguing with a fellow like this anyway and I was growing uncomfortable with the steady look and the finger-pistol which Gally was fastening on us from the corner. He seemed to be amused by the whole scene. My estimate of Peter had gone up and, faced by such an enemy of the theatre, I felt a little penitent. I'd been patronizing towards my friend, or at least not taken his playing ambitions seriously enough. That probably accounted for what I said next.

"I've another rehearsal to get to this afternoon, Peter. Dick Burbage really will use my guts to tie his points if I'm late this time. We're over the water. Why don't you come along too?"

"Your Burbage might decide to use my guts instead," said Peter, "if I appear unannounced."

"I'll have a word with him," I said, by no means as confident as I sounded of the senior's response. "You can be presented as an apprentice."

I stood up. The old fellow who didn't like plays or players look aggrieved that we were no longer paying attention to him. Whether he intended to or not, he was blocking our exit between bench and table.

"Do not go down that road, young man. Playing is the primrose path to perdition."

Peter made to go forward but the other put his hands out and shoved against his chest. For an old man, he was strong. My friend stepped back sharply and would have fallen if I hadn't been there to prevent him.

"You shall not join those saucy stinkards. I shall save you despite yourself."

I sighed. We weren't going to get out of the tavern without a tussle. Then I grew angry with this insolent person who interfered with honest citizens going about their lawful business. I looked towards Tom Gally. If he was at all friendly with this strange being then surely he'd step in to save us from his company. Gally, however, continued to look down his index finger as though we were providing him with entertainment – or easy targets.

Now help came from an unexpected quarter. The boatmen, who'd also lost interest in their card game to follow the argument, now rose from their table and moved towards us. Without a word, the foursome split into twos on either side of our tormentor and picked him up bodily, as if he was a piece on a chess board. Still without speaking they carried him towards the door of the ale-house and then through it, in a sideways shuffle. The door closed. There was a pause. I waited for noises off: the thumps, the yelps, the oaths. But none came.

The boatmen reappeared with looks of barely concealed satisfaction. I hoped they hadn't harmed him, too much. Surreptitiously I looked for marks of blood. There were none. Perhaps they'd just given him a good talking-to. The leader, a broad-shouldered fellow, raised his hand and, twining together his index and middle fingers, said, "Players and boatmen." The others nodded behind him in silent agreement.

I nodded too but it took me a moment to realize what he meant. That players and boatmen were eternal friends, surely not; but that the interests of players and boatmen were as interlinked as his fingers. We depended on them (to ferry our patrons across the river), they depended on us (to attract those patrons across the river in the first place). Even so I was surprised, not so much by their action – watermen always enjoy flexing their arms, in or out of their element – as by their near-silence. Your average boatman is as full of filthy words as his bilges are of Thames water.

Nodding again to our rescuers, Peter Agate and I made our way out of the Goat & Monkey. I noticed that Gally followed us with his gaze out of the door but didn't otherwise acknowledge any of what had passed. I hoped that by this time the pale-faced old man would have vanished into the fog, to lick his wounds. There was no sign of him in the dirty air that enveloped us. There was no sign of anybody at all on this ghostly afternoon. We might as well have been going blindfold or, more fancifully, walking on a thoroughfare in the clouds.

Perhaps Peter felt this too because from time to time he grasped me by the arm or I grasped him, as if each of us was fearful of getting lost. In fact I could have found my way through this stretch of town on a starless night, as I had done on many occasions. With the river to our right we paced beyond Paris Garden and along Upper Ground in the direction of Barge House Stairs, the closest crossing-point to our destination. Our footsteps echoed unnaturally loud. As we neared the Stairs I was pleased to hear the muffled chime of church bells and to pass other shadowy human shapes in the fog as well as the occasional cart and clomping horse.

The steps were deserted. It was low tide and I sensed rather than saw the presence of the water below. I wondered whether the constant to-and-fro traffic across the river had been interrupted by the fog, before deciding that the ferries were doubtless working to their usual principle: that when you wanted one, none was to be found, but that when you had no desire to cross the river and were simply enjoying a stroll along its banks there was sure to be a whole fleet of them idling off-shore.

"You are certain of this, Nick?" said Peter. "That I will be welcome at your company rehearsal?"

"As I said back there, you're an apprentice come to learn the craft."

"And craft is what we want now. A river craft."

"Oh, yes, ha. There's never a boat around when you need one."

But at that moment I heard a creaking sound and spied a tall shape taking on definition through the yellow-grey gloom. And the moment after that something strange happened, happened to me, I mean. I felt my scalp prickling and the hair stir on the nape of my neck.

It must have been the lurid gloom and the grinding of the oar against the side of the boat and the way in which the boatman's outline was distorted by the foggy vapours. It must have been all these things as well as the steady, undeviating approach he was making towards our wharf. Whatever it was, it made me think of that other boatman.

You know the one I mean.

In the old stories it is Charon who ferries the souls of the dead across the river Styx to the underworld. It doesn't matter that he is a man of unprepossessing appearance for he does not have to win his clients. They have no choice, since there is a river to be crossed and only one ferryman to take them. To pay him they have a coin tucked into their mute mouths. I shivered at the grizzled features of the boatman as they emerged below us in the haze. The taste of the fog was like a coin laid on my tongue.

And then the spell was broken.

"Hop in, gents."

Peter and I scrambled down the slippery stairs and took our places on the damp, padded seats in the stern.

"Where to, gents?"

"What? Oh, Temple Stairs."

"Rightaway."

We swung out, bobbing into nothingness. The boatman, the soul of cheerfulness, hummed tunelessly under his breath and plied with a will. At least he seemed to know where we were going. Pulling my cloak tighter about me, I noticed that there was a fire-fly of a light hanging above our heads in the stern as there would have been for a night crossing. The sight of other smudges of light around us and the sound of other oars creaking away across the water were reassuring.

I laughed (in my mind) at my fears and premonitions and was glad when Peter resumed his account of how and why he'd quit his family home. He'd hinted in the tavern that there were other things apart from his father's hostility which had driven him out. In confidential tones, while we sat shoulder to shoulder in the back of the boat, he now told me what they were. After a period of violent mourning his father Anthony Agate had taken him a new wife – or rather been taken by a new one. She was a well-practised widow with, according to Peter, all of a widow's wiles.

"I don't like her, Nick. She's already seen two husbands into the ground."

"She can't be blamed for outliving them."

"And I can't be blamed for not liking her."

"That's not so unusual with stepchildren and step-parents, I suppose."

"She seized on my father like a – like a harpy, with her claws out and her wings flapping."

Peter almost whispered this, although I don't think the boatman, humming away, plying his trade, was listening.

"But my father seemed happy enough with this. Or at least his raging moods went."

Anthony Agate might have been as opposed as ever to the notion that his son could turn player, Peter explained, but now he was distracted with a change of wife he treated his children better than he had done in the aftermath of their mother's death. That is, he largely ignored them.

"I will say this for Mistress Gertrude Potts, even though it goes against my teeth to do so – "

"Gertrude Potts?"

"The harpy. My father's new wife. She was formerly married to Randolph Potts of Peckham. And there was some other unfortunate before Randolph."

"Gertrude is a pregnant name for a stepmother."

"Why?"

"There is a play by William Shakespeare . . . "

"*Hamlet*? Oh yes, I know it. Well, whatever her reasons she has been . . . *attentive* . . . towards all of the girls, particularly my oldest sister. Perhaps she sees it as a way of winning my father's approval. But she already had him in hand, I think, before that."

Sensing something here, I said, "And towards you she has also been attentive?"

I felt Peter tense beside me.

"More than attentive."

Before he could say anything else in this teasing vein we

jarred gently against the base of Temple Stairs, and our brief voyage was over.

I thanked the boatman, tipped him handsomely and groped my way up the greasy steps. Peter followed.

"Where exactly are we going, Nick?" said Peter, catching up with me in the fog.

"Only a little way in this direction along Middle Temple Lane. If your story doesn't take more than a few minutes you might as well complete it. No danger of a boatman eavesdropping now."

"Story?"

"Of the young man and his stepmother."

"You expect some filth, eh?"

"I live in hope."

"Then I'm afraid you'll be disappointed. Evidently my father wasn't enough for my new stepmother – or perhaps she is one of those hot-livered women who must subdue every man within her reach."

"I should like to meet her."

"You should not. Mistress Gertrude is a harpy, as I say, all claws and leathern wings."

"You're protesting too much, Peter. I suspect you have fallen in love with her. Or in lust."

"Oh yes, she wore low-cut dresses for all that she was married to my father, and pressed her boobies against me within a few days of arriving in our house – "

"And you had no say in this matter. You didn't invite her booby presses."

"Wait. It gets worse."

"Better, you mean."

"I mean what I mean. Be sure my stepmother would often be up night-walking when I was not yet in bed."

"She couldn't sleep?"

"She was wide awake and in search of *night*-work to put my father in his *night*cap."

"What do you mean?" I said though I half knew.

"Why, she was out to cuckold him, when she made to thrust my hand through her silken placket."

His tone was half-way between being amused and bitter, but with a dash of something else.

"That would have been a good revenge," I said, "against your father."

"It's not a matter for levity, Nick. She is loose in the hilts. And she has a son of about my age too. She told me. That makes it even worse."

There was something a bit priggish about Peter. Naturally I didn't say so. Instead I tried a little light flattery.

"Have you considered that you're an attractive young man, Peter?"

"Her very words, as I recall."

"I meant them mockingly."

"She did not."

"Of course you loyally refused her thrusts and her plackets?"

"I was too afraid that I would succumb to them, if I'm honest," said my friend. "That is partly why I left Quint House. That, and my father's continued refusal to countenance my ambitions in playing. I left home in a hurry. Then it took me some little time to screw up my courage and come to London. But I did come. And here I am."

"Exit, pursued by a stepdame."

"Only in my dreams. I dream of her. Have nightmares I should say."

I wouldn't have said it for the world, but I was amused by the picture of my friend fleeing his stepmother's overtures. I imagined her hot-breathed behind him, with nightgown loosened and flapping.

By now we had reached our destination, as I informed Peter.

"*Where* are we though?"

"Countryman that you are, Peter, even you must have heard of Middle Temple."

"I think so. But you may enlighten me."

If you asked me for my ideal audience I suppose it would come close to being the law students of the Inns of Court. Or so I would have thought before I had much experience of them. I've no time for them as would-be *lawyers* but speak of them now only as an *audience*.

Like the apprentices, these young men have a riotous reputation but because they're usually well born they get away with it (unlike the apprentices). They are also players in an amateur way. Training to be politicians and pleaders in court, they no doubt regard the drama as a good preparation in rhetoric and deceit. They are inclined to the theatrical, and enjoy debate, word-play, innuendo, love-making, and dressing up. In addition these students of the law are more than happy to see men beating each other over the head. There's nothing that the sedentary like more than a good fight, seeing other people fighting, that is. And when a lawyer is involved there is always a good chance of an action for battery, and therefore profit.

As it happened, the play we were going to stage, William Shakespeare's *Troilus and Cressida*, contained all this and more. To wit – wit (of a sour sort), love, lust, argument, filth, battles, treachery, and sulking in tents. As a backdrop, there's a war, the one between the Greeks and the Trojans. It may even be the original war, for all I know, the very first to darken the face of the earth. It certainly goes on for a long time, all of ten years. And then there's the cause of that war, the seizing of Helen, wife of Menelaus the Greek, by Paris, the son of King Priam of Troy. But the story of Troilus is not really to do with *them* – and I should know since this was my part.

Yes, Nicholas Revill was playing Troilus, the love-sick young Trojan prince who, like Paris, was a son of King Priam. It was the first time, incidentally, that I had appeared in the title to a play.

I am a warrior and in love with the beautiful Cressida, daughter of Calchas the priest. Calchas is a Trojan blessed or cursed with second sight. Forseeing his city's ruin, he has abandoned Troy for the Greek camp outside the walls but somehow forgotten to take his daughter with him. Comes a time, during which Troilus after a long and laborious wooing is enjoying his Cressida, when Calchas arranges for his daughter to be brought to him in an exchange of prisoners. The young lovers must part, although not before they have sworn eternal fidelity. Do they keep that faith? You shall see (even though you already know the answer).

Meantime – in the foggy by-ways of London rather than on the sun-kissed plains of Troy – Peter Agate and I groped towards our destination beyond Temple Stairs. I knew the area just to the west of here for it was the site of Essex House, the London palace of Robert Devereux, the now disgraced Earl, and a place which I had twice visited at some peril to my life. In the shadow of Temple Bar we entered the jumbled precincts of the Inner and Middle Temples. It was only about two in the afternoon but it seemed as though evening was already approaching. I identified ourselves to a gatekeeper as members of the Chamberlain's – adding "the players" in case he pretended ignorance – and Peter and I were directed round several corners and through several courts. Dark-gowned figures were flitting about in these spaces, like crows, and adding to the general cheerfulness of the scene. I supposed they were Benchers or juniors. A grand red-bricked tower and entrance, crested with the lamb and flag symbol of the Temple, loomed up in the murk. We climbed a few steps. Pushing through a weighty oak door, we left the damp fog and entered a great hall with an elaborately beamed ceiling and candles massed in sconces along the walls. The tables and benches which had been shifted to one side indicated that when this room wasn't being used for playing its real purpose was for dining, probably of a grand sort.

Inside this hall were my fellows and that air of bustle and excitement which I've long associated with a play in its real beginnings – any play, it doesn't matter what. The run-through that morning in the Globe tire-house had been a bare affair and now we were going to clothe that skeleton with action, expression and gesture. I pointed out to Peter the area at the end of the room, telling him that this was the very spot where the law students mounted their own performances and where our own *Troilus and Cressida* was to be staged. I enjoyed playing the expert.

First, though, I had to gain approval for Peter's presence here. I looked about for a likely senior, that is, one who wouldn't raise objections. Fortunately the playwright himself was in attendance. He hadn't been with us at the earlier chamber practice. Now he was standing, as he often did, a little to one side, regarding. His acting days weren't quite over but he was always more prominent backstage than on the boards.

WS looked up and nodded slightly at my approach. He seemed preoccupied but greeted me courteously enough.

"This is Peter Agate, a friend of mine arrived from the country," I said. "He has come to see how we do things."

"He is welcome."

"Peter, here is our playwright – and senior – and shareholder – and sometime player – Master Shakespeare."

Peter looked abashed – he knew who it was standing opposite him for WS's fame had spread quite far among the lettered classes. No words came out of his slightly open mouth but he stuck out his hand in response to WS's own. I took some pleasure in seeing an old friend shake hands with a man I greatly admired and liked. And I took a more covert pleasure in the thought that now Peter knew that *I* knew a man like WS. Reflected glory.

"Peter wishes to become a player."

"He is doubly welcome then," said Shakespeare, sounding as though he meant it.

Peter looked even more abashed, as though I shouldn't have revealed this ambition. WS's warmth contrasted with my own coolness back in the Goat & Monkey, and I regretted having been discouraging to my friend, even briefly. I wondered whether to amuse WS by telling him of the tavern encounter with the chalky-faced old man and of our rescue by the boatmen. But there were other more serious matters running through the author's head.

"You can read, Master Agate? I mean, read with feeling rather than by rote?"

"I hope so, sir," said Peter, seeming unsurprised by the question.

"We have a sudden gap in our ranks, Nicholas."

"Somebody's late?" I said hopefully, wanting Burbage's waspishness directed elsewhere.

"Not late now – but I fear that our patron will be shortly."

Deliberately or not, Shakespeare had misunderstood me. We were all aware that our patron Lord Hunsdon – who had succeeded his father to the post of Lord Chamberlain only a few years earlier – was sick, too sick to attend the Privy Council. This meant that the Chamberlain's Company was without a voice at court or in the highest circles of the land. I had glimpsed this great man on a handful of occasions but knew nothing of him except that he had a great fondness for music. What I knew besides was that every company needed a patron and protector. During any sickness of Lord Hunsdon, we might have looked to the Queen to be our guardian but rumour whispered that the royal decline, hitherto slow, was gathering pace.

"Thomas Pope has gone off on a visit at Hunsdon House," said WS. "It is a delicate business. He left for Hertfordshire this very afternoon."

I nodded. It must have been an urgent departure if Thomas Pope was compelled to travel in this weather. He'd been present at the morning practice. I noticed that Peter Agate looked both interested and baffled, as well he might. I was a bit baffled myself.

"We want a first-hand account of our patron's health," said

Shakespeare. "And our obligation to Hunsdon demands that a senior visit him."

This was surely a sudden decision on the part of the shareholders, the seven men who between them had control of the Globe playhouse. Perhaps they had received news of some crisis. Underneath the courtesy of visiting an ailing man was, of course, the unspoken desire to determine whether we needed to look about for a fresh patron now or whether this might be postponed for months or even years.

"But it means that we're without a Thersites for the afternoon," said WS, looking at Peter. "Only for this afternoon. We can make other arrangements before the next rehearsal."

He said no more but let his words sink in.

"Peter – play Thersites!"

I couldn't help myself. I spluttered loud enough for one or two near us to stop whatever they were doing. If there's any one character in *Troilus and Cressida* who'd be beyond the reach of my friend it was Thersites. My acquaintance with Shakespeare's creations was by this time fairly extensive and, however brilliantly they were realized, you generally knew where in the catalogue of men (or women) to place them: soldiers, sages, lovers, shrews, & cetera. But I'd never encountered anyone like Thersites before, either in real life or on the stage.

So I half laughed, half exclaimed, and Peter became a little indignant, at least in his looks.

"Master Agate," said WS ignoring my reaction, "I don't know you, although you come with the recommendation of being Nicholas's friend."

Peter hardly knew where to put himself. He actually blushed.

"And you want to be a player?"

Peter nodded.

"You know what is the hardest part to play?"

"Oneself," said Peter.

"Why yes," said WS, the pleased pedagogue. "And the

opposite is generally true too. That is, we find it easiest to play what we are not. And, believe me, when I ask you to read – *read* not play – the part of Thersites, I'm asking you to be the very opposite of what is most likely your true self."

"Who is Thersites?" said Peter.

"A deformed and scurrilous Greek," said Shakespeare. "One who rails on the wars and satirizes his commanders. One to whom the whole world is a mass of fools. A nasty, cynical fellow but a necessary one perhaps."

"Thomas Pope has the part," I added, seeing the drift of WS's words, "and he is not like that at all."

"Nor are you, Master Agate. Not a scurrilous, cynical fellow, I think. Are you?"

What answer can you give to a question like that? Peter duly shrugged and reddened and looked abashed all over again.

"So you are well suited to read the part of Thersites this afternoon, since that Greek gentleman is your opposite in every respect."

The playwright paused for an instant to allow Peter to disagree but my friend naturally said nothing.

"That's settled then."

WS clapped Peter on the shoulder and smiled. Peter smiled back. Shakespeare had got his way. He usually did get his way, and without stirring up resentment or a sense of grievance, even though it was sometimes hard to see how the trick was done.

"Nick," he continued, "if you take Peter across to see Master Allison, he'll supply this fledgling player here with his part. I'll speak to Dick Burbage and make the way smooth."

WS moved off to explain to Burbage that we now had a man to play Thersites for the afternoon. Peter gazed after him. I looked around for Geoffrey Allison and eventually spotted him ensconced behind a table in a corner, with sheaves of paper and a mound of scrolls. I tapped Peter on the shoulder to get his attention – he was still staring, bemused, at Shakespeare who was now talking in low tones to Dick Burbage – and we crossed the banqueting hall to see the book-keeper.

Master Allison is the conscience of the Chamberlain's, or perhaps our recording angel. He remembers our good actions and our bad ones, that is, the good and bad performances. He keeps our parts and doles them out, grudgingly. He remembers who we've played even after we ourselves have long forgotten our lines. No one, not even Dick Burbage or William Shakespeare, knows as much as Allison does about the playing history of the Company.

I introduced Peter to him, informing him that this 'fledgling player' was to assume Thomas Pope's part of Thersites for the afternoon session, by order of WS. Master Allison paused from his note-making to scrabble among the mound of scrolls on the table and, selecting one more by instinct than inspection, held it out to Peter but without letting go of it. He cast his eyes up and down my friend.

"Fledgling player, eh. Well, here is a feather or two will help you fly."

He waggled the scroll but didn't release it into Peter's outstretched hand.

"Mind you return it straight after the practice is over."

"I will."

"You have an honest enough face," said Allison, and it occurred to me that Peter might be growing weary of being complimented on his honesty. Still reluctant to part with the rolled-up paper, the book-keeper continued, "Understand that these parts are like gold, young man, but more valuable since they are mined, not from the earth . . ."

"Mined?"

" . . . but rather from the *mind* of our author – as you might say."

Fortunately my friend smiled at the pun. And only then did Geoffrey Allison allow Peter to take the scroll. Then, dismissing us with a wave of the hand, he resumed his note-making.

Without any signal being given, the rest of the company was moving towards the hall-screen. It was in front of this partitioned-off area that we'd be practising and later performing *Troilus and Cressida* since, with its double entrances and gallery above, it was the nearest thing to the layout of the stage at the Globe. As we ambled across to join our fellows, I said to Peter, "Well, you can never have thought that within a few hours of arriving in my lodgings you'd be reading with the Chamberlain's Company."

"I'm speechless, Nick."

"Not for a couple of hours, I hope."

"So when do I come on?"

"It's all down there on the scroll. The lines immediately before your entrances. But Burbage'll cue you anyway. You're only reading. This isn't your part, after all. You're not Thersites."

I said this to soothe his nerves or rather to temper his growing excitement. But something inside me also wanted to put my old friend in his place. I had been many months in London before achieving even a hearing from the Chamberlain's. I didn't want Peter Agate to believe that theatrical success came too quick and easy. It wouldn't be good for him. (It wouldn't be good for me either.)

After all this, I expect that you expect to read how Peter gave a brilliant reading as Thersites, the Greek with the foul mouth and fouler mind. Or how he was execrably bad in the part. The truth is that he was neither. When he got into the part and saw what he was dealing with, he gave a solid account of the character, sneering and fleering with the best of them. But every so often glimpses of good, honest Peter shone through, so that lines and sentiments like 'I am a bastard' were quite decorously delivered, rousing the wrong kind of laughter.

Still, all went well. Well enough for it to be arranged that, if Thomas Pope hadn't returned from his visit to Hertfordshire and Lord Hunsdon by the next *Troilus* rehearsal in a couple of days' time, then Peter would once again speak for Thersites. I noticed that Shakespeare went out of his way to say something to my friend. By his look and gesture it was complimentary. But then WS was always complimentary, I consoled myself. Almost always.

After the play practice some of us repaired to a local tavern, a rather more salubrious one than Southwark's Goat & Monkey (but we were in north London and in lawyer-land after all). The place was called the Devil, spawning plenty of jokes about 'going to the . . . ' and 'talking of the . . . '. The story went that the tavern owed its name to the church of St Dunstan which stood nearby, and that an old inn-sign had once depicted that saint pulling the devil by the nose (what the devil had done to deserve this, I don't know). Now the painted sign was duller and vaguely legal-ish, showing a scroll and a seal and a quill. Even so I considered that the devil's name was a fitting one for a tract of London where so many lawyers and would-be lawyers congregated.

Peter got on famously with those of my fellows he chatted with in the Devil. We were in that high-spirited mood that comes after a successful practice or performance and we welcomed a newcomer to our ranks. I was split between pleasure that my friend was being so graciously received by the Company and anxiety in case he thought it was always like this. And of course there was a little touch of resentment too. No patron likes to see his client go too far too fast.

We didn't get free of the Devil until late evening. Peter was reluctant to leave and we reeled out with the other unwived, unloved, un-bed-warmed members of the Chamberlain's, mostly the younger ones. The fog had cleared and permitted a few stars to gaze drowsily down on the two of us as we reached the river, caught a ferry and, on the far side, retraced our steps to Dead Man's Place. No Charons or chalk-faced old ranters in sight.

It was generally assumed that Peter would share my lodgings for the next few days until he could find his own. Assumed by him, that is, and acquiesced in by me. I didn't think Samuel Benwell would make any difficulty. More likely he would be drooling to imagine two members of his favourite profession sharing a bed. So it proved. My landlord was still in the little lobby, leaning into a corner – I wondered if he'd been hanging around there all day waiting for some surprise visitor. He was holding a candle of stinking tallow whose waste oozed into a grease-pan. For a moment I thought of a mother, or perhaps a wife, waiting for two naughty boys to come back home after a night on the town.

I shut Peter up just after he'd started burbling and slurring on about his fren'ship with Willum Shakeshpeare and his discovery that the Chamberlain's were wunnerful men. Revill, relatively sober, swiftly negotiated with Benwell the provision of a spare mattress rather than a new room. The landlord simultaneously looked disappointed and raised his eyebrows in surprise – insofar as one could read all this expressiveness by a single smoky candle – but he must have known that my bed was small and mean, not really comfortable enough to share with anyone, even with a woman. He must have known, I say, because I think he was in the habit of spying on me.

We settled on one and a half pennies a night extra. I already knew that Peter was in funds, having seen his largesse in the Devil. The bargain struck, Benwell graciously handed over his odorous candle, now more grease than illumination, so that we might see ourselves to bed. Then we went single file up to my room, I almost pushing Peter up the stairs with one hand and holding on to the light with the other. I retrieved a leaking straw mattress from some unregarded corner, tugged it into my little room, laid it out beside my own bed (there was no space for it to go anywhere else), and felt simultaneously virtuous and resentful, as if I'd done everything and more that could be expected of me in relation to my old friend.

Peter had bashed his forehead somewhere in his progress to my room, probably at the entrance. The lintel was low but I was used to it. I should have warned him but the blow seemed to do him a favour and clear his head a little, even as the blood leaked slowly from his noddle. He was disposed to go on talking. He was still the worse for drink although the slurring disappeared.

I didn't much want to talk. For one thing, I had to work the next day, not on *Troilus and Cressida*, which would henceforth be rehearsed in Middle Temple, but on an actual play for the following afternoon and a practice for a different one in the morning, both of them at the Globe. So when Peter, half sitting up on his straw mattress and wiping abstractedly at his bloody forehead, said, "You know what Master Shakespeare said to me?" I merely grunted. This didn't deter Peter, who continued, "He smiled at me and said I had the makings of a player. He smilingly said."

Anyone not absolutely dead could be said to have the makings of a player. I didn't tell Peter that from WS these words were faint praise. If they'd been said to me I would've packed up straightaway and headed home to Somerset. Then I felt guilty for thinking such thoughts. Instead of grunting again, I asked Peter a question which had been nagging at the edge of my mind during the day.

"How did you know where to find me this morning?"

Now it was Peter's turn to grunt or make some similar non-committal noise. He lay down on his penny-and-a-half-a-night bed. I'd been about to snuff out the candle. The wick was guttering like a very small man drowning in a great greasy sea. It was my curiosity that flared up instead.

"I mean, you didn't go to the playhouse first, did you? It wasn't one of my fellows who told you where I lived?"

"Not exactly," said Peter.

"Who then?"

I looked down at him lying there, his forehead painted with blood which he'd wiped at ineffectually and which showed up dark in the little light.

"I'm bleeding."

"A flesh wound only," I said. "Who told you about my lodgings?"

Peter tried to avoid my eye. What didn't he want to tell me?

"I reached London yesterday," he said finally. "Not knowing where you lived of course, I thought I'd apply at the playhouse. And I had to ask where *that* was first. On the way to the Globe playhouse I passed a place called Holland's Leaguer . . . "

Oh, I saw where he was headed now.

"I suppose you're going to say, my friend, that you wandered in there all innocent."

The remark came out sharper than I intended and Peter seemed to bristle.

"I had heard of the place, naturally. Even in the depths of the country I had heard of it."

"And you thought you'd just have a taste."

"It seemed an – appropriate thing to do on arriving in a new town," he said. "And I'd had a drink or two."

"Of course. I've done the same."

"Had a drink?"

"Visited a brothel early on."

Had I? I couldn't remember. Did I enter a brothel on my first night in London town? The second or third night possibly – it could take that long to summon up the nerve – and then it would've been somewhere modest, where one could blush unseen, and not the famous, semi-fortified place known as Holland's Leaguer. Anyway, my comment had the effect of putting Peter at his ease, even making him combative.

"Yes, you *have* done the same, Nick, so you can get off that high horse."

No use to contradict him so I said nothing. I was very much afraid that I could see where he was headed now.

"I met a friend of yours in Holland's Leaguer."

"A customer, you mean?"

"A *resident* of the place."

"Any whore is friend to half the men of London, to hear them talk. The whores, that is."

"No, this was a very particular friend of yours. After we had finished the business which we had contracted for, we exchanged a few words. Since she could see I wasn't a townee she asked me where I came from. And when I told her it was a Somerset village she grew attentive and when I told her the name of the village she grew more attentive still. She even asked me if I knew one Nicholas Revill, the parson's son."

I rather wished that Peter had bashed his head hard enough on the lintel to knock himself right out. Or perhaps I should hit him over the head myself to stop him going on.

"'Know him!' I exclaimed," said Peter. "'We have known each other since we were boys. I have come to London expressly to see him.'"

"Whores are sentimental," I said. "I suppose she wanted to know what I was like as a youngster in that Somerset village."

"She didn't seem very interested in that. She was more interested in what I was doing here in town. So I told her of my ambitions to become a player."

"She likes players . . ." I said weakly. (I could in truth think of nothing else to say.)

"You may well say so, Nick. She gave me a free turn after that. I paid only once."

" . . . and she has a heart of gold."

He ignored my irony, pursuing a different train of thought.

"I think it may have been my freshness, my ambition. That seemed to touch her."

"She is easily touched," I said, this time without irony. "If you are talking of Nell."

"Nell, yes. I didn't know if it was her real name."

"It is."

"Not only was she able to tell me where you live but she had a message for you – if I managed to find you."

"Well, you have found me, Peter, and pretty soon I must sleep in order to rise fresh for work tomorrow. So tell me Nell's message and then I'll snuff out this filthy candle."

"Didn't make much sense to me," said Peter drowsily.

The excitement of the day – the playing – the drinking – the blow to the head – were at last getting the better of him.

"Nevertheless, tell me what Nell said."

"She said to tell you, 'A recovery would be fine.' That's all."

"A recovery would be fine?"

"Her words. Sounds legal to me."

"It probably is," I said, leaning across to extinguish the dirty light.

If this comment about fines and recoveries was Nell's way of re-establishing friendly relations, I didn't think much of it. Or, more accurately, I wasn't sure what to think of it.

Nell – for all our years together I never had discovered what her surname was (I'm not sure that she knew either) – Nell was a flesh-pedlar at Holland's Leaguer, as you'll have gathered. The Leaguer was the chief stew in Southwark, got up like a fortress with a moat and battlements, but all in a pissy play-acting style that wouldn't have kept out a band of children equipped with pikes of straw. (Oddly enough the Leaguer had a connection with the current patron of the Chamberlain's Company, the ailing Lord Hunsdon, since it was his father who'd owned the place when it was just a straightforward manor house.) The residents of this house of ill-fame were higher-priced than the members of the profession in other places like the Cardinal's Hat or the Windmill, and they accordingly adopted a more lady-like air as though they were doing you a favour in accepting your coin.

Not my coin, though. I got in free. And I could hardly object that Nell gave me what others paid for, nor that she was willing to give me in addition something you might have come close to calling love. I loved her too, in my fashion. Or perhaps it was that I was merely pleased to have her at hand, winning and grateful.

But as we grew more familiar with London our paths began to diverge, Nell's and mine, after a couple of years. The itch of respectability started to make me restless. I grew familiar enough with great men and their houses, two or three of them anyway. I considered that I was moving up in the world. I wasn't the only one to feel this. When we'd first met, Dick Burbage said that players were crawling towards respectability, even if slowly. Many of our seniors in the Chamberlain's were married men with children, in some cases happily so. They were shareholders, men of substance. Wasn't that what I was aiming at too?

In other words, I was growing up (or merely growing older).

Nell too must have been feeling this itch for respectability. It's even harder, though, for a doxy to get a leg up in the world than it is for a player. They start from further down the ladder, you see. True, there were stories that circulated around Nell's work-place about girls who'd been favoured by rich old men, so favoured that they'd been fished out of the stew and set up in comfortable establishments, with jewellery and servants and fine linen. Nell and her particular confederate in night-work, a girl called Jenny, often talked about these rich old men as if they actually existed. The best part was that, in the triumphant climax to the stories, the old men were persuaded to marry their dolls on their death-beds. These dolls – still comparatively young and fresh but wealthy and widowed – had worked themselves into an enviable position. Mind you, I'd never met any of these newly respectable widows, and neither had Nell or Jenny. They always turned out to be acquaintances of aunts of neighbours in the next street.

Now my Nell knew how the world worked, she knew what was what. And, since these rich young widows were nowhere to be found, she also realized that the rich old men were as real as the unicorn. Less real perhaps, because who is to say that the unicorn is not roaming somewhere on the far side of the world, even at this moment?

Therefore Nell was well aware that the way ahead was a rocky one. Unless she transformed herself into a madam or bawd, what lay in the future for the whore but fading charms and the pox? She must attach herself respectably, must find a protector. Maybe not a wealthy dotard who would peg out straightaway after the marriage but a younger gentleman with a bit of influence, with a prospect or two in the world. A player doesn't have influence or prospects, not really.

So my Nell too was growing up (or merely growing older).

Our friendship had been cooling for many months, although we still met from time to time for conversation of every sort. Our last encounter had been in her place of work, Holland's Leaguer, since she pleaded a busy-ness which prevented her from visiting me in Dead Man's Place. Really I think she didn't like Master Benwell's prying eye. It was a mark of her increasing fastidiousness.

Another sign of this was her desire to impress me with her ability to read. "Jenny can't read as I can read," she said proudly. This was a turnabout from the old days when she'd claimed, probably rightly, that being able to read and write wouldn't add a scrap to her earnings. Now it was a different Nell. I didn't respond – as I might have done once – "What business has a whore with words?" It would have been an illiberal remark, an ungentle one. Besides I was afraid she might hit me. She had a neat little fist.

"Nicholas," she said to me on this occasion. She always called me Nicholas these days, never the familiar old Nick.

"Yes?" I said, poised between abandoning her bed and the chances of another (free) session.

"Nicholas, do you know the meaning of *bona roba*?"

"It sounds like Latin, or Italian perhaps."

"I have been so described," she said.

"Oh good," I said.

"It has a handsome ring, hasn't it? He termed me a *bona roba*."

"He?"

"A particular individual."

"A fine piece of skirt, it must mean."

"I believe so but I prefer the original. *Bona roba*."

"Soon you'll be talking in tongues, Nell."

"I have another word for you. What about *quaedam*?"

Quaedam. Now, I knew that this was a learned sort of way of referring to a whore, one of Nell's profession. It meant no more than 'a certain woman' or *one of those*. It wasn't so much respectful, but more sneering, in my opinion. But my friend seemed pleased enough, to judge from the way she was preening herself.

"Another description? From the same man who described you as a *bona roba*?"

"The same *gentle*man, yes."

"And I am not a gentleman, Nell?"

"You are a player."

I ignored the implicit insult and said, "I'm not going to change trades to suit you, but what would you have me instead? For the sake of argument."

"What would I have you? Oh I don't know . . . perhaps a lawyer."

"So that's it! You are consorting with those fellows from the Inns across the water."

I meant the nests that the lawyers had built for themselves around Holborn and Whitefriars. It was a guess but one of those guesses that are certain things, and her next words showed I was right.

"Better than those that you consort with in *your* inns – I mean the Goat & Monkey and the Knight of the Carpet. And most of my trade is from the other side anyway, I'll have you know."

No chance of another bed-session with her now. She stiffened next to me and all but shoved me off her couch. It was irritation – and a touch of jealousy – which kept me going.

"It's a lawyer, is it, Nell?"

She said nothing and, lawyer-like, I took her silence as an admission of guilt.

"Tell me, is he young and springy, or old and vile with sagging dewlaps and gallow's-breath?"

"He is clever," she said finally. "Oh yes, and he is not old or vile or the other things besides. He has a liquid tongue."

"A *liquid* tongue?"

"Which he does not waste on groundlings in the pit, spouting other men's cheap words. He is clever, I say."

This slur on players (and incidentally on playwrights) was too much.

"Clever enough to negotiate with you for fee-simple? With that liquid tongue. Or is it fee-tail? Or free tail?"

By now I was out of her bed and struggling to fasten up my points and be on my way. I was surprised at my own anger. That she should instal another in my place as her favourite! Something told me that this was exactly the situation. Call it an ex-lover's intuition. To be free with her in her bed – and for free! I would have preferred a rich old man, preferably an impotent one.

There was not much logic in this response, but when did logic, love and lust ever go together hand in hand? I might at any time have walked away from *her* and felt justified in doing so – we had largely walked away from each other already – but that she should walk away from *me* like this! And with a young lawyer!

"Well," I said at the door of her little chamber, "I will leave you to your friend and his fines, and recoveries, and statutes, and recognizances – and – and all his other dusty stuff."

And I shut the door hard so that I couldn't hear what, if anything, she said in reply.

It was a very brief fit of temper because, once I was outside Holland's Leaguer and walking towards where the road crossed Gravel Lane, I had nearly calmed down. A brisk wind was coming off the river. I almost thought of going back and apologizing to Nell.

But of course I didn't go back. Hadn't been back since.

All of this – this *scene* – had taken place a couple of months earlier at the beginning of the autumn season. Naturally, when it was announced that the Chamberlain's *Troilus and Cressida* was to be rehearsed and performed at Middle Temple, that nest of young lawyers, I was curious as to whether I would encounter her new paramour. But I didn't know which Inn he was a member of – there were four of them altogether – and even if I had known the Inn, then I still had to locate my rival among many dozens of students. I could hardly go around these well-born gentlemen and ask which of them had acquaintance with the trulls of Holland's Leaguer. (For sure, the answer would run to a fat figure, students of the law being as human in this respect as any other young men.)

You may think it very strange that I was ready to accept Nell's entertainment of many Londoners in the way of business but that I should grow aggrieved when she seemed on the point of giving away a portion of her heart. Her heart, which I had thought all mine. Well, if it was strange what of it?

As I lay in my own bed with Peter Agate snoring heavily at my side on his thin mattresss, I reflected on Nell's message about fines and recovery.

'A recovery would be fine.' Was this her way of signalling that she wouldn't mind seeing me again? Was I to recover her, and re-cover her once more? And then all would be fine? Was she using the legal terminology to remind me of our little quarrel over her lawyer friend and to turn it into a joke?

If she was still averse to players, who did no more than spout other men's words like gargoyles, then she'd made an exception to my friend from Miching, hadn't she? He was only an apprentice player and yet she'd given him a free turn in the bed, if he was to be believed. (I did believe him.) Perhaps players were back in favour with her. Perhaps her lawyer friend, he of the *liquid tongue*, had fallen into disfavour. I swiftly constructed, in the confines of my head, an episode in which Nell had given him his quittance. Or perhaps it was the other way about and he had given her hers . . .

Something in me warmed towards Nell as I lay in the darkness. I sniffed at my fingers, disagreeably scented from snuffing Benwell's rancid candle. Well, I wouldn't hurry to recover her, but in my own good time – say in a week or so – I'd stroll across towards Paris Garden and Lord Hunsdon's old manor house, just to see how the land lay with my friend.

Corpus Delicti

But the next day something different came to trouble me, apart from Peter Agate's connection with Nell. It was to do with another old friend, the playwright Richard Milford, and a little piece of work which he'd contrived. A dangerous little piece, as it turned out.

How about this for a plot?

There was once a Duke of an Italian city, somewhere with the name of Malypensa. Duke Ferrobosca was a tyrant who ruled with a rod of iron. He killed his enemies and then had waxwork effigies made of them to tease the dead men's families. This Duke Ferrobosca had a duchess. But then he took a fancy to a younger unmarried woman called Virginia who would not capitulate to him. So he determined to make her his next duchess, thinking that if she would not be wooed with words she might be won with wealth.

The only problem for Ferrobosca was what to do about the woman who would soon be his last duchess. Of course – and why didn't he think of this before? – he would have her killed. So Ferrobosca hired an assassin called Vindice. What he didn't know was that Vindice was the brother of Virginia, and furthermore her lover. Yes, sister and brother were passionately and incestuously in love. This was Virginia's real reason for spurning the Duke.

Vindice the assassin therefore had every reason to reject the Duke's murderous commission and to keep the original duchess alive, in order that Ferrobosca couldn't get his hands on his sister. But, naturally, Vindice did not wish to reveal the true state of affairs between himself and Virginia, nor did he wish to have his reputation as an honest, reliable assassin compromised by an apparent inability to do the job. In addition he needed the money. Therefore he must kill – someone. Fortunately, there was a spare body at hand. Vindice knew (in the Biblical sense) a loose woman named Sostituta who bore a passing resemblance to the original duchess. Now, his amour with Sostituta being long since over, Vindice, villain that he is, contemplated murdering Sostituta and presenting her body to Ferrobosca in a dimly lit room, putting the cash in his purse and making an exit before the imposture was discovered. Meantime he had warned both the original duchess and Virginia to make themselves scarce while this trick was being played.

So Vindice murders Sostituta . . . displays the body to Duke Ferrobosca in that dimly lit room . . . purses up the cash . . . and makes his exit. All is going according to plan. *Unfortunately*, the dead Sostituta has a lover who is a Cardinal of the Church, and therefore a powerful man and a vengeful one too. Now this unholy Cardinal, Carnale by name, finds out what's been happening and he decides to . . .

Well, you get the picture – or the stage-play, which is what it is. I haven't the time to detail other aspects of the piece, like the severed limbs made of wax, the dance in the lunatic asylum, the poisoned nightshirt, the bleeding head, and the torn-out heart. It's a tragedy of a rather ridiculous sort and it all ends in tears, with a pile of mangled corpses, comprising the guilty and the innocent. Comprising just about every character in fact. The last ones to die are Virginia (the tainted heroine) and Vindice (the not insensitive villain), with words of undying love on their lips. This is the most affecting part of the action, even if my eyes stayed dry. Indeed the love between brother and sister, sinful though it is, is well suggested throughout.

This play, called *The World's Diseas'd*, was written by the aforementioned friend of mine, Richard Milford.

"It's a good title, Richard," I'd said to him. "It captures the spirit of the thing. You have painted a sick world."

"I merely show mankind his face in the mirror, you know," said Richard. He might have been talking about a species quite distinct from himself.

Richard Milford had made great strides since his early association with the Chamberlain's Company. He came from near the town of Warwick, the same part of the country as William Shakespeare, and it was sometimes said that he was treading in the master's footsteps. His first play, the first to be performed at least, was *A Venetian Whore*. I'd caught him out in a little bit of borrowing here, since I'd come across a similar piece in the manuscript-chest at the Globe playhouse and we fell out over this sharp practice.* But the borrowing went undetected by anyone else, it seemed, and *A Venetian Whore* was mounted to general acclaim. This success seemed to open a creative vein in him. He speedily drafted a play about a murder in a garden (this one was all his own work, he assured me) and he even brought out a volume of poems called – with artful simplicity – *A Garland*. Richard was possessed by literary ambitions and he knew that an enduring reputation was to be gained through verse, especially lyrical lines about love and transience, rather than through the more ephemeral effusions of the stage.

We were on good terms once more, the rift over *A Venetian Whore* having long since closed. He was a friend, although I could never take him entirely seriously – or not as seriously as he took himself.

Either because he trusted my judgement and sought my approval or perhaps because he wanted to prove that the work of his hand was truly the product of his brain, Richard was in the habit of presenting me with early copies of his

*see *Death of Kings*

most recent pieces. So it was that I'd seen a 'foul paper' copy of *The World's Diseas'd.* I knew it was genuine. The foul paper was the earliest stage of finished composition, before the material was sent to a scrivener to make fair copies, and this one was covered with sufficient splotches and crossings-out to attest to the author's struggle to express himself. Anyway I'd read this piece many weeks before the Chamberlain's were due to present it on stage. At least I assumed that our Company was going to do it, Richard having established himself as something of a favourite with our audiences. But Milford told me that one or two of the seniors were doubtful about the new play. They didn't like the incest in *The World's Diseas'd* and considered that it might be offensive. Richard was baffled.

"After all, the brother and sister in my piece are punished," he said. "They die in the end."

"So does everyone else," I said.

"Of course everybody dies. It's a tragedy."

"What's the problem then?"

"It is rather that Master Burbage and Master Heminges object to the fact that my Vindice and my Virginia are without conscience in their love."

"Your lovers don't say 'sorry' often enough."

"You have hit it, Nicholas. I might have a brother and sister fall in love and couch together as long as they constantly lament their sinful state. However they don't, rather they enjoy it."

"Indeed, they seem somewhat earthy characters."

"Oh come on, you know that audiences like nothing more than a spot of filth. Which is just what the shareholders object to. They're getting old."

"But it is the better part of the play, the brother-and-sister love," I said.

He took this for more of a compliment than it was.

"Thank you, Nicholas. I knew I could rely on you, with your ear for true feeling and real poetry. We men of taste must stick together, you know. Even if Burbage and Heminges don't appreciate my work there are others who do. But you say 'the better part' – does that mean that there are aspects of *The World's Diseas'd* which you consider to be, ah, not so good?"

Richard Milford was still a sensitive creature underneath. The shell of his success was thin. He fixed me with a hard stare. He had a little peculiarity in his eyes which was disconcerting when you first noticed it: one of the irises was heavily flecked with green while the other was pure blue.

"I thought that some of the matter was . . . a little sensational."

"Such as?"

"The severed head and the cut-off arms together in the one scene perhaps."

"It is a satire on cruelty."

"I thought it was a tragedy."

"A satirical tragedy. Or a tragical satire. Or what you will. Those limbs are made of wax, by the way, designed for torment by the cunning of Duke Ferrobosca. They are not real, you know."

"But the heart of the wicked Cardinal torn out at the end and brandished before the audience, that is real."

They'd use a sheep's heart but it would still be real in the sense I meant.

"Nicholas, I tell you," Richard told me, "this is the way the drama is going."

I had to acknowledge that he might be right. You could never lose out by underestimating the taste of an audience, at least when it came to violence. Audiences are funny things though. If you offended them in their proprieties – by advertising the blessings of incest for instance – you ran the risk of failure.

Even so, I was surprised at the direction Richard Milford's writing had taken, from the lightness and sugariness of his early pieces to the violent colouring of this latest offering.

He might well be correct that the drama was getting darker. By contrast, his own personal circumstances were nothing but sunny. For one thing, he was achieving some professional success. For another, he'd recently married. His wife, Lucy, was a pretty, demure piece. She was a gentlewoman.

And not only had Richard Milford got himself a wife, he'd acquired a patron too. I've mentioned already that he seemed to model himself on William Shakespeare: coming from the same country, setting himself up as a playwright and also trying to establish himself as a pure poet. And the one thing a poet needs above all is a patron.

In his early days William Shakespeare had a patron – Henry Wriothesley, Earl of Southampton. Even I, a relatively unknown actor, had exchanged words on two occasions with Wriothesley. I remembered his candid gaze. Shakespeare was still, as far as I knew, friends with the Earl although Southampton had been lucky to escape with his life after the Earl of Essex's rebellion and he yet lived in the shadow of disgrace. WS had dedicated his poem of *Venus and Adonis* to this nobleman, when he was young, when they were both young.

A little while ago Richard Milford decided that he too required a sponsor and fastened on a noble sprig to garnish his first book of verse. So in the front of *A Garland* appeared a florid tribute to one R.V., Robert Venner. Venner was the son of some obscure lord from some backwater Loamshire or Clod Hall. Whatever furrow he'd sprouted from, Venner was entitled to be addressed as Lord Robert. He was no Southampton though. No great port, he was barely a tiny harbour. He wasn't charming and beautiful and dashing like Southampton. Venner was highly undistinguished in appearance, squat and straw-haired. At most a lordling or a lordlet. He was an occasional attender at the Globe playhouse and I'd met him once, very briefly. I thought that Richard Milford ought to have spent longer looking for a patron. I didn't imagine that Venner had too many poets clamouring for his patronage. Still, it was none of my business.

All of this – Richard Milford's new play, titled *The World's Diseas'd*, and his connections with his patron – came together for me in an unfortunate conjunction on the following day, the day after Peter Agate's arrival in my lodgings.

I left Peter asleep in my room in Dead Man's Place. It was nine o'clock but he was still flat on his back, a combination of last night's drinking in the Devil and, no doubt, general excitement at finding himself consorting with real players in the big city. I assumed he'd find something to do to while away the day. I wondered whether he'd pay a return visit to Holland's Leaguer and Nell. I hoped not.

The fog was still creeping around Southwark like a disgraced guest. The sound of church bells came muffled through the gloom. Passengers passed like wraiths in the streets.

In the Globe playhouse it was business as usual today. We played less frequently at this time of year – on the previous day, for example, we'd only had our *Troilus and Cressida* rehearsal at Middle Temple – but we did continue to perform for the public. Our audiences were loyal.

In the morning we rehearsed in the tire-house for some play or other – I've forgotten what it was now – and in the afternoon there was the revival of a drama called *Love's Diversion* by William Hordle. This was a companion piece to his earlier *Love's Disdain*, which had also done well for us. Not a bad house for a revival, all things considered, more than half full. The penny-payers in the pit stamped their feet and huddled together near the stage while their plumy breaths and the smoke from their pipes added to the dank fug of the yard. The twopenny- and threepenny-payers in the galleries were tightly swaddled up on their seats. All their attention was held, I think, by William Hordle's drama of love rewarded. And not a severed head or limb in sight.

A small part of our audience was secured quite tight against the weather, however. The Globe offered a few boxes in the upper reaches of its galleries. These boxes made up in comfort and privacy what they lacked in a near view of the stage. Indeed, they were furnished with curtains that could be pulled to shut out the sun or the rain or the more tedious parts of a play. You could even enjoy your own private fire in your own private box. (Not a good idea in this humble player's opinion. If I'd been a shareholder I would have worried that the wooden Globe might one day be reduced to a mountain of ash.)

After *Love's Diversion* was done I headed for a box in the uppermost gallery. Before the performance began Richard Milford had invited me to join him in a box which his patron had hired, to join him for a glass to drink and for some close conversation. Little Lord Robert was holding court up there. From the stage I'd glimpsed two or three figures aloft in that box. At least the curtains hadn't been drawn, so presumably these people had been attending to the play.

I don't know why I accepted his invitation. Amusement and curiosity perhaps. Still wearing my costume, I tapped at the door to the box and went straight in.

"Ah, Nicholas," said Richard Milford. "May I present you to Lord Robert. My patron, you know."

Oh, didn't I know.

It was late afternoon. Standing in the rapidly dimming daylight in the middle of the box was Richard's stubby patron, his Southampton-substitute. A sea-coal fire threw a flickering glow on the whitewashed walls and kept out the damps. A small woman was sitting at the edge of the little room overlooking the stage. I could see her only in outline. For a moment I hoped that it was Richard Milford's fresh young wife, Lucy. I inclined my head, very slightly.

"Nicholas Revill, my lord," said Milford. "You have met, I believe."

"We have met, I believe," parroted Lord Robert.

"A promising young player, you know," added my friend Milford.

Now, this was the kind of remark sure to gall my kibe. You know you're getting on in experience, if not in years, when you no longer like being called 'promising'.

"Not so young any more, Master Milford," I said neutrally, "but about your age."

"Nor so promising neither, Master Revill? Haw haw."

This was Lord Robert speaking. I found it very difficult to think of him as Lord Anything. Lord Bumpkin perhaps. He had a twangy, rusticky sort of voice, with burrs and thistles clinging to it.

"That is not for me to judge, my lord, how 'promising' I am. You have just seen me perform, after all."

I indicated my costume. In *Love's Diversion* I played a lover – a satisfied lover, unlike Shakespeare's Troilus – and was wearing something smart but unshowy.

Lord Bumpkin came forward and felt the material of my doublet. He had little pig-like eyes, hair like a hay-rick and powerful, meaty hands. He stood back and sized up the overall effect of my costume, as if he might be about to buy it. Then he turned towards the woman sitting by the outer rail. Now I saw that she wasn't Lucy Milford and was disappointed. This woman was much stouter, much thicker. She was also dressed in a style which gave much away, whether you wanted what she was giving or not.

"Whaddya say, Vinny? Do you like the cut of his cloth?"

"I am not a tailor, dear."

"I mean, is Master Revill's performance *promising* – or has he shot his bolt? Haw."

"It depends on what he's promising, don't it, dear?"

Her voice was as ugly and countrified as her husband's.

"Or what he's performing, haw haw," said Lord Bumpkin.

I said nothing, not feeling up to these rallies of wit.

Richard Milford, as if he saw that his aristocratic friends

were not making a favourable impression, busied himself at a little table and handed me a glass of something spiced with ginger.

"Well, *I* thought you did well this afternoon, Nicholas," he said.

Well, thank you, Richard, I thought.

"It is a thin play, this *Love's Diversion*, you know," he added. "It wants a bit of blood and sinew."

"William Hordle is a good craftsman," I said. "Master Shakespeare thinks highly of him."

"Oh, Shakespeare," he said.

"Tell me, Master Revill, you're a player . . . "

"I am, my lord."

Bumpkin Venner seemed to be having difficulty in ordering his thoughts.

"As a player . . . you are able to say . . . regarding these Shakespeares and these Hordles now . . . they don't match up to our playwright, do they?"

"*Our* playwright – I am not sure who – "

"This gent here. They just don't match up, do they?"

Squat Lord Bumpkin slammed a meaty paw into Richard's back, causing him to spill some of the contents of his glass. Even in the dim light of the box, Richard had the grace to look uncomfortable.

"Oh, Richard is without equal," I said.

O Nicholas, master of the diplomatic equivocation.

"And he is not merely our playwright. He is our poet as well. Look."

And from out of a pocket Lord Bumpkin produced a slim volume which I recognized as Richard Milford's *A Garland*. He opened the poetry book near the frontispiece and jabbed a stubby finger at a paragraph. I couldn't make out much in the half-light of the box but Bumpkin saved me the trouble by reading the words aloud, after a bout of throat-clearing to get rid of the burrs and thistles.

"'TO R.V. THE ONLY BEGETTER.'"

These first words were boldly uttered, fitting the capital letters they were printed in. Then the speaker moderated his delivery, imparting a tender, almost trembling quality to what followed.

"'*As the weaker growth must needs find some stronger plant to prop it up, so I turn respectfully but fearfully towards your lordship in hope of your favour, since only in the sun of your gaze can my lines thrive and my verses grow. If these first fruits of my brain prove deformed, I shall be sorry they had so noble a godfather, and vow no more to plough so profitless a furrow, but if posterity find in them some scrap of worth, then may all the honour and praise be his to whom these lines are dedicated.*'"

There was a pause. When he'd first opened the *Garland*, I expected Lord Bumpkin to read one of Richard's poems but he had chosen instead to read the dedication – the dedication to himself. R.V. THE ONLY BEGETTER, Robert Venner. A dedication may be a kind of poem, I suppose, with a similar degree of pretence and deceit in it. In fact Bumpkin hadn't so much read as recited it, and I realized that he had the words off by heart. Well, if a volume of verse was dedicated to me I expect I'd know the words pretty thoroughly too. Although I probably wouldn't read them aloud to a stranger. Not unless I was very self-assured – or stupid.

"Very good," I said.

Richard Milford coughed, as if with embarrassment.

"Our poet, eh, Vinny?"

"Some of those verses are about me, they are," said the woman called Vinny. She hadn't moved from her seat in the corner. I wondered that she didn't need to wear more clothing on such a cold and dank afternoon. Now she made a give-me gesture to her husband. He handed over the precious volume. Without opening it, she brandished it like a prize. "About me these verses are. Master Milford told me so."

Another compromised cough from Milford.

"Better than having words about you scrawled up in the jakes, eh, Vinny?" said Lord Venner.

I expected the lady to object to the imputation that people wrote items about her on the walls of a privy, but to my surprise she found her husband's remark extremely witty. Her large tits quivered. Her cheeks puffed out in delight.

"Especially when you wrote those words in the first place," said this lady to her beloved.

"One must do something when one is at stool," said my lord.

"The devil finds work for idle hands," said his lady.

They guffawed together. Then, glancing down at the book in her hand, she made an effort to elevate the conversation and repeated, "But these verses *are* about me. Master Milford says so."

"Then they must be, my lady," I said, "since we all know that poets never lie either in their verses – or in their persons."

I gulped at my glass. Whether from the ginger in the wine or from some other cause I felt my face growing warm in this little sea-coal-heated playhouse box.

"We are informed that Richard has written a new play," announced Lord Bumpkin.

"*The World's Diseas'd*, you know, Nicholas," said Richard Milford, the complacent satirist.

"What? Oh yes. I do know it. I have been privileged to receive the foul papers."

"Foul papers? Is it horrid?" said the lady. "Is it dirty?"

Richard hurried to explain this piece of theatrical jargon, before someone could make some fresh comment about privy walls.

"You've seen it," said the lord in surprise.

"Not only seen it, I've read it," I said.

"It is a great work, though, is it not?" said Lord Bumpkin to me. "Fit to rival Master Shakespeare's."

"Never thought much of *him* meself," said his lady.

"*The World's Diseas'd* has blood and sinew, certainly," I said.

(And the odd severed limb and head.)

"I look forward to reading it – fair or foul – guts and all," said the woman called Vinny.

"I don't have time to read, not even to read the works of our poet," said Lord Bumpkin, "I am too busy with more important things. I rely on Vinny to read for me. She is a lady of discrimination."

She was so obviously the opposite that I waited for the heavens to fall or at least for Richard Milford to intervene with a soothing platitude, but he had apparently given up, even on his coughing.

"I am sure that is the case, my lord. Her appearance alone is a warrant of her good taste," I said, bowing slightly in her direction. Lady Venner twinkled in return, showing a good amount of bad tooth and heaving booby. I couldn't endure another instant in this box. Luckily I had an excuse to hand.

"Now I must return these clothes or I'll be in trouble with the tire-man."

"I'll come with you, Nicholas," said Richard. "I also have some business with the tire-man. If you'll forgive me, my lord and lady. Please stay as long as you like."

"It's our box, we've paid for it, we shall stay," said Bumpkin.

We made our adieus to the elevated couple in their rented box. As we left Richard interjected an oddly domestic note when he asked the Bumpkins to ensure that the small fire was doused before they departed. Perhaps, in the midst of more important considerations, he too had remembered that the Globe playhouse was built of wood.

"How should I do that, extinguish a fire?" said Bumpkin, evidently considering this a servant's task. "What instrument should I use?"

"Piss on it, Robbie," said his noble lady. "You have an instrument to hand."

"Haw haw," said Bumpkin.

I didn't wait to see whether he was going to act on her suggestion. I was rather afraid that he might. I clattered down the stairs to the ground floor, aware that Richard Milford was at my heels and aware too that he wanted to *explain* things to me. Visiting the tire-man was just an excuse.

He caught my arm as we were in the passageway outside the tire-house. He raised his eyebrows as if to signify, 'Yes I *know*.'

I said nothing.

"Poets and playwrights need patrons," he said. "We can't all have Southamptons at our beck and call. Young men in possession of all the graces are hard to come by, those with wealth *and* connections *and* refinement."

"But Lord Robert Venner does have *one* of the graces, surely? Let me guess which one it is. I have it – he must be rich."

"You know, Nicholas, you should play the prig more often. You do it so naturally. But to answer your question, yes, he is rich – rich in expectation."

"Then he lives on the air, promise-crammed. And I assume others will live on *his* promises."

"Don't assume. He's not like some of your more high and mighty patrons. Lord Robert has done more than ply me with promises. That gentleman you have such a low opinion of, he is paying to have some copies of my play circulated privately. *The World's Diseas'd*, you know."

"Printed, you mean?"

I was as surprised as I must have sounded. The only plays which were honoured with publication were the established successes, and then not invariably. Yet Richard's hadn't even been performed yet.

"Yes, printed and bound by Master Nicholson over in Paul's."

"Immortality guaranteed?"

"A little fame, local fame. Immortality is another thing, you know."

"I'm sure you'll live to see it," I said. "This next book will have an appropriate dedication?"

"You have heard of a *quid pro quo*, Nicholas, you with all your learning. You may also have heard the saying in the marketplace that you can't lure a hawk with an empty hand. In fact, to show you how . . . unabashed I am by all of this . . . I will tell you that I am dedicating *The World* to *both* of my patrons. It was that, I believe, which encouraged them to have the play printed. "

"You have a generous patron – sorry, patrons."

"And there's another thing," said Richard. "We writers have many weapons in our armoury, many arrows in our quiver."

"As many as you have metaphors," I said.

"It is possible to take the money with one hand – to put it crudely – and yet to pay back with the other."

"I don't understand."

"We may love our patrons in our prefaces and dedications, yet convey a truer message elsewhere. A hidden message."

"That's subtle," I said.

"So tell me truly what you think of them," said Richard, jerking his head in an upwards direction. I wondered if Lord Bumpkin had pissed out the sea-coal fire yet.

"A delightful couple, if somewhat earthy."

"I do not think you really think so, Nicholas. You are being ironical. Though I would sooner you were ironical than priggish."

"Inform me of one thing, though, before I return this costume," I said, beginning to undo my points and making for the tire-house. "Those verses in your *Garland* book, they are not really about that woman in the box, are they? She's not exactly the nonpareil of beauty."

"Beauty is in the eye of the beholder," explained the poet. "I am happy if she thinks that the verses are about her. And if she thinks that they are, they are. But whatever you do, don't say a word to my wife."

At once I became interested.

"Lucy? Why not?"

"Because, you simpleton, I have told her that the lines are hers, some of them at any rate. It's easy to see that you've never written a love-poem."

"Can't she share the lines with Venner's wife?"

"Wife?"

"The lady in the box."

"She is his sister."

"I assumed that she was his wife."

"Assuming again, Nicholas," said Milford, turning on his heel.

As I exchanged the play clothes for my street garb in the tire-house – half-listening to the grumble of the tire-man Bartholomew Ridd that I was the last one from *Love's Diversion* to bring my costume in – I ran over what I'd discovered from Richard.

That the playwright had a generous patron, there was no denying. Whatever Lord Bumpkin's reasons for wanting *The World's Diseas'd* published, the fact remained that Richard's little book would actually be launched on the world, watertight and ship-shape, and with a much better chance of survival than it would have had as a pile of paper languishing in some corner of the playhouse.

I couldn't make out Lord Bumpkin and his sister though. Why had I taken them for man and wife? They looked a bit alike, hay-rickish and toothy. They had the same expensive but slightly coarse clothing and very coarse manners, while claiming refinement. On the other hand they hadn't seemed particularly intimate (sign of one kind of marriage) or distant (sign of another kind). But, since I'd only seen them together for a few minutes, what did I know about Robbie and Vinnie Vennor of Clod Hall, Loamshire?

Robbie and Vinnie. I smelled the nursery here. The clutching at slippery syllables, the lisping of names. I thought that Vinnie was most likely a diminutive – an affectionate, babbling child's diminutive – for Virginia. A brother's blubbery attempt to get his fat baby lips around 'Virginia', and then a fond name which had stuck between them since.

Next I thought of Richard Milford's latest play, *The World's Diseas'd*, and of the brother and sister in that drama. The passionate and earthy brother and sister, Vindice and Virginia. Well, what's in a name? A rose would smell as sweet & cetera. Nevertheless it was perhaps a little . . . *tactless* . . . of Richard to name one of his characters after the sister of his only begetter. And then to plunge that character into the toils of an incestuous love affair. Perhaps the playwright considered that he was paying them a tribute? No, Richard was obtuse sometimes but not that obtuse. Perhaps he was simply oblivious to the coincidence of names? I didn't think that was likely either. No, I considered that Richard was probably doing what he'd boastfully hinted at to me just now. That is, he was getting back at his patrons, whose coarseness and stupidity he was well aware of, getting back at them in the only way he could – through the power of his pen. I'd called it 'subtle' but really I thought it was foolish.

I hoped that the real-life brother and sister, if they found out, would not take amiss this 'accident' of naming, especially since they were paying to have the work printed and circulated. Maybe neither Lord nor Lady Bumpkin would get beyond the title-page. There are advantages sometimes to having stupid and unbookish patrons.

I'd more or less forgotten about my friend up from the country, Peter Agate. When I returned to Dead Man's Place, however, I found him eager to tell me of his latest London adventures. Not with Nell of Holland's Leaguer, as it turned out. Rather he'd spent part of the day in friendly conversation with the zealous, chalk-faced individual who'd been ejected from the Goat & Monkey by the boatmen. This conversation was surprising, given that Peter had previously rebuked Chalk-face, cast aspersions on his ears and generally acted as though he had neither time nor patience for the man's anti-drama zealotry.

"It wasn't an argument this time, Nick. He was once as we are."

"Sane, you mean?"

"He was a player. With Lord Strange."

Why wasn't I surprised that the old man should have been on stage? Converted sinners make the best preachers.

"His name is Chesser," Peter continued. "He was a player, I say, but then he saw the light."

"Listen to him long enough and you will see it too."

"He was trying to get me to see it, yes. That was also why he was talking to that man from Philip Henslowe's company. Seeing he was getting nowhere in that quarter, and having an ear out for our conversation, Master Chesser could not help trying to convert me to his cause instead."

"I didn't know you wanted to be converted from playing."

"But today he was talking about the old days instead," said Peter, avoiding my question. "I was interested."

"Plenty of people in the Chamberlain's could provide you with tales about the old days, if that's what you want," I said. "You were speaking to one or two of them last night in the Devil."

"Master Chesser has a tale about the devil too, not the tavern one either."

"He probably does. Most of us can talk of the devil."

"It's not only that, Nick."

Once again I sensed that Peter had something to tell me. I waited.

"I have been reviewing my behaviour. My London behaviour, I now call it. I was discourteous yesterday in the tavern, the first tavern, the Goat & Monkey not the Devil. At first I thought it must be the fault of the drink. No . . . my own fault rather. I think I've been drinking ever since I arrived in this town. I can remember only a little of what I've said and done. One thing I did remember though was that I had been discourteous to Master Chesser. I recalled my words to him in the Goat & Monkey – and I rued them."

"Rued your rudeness."

"I wanted to atone," said Peter, ignoring my little joke. "So when I saw Chesser – or rather when he loomed out of the fog today and grabbed me by the arm, and when I'd recovered from the surprise and recognized him – I thought that the least I could do was to give him a hearing. To atone for my jibes of yesterday."

"Well, you have paid for your jibe about his ears by now – by giving him yours for several hours."

"But I have been rewarded, Nick. He has much to say that is worth listening to. His time with Lord Strange's men. The great days of playing in the '80s."

"Well then, I am glad," I said. "That's that."

I respected the penitential mood in Peter Agate but didn't necessarily want to hear any more of it. So, to change the subject, I reminded him that he was due to take part in another rehearsal of *Troilus and Cressida* at Middle Temple the next day, since Thomas Pope still hadn't returned from his visit to Lord Hunsdon's house. But Peter wasn't finished yet.

"I am wondering whether this is the life for me after all, this playing life."

"But you came to London expressly to be a player."

"A man may change his mind."

"After two or three days?"

"Better now than later."

"Is this the result of meeting old whatisname? Chesser?"

"No, or not much. It's more that I am not sure I like my London behaviour."

"That's the second time you've mentioned it. There's obviously something in the air here, some contagion."

"You speak in jest – "

"Look, you got drunk, you visited a whorehouse. You can do these things anywhere, although it's easier in London. And the goods are better here even if they're more expensive."

"Too easy. I say nothing of the expense, at least in terms of money."

Oh dear. Peter was having a little attack of conscience. I wondered whether to tell him what a friend (Nell in fact) had once told me: that the best way to survive such an attack was to harden your heart and sit it out. The trouble was that I suspected Peter enjoyed being conscience-struck. You can indulge your conscience just like anything else. A thought occurred to me: that maybe this was Peter's grandfather (another Peter) peeping out, the one who had presented the living of Miching to my father and who had reputedly been a pious and severe man. Perhaps these traits had been inherited by his grandson, who was now fierce in condemnation of himself. But it would not have been tactful to raise these ideas with the young Peter. So I changed direction again.

"What would you do instead?" I said. "Slink back to Miching and your play-hating father – and your rapacious stepmother?"

I was pleased to see a twitch which almost amounted to a grin tug at Peter's face.

"You're right, I suppose. I can't go home to them – or not quite yet. I don't believe they'd welcome me back like the prodigal son. Though, God knows, my London self has been prodigal enough."

I made no reply but noted how Peter was now talking grandly of his 'London self'. Well, if my friend wanted to think that the reprehensible acts he'd committed, such as drinking and whoring, were somehow to be laid at the door of his 'London self' while a purer Peter was elsewhere at his prayers, that was his business – or his delusion.

It was odd that, whereas the day before I'd tried to dampen

his enthusiasm for playing, now I was trying to prop him up. But I wish now that I had encouraged him to go home straightaway, or to leave London and have nothing more to do with plays and playing. It would have been for the best after all. He might have lived.

This *Troilus and Cressida* is a funny piece, a sour piece. I don't know whether WS was in a crabbed mood when he wrote the play or was exorcizing some internal imps of mischief and cynicism but for sure there is something unaccountable at work within it. If I knew him better I'd ask – but perhaps he doesn't know himself.

Still, there was something about the Trojan play which fitted that damp, foggy, bone-aching autumn. My own fortunes seemed to be going well enough but apprehension hung in the air. Our patron Lord Hunsdon was sick, the Queen was dying by degrees, and nobody knew what the future held. The age of heroes, whether Trojan or English, the period of gallant deeds by land and sea, all of this was done. An air of spiritless exhaustion hung over the town, as if London herself had endured a ten-year siege and could expect no relief from any quarter. (Some say London and Troy are linked. There is a stone set in the middle of Candlewick Street and brought here by Brutus, who was descended from Aeneas of Troy. I have seen the stone and can vouch for it. As long as the stone is preserved our city will flourish, they say.)

And if *Troilus and Cressida* fitted that dying season, it also fitted the tastes of our audience at Middle Temple, as I quickly realized at an early rehearsal. Although we weren't due to perform for a week or so, word of this witty and scabrous piece had got abroad among the law students, and they started clustering around us players in the banqueting hall until Dick Burbage or one of the other seniors shooed them away because a practice was starting. When I arrived at the next rehearsal I saw Peter Agate, who'd decided not to abandon the Chamberlain's for the moment, happily passing the time with some of my friends and with a couple of the law students. There was a gust of laughter from the little assembly of players and young lawyers.

"Helen of Troy is only a piece of property after all," said one of the law students. I could identify him as such by his gown and the plainness of his clothes. The Inn lawyers were not permitted to wear finery.

"Hotly contested property," said the other student, also gowned and plainly garbed.

"*Property*? Where are your hearts and souls?" said Michael Donegrace. "Helen is the non-pareil of beauty. I would have played her once."

Michael had been one of our boy-players, specializing in women's parts. But over the past few months his voice had gone down while his height had gone up, and he was no longer fitted for women's parts. Now he was acting the young Greek warrior, Patroclus.

"Lawyers don't have souls. And about their hearts there is some doubt," said the first student, but in such a way that I wasn't entirely sure whether he was joking. He had a beaky face.

"Helen of Troy could be as ugly as sin," said the second student. "Her beauty is not *in* question. Nor is it *the* question."

"The question is one of possession, prior possession," said the first student.

"The question is rather that of *spolia opima* – and also one of damaged goods," said the second student. This young lawyer was round in the face, with carroty hair.

"Ah, a debate," said Jack Wilson, rubbing his hands. "It could be good, if we knew exactly what they were talking about."

I watched Peter Agate as he looked intently from speaker to speaker. His expression was absorbed, intent. My fellow Chamberlain's men, Jack Wilson and Michael Donegrace, also looked as though they relished the chance of seeing fledgling lawyers debate, for nothing.

The two young men acknowledged my presence – it struck me that they were waiting for a larger audience before they opened their 'debate' – and Jack took the hint to introduce me. One was called Michael Pye, he of the beaky countenance, and the other, the carroty one, was called Edmund Jute. When it was clear that we were all ears, Pye and Jute opened their gobs to begin the debate, just as they'd been trained to do in this very hall, but Jack Wilson got in first.

"One word," said Jack, "if we're to follow you gentlemen you'll have to talk in good, honest English. We're not in a court of law now."

"Very well," said Master Pye, with a slight sigh, "to put it plain. The Trojan prince Paris has seized Helen from her husband Menelaus, the King of Sparta. Now Menelaus and the other Greek kings want her back. And the law of nature and the law of nations speak aloud to have her returned."

"No," said Master Jute. "The beautiful Helen is a prize of war, seized by the sword and retained by the sword. The spoils of war go to the victor. We are talking of heroes here. And this lady's not for returning."

"The age of heroes is dead," I said and the others looked at me in surprise.

No, I don't know why I'd said it either (although it had been in my mind earlier in the day). In order to cover my confusion I added a lighter remark, "But I agree the lady's not for returning. Spoils of war or not, she is a little *spoiled*."

Now Master Pye glanced disdainfully at me as if I had blundered into a complicated game and shown complete ignorance of the rules. But Master Jute looked pleased.

"Exactly so, Master . . . Revill, is it? Helen is the prize of war but she's also spoiled goods, damaged ones."

"Only a little handled, a little fondled," said Michael Donegrace, the ex-boy-player. "She retains her beauty still."

"But we don't return a half-eaten sweetmeat to the cook, do we?" said Jute. "We don't return soiled goods to the shopkeeper. So how can Helen be returned with any honour?"

"She's only been nibbled at," said young Donegrace.

"A rare piece of goods," said Jack Wilson.

I could see that the high-minded debate about rights and wrongs, about the spoils of war and spoiled goods, was breaking down into excited contemplation of Helen of Troy. What exactly did the woman have about her person that caused a ten-year war – that launched a thousand ships, in Kit Marlowe's words?

"Helen's a hot morsel," said Michael Pye.

"The Trojans' strumpet," said Edmund Jute. "Or their *trumpet*, you may say, for all the Trojans blow at her, or on her, or down her, or want to blow at, on or down her."

"A *quaedam*," said Pye. "A certain woman."

"A *quicumque vult*," said Jute, not to be outdone in Latin wit.

It was perhaps rather a relief to see these two fledgling lawyers being young men too, enjoying their cracks (of a learned kind) about women, and being prepared to snigger along with the rest of us.

At this point our jollity was cut short by Dick Burbage who announced that he wanted to get on with the business of playing in a few minutes. The scattered law students started to drift reluctantly towards the door. Pye and Jute, however, showed no inclination to move. It's odd how eager the laity – if I can use that term to describe non-players – are to hang about on the margins of the theatre world. They even seem to enjoy attending rehearsals.

I'd noticed, of course, that Master Pye had used the expression *quaedam* to describe Helen of Troy. It was a term more usually applied to a strumpet (or trumpet) than to the wife of a king. I remembered that Nell had taken pleasure in telling me that she had been so described – as a *quaedam*, as a *bona roba* – without seeming to be aware of the sneering strain in such descriptions. I remembered also that her fresh lover and protector was a gentleman from one of the Inns of Court across the water. So naturally I couldn't help wondering whether, in the person of Middle Temple's Michael Pye, he of the beaky face, I had stumbled across the new occupant of my old friend's bed. My rival.

And with the certainty of intuition I was at once sure that I had identified my rival. Master Pye, with his prominent nose and cocky manner. Who did he remind me of now?

And, of course, if I had (perhaps) identified *him* wasn't it possible that he had recognized me, although we'd never met? Nell would have mentioned me, wouldn't she? Revill's a young player with the Chamberlain's, she'd have said – a pleasant, witty fellow, she might have said, even if we were no longer on such good terms. Or maybe I was deluding myself? Perhaps she never bothered to mention me at all.

They say that the purpose of art is to hold the mirror up to nature but it often seems to me to be the other way about. Life has a way of imitating art. Take this *Troilus and Cressida* play. I act a young lover who grows to suspect and then to hate a rival in the Greek camp, one Diomedes. Troilus suffers the violent anguish of betrayal when his Cressida switches her allegiance. Now, believing I had a real-life rival in my gaze, I wasn't certain what I felt. No grand heroic response, for sure. But then it is hard to strike heroic poses over a whore.

"Let me show you something before I leave, Master Revill."

I felt a touch on my arm. It was Edmund Jute, the red-headed law student.

"I would not like you to think that we lawyers are without hearts and souls, not completely without, whatever my friend Pye says."

"I took that for a jest. I know you are not really dry fellows, but lusty and full of juice."

This was perhaps a rather fuller commendation of lawyers than Master Jute had been looking for but he beckoned me to follow him down the banqueting hall, saying it would only take a moment. Out of curiosity I went after him.

At the raised end of the hall, the opposite end to where we were about to rehearse, was a great table set beneath a mighty bank of portraits. The table was made out of a single oak tree from Windsor Forest, Master Jute told me, the gift of the Queen. She had once dined at Middle Temple. It wasn't this, however, which the student wanted to show me but another table below it, a smaller one and rather battered-looking.

"If this wood could talk," said Edmund Jute, rapping the top.

Seeing that he needed to be humoured, I simply nodded and looked attentive.

"It has circumnavigated the globe, this piece of wood, travelled further than we ever shall. It comes from Drake's boat – I believe it is a hatch-cover."

"Sir Francis Drake?"

"The very same. Drake of The *Golden Hind* that is now laid up at Deptford. He dined here many years ago after he had sailed round the world. Now his hatch-cover is used for ceremony, for signing the roll of members and so on."

I ran my hand over the surface of the table.

"There was a hero for you, Master Revill, if you are searching for heroes now . . . "

"I wasn't, particularly. The remark I made earlier came from nowhere."

"He was from your part of the world if I'm not mistaken."

"Who?"

"Drake. From the West Country. You still carry a trace of it in your voice."

Once I'd have been irritated to think that my roots still showed, however faintly. Now it didn't bother me so much.

"And Master Agate also, I'd say," said Edmund Jute. "From *his* voice."

"We come from the same village," I said. "Not Sir Francis Drake, but Peter and I."

"A small world," said Jute musingly.

"If that hatch-cover spoke now, Master Jute, it would tell us that your small world was rather a great globe. Doubtless."

Jute gave a small, snorting laugh. Then he said, "And if we're talking of the Globe now – the Globe playhouse, that is – Master Agate tells me that he is here to play too. Your village must breed players."

"I am glad that Master Agate is so resolved. A little while ago he was all for quitting London and making for home there and then."

"London is a fine place for a young man, full of opportunities."

Jute was obviously referring to himself, but it was a curiously middle-aged thing to say. Not having exhausted the subject of the city, he went on, "Some of those who come to London expect to find the highways made of gold. They never recover from their disappointment. Perhaps Master Agate is of that company?"

"Do you count yourself in that company, Master Jute?" I said, unwilling to say more about my friend.

"Oh, I have long since recovered, Master Revill."

"You sound old beyond your years."

"You could not pay a greater compliment to a lawyer," he said, smiling.

At that instant there was a second, urgent summons from Dick Burbage. Even Edmund Jute could see that he had to leave the hall. I thanked him for showing me Francis Drake's table. He told me that he was looking forward to seeing *Troilus and Cressida*. We shook hands and parted. I walked to the other end of the hall, the screen end. The prologue was beginning.

In Troy there lies the scene. From isles of Greece
The princes orgulous, their high blood chafed,

> *Have to the port of Athens sent their ships,*
> *Fraught with the ministers and instruments*
> *Of cruel war . . .*

Then it was my turn, since it is the love-sick Troilus who fires the first shot in this campaign.

At the end of the rehearsal I was briefly detained by Shakespeare. With his usual consideration he wished to tell me that, since Thomas Pope was returning on the following day from his visit to Hertfordshire and the Chamberlain's patron, Lord Hunsdon, there would be no more lines for Peter to read in rehearsal. Pope would resume the role of scurrilous Thersites. Perhaps I could pass that message on to my friend?

"I'd be pleased to," I said, not entirely displeased that Peter was no longer required.

"Though Dick Burbage won't mind if he remains on hand for the time being. He might be useful. He has found some friends in the Company, I think."

"He has an easy, open nature," I said.

"He will make a player one day, Nick, if that's what he wants. Does he?"

"I'm not sure. Part of him does."

"If that part persists he will make a player. Tell Master Agate that also."

"Thank you, William. He'll be – reassured. How is our patron?"

"Either at the point of death or out riding twenty miles every day. Rumour sleeps in the sick-bed. So we are waiting for a first-hand account."

I would have liked to press for more information – or rather I wanted to know what the Chamberlain's were going to do if Lord Hunsdon died suddenly and left us without a protector – but it wasn't the kind of question I could easily put to WS. So, after a few aimless remarks about Windsor tables and Drake's hatches (both of which

WS already knew about), I made my way into the foggy evening.

The next few days passed in a blur of rehearsals (for *Troilus and Cressida*) and occasional performances (of other things) at the Globe, although the weather tended to thin our audiences. It was a relief to get inside the Middle Temple banqueting hall, away from the unhealthy damps and the cold. I looked forward to the performance, knowing that if those young lawyers, Edmund Jute and Michael Pye, were typical of our audience then we were assured of a warm but not uncritical reception. Perhaps our future, or part of it, lay in these privileged indoor performances. Thomas Pope, the senior and shareholder, came back from Hertfordshire and reported that Lord Hunsdon probably had a year or two more left in him but that he would no longer be a vigorous protector or promoter of our interests. This was an unsatisfactory conclusion.

My friend Peter was still quartered in my room, paying his penny-and-a-half a night direct to Master Benwell. I didn't object to this. He continued to consort with members of our Company, hanging around at rehearsals, drinking with us, listening to our talk, sometimes adding to it. I couldn't have said what his plans were. Probably he couldn't have either. Perhaps his London half and his country half were fighting out a civil war inside him. There was no opening with the Chamberlain's at present, even had the seniors been inclined to employ him, but he did go and enquire one day of the Admiral's Men, Henslowe's crowd. If he returned to visit Nell at the brothel known as Holland's Leaguer, he didn't tell me of it.

Then one afternoon, about a week after his arrival in London, Peter was killed.

I can be precise enough as to the time of his death. It must have occurred as I was turning down Clink Street, perhaps five minutes away from my front door. I can't remember what

I was thinking of just beforehand, because everything was wiped from my mind when I reached the entrance to my lodgings. The door was unlocked and slightly open. I don't even know whether this struck me as odd. It should have done since Master Benwell believed in that tight-lipped householder's proverb, 'fast bind fast find'.

I tried to push open the door to the small lobby but it moved only a little way before jarring against something. Impatiently, I shoved harder. Again it seemed to stick. I peered round the partly open door to discover what the impediment was. The light was very poor but I could make out a huddled human shape half propped against the inside of the door, with its legs stretched out across the floor.

I think I knew that it was Peter Agate. For an instant I must have assumed – or hoped – that my friend was drunk. Coming in befuddled from the Devil or the Goat, leaning against the entrance, sliding down stupefied to end up on the floor. I said his name several times, loudly at first then softer. His doublet was unfastened. I leaned over and grazed my fingertips across his shirt front, which was sopping wet. I knelt down. The floor was wet too. For sure the fool had spilled drink all down himself or had puked up his guts after a few pints too many. Only there was no stink of drink, but another smell. The wetness on his front was dark and pooling and slightly sticky and of course I knew. Knew also from the way his head lolled haplessly in my direction, as if to impart a confidence.

Then there was a human noise behind me, somewhere between a cough and a snort. A smoky light swelled to fill the little hallway. But it did not take the illumination from one of Master Benwell's cheap tallow candles to tell me that my childhood friend was dead. On Peter's forehead I saw the mark, now nearly healed, where he had struck the lintel to my room. I wanted to touch it and reached out my hand to do so but faltered at the last instant. *Vita brevis*, I thought. He would never be a player now. I wished that he had waited to die until that little wound on his forehead was all healed.

Post Mortem

"Did you kill him?"

"I did not."

"Do you know who did?"

"No."

"So all you know is that you did not kill him."

"Yes."

"Did you mean to kill him?"

I started to say something then realized that any response to that question was dangerous. So I merely shook my head.

"Did you want to kill him?"

"He was my friend. He was an inoffensive fellow. Without enemies."

"That is not the answer to what I asked, Master Revill."

"Even so, it is the only answer I can give, Master Talbot."

Master Alan Talbot was questioning me about Peter Agate's death and it was evident that he considered me not so much as a witness but as a potential murderer. Perhaps the Middlesex coroner saw most of his witnesses in that light. He had cold, ungiving eyes, like the corpse's which he examined in the way of business. He was a dangerous man too, from my point of view, since he had the authority to lay an indictment and to order an arrest – the arrest of N. Revill, for example. Talbot had indicated that this was a preliminary examination but had hinted, more by looks than actual words, that an unsatisfactory answer would land me in trouble. But, in my opinion, the only satisfactory answer as far as he was concerned would have been a straight confession.

I sat awkwardly facing Talbot. I had been summoned to his house in Long Southwark where a silent servant-girl showed me to his first-floor study. The fog had finally lifted and a glittering sun shone low into my eyes through the window behind the coroner. I shifted my head slightly to escape the light. I wondered if he'd deliberately positioned me here to increase my discomfort.

"Tell me again, Master Revill, why you crossed the bridge. If you were coming from the Middle Temple."

"I *was* coming from Middle Temple, sir. You may ask my fellows in the Chamberlain's. I was at a rehearsal there which occupied me until the last moment."

"I may ask them, though I don't doubt you were at a rehearsal. My question is why you didn't cross the river from Temple Stairs rather than going the long way about and walking over the bridge. Aren't you familiar with London?"

"I know my London."

He consulted a sheet of paper in front of him.

"Yet you're a country lad from the parish of Miching. Where is that?"

"In Somerset."

"Do you wish you were back there now?"

This was such an odd question that I didn't know how to respond, but perhaps my hesitation was answer enough.

"To return to the business of the river crossing," he said. "Didn't you have the money to pay the ferryman?"

In normal circumstances I would have bridled, slightly, at the imputation. Was he suggesting that players were poorly paid artisans? But these weren't normal circumstances. I couldn't afford to bridle or to get on my high horse. So why hadn't I taken the ferry across the Thames that late afternoon? Why had I chosen to trace a roundabout route through the city and then across London Bridge to Dead

Man's Place? I didn't know. It's hard to account for unexamined moments, for decisions so small they hardly deserve the name of decisions.

"I had enough money. But, if I'm honest, I can't recollect why I walked instead of being ferried. Is it material?"

As soon as these last words were out of my mouth I realized I'd made a mistake. I was calling into question, however mildly, the coroner's right to ask whatever questions *he* chose to ask. Talbot brought his palms down flat on the desk which was between us.

"Very material, Master Revill, leaving the question of your honesty to one side. It would have taken you, what?, an hour or more to walk through the city and back to your lodgings, a tedious hour on a damp, foggy afternoon. But it would have taken you less than half that time to hire a ferry at Temple Stairs, be landed on this side of the river and return to those same lodgings. You would then have had a spare half-hour or more at your disposal . . . "

"To kill my friend, you mean?"

"Your words, Master Revill."

My skin broke out in goosebumps. My mouth was dry.

"What reason – I mean – "

"That is what we are here to determine, the reason," said Master Talbot. "According to your landlord's testimony, he heard bumping sounds from the lobby, as of a struggle, and then heard you calling your friend's name several times over. He came out to find you stooping over Master Agate while his chest was still pumping out his life's-blood."

"You've already heard my story. I had just come through the outer door myself. It was stuck and I had to push it – against – against Peter's body."

"You did call out the name of the dead man, repeatedly."

"I thought he was drunk and had fallen down and hurt himself."

"His blood was on you."

"That couldn't be helped. It went everywhere."

"It went everywhere," echoed Talbot.

I went colder still at the tone of the coroner's voice and at the memory of the murder. Peter had been stabbed through the heart. I had caught him within minutes of his dying. The sounds that Benwell heard must have been the sounds of some desperate struggle.

"Master Agate was freshly killed. And if not by you, Master Revill, then by someone else. Yet you saw no one running from the house? Did you see anyone running from the house?"

It would have been easy to make up a figure fleeing from the front door and into the murk. Easy to imagine that I had actually seen such a figure. Easy but dangerous. Stick to the truth. Say no more than you have to. Avoid speculation.

"It was foggy. I don't think I saw anyone. I was probably walking with my head down."

"Ah yes. It was a good afternoon for a stroll, wasn't it. Tell me, Master Revill, what did you do with the weapon?"

"I did not kill my friend, sir. I have no weapon. I am not permitted to carry a sword."

"No matter. We are not talking swords or rapiers here. A knife or a bodkin is easily hidden, and quickly discarded. You are certain that you saw no one running away into the fog, perhaps throwing down an object? You heard nothing?"

Now I did suspect a trap. For sure, Master Talbot wanted me to create a shape out of the mist, a shape that ran off and threw away a little dagger so that it clattered on to the icy ground. Not because he believed in such an apparition but because he wanted to see whether I could be persuaded to invent a story to draw blame or attention from myself.

"I saw nothing. I heard nothing. I was in a mist."

"Did you not threaten your friend?" said Talbot suddenly. "Threaten his life?"

"No, sir. I had no reason to."

"That is not what your landlord, Samuel Benwell, says."

"Master Benwell was not privy to our conversations."

"He says otherwise. Sometimes you talked so loud that he couldn't help hearing, willy-nilly."

Couldn't help having his ear pinned to my door, you mean, I thought but did not say.

The coroner picked up another sheet of paper from the desk-top.

"He deposes this: that you said that if he – that is, Master Agate – went any further you would kill him. Is that so?"

"No – I don't think . . . but it's possible that I might have made some such comment in jest."

And indeed I had a half-memory of telling Peter, soon after his arrival in my room, that if he didn't stop apologizing I would kill him. It was only a joke, a joke that was simultaneously callous and feeble. And an unfortunate remark, doubly unfortunate now.

"You had a dispute . . . about a whore," said Master Talbot.

I realized that Samuel Benwell must have spent all his time listening outside my door, probably in the hope of picking up players' tittle-tattle.

"Not a dispute, no."

"Let us call it instead, a fight. Didn't you fight with your friend and strike him on the head?"

"He hit himself on the doorway to my room when he came back drunk one night. I had nothing to do with it."

I would have said, ask Benwell, but the landlord was probably the source of this story. Talbot was silent.

"It is true that Peter visited a – a friend of mine – in Holland's Leaguer," I said at last.

"A friend? You mean a whore?"

"What do you suppose, a Puritan?"

Talbot said nothing.

"Of course it was a whore."

"Do you players often visit whores?"

"It is not a habit confined to players, I believe."

"Say vice rather than habit."

I shrugged. It was evident that Alan Talbot didn't much

care for players. He'd already made that clear in one or two preliminary remarks in my examination. Like many in authority he probably blamed us for encouraging immorality and undermining law and order. I don't suppose he cared for whores either.

"You were jealous of your friend, Master Agate?"

"Jealous over a whore! That is like being resentful of the wind for brushing your enemy's face as well as your own. The wind goes where it pleases."

"Very poetical, Master Revill. Why do you say 'enemy'? Was your friend your enemy?"

"He was not."

"I ask again, did you kill him?"

"I say again, I did not."

"As you say."

Talbot surprised me by rising from his chair. Apparently the interview was over. But, suspecting a ploy, I did not trust him. I no longer trusted myself. I wasn't sure what I'd be betrayed into saying next.

"That will do for the time being but I may recall you later."

It was over. But I very much feared that if he did recall me it would be before an impanelled jury, and that the stages after that would be arrest and arraignment. My legs felt shaky. The coroner ushered me from his room and we descended the stairs together. For an instant he seemed to be acting more as a host than a questioner. Half-way down the stairs was a window opening on to a northern aspect. Not far off could be glimpsed the top of the battlemented gate which stands at the near end of London Bridge.

Alan Talbot grasped me by the elbow. With his other hand he gestured at the view.

"You see that?"

I nodded. What did he want?

"You see the heads."

Several mast-like poles stuck up into the cold sky. They were topped by dark blobs. I hardly needed to be told that they were the heads of traitors. Every Londoner, and most visitors, knew that. Some of us passed under those severed heads regularly and – since custom can harden you to almost anything – we didn't trouble our own heads about them.

"Do you know how they are preserved?" said Talbot. His eyes, as cold as the sky, fixed on me.

"I don't know," I said, while thinking that this odd consideration was perhaps a natural one for a coroner. "I am not so curious."

"They are first parboiled and then dipped in tar. That way they can be kept safe for many years."

"The Earl of Essex is up there," I said, almost despite myself. I had once heard that head talk.

"The third from the left-hand end, I believe," said Talbot. "Next to him is Sir Christopher Blount."

"You make a study of them?"

"I do not make frivolous play of them as you do. I mean you players. Your pieces are stuffed with severed heads, aren't they, booted about the stage for the gratification of the groundlings."

I thought of Richard Milford's unperformed play, *The World's Diseas'd*. The coroner had a point. Still, as Richard would say, it was what the customers wanted.

"This is the view from this window whenever the day is clear, the inevitable view," said Talbot, as he led the way down the rest of the staircase. "It reminds me of the law and the law's penalties."

If he'd meant to alarm or intimidate me he had succeeded. Once outside in Long Southwark I breathed deep and set off walking briskly in a south-easterly direction, away from my lodgings, away from the Bridge and the traitors' heads.

I soon got beyond the packed houses and streets and in among clear fields and hedges and bare trees, with only a straggle of buildings here and there. I walked and, while I was walking, I thought.

I started with what I knew. It was a single thing only but a thing highly significant to me. I had not killed Peter Agate.

Circumstances were against me though and it looked as if I might have killed him – and this could be enough to cause me to be arrested . . . arraigned . . . convicted . . . executed. I shivered at this dreadful sequence and its inevitable end-point. The landlord's testimony, accurate as far as it went, was that, after hearing the sounds of an apparent struggle and my repeated calling out of my friend's name, he had emerged from the interior of his house to find me crouched over Peter's body. Benwell had also deposed, less accurately, that he'd heard me threaten Peter and that there'd been some dispute about Nell. I wasn't sure whether the landlord genuinely believed this or whether, from some private or malicious purpose, he had chosen to misinterpret the conversations which he had eavesdropped on.

If the case against me appeared so strong (though circumstantial) then why hadn't Alan Talbot the coroner moved to have me arrested? Either because he was waiting to assemble more evidence against me, I surmised, or because he was not so sure of his ground as he pretended to be. Under this more hopeful interpretation, those sudden questions – "Did you mean to kill him?", "What did you do with the weapon?" – had proceeded not from certainty but a desire to startle me into a confession.

Looking at the affair in this way I grew slightly more cheerful – or slightly less gloomy, rather like a man who's been told he will be executed in a month instead of a week. After all, I argued with myself, no weapon had been found on me nor had I had the time or opportunity to dispose of one. Or not much time, not much opportunity. More important, I had no motive to wish my friend dead, let alone actually to kill him. He was no rival of mine in the Company, he was not about to supplant me. And, although Peter had occupied my place next to Nell in her crib, so had hundreds of other men besides. Was I supposed to go around slaughtering half of London's males? If there had to be a rival then the authentic one in this matter of Nell's bed (and heart) was the young gentleman from the Inns of Court across the water. And if that man was Michael Pye, he could rest easy. Magnanimous Revill had no intention of running him through. What was Nell to me? Once she was much to me, then she became less, and now she had dwindled into something . . . something not worth killing or dying for, at any rate.

Anyway, I was no killer, it was not in my nature.

The question was, who was? Who had killed Peter Agate?

Under the bare autumnal sky, I turned to look back over London. On this side, the Southwark side, the city lumped and swelled like a living thing under a thin veil of smoke and smut which the sun only served to bring out. The grander buildings with their spires and towers and battlements were mostly on the far bank. Out in the open I tried to shake off the taint of suspicion and guilt but it clung like the London air. I felt guilty. In one corner of my mind, I wondered what I'd feel like if I really was guilty. More guilty still, presumably. But perhaps genuine murderers are unfeeling, have no consciences, suffer no guilt. So that if I really was guilty, I would actually feel less bad than I did at this moment . . .

It was a useless speculation. My mind would be more profitably occupied in trying to establish who had murdered Peter.

Not me.

Good. That only left the rest of the world.

Start with the obvious . . . it must have been an enemy.

Good, an enemy. And then what?

The problem in starting with the obvious is that it doesn't really get you anywhere. Another problem was that, as far as I knew, Peter had no enemies. He'd been in London little more than a week. You'd have to be a dedicated trouble-seeker to make a mortal enemy inside seven days. A man he'd insulted in a tavern or elsewhere, if his 'London side' was to the fore? I remembered the chalky-faced, superannuated old player who had objected to our trade. But hadn't he and Peter met later and enjoyed a courteous talk?

Had his murderer been someone from our native village of Miching, then? Most of the villagers were dead. His father Anthony might have opposed his wish to go on stage but that would hardly extend to having his only son cut down in cold blood. Anyway did they even know (or care) where he was? Peter had a stepmother – Mistress Gertrude, like the mother of Hamlet – and she had reportedly pursued him not with a bare bodkin but with flapping dugs and lascivious intent. He had little sisters, not so little now perhaps. They were deprived of a brother. Anthony Agate had lost his son. I could not think of anyone else who would break the news to Peter's family. I resolved to write to them that night. They would get the news in three or four days.

The part played by Samuel Benwell in all of this did not escape me. It was convenient for Talbot the coroner that my landlord had been on the premises with his sharp ears. He'd been able to report on the comings and goings of his two lodgers, been able to repeat their 'arguments'. Then he had appeared on the scene at the right moment, just as I was huddled over Peter's corpse, covered with my friend's blood. The wrong moment for me, of course. How had he responded to this shocking picture? Calmly, quite calmly, certainly by contrast to my own surprise and terror. Still clutching his smoky candle, Benwell had passed within feet of where I was huddled and gone outside into the foggy street. There I heard him calling for help. Shouting, I think, "Help! Murder! Murder! Help!"

Within a few moments he returned with a clutch of neighbours, avid for catastrophe. We stood around awkwardly, half in, half out of the doorway. A couple of people stretched out Peter's body to its full length in the lobby. The blood no longer flowed, as if he was all emptied. No one attempted to detain me, although they might have done so if

I had made to leave the house. After a time the headborough was summoned or perhaps he simply appeared, drawn by all the commotion. This headborough was a stupid man called Doggett. He had once fined me over non-attendance at church. Now Doggett studied the scene and pronounced it unwholesome, foul and villainous. Then he made to detain one of the neighbours until Benwell whispered in his ear and gestured at me.

I don't know why the headborough didn't take me in. I protested my innocence, of course, explained how I too had stumbled on this bloody scene. I think that murder was probably out of Master Doggett's realm. It is out of most of our realms, fortunately. Doggett said again that the deed was unwholesome, foul and villainous, and appeared to think he'd done his duty. These headboroughs are elected by their fellow householders and it's sometimes seemed to me that, particularly in a slippery suburb like Southwark, it might suit the locals to have a man who will not be too officious – or not too effective anyway – in enquiring into wrongdoing. Not that they're expected to wink at murder . . .

Anyway Master Doggett contented himself with condemning the deed for a third time – now calling it unfair, filthy and felonious – and then went off to report the matter to higher authority. So it was that Master Alan Talbot took over the investigation of Peter Agate's death.

Relations between Master Benwell and myself were constrained. I had not moved out of my lodgings in Dead Man's Place, nor had he asked me to, but he was no longer eager to hear the titbits of gossip or even to talk to me at all. I couldn't really believe that he thought he was harbouring a murderer under his roof. Perhaps he was merely paying me back for that earlier rebuff when I had brushed aside his hovering hand, stared down his glazed eye. Benwell himself might have appeared a suitable suspect for this crime. Had he accosted Peter as he had once accosted me, been rejected, and in frustration or fury stabbed my friend? I took care to secure my door at nights but, even so, did not sleep well.

Through my head, when I lay down, ran that scene when I'd come through the door and found my friend's body. I seemed doomed to repeat it again and again, like imperfect lines in a rehearsal. And there was another memory which recurred and which in retrospect began to seem like an omen or harbinger. It was much more minor than murder but strange and disturbing nonetheless. It had happened as I was leaving Middle Temple one evening, the one when Shakespeare had told me that Thomas Pope was about to return to the Company. I'd stepped out in the dank courts. It was foggy of course. We had been floundering in this fog-sea for days. Sometimes, for brief moments at night, it cleared enough to allow a glimpse of the stars but otherwise we might have been at the bottom of the ocean. The world had grown as small as Master Jute claimed it was when he showed me Drake's relic – or even smaller since everything had shrunk to the few visible yards around you. A handful of lights were diffused through the gloom. Passers-by, some carrying lanterns, swirled up and then evaporated. The dankness clung to your face and the brassiness of the fog filled your nostrils.

My footsteps had rung hollow as I wound my way through the courts and alleys of Middle Temple. By now I knew the place a little. This legal temple was like a village, a deserted village. But not so deserted after all, because through the murk I detected a shape moving rapidly towards me along a walk. I gasped for, in the darkness, it seemed that the shape had no head. But it was merely that the man had his head right down looking at the ground, while the collar of his cloak was pulled up high.

He didn't see or hear me, despite my involuntary gasp, and before I could shift to one side we collided heavily. I fell back and sat almost comically down on the dank paving. I couldn't help it, he was broader and heavier than me, fleshier altogether.

"For God's sake, man, can't you look . . . "

The words died on my lips because the shape had already gone several yards beyond me, swallowed up by the night and the fog. Either he hadn't heard me or had chosen not to hear. Perhaps he wasn't even aware that he'd struck someone in his rushing passage. He must have been, though. If I was bruised after the encounter so should he have been. Was he a lawyer? His cloak had been lawyer-like, so far as I'd glimpsed it in the gloom. I thought of scrambling up and running after him and holding him to account. But I stayed where I was on the cold ground, overcome by a strange reluctance to move.

And by a slight fear perhaps. There was a scent in the air, quite apart from the smell of the fog. It was a rank, vulpine smell.

Preparations for the Middle Temple production of *Troilus and Cressida* ran smoothly enough. It was a pleasant distraction to play a Trojan prince who has lost his love to a rival and his friends and brothers in battle, and then goes out to slaughter everyone he can lay his hands on – reality was kept at bay. Although I heard no more from Alan Talbot, I wondered whether this might be the last time I would play with my Company. He could order my arrest at any time.

There was genuine sorrow among the Chamberlain's at Peter Agate's violent death. In a few short days they had got to know and like him. Both Dick Burbage and WS spoke warmly about him to me, and I was doubly grateful, not only because they too had liked my friend but because they plainly did not believe that I was implicated in his death. (Word had quickly spread of how I'd found the body and been questioned by the Middlesex coroner.)

I felt – curiously perhaps and unaccountably – that I had brought shame, even dishonour on my Company merely by incurring the suspicion of the authorities. It was not my connection with death and violence. Ben Jonson, who was sometimes involved with the Globe both as poet and player, had killed a man only three or four years previously, and furthermore that dead man had been a fellow player. But Jonson disposed of Gabriel Spencer honourably in a duel, even if he was hauled off to court for it and nearly paid with his neck. No one in the theatre world thought any the less of him for what he'd done. In fact, I'd been told that Spencer was regarded as a troublemaker. There is a world of difference between facing a man front-to-front in the open field and sneaking up on him in a lobby to stab him through the heart. While none of my fellows considered that I was capable of such a dishonourable and treacherous act, it pained me to know that there were outsiders who would believe it, and that the Chamberlain's Company would be tainted by association.

The only person who was interested in a prying way in Peter's death and the grisly details of it – or the only person who didn't bother to conceal his naked curiosity with a show of fellow feeling – was Richard Milford, poet and playwright. We met by chance late one morning in the precincts of Paul's Yard. He was in the company of his wife and, oddly, Henslowe's unofficial agent, Tom Gally, the man who'd been in the tavern with Chesser. Gally said nothing directly to me but continued to gaze down his pointed finger in the direction of whoever was speaking. Richard Milford asked me so many questions about the murder that I wondered whether he was seeking new material for some violent and sensational drama. I kept my patience for a time but eventually retaliated. I asked him how things were going with his story of incest and double-dealing, *The World's Diseas'd*. Had the seniors in our Company relented? Were they willing to stage the piece?

"Oh, there are plenty of takers," said Richard airily, but with a sidelong glance at Gally. Aha, I thought, that's the way it's going. He's negotiating with the Admiral's Men, and this man is a go-between. The suspicion was almost confirmed by his next comment. "If Burbage and Heminges and the rest don't want quality, if they're too short-sighted to see it, there are many others who will. Who do."

Tom Gally nodded vigorously at this point but kept his finger under his eye.

"So they've turned you down?" I said.

"It is a difficult thing, Nicholas, to be always ahead of public taste, a little way ahead."

"But you were confident you were providing what the public wanted."

"The public doesn't always knows what it wants until it gets it."

"Then it's as well you have your patron – patrons, I should say."

"Whatever your private opinion of Lord Robert, he and his sister have been all grace to me. Haven't they, Lucy?"

He turned to his wife who was standing quietly next to her husband. She was, if I'm honest, the real reason I'd been willing to stop and subject myself to Richard's questions. Not for his company but hers. I'd even been willing to talk about Peter Agate because she was listening. Perhaps I hoped for her sympathy. So far she'd made no comment. She had a way of glancing up through her long lashes which was as interesting as any speech might have been. Now she simply said, "They are good friends to my husband, Master Revill."

"Ben Nicholson is printing the play, even as we speak," said Richard, gesturing across the Paul's precinct. There was a great concentration of publishers and booksellers in this part of town. "We have just been to see him. It will be a handsome volume. You know it was he who published my *Garland*."

I visualized Richard as someone who would be constantly running to the publishers, checking that all was well. I owed money to Master Nicholson. He was a genial, white-haired tradesman who did business with the Chamberlain's and was tolerant about players' bills.

"A precious volume, that *Garland*," I said. "The more so because it contains verses about you, madam, I believe."

I bowed slightly at Lucy Milford and was pleased to see a blush filling her cheeks. She looked up at me – those long lashes! – but said nothing. I'd meant the remark sincerely, insofar as one means any near meaningless compliment paid to a pretty woman. In truth I liked Richard's poetic effusions, his slightly self-centred verses about love, transience and mortality. I thought they were truer to the character of the man than the violent actions and severed limbs of *The World's Diseas'd*. But I'd also wanted to remind the poet-playwright of what he'd told me recently, that Venner's sister was the supposed object of his love-lyrics. Or so he had informed her (while telling his wife something else). The duplicity of poets! Their shamelessness! But then I'd do the same thing if I was lucky enough to be a poet. I couldn't be a poet. I knew, I'd tried. Even so, to be able to say *I wrote these verses for you*.

Richard didn't respond to my compliment to his verses and his wife, other than by a tight smile. She smiled too, slightly, amid the blushes. We exchanged a little more small conversation. Gally still hadn't said anything although he had been attentively following our words. Milford announced that the two of them, he and Lucy, would be attending the Middle Temple performance of *Troilus and Cressida*.

"I wouldn't want Burbage and the rest to think I bear them any hard feelings for their frostiness towards *The World's Diseas'd*, fools though they may be."

The last thing Burbage and the rest were were fools, but I held my tongue, said goodbye to the Milfords and moved off. I hadn't gone many yards when I became aware that Tom Gally had left them behind and was keeping pace with me. He kept his head screwed sideways and, from time to time, brought up his hand and sighted at me along his forefinger. Gally had long, soft, unkempt black hair. It reminded me of a sheep's fleece. But I sensed the wolf beneath.

I smiled, grimaced rather, and walked quicker. But he wasn't to be shaken off.

"Master Henslowe sends his commiserations over your recent troubles."

"I thank him."

"He knows that you are no murderer."

I'd worked briefly for the Admiral's Men soon after my arrival in London. I didn't care much for Philip Henslowe, their manager. He was a hard-headed businessman who preferred to keep people in debt to him rather than be paid off, since they would then be out of his power. He was always looking for money-making opportunities outside the theatre, in brothels and bear-baiting gardens. During my early, priggish days I'd tended to disapprove of this. The Chamberlain's Company seemed purer and more whole-hearted in their dedication to the drama. Nevertheless Dick Burbage and some of the other seniors seemed to get on well enough with Henslowe and, as I've said, a friendly rivalry existed between the two companies.

Tom Gally, however, with his squinty glance and pointy finger, was an unwelcome companion. To be told by him that my former employer did not consider me a murderer seemed a somewhat feeble form of praise. Even so, I just about managed to squeeze out more thanks.

"Master Henslowe is sorry too to hear of the sickness of your patron. These are difficult times for us men of the theatre."

I doubted that Henslowe was that sorry about Lord Hunsdon's condition but half smiled in acknowledgement, even as I considered how Gally was no real 'man of the theatre', but a hanger-on, a parasite. A self-appointed agent of our rival.

"The Chapel Royal boys," he added. "They're a danger, now."

These were the acting children who'd been doing so well at Blackfriars recently. They were our competitors, true, but few in the Chamberlain's considered them to be a real threat, or not that much of a one.

"Those little eyases couldn't take the bread from the mouths of grown, experienced men," I said, not as sure as I sounded.

"They are all the fashion. There are many boy-lovers."

"Fashions come and go. We should welcome rivalry. You know what they say, Master Gally. It's the storm that proves the roof."

"Of course. How is he, by the way?"

Gally gazed at me down his finger-gun. By now we had almost completed a circuit of Paul's Yard.

"How's who?"

"Why, George Carey. Lord Hunsdon."

"Strong. Vital. He will live to be as old as Moses."

"I hear otherwise."

"Master Gally, if you expect me to report on the health of our patron, you're talking to the wrong person. I suggest you address yourself to Master Shakespeare or Dick Burbage for an answer."

"Forgive me, Master Revill, I was not aware that a great man's health or sickness might be a subject for secrecy."

"And you must forgive me, Master Gally, if I'm suddenly overcome with my own sickness."

"I am distressed to hear it."

"Its chief sympton is a violent aversion to continuing in your company. Goodbye."

And I veered off from him, angry inside myself that he should have gone this roundabout route to try to discover how close to dying our patron was.

It took me several minutes to recover my calm. I was glad to see, though, that I had shaken Gally off, or at least that I could no longer see him in the throng of the Yard. He was a troublemaker who would do his best to do down his – or Henslowe's – rivals. Someone to be watched. A dishonest fellow.

As if to prove my own honesty to myself I thought of walking over to discuss my small debts with Benjamin Nicholson, who was printer, publisher and bookseller all in one. I had bought several volumes of verse over the last few months, partly out of a wish to read the latest thing but also to see if I could learn the craft of verse-writing. Poetry is surely a skill like any other, it can be learned – or grasped – in its outward manifestations. But there is also something inside it that you can't get at, like the kernel in a nut. Can't get at without smashing the shell. And the kernel is not only in the poetry, it is also in the poet. If you do not already possess the kernel inside you then there is little chance you will pen anything but the most mediocre verse. So I'd concluded.

And as I walked across the Yard I paused in the vicinity of the great Cross that stands in its centre and concluded something else: that I would not settle my bill with Master Nicholson, not just yet. You see, I didn't know whether I might not at any time be arrested by Master Alan Talbot. He had it in his power to cast me into prison, to bring me before magistrates for trial, & cetera. Why settle my debts now if my future was so clouded? A man who is about to be hanged smiles at petty obligations. Besides I hadn't got the money.

In this way I toyed with my prospects. Did I think I was about to be accused of my friend's murder, convicted and hauled to the scaffold? I didn't know. Maybe I thought I could avert that possibility by imagining in detail how it might happen and so, by fearing the worst, placate the Fates (who delight in taking us by surprise).

And talking of surprises . . .

"Master Revill!"

A hand clutched at my arm. I looked into a lined, chalky countenance. It was the alliterating man from the Goat & Monkey, he who had warned Peter against stepping out on to the stage. The ex-player. His ears stuck out from under his cap. The last time I'd seen him had been as he was hauled out of the ale-house by a crew of boatmen.

I shook my arm free but he too kept pace beside me. Yet another eager, talkative companion. I'd had enough.

"You are a friend to Peter Agate?"

"Was a friend," I said.

"Alas," said this gentleman. "There is woe in the world."

I stopped, turned towards him and said, "Sir, have you anything to say to me? If so, say it and be done. I have had sufficient conversation for this morning."

"I was a player once," he said.

"I know, with Lord Strange."

If he was surprised that I was aware of this he didn't show it.

"Until I saw the playhouse for what it was."

"We've been here before," I said wearily. "You will say that it is a place of perdition, and I will respond that it is a bower of bliss. Can we leave it at that, Master Chesser?"

I was only giving him this much of a hearing because he had been, once, a member of my trade in a way that Tom Gally could never claim to have been. I had recalled Chesser's name from Peter's account of their second meeting. We stood in the centre of Paul's Yard near the big Cross and the world, woeful and otherwise, flowed round us.

"It is the devil's hole," said Chesser. "But it is not too late to climb out."

"Of course."

"I saw him once. In Derby."

"Saw him? Saw who?"

"The devil."

I might have moved on but this superannuated player gripped my arm again with a hold that was almost painful. His eyes glared, yet he no longer looked so absurd. Despite myself, I was attentive.

"You are familiar with the tragical history of Dr Faustus, the hellish Conjurer?" he said.

"Kit Marlowe's play?"

"A sacrilegious man. He denied the divinity."

I wasn't sure whether he was referring to Christopher Marlowe, dead and murdered these many years in a tavern brawl in Deptford, or to his creation Dr Faustus who sold his soul to the devil in exchange for all earthly knowledge and delights. Either Marlowe or Faustus would have fitted the description of godlessness.

"We were in Derby," said Chesser, "about that cursed play. A certain number of devils were keeping their circles on our stage, and Faustus was busy in his magical invocations, when on a sudden we players were confounded for we were all persuaded there was one devil too many amongst us."

These tales of extra demons on stage during performances of *Faustus* were well known in the theatre world. This was the first time, though, that I'd met anyone who'd experienced it. There was something impressive about the steady tone of Chesser's narrative. It was cold in the morning air but I grew colder still.

"After a little pause," he continued, "we requested the people to pardon us, since we could go no further with this matter. Those people knew well what we were about, and every man hastened to be the first out of doors. We players broke up in confusion and spent the night in reading and prayer."

"After that you turned your back on the stage?"

"My fortunes faltered. My eyes were opened, Master Revill. I pray that yours may be."

"I have need of being in others' prayers at the moment, Master Chesser," I said, glancing up at the Cross which stood overhead. "I thank you."

He gripped my arm even tighter. I was surprised that an old man should have such an iron grasp.

"Avoid the fate of your friend."

"What do you know about Peter's death?"

"Avoid the foul fiend."

I finally broke away from the pale-faced man and sped off across the Yard. When I looked back, Chesser was gazing after me, his arm half held out, in warning, in entreaty.

It was harder to shake off Chesser's unsettling words than it was to rid myself of his person. WS's Trojan drama of *Troilus and Cressida* was in my mind and the ex-player seemed like some combination of the doom-laden Cassandra and the bitter Thersites. Nevertheless his words had this little conscience-niggling effect. Passing Master Nicholson's shop among the tightly packed row of booksellers, I went in to reassure that tolerant tradesman that I would pay him as soon as possible. He was standing there, puffing at his pipe and looking benevolent. He added to my guilt by casually waving aside my little debts as if they were so much pipe-smoke, and made me feel that the world wasn't such a bad place after all, despite its Gallys and Chessers and its cold coroners and unknown murderers.

Since I was on Nicholson's premises, I also asked about Richard Milford's play, *The World's Diseas'd*, mentioning that I'd just seen the playwright and his pretty wife. I was curious to know how generous a patron Lord Robert was; whether he was paying to have this immortal work bound in vellum or leather, or even gold-clasped. Perhaps it depended on the degree of gratitude and fawning in Richard's dedication to his 'only begetter'. But Master Nicholson merely confirmed that the work was in preparation. It was no more than a commission to him. If I'd expected a little laughter at Richard's expense – or Lord Bumpkin's – I was disappointed in my meanness (and deserved to be). I walked off, discontented and dissatisfied with myself.

In this current mood I wished to see my friend Nell, not entirely for the obvious reason but also to receive some words of comfort from her. Did she know that her old bed-companion was suspected of murder? Probably. Everyone else seemed to know. Southwark was a small place.

I made my way towards the Bridge but, once on the other side, my resolution faltered. Suppose she was not happy to see me? Suppose she was entertaining one of her clients or even her clever lawyer friend? Instead of progressing towards Holland's Leaguer, I turned in at my own door. I passed rapidly through the lobby where I'd found Peter's body. It was a place of blood and shadows. I crept up to my room and shut the door. But I could not shut out my troubling thoughts.

My suspicions about Tom Gally and his trouble-making propensities were confirmed the next afternoon. As I've indicated, we were continuing to play at our home, the Globe playhouse, despite the foggy season and the fact that we had other legal fish to fry at Middle Temple in a few days' time and even bigger royal fish at Whitehall later in the winter – if the Queen was still living and inclined to watch a play. But the Globe was our daily bread, our commons.

I was approaching the playhouse in order to prepare for that afternoon's performance of *Love's Diversion*, in which I played – what else? – a young lover. The fog had returned, though not so thickly as earlier in the month, and at first I didn't notice anything odd about the crowd gathered in front of the main entrance. It was just a blurred, shifting mass, making a deal of noise for such a dank day. We are lucky, I thought, to have such loyal followers.

But closer to, the shoving and the shouting were not so good-humoured.

"Let's hear you, then."

"Out with it, Lowlander."

"Pipe up, Dutch! Give it voice!"

From the raucous tones, as much as from the comments, I guessed what was happening. I'd seen it often enough before. A crowd of apprentices had discovered a foreigner, presumably a Dutchman, and were giving him a London welcome. That is, they were jostling and jeering at him for the crime of being foreign or, more precisely, for the crime of not being English. If this had been occurring anywhere else in town I'd have walked quietly on, hoping to go undetected by the apprentices. But their presence on the doorstep of our theatre made such an evasion harder, although still possible. I might have slipped unobtrusively round the back. The players used a rear entrance, which gave on to the offices and tire-house behind the stage, while the audience came in together through the main door and into a lobby. (Once inside they were separated sheep-and-goat fashion into the pit-dwellers and the gallery-climbers.)

"Give us a taste of your Dutch tongue."

"Double Dutch."

"Else give us a taste of your Dutch wife."

"Just a lick."

"Your Dutch widow."

I now saw that there was a circle of these lewd young men and, in the centre, a man and woman who were their sport. From the couple's dress they were not English; from their looks they were frightened and bewildered. I guessed they were on their way to see *Love's Diversion.* We had occasional visitors from overseas to watch our productions, and were proud to count ourselves among the sights and attractions of the town. The treatment of this foreign couple was a slight on the Chamberlain's Company, on the honour and good name of the Globe. I looked around for assistance but could see not a single one of my co-players. No one else was about. If we had a prospective audience for that afternoon's play they'd surely be put off by this stir outside the playhouse entrance. There was a gatherer or money-collector in the lobby, but Sam was old and lame and could hardly be expected to sally forth and defend our customers from the rude natives.

No, it looked as though Revill was going to have to do his bit, do his best. I sighed, for you'd be a fool to take on the apprentices single-handed. I was likely to receive a few blows and thwacks in recompense. Still, what was that to a man who might, any day, be arrested, tried and executed for a murder he didn't commit . . .?

"*Veni, vidi, vici*," I called out through the foggy air. Julius Caesar's claim of 'I came, I saw, I conquered', not really apt for the occasion but the only thing I could think of. I can project my voice (it's an actor's trick, you know). I called out the same words once more, adding, "You wanted to hear some Dutch, masters? There it is."

The group of apprentices surrounding the couple pulled back a little and peered through the mist to discern where this new diversion was coming from. There were perhaps eight or nine of them. They had cropped hair and plain, almost severe clothing. They turned their badges of rank to a threatening kind of advantage. Something flickered in the corner of my eye. I turned quickly, hoping that a passer-by or a fellow from my company might be coming to our aid. Through the murky air I saw Tom Gally, he of the pointy finger and hair like a sheep's-fleece. I wondered what he was doing there and had my suspicions. Gally receded into the mist, apparently reluctant to interfere.

By this time two of the apprentices had moved to stand directly opposite me. They were evidently the leaders. Their breath was garlicky. One had ginger hair which was no more than a thin pile on his scalp.

"If you're a Hollander, I'm a Dutchman," said this ginger-head.

"'e's not from the Low Countries," said the other. "I've seen 'im in 'ere."

He jerked a thumb over his shoulder in the direction of the playhouse.

It's gratifying to be recognized – most of the time.

"I hope you enjoyed the performance," I said. "I am always pleased to meet a playgoer, whatever the circumstances."

"Oh, a gentleman," said Ginger-head, "from his voice."

"If 'e's a player, which 'e is," said the other apprentice, the one who went to plays, "then 'e's a gen'leman *o' the back door*. They all are. I know."

"Wherever I may come from, it's easy enough to tell your origins," I said.

"Good English stock," said Ginger-head. "You would not dare to say otherwise."

"Not so, for you are in fact from the Low Countries, that is, from Hole-land," I said, pleased at my wit in this emergency.

"I'll give you a 'ole," said the playgoing apprentice, "to add to those you 'ave already."

"Another hole in your netherlands," said Ginger-head, developing his friend's idea.

So might we have continued through the live-long day exchanging witty insults until we descended to unwitty blows. I saw the other apprentices drawing nearer. The only good result of all this was that the Dutch couple would have had the chance to make their escape, either into the playhouse or off down the street. I hoped they'd taken it. Being distracted, I couldn't see them. Perhaps they'd acknowledge what they owed me by coming to my funeral.

The two apprentices advanced even closer. I was enveloped by their garlicky breath. It was the moment to fight or run.

"Keep up your bright words, gentlemen, or the fog will rust them."

I recognized the voice and the outline which had suddenly appeared by my side, and was surprised as well as pleased – and not a little relieved.

The two apprentices turned their attention to William Shakespeare. He looked his usual self, largely at ease with the world and most of its occupants.

"Shog off, won't you," said Ginger-head, but a little uncertainly.

"'e's another of 'em back-door gen'lemen," said my playgoing friend, once more flinging his thumb over his shoulder. "I've seen 'im there too."

"Yes, I've trodden the boards from time to time, I'll own up," said WS. "But I also write the lines that players speak."

WS mimed writing in the air. There was a pause then he said, "Now, since you know my trade, tell me what yours are."

He spoke with what seemed to be a genuine curiosity.

"Carpenter," said Ginger-head mechanically. Perhaps he was too taken aback by the question to produce an abusive reply.

Shakespeare looked at the other apprentice.

"Cobbler," he said.

Though I was mightily relieved that WS had turned up on the scene, I was half afraid that he was now going to try to amuse these two apprentices with some punning diversions connected with their trades, probably along the lines of living according to 'line and rule' or attending to the 'mending of souls'. That would be typical of him. I'd been in this situation before, seen that trick played once on a threatening boatman. It had worked then – but twice?

"And you are a playgoer too, my friend?" said WS.

"I 'ave attended now and then, yeah."

Ginger-head nodded, as if he didn't want to be left out of the reckoning. The half-dozen or so of their companions had stopped closing in on us and were listening to the exchange, seemingly more interested now than intimidating.

"Whatever your day-trades, I can see that you're word-smiths, like me," said William Shakespeare. "With all that talk of the netherlands and Hole-lands. That's good. Also a touch bawdy, a thing which is very natural and proper in young men. I will make a note of it and perhaps use it one day."

He patted his upper garments slightly more showily than was strictly necessary.

"Alas, I have forgotten my notebook. But I am sure my good friend Nicholas here will remember the jest so that I may write it down later on."

I nodded. I did not point out that it was I who had first made the joke about Hole-land.

"And then, my friends, you will perhaps hear your own jests coming back at you from the stage of the Globe playhouse."

Ginger-head scratched his bonce. I almost expected the pile on his skull to come off like rust. The other apprentice wore an expression somewhere between pleasure and surprise.

"Now, if you'll forgive us, gentlemen," said WS, "we have business, playing business, to attend to."

The playwright grasped me firmly by the upper arm and we moved away from the apprentices. The fire had gone out of the gang or been doused. As we were leaving, WS stopped and said, "You are very welcome to attend our performance of *Love's Diversion* this afternoon. We require quick-witted spectators. Simply bring your brains – and your pennies."

He ushered me round the side of the Globe towards the players'entrance. (There is an innocent sense in which we are all of us *gentlemen of the back door.*) I thanked WS and rapidly explained how this confrontation with the apprentices had come about. I didn't want him to think that I went around provoking trouble. I mentioned that I'd seen Henslowe's man, Tom Gally, hanging about earlier and voiced my suspicion that he might have been stirring up the apprentices so as to damage our business. WS said nothing and I couldn't be sure whether he credited this. With his generosity, he tended to think the best of people. I then expressed the hope that the Dutch man and woman had made their escape.

"They are safe inside the playhouse. By chance I was in the lobby when they entered. The Hollanders indicated what was happening by the entrance so I came out."

By now we too were safe inside the playhouse. We loitered in the passageway by the tire-house.

"Thank you, William," I said again. "I don't know what

would've happened if you hadn't arrived. It is not the first time you have saved me."

"Don't underestimate the apprentices, Nicholas."

"I don't . . . I didn't stumble into this unthinkingly. I was trying to protect our foreign visitors."

"Though it wouldn't have been much use if you'd had to appear on stage with real injuries and not just those of Cupid's dart – if you'd appeared at all, that is. I meant, though, don't underestimate the apprentices in a different way. They are young and given to riot but they're also quick spectators. We should welcome them."

"I thought you were merely . . . flattering them."

"I was. But they are not fools. Some day some of them will climb the ladder. Why, one of those fellows we were talking to might become Lord Mayor in the future and receive foreign guests with all ceremony and courtesy. If he remembers his rough-house days at all he will look back on them and laugh – or be ashamed of them. And he will be a very severe judge of the excesses of the apprentices."

I tried hard to visualize the red-headed carpenter or the playgoing cobbler rising to the heights of Lord Mayor and conversing gracefully with Dutchmen and Italians & cetera but couldn't do it. I suppose that's the difference between someone with imagination, like WS, and a common player, like N. Revill.

"Did you want to note those bawdy jests down? You hadn't really forgotten your notebook, had you?" I asked. I was eager, I must confess, that WS should know how I had been able to retort upon the apprentices with the 'Hole-land' pun. I wanted to claim this original remark, made in the stress of the moment, for my own.

"I rather think I've used those jokes already – and will probably use them again," he said. "And I wasn't the first to make word-play with nethers and the rest, either. The old jokes are the best ones."

"Oh yes," I said.

"You must go off to do your work, Nicholas, as a young lover in *Love's Diversion.*"

I considered that I hardly needed reminding of this but WS had another purpose in making the remark and was only preparing the ground.

Shakespeare continued, "To do your work as a lover – to wit – "

"To wit?" I said, baffled.

"To wit, to woo," said WS, looking immensely pleased with himself. And then, in case I hadn't got the joke, he flapped his arms and delivered it hootingly, "To wit, to woo. To wit, to woo."

"Very good," I said, feeling as old as a grandfather in the presence of a small child.

"Well then," said WS.

Sensing that our dialogue had come to an end – and where could it go after that? – I went off to change for my part in the play. When I was on stage during that cold, dank afternoon I cast occasional glances down into the groundlings' area to see whether any of the apprentice gang had taken up WS's invitation to watch our play. I thought I spotted a rusty head somewhere in the middle of the pit but couldn't be sure. I marvelled at WS's dexterity, even as I was astonished at the depths to which he'd sink in quest of a pun. Not only had he rescued me outside the theatre from an almost certain beating, but he had won the interest, even the respect of the two young men – and he had probably swelled our audience by a few too.

For a time I even forgot that a cloud of murderous suspicion was hanging over me.

Alibi

The Chamberlain's Company fought out the battle of Troy in the hall of Middle Temple – or a chunk of the battle anyway, since the real thing lasted for ten years. During one dank and foggy night in the early part of November the students and benchers lapped up *The Famous History of Troilus and Cressida*. The dining tables were piled to one side and our audience either perched on bum-numbing benches in the well of the hall or, in the case of the higher-ups, were seated more comfortably on the dais at the far end.

The great room glowed with its own lustre. The bank of varnished portraits, magnified versions of the worthies sitting beneath them on the dais, caught the rays thrown out by the clusters of candles. The mighty roof, with its tiers of beams, disappeared into mysterious shadows. There was a dark sheen over everything, a sheen which bespoke quiet learning and modest wealth. Not that the behaviour of the students was quiet or modest. If they were affected by the presence of the justices, coroners, benchers and serjeants-at-law on the dais or by the fair number of lady guests they didn't show it. For all the soberness of their dress, these fledgling lawyers were loud before we started and loud throughout. They sighed windily at Troilus's love-sickness, guffawed coarsely at the bawdy of Pandarus, sniggered cynically at Thersites' satires on the Greek commanders. They especially enjoyed the blood-letting at the end when we squeezed hidden sponges or burst bladders concealed under our clothes to simulate the carnage outside Troy gates.

In other words, the law students weren't so different from the other audiences we play to. But they did fall silent and pay particular attention in those places where a less educated – or less arrogant – lot might have permitted their ears, eyes and minds to wander. That is, during the debates in the Greek and Trojan camps on warfare and honour, on time and memory. As I'd grown more familiar with the play I saw how artfully WS had tailored the action to his watchers and listeners. For what most of these people, these Greeks and Trojans, do most of the time is to sit, stand, talk and debate. And what is it that lawyers do but sit, stand & cetera? The cut-and-thrust of argument is the very air which these people breathe – even if it is a somewhat refined air for the rest of us.

One part of my part as Troilus had a particular flavour for me, playing in this place. As I've said, I suspected one of the students, Michael Pye, of usurping my position in Nell's favours. Tell myself as I might that I had no right to feel this way, I couldn't help seeing a very faint shadow of my situation in Troilus's. His plight is infinitely worse, of course. The Trojan prince has been betrayed by the woman to whom he has surrendered his whole heart and soul. Revill, on the other hand, was merely passed over by a whore even while he had been thinking of rejecting her himself. Nevertheless I felt just a touch of Troilus's agony as he spies on his rival, the Greek Diomedes, making overtures to Cressida. And worse, as he sees her give way before his eyes.

I knew that Michael Pye was in the audience, having glimpsed him in the company of his friend Edmund Jute. As Pye watched me playing the heart-sick Troilus, I wondered whether he knew me for a rival – if that was what he was. I resolved to see Nell for a final time and settle things one way or the other.

But it was not that moment in the play when I spy on my faithless Cressida which I had especial cause to remember. Rather, it was an earlier point in the action which haunted me for a long time afterwards, and which had consequences too.

This is how it happened. When Cressida is claimed back by her father she must depart straightaway from Troy for the Greek camp. The parting lovers swear hurried vows of fidelity. As tokens of their eternal faith, Troilus unfastens the sleeve of his doublet and gives it to his love while she hands him her glove. As far as Troilus is concerned, although of course he's not to know it at the time, this giving of a sleeve is what they call a 'sleeveless errand' or a useless gesture, since he gets no reward for his token of love except betrayal. I'd wondered whether the presence of this joke – a kind of visual pun – had occurred to WS as he was writing the scene. Perhaps I should mention it to him.

(By the by, this habit of giving away one's detachable sleeve is all very well for gentlemen in the moneyed and leisured classes who can afford to replace their doublets or get new sleeves as often as they like. I can't say that I've ever done it myself though. I can't afford to. I only possess one doublet. What do those other fellows do with the remaining sleeve, anyway? Give it to their second, secret mistress? You don't see men going round with one-armed doublets. No, I've never had the resources to wear my heart on my sleeve. Or to receive a glove in return.)

I was playing opposite Peter Pearce, a boy-player who was fast making a name for himself in our Company. Ever since we'd had to face the rivalry of the child actors in Paul's or Blackfriars, our seniors had paid a little more attention to the recruitment of our young players – that is, those who would take the women's parts – recognizing that an audience can be drawn by quality here as elsewhere.

We were saying our urgent goodbyes. Peter's voice hadn't yet broken, of course, but he delivered his lines with an adult tremor.

O, you shall be exposed, my lord, to dangers
As infinite as imminent! But I'll be true.

In his protestation of truth was a world of hope and fear. And I – or rather Troilus – reply,

And I'll grow friend with danger. Wear this sleeve . . .

. . . as I unpick the sleeve of my doublet to present to Cressida as a token. And then something odd happened.

My doublet was made of brocade with figures of gold thread. It was a lavish garment appropriate to a prince. The light from the sconces and the hanging candles was concentrated around our playing-area in front of the hall-screen. Now the lights all seemed to gather and glitter on the rich sleeve and my eyes were so taken up by the dazzle that I forgot what I had to say next. I dried. At the same time I felt the hair on my nape bristle as if the sleeve were a dead thing. Mostly I was conscious of the golden sleeve dangling from my hand, but with one small quarter of my mind I knew that Peter Pearce, as he thrust at me with a finely worked lady's glove, was saying the lines which had been written for him.

And you this glove. When shall I see you?

Still he gestured with the glove.

When shall I see you?

Cressida's question echoed in my head, and no answer came.

When we're playing at the Globe our book-keeper, Master Allison, or one of his underlings acts as our prompt from one of the points in the tire-house where he has an eye-hole on to the stage. But in the somewhat more awkward circumstances of the Middle Temple hall, not designed expressly for playing, the prompter was behind one of the entrance doors. It might not be immediately apparent that I'd lost the thread, even though an experienced prompter can usually tell from a player's tone or from that pause which lasts half a beat too long that things aren't going as they should.

This time no prompt came. The pause, which can only have lasted seconds, seemed to stretch to infinity. I was aware now of the shadowy vastness of the banqueting-hall, of the crowd of watching dark-suited figures, and of a roaring in my ears. The world spun. I shivered slightly. Then, as abruptly as the fit had arrived, it departed. There was Peter Pearce standing before me, holding out the glove and mouthing *When?* like a fish out of water. There was the audience hanging on my reply – and here were WS's words come fresh into my head.

> *I will corrupt the Grecian sentinels,*
> *To give thee nightly visitation.*
> *But yet, be true.*

. . . and, so saying, I at last surrendered a golden sleeve in exchange for a delicate glove.

After the play was over, I was expecting a rebuke or at least a comment from my fellows. It's natural to pick over the performance for its good and bad passages. Instead I received compliments on my playing as Troilus and particularly for the scene when Cressida and I swapped love-tokens.

"That was a poignant moment, Nick, when you and Cressida parted," said Michael Donegrace, the boy-player who'd graduated to men's parts and who was still attentive to those scenes in which he might, until recently, have been playing the female role. We were changing out of our costumes in a makeshift tire-room behind the hall-screen. "It was as if you could glimpse into the future and knew that you would not be seeing your Cressida again, or not be seeing her in such a loving light. By your pausing and the little shake you gave you seemed to say so."

"Thank you, Michael."

I shrugged off the compliment in a grateful way and marvelled at how my incompetence could be transformed to artistry. I think that Peter Pearce alone was aware of how I'd lost my lines but he was too generous or too sensitive or too ambitious a young soul to give me away.

Troilus and Cressida was done and not to be repeated, at least in Middle Temple. I wondered whether our seniors would transfer it to the Globe playhouse. Perhaps not. It might be caviar to the general – too crabbed, too inward and talkative for the public taste. It may seem strange, almost spendthrift, to mount a play for one night only, but the Chamberlain's was no doubt being well remunerated for it. (I didn't know. I simply and gratefully accepted my shilling a day.) We also had to bear in mind the calibre of our audience; men who were rich and powerful or who would be those things one day. At this time of uncertainty, with a sick patron and a Queen who could not live much longer, it was useful to have friends with influence.

So the play was over, the costumes, props and scrolls packed away. But our revels were by no means ended. Perhaps it's the intentness of their studies which makes these law students take their pleasures so seriously – and noisily. The rafters rang. The air grew hotter and thicker with smoke from the pipes and guttering candles. There was drinking and singing and music and dancing and more drinking, and much consorting with the players and guests.

A full tankard was thrust into my hand from somewhere and I drank copiously to cool myself down. But it had the opposite effect of heating me up. Never mind. Looking around, I was pleased to see Richard Milford or, more particularly, Richard's pretty young wife, Lucy. Not so pleased, however, to see that they were accompanied by his patrons, the Bumpkins, Lord Robert Venner and his sister Lady Vinny. Brother and sister seemed already far gone in drink and clung to each other for support, like two squat, fleshy pillars. The porcine eyes of Lord Robert squinted warily round the room. He seemed to be regarding me with particular suspicion. Once again the lady was showing a good deal of undesired flesh. It could be that she was hoping to attract some well-connected lawyer. Even as I watched I saw Pye and Jute and a couple of other students ogling her, but in a mocking way. Eventually they came right up and peered down at her bosom. She didn't seem to mind and nor did her brother, but Richard Milford, more mindful of his patrons' honour than they were of their own, shooed the young lawyers away with a few choice words.

I wondered whether this delightful couple had yet read Richard's play of *The World's Diseas'd*, that tale of incest and Italian double-dealing. Of course the brother lordling didn't read because he had more important things to do. But his sister might spell her way through the text, finger underlining each word, tongue protruding from the fat purse of her mouth. She might actually read *The World's Diseas'd* if she thought it offered the chance of a bit of dirt.

I really should advise Milford to change the name of his female heroine, just in case Robert and Vinny saw themselves in the lurid mirror of his characters. He wouldn't listen but it would salve my conscience. It wasn't too late to change a detail, even though the text was at the printer's. (The book trade is used to dealing with the last-minute whims of authors.) I looked in Richard's direction and he caught my eye. His gaze seemed to convey a mixture of defensiveness and hostility – or maybe I was imputing these feelings to him. I was certain now that the naming and the crude characterization of the incestuous brother and sister in *The World's Diseas'd* were quite deliberate. From what Richard had said about taking money with one hand and paying back with the other, as well as the references to hidden 'messages', he secretly resented the necessity for patronage. Therefore he conveyed his real feelings about the absurd brother and sister in this oblique fashion, never imagining he'd be detected because his patrons were so stupid, so thick-skinned. If this was his opinion he was likely to be wrong. The insensitive may be blind to the world around them but they're often very sensitive and watchful over everything connected to themselves.

Anyway, in the matter of this play, I thought I'd leave well alone. What business was it of mine?

While Richard was having to listen to the drunken meanderings of his rustic patron, I took the opportunity to accost Lucy Milford. She was standing near her husband but also separate from him, if you see what I mean. She half glanced at me – through those long lashes!

"Did you enjoy the play, Mrs Milford?"

Even in the hazy dimness of the hall I could see the blush that crept into her cheeks. She inclined her head slightly and said, "I did."

Her voice was gentle.

"You do not find the taste of the lawyers too coarse and cynical?"

Still looking down she said, "No."

"I rather thought – it seemed to me – "

I had been intending to turn a compliment here, contrasting the roughness of the play or the witty crudity of its humour, with her delicacy and refinement. It's safe enough to pay compliments to a married woman, they enjoy them. But Lucy's near silence, her downcast gaze, made me stumble.

" – it might be too much for you," I ended feebly.

"Oh no."

"Oh well," I said.

I wondered how Richard Milford had courted her. Had his stream of words – for he was a voluble, self-explaining fellow (not unlike me) – met the dam of her silence? How had he prevailed?

Seeing I would get no further here, I made to turn away. Then I felt a firm hand on my arm and was surprised to see that it was Lucy's.

"Master Revill . . .?"

"Yes?"

"There was a man murdered."

I bent my head towards her. I couldn't be sure that I'd heard what I'd heard, her voice was so soft.

"A man – ? You mean, Peter Agate."

Her grip tightened on my arm.

"No, not your friend."

"Who then?"

"I don't know," she said.

"Ah madam," I said, moving to detach myself. I felt sweat breaking out on my face. The heat of the room, the drink I'd already taken.

"Look how he dies! Look how his eye turns pale!" she said. Her voice did not vary from its low pitch but she shuddered.

My skin crawled. The hair prickled on my nape. She seemed to be looking over my shoulder. I was afraid to turn round in case I saw what she was seeing.

"Look how his wounds do bleed at many vents!"

And then I recognized the lines. They are the words of the mad prophetess Cassandra in Troy, as she foresees the death of her brother Hector on the battlefield outside the city. Well, I suppose there are different kinds of prophetesses, the raving ones and the quiet ones. Obviously Lucy Milford had been more deeply affected, not to say afflicted, by *Troilus and Cressida* than she'd let on at first. If she was a Cassandra then she was a whispering one rather than of the breast-beating variety.

"It was only a play, Mrs Milford, only a play," I said, my tone almost matching hers for softness. I glanced sideways to where her husband was in close conversation with Robert and Vinny Venner, their red countenances framing his paler face. He was oblivious to his wife's strange mood. "Those are words from the play you have just seen."

"Stop him," she said.

"Stop who? Stop Hector? But he will go out to battle and be killed. He has already gone. The warrior's fate. It is written."

"No, not him," she said for the second time. She moved closer. "*You know.*"

"I don't know."

"But you have it too."

Before I could ask what she meant or what it was that I was supposed to have too – if she knew it herself – we were interrupted by Jack Wilson.

"A fine performance, Nick."

"What? Oh, thank you, Jack. And you as Hector."

I gestured at my friend, as if to say to Lucy Milford, look here is the player who impersonated Hector, alive and well.

But whatever strange mood had seized her seemed to have passed. She inclined her head and said, with only a faint blush, "You make a fine warrior, Jack."

"Though I am not a martial man by nature," he said.

I felt a twinge of – yes, admit it – a twinge of jealousy that she should be complimenting my friend on his acting as well as the fact that she called him by his first name. Yet it was not surprising. Jack was liked by all for his easy openness.

At this point I was swept off by a gaggle of law students, among whom I identified Michael Pye and Edmund Jute. It was that stage in the evening when I had to stop a moment and identify people. To be honest, I wasn't altogether unwilling to be drawn away from Lucy Milford's company, especially now that Jack had turned up. There was an unsettling quality about Mistress Milford. Perhaps that was part of her attraction.

My tankard was refilled by someone or other. I hadn't been aware of finishing it. Normally I drink sparingly, in sips like a green girl. Not tonight though.

"Well, was our Helen made of hot enough stuff for you, gentlemen?" I said to the young lawyers. "Worth fighting a war over, was she? Or going to law for?"

"We hear that the law has rather come to you, Master Revill," said Michael Pye.

Was there anyone in London who didn't know my circumstances? Was I walking round with a dark cloud of suspicion over my head? Next I'd find myself the subject of a broadsheet ballad!

"Let Master Revill alone," said Edmund Jute. "He has just wrung our hearts as Troilus. What he does in his spare time is no concern of ours. In law a man is innocent until proven . . . otherwise."

This was a two-edged compliment, like being told by Tom Gally that his employer Henslowe did not regard me as a murderer. But it was more acceptable because Jute had coupled it with praise of my playing. But then, what did the opinion of these law-chicks matter? They had such good judgement that they thought it a good use of their time to ogle Vinnie Venner's tits.

"My question was about matchless Helen, gentlemen," I said, trying not to slur my speech. "Whether she was worth it."

"I grant she had a ready tongue," said Edmund Jute, "though the face that surrounded it was not one that would ever launch a thousand ships, in my opinion."

"Or only a little ship, just a bark," said another student.

"Maybe a cock-boat," said a third.

"Who is the boy that played Cressida?" asked a fourth student, a solid fellow. I detected a level of interest here, it was more than a casual query. "What is his name, Troilus? You must know him, know him well. Tell me his name now."

My head was muzzy from the heat and drink and that odd combination of excitement and tiredness which comes after a play. I had to struggle for a moment to think of a name for Peter Pearce.

"One of our apprentices. Let me see, what is his name, my head is thick . . . his name is . . . Matthew Goodpiece."

"Named for his mother? He has a feminine cast."

"Boys make better women than women," I said.

"It depends on the end you have in view," said Jute, whose carroty hair had taken on a flaming quality in the artificial light of the hall.

"On the stage, I mean."

"Women for duty, boys for pleasure," said the stocky student, licking his lips in a manner that reminded me of Samuel Benwell.

"Your Goodpiece had a fetching eye, though I preferred the one who was Helen," said Michael Pye.

"Then you have the worse taste," I said. "Cressida is young and fresh, not used goods."

"You may be right," said Pye, cocking up his large nose. "As for Helen, she was a king's wife and the mistress to a prince – but she was still a whore."

"What do you know about whores, Michael?" said the Benwell-like student.

Yes, I thought, *what do you know about whores?* Answer now. Are you familiar with one by the name of Nell?

"I know the breed, which is more than you will ever know, Master Miller."

"Oh, the Miller grinds on, careless of who comes to bring him their corn, boy or girl," said the one called by that name. He lurched in my direction. "Let me take your flour, Troilus."

I smiled, slipped out of reach and slopped my drink on the floor.

"Just make sure you don't get caught between his upper and nether stones, Master Revill," said someone else, Jute, I think.

So the evening wore on with this unrelenting kind of raillery, and with drinking and more drinking still. Was the chat of these educated young lawyers – their pleasure in suggestion and bawdy – so different from what the lewd apprentices enjoyed? Not really.

At some later point a band of us, students and the younger players, shifted to the nearby Devil Tavern, there to go on drinking and singing and swapping bawdy talk, with occasional intervals to go outside for a spew or a piss (or both at once). I couldn't help remembering the last time I'd been here with Peter Agate. His murder seemed distant but not distant enough. If I drank a little more I could make it more distant still. I craved oblivion. In our play of *Troilus* the Greek Ulysses tells of how time stuffs the deeds of the past – good deeds and bad deeds, heroic ones and mean ones – into the wallet which he carries on his back. Everything is destined for oblivion. Alms for oblivion. Just give it all to time. Well, I hadn't got the time at the moment so, in the interim, drink would do the job well enough.

The stocky boy-loving student who went by the name of Miller snugged up to me on the bench, and insisted on buying me another drink or three. He wasn't interested in me or only interested insofar as I might be a conduit to younger, fresher flesh. He pressed me for details about young Matthew Goodpiece. Given fluency by the ale, I invented a few facts, just as I had already invented another name for Peter Pearce. I felt protective of my Cressida, and didn't want this fellow going in pursuit of her or him. Besides, our boy-players – with one or two exceptions – lead clean lives, often lodging with our seniors, the best of them being brought on to inherit the dramatic mantle which their elders will one day pass over. Often, they are quite well born and their parents have entrusted them to the care of the Company.

At an even later point during that evening the interior of the Devil Tavern started to spin and swirl. The faces of my companions danced in front of my own. I began seeing things. I was sure that in one corner of the place I spotted Tom Gally in conversation with the old player Chesser, the one who had seen the extra devil on stage during *Faustus*. Well, he's in the right place, I thought. There are plenty more devils, young and old, in the Devil . . .

I could no longer distinguish between what was real and what wasn't. I knew this because Lucy Milford's face and body floated before me and the words coming out of her mouth asked me if I would like her to tear her clothing and bare her breast, like a true Cassandra. I knew this wasn't happening, since I had earlier left her and her husband with the Venners in the banqueting-hall. I also knew it wasn't happening because she would never have uttered those words. So I said yes. But she must have been teasing me for she shook her head and said that she couldn't do it and when I asked her why, she repeated, as if it was reason enough, "There was a man murdered." I nodded, since this did seem a good reason.

And then I decided that the floor would be a more comfortable place on which to spend the next few hours, or years, and accordingly I slid off my bench and took up my position among the dust and dregs. From lying down it was a short step to sleeping or stupor.

I dreamed that I'd died and gone to the underworld. It was a mazy place of alleys and arches. Although this underworld was nearly deserted, I did recognize one of the passers-by. It was the headless figure who had knocked me to the ground in Middle Temple. He too was out and about and striding through the streets, regardless of anyone who stood in his way and exuding that strange, feral smell. Then I was being ferried across the river Styx by Charon, the boatman who is at everybody's service, like it or not. I recognized him. That thin shape taking on definition through the yellow-grey gloom. I heard the grinding of the oar against the side of the boat . . . I knew that steady, undeviating approach.

Then there were hands helping me into his boat and even a body sitting in the stern next to me, and I was filled with gratitude that I had at least one friend prepared to accompany me on this last ride. We reached the far side and my friend – from his voice it sounded like Jack Wilson – had Jack died as well then? – helped me up some stairs and through some more mazy streets. I tried to tell Jack about the headless figure as he helped me up yet more stairs to my room in the underworld, but I don't think that my friend was listening. Instead he clapped me reassuringly on the shoulder and told me to sleep sound. There is kindness in the afterlife after all, I thought. Then I sank into a true oblivion.

"Wake up, Nick!"

I'd only been asleep for five minutes, it seemed. Yet here was a little daylight squeezing itself through my pinched window, and here was my friend Jack Wilson come again, this time not to clap me reassuringly on the shoulder but to give me an urgent shaking up. Had he stayed in my room all night?

"Wake up!"

"I am awake. What do you want?"

My voice sounded queerly disembodied. My mouth tasted like the bottom of the bear-pit.

I made to sit up. The bed swayed slightly. I was a stranger to myself. My head felt as though it was balanced precariously on my body, like a heavy ball of stone on a crumbling pillar. I lay down again. The bed lurched. I closed my eyes, and hoped that Jack would go away.

"Nick, you must listen."

"Why?"

"Richard Milford is dead."

Now I opened my eyes and sat up. The next instant I'd stumbled out of bed and, clinging to the wall, was attempting to stand upright.

"What?"

"He has been foully murdered. We must go."

Jack was standing in the doorway.

"But I saw him yesterday at the play," I said.

"We all saw him yesterday at the play, Nick," said Jack. "Now you must come to the playhouse. Dick Burbage has summoned all of us."

"Who murdered Richard Milford?"

"I don't know. Nobody knows. Come on."

"The murderer knows," I said.

"Eh? Hurry up, Nick."

I remembered Lucy Milford's words, *There was a man murdered.*

"Lucy Milford is not harmed, is she?"

"She found him."

"She knew too," I said.

My sight was fuddled but, even so, I was aware of Jack looking at me oddly.

"She is a delicate lady," he said.

I was fumbling to take off the shirt I'd fallen asleep in. I was ashamed to see that it was heavily stained with last night's revel. I couldn't go to work like this. Even my blunted sense of smell informed against me. I scrabbled in my chest for my spare shirt, hauled it on and, hastily flinging on some outer garments, clattered downstairs after Jack and out into the street.

The morning was dank and foggy, as usual. When would these blindfold days be over?

I was still half-numbed from last night's drinking. The surprise and horror of Richard Milford's murder had yet to sink in.

As we paced quickly through the streets towards the Globe, Jack told me what was known of Richard's death. It wasn't much. The Milfords had recently moved to lodgings on the north side of the river, in Thames Street. Though not a grand thoroughfare it was more respectable than most of the places on our side of the water. Obviously Richard and his wife were on their way up in the world. At the end of the previous evening they'd left Middle Temple in company with their patrons, Lord Robert Venner and his sister. These noble siblings had in turn left the Milfords at the door of their lodgings in order to return to their town-house which, Jack believed, lay somewhere in Whitefriars.

It wasn't clear precisely what had happened after that. Either Lucy Milford had gone to their part of the house alone while her husband remained in the lobby for some reason, or both had retired to their chambers until Richard was summoned back to the lobby by a knocking at the front door. In any event, Richard Milford had opened the door and been violently attacked, probably with a knife. His wife was drawn out by the sounds of struggle and by shouting and discovered her husband dying in a pool of his own blood. The door to the street was open. No weapon was to be seen. The head-borough, a more capable man than Doggett of Southwark, was alerted and had rapidly established the bare bones of the story, even down to the hour. The murder had taken place some time after after one o'clock, as called by the watchman on his rounds.

I thought of the watchman's refrain.

Past one o'clock and almost two,
My masters all, good day to you.

For Richard Milford it had been the bellman's fatal goodnight.

Then I thought of Lucy Milford.

Look how he dies! Look how his wounds do bleed at many vents!

She had surely foreseen her husband's death, just as Cassandra glanced into the future and there witnessed the ruin of Hector. I said nothing of this to Jack Wilson of course. The merest suspicion brushed past me that, if Lucy had foreseen Richard's death, then she might also have caused it. But she was meek and gentle, she did not look like a murderer. What did a murderer look like? Not like her, for sure . . . or like me either.

Another aspect of this dreadful business was, in its way, to my benefit, since it dispelled some of the suspicion which hung over me for Peter Agate's death. I wasn't so heartless or cold as to think of this while Jack and I were hastening towards the Globe playhouse for Burbage's meeting (of which I shall say something in a moment). But these ideas occurred later, when I came to mull them over, sitting by myself in the Goat & Monkey ale-house. It was the evening of the same day. I wanted no one's company. I was still experiencing the effects of the previous night. Someone in the Company who prided himself on being able to hold his liquor told me that the best cure for crapulousness was to take yet more ale. This remedy he called 'the hair of the same wolf'. It didn't seem to be working with me since I was still queasy and out of sorts, although that might have as much to do with the events of the last few days as it did with the drink. Anyway I might as well feel sick in a tavern as sitting solitary in my room. So, sipping slowly at Master Bly's ale, I considered the unsatisfactory state of my life and my connection with the sudden deaths of two men.

The circumstances of Richard Milford's death were similar to Peter Agate's. Both men had apparently been taken by surprise in the lobby of their lodgings, both had been stabbed. The assailant had fled under cover of night or fog, leaving no weapon behind. In neither case was there an easily discernible motive for these men's deaths. Peter was newly arrived in London, a would-be player and – in my judgement – an offence to no one. Richard Milford was a rising playwright and generally popular, although he had the knack of rubbing people (like me) up the wrong way sometimes. However, it was hard to maintain dislike for him for long. There was something open about his vanity and self-concern. And there was no doubting that as a budding poet and playwright he had promise. Had had promise . . .

Here I paused in sipping my ale, and came over cold as I thought of Richard's death. And Peter's. I wiped at a moistened eye, uncertain who this little water was in aid of, and then tried to bring my thoughts to order once more.

What had linked these two men? Nothing as far as I could see, apart from the fact that they'd had connections to the Chamberlain's and also that I'd been a friend to each of them. However, the details of this second violent death in Thames Street so paralleled the first in Dead Man's Place as to suggest that a single individual might have been responsible for both. Must, surely, have been responsible for both. Now, the finger of suspicion was pointing at me for Peter's murder. But it would have to point elsewhere for Richard's. If he'd been killed around one o'clock in the morning or shortly afterwards then I could prove that I was elsewhere at the time. Exactly where I couldn't have said, being drunk and incapable at the time. But I was somewhere in transit between the Devil Tavern and Master Benwell's lodgings, supported by my good friend Jack Wilson. Jack could testify to my helpless condition. Or – if I had arrived back home (home, ha!) before that time – then I was safely wrapped up in a drunken stupor. Any number of people would be able to vouch for my perplexed state during that evening. I couldn't have lifted a pint pot in the latter part of it, let alone a knife.

I prepared my defence in these terms, just in case I was questioned by Alan Talbot or another coroner, you understand. And naturally my thoughts turned to the question of who had actually done the killings and whether it was indeed one individual or whether the murders were unconnected. One thing was indisputable. The two deaths had cast a pall over our Company.

The mood at the meeting in the Globe tire-house that morning was sombre and subdued. Dick Burbage looked unusually grave. He was famous for his tragic parts and was good at looking grave, but this was no act. At least, I don't think it was. He expressed our collective grief over the death of Richard Milford, talking of the tragedy of a promising life so brutally terminated. Burbage addressed us standing on the platform from where he oversaw the chamber practices. Standing beside him was Thomas Pope, another of the shareholders. Our thoughts, said Burbage, were with Richard's widow, Lucy. (Mine certainly were, from time to time.) He went on to say that some of us might be examined by the authorities in the matter of Richard's death. This was because the playwright had been, in a manner, one of the Chamberlain's Men. We'd been among the last people he'd talked with. Then Burbage paused, and I sensed that whatever he was about to say was the real reason we'd been called together.

"Gentlemen, I have heard it whispered that there was bad feeling between Richard Milford and the shareholders. The story has got about that we turned down his last play, that we rejected him. The truth is that we had not yet decided whether to stage this piece. And he knew it. Richard knew also that, even if we chose not to stage this particular play at this particular time, then we would still look with favour on his work. Why, almost everybody here remembers his *Venetian Whore* comedy. More in that vein would have been very welcome."

There was something constrained, almost defensive, about Dick's words. I didn't quite believe him or the confirmatory nods which Thomas Pope was making on the platform next to him. I was almost certain that Richard *had* been turned down over *The World's Diseas'd*. Burbage's comments about *A Venetian Whore* were pretty good evidence of the kind of thing the shareholders would have liked from Richard Milford, light pieces which worked by suggestion rather than sensation. But why was Dick bothering to justify himself and the other shareholders over the choice of plays, anyway? It wasn't, strictly speaking, the business of the rank-and-file players. We had opinions, sometimes very strong opinions, but were content to leave the selection to our seniors, trusting in their judgement and experience.

"These are difficult times, gentlemen," Burbage continued. "Our patron Lord Hunsdon is . . . not well. [*Another series of nods from Thomas Pope.*] We face competition from the Paul's Children. We face the usual enemies of bad weather and creeping plague, and the displeasure of the Council if we overstep the mark. All of these things we can deal with singly. But – as William has observed of sorrows – when troubles come, they come not single spies but in battalions."

Burbage paused. There was a murmur of subdued recognition at his using Shakespeare's expression. WS was nowhere in sight on this dank morning but the closeness between the principal player and the principal writer of our Company was familiar to us.

"But you are aware of this," he said carelessly. "I won't weary your ears with more. I wish only to warn you against a certain individual named Gally, Thomas Gally. Some of you have already encountered him. He is a kind of playhouse moth, drawn to us by our light and warmth. I know that he and Richard Milford had been . . . seen together. This Gally claims to be an agent for Philip Henslowe of the Admiral's. It may be true that he works for our rival in some capacity, I don't know. But his real business is to interfere in matters that are none of his business.

"Gally is eager to know our plans, to ascertain our patron's health, to find out about our takings. Whether Master Henslowe has explicitly asked this dog to report to him on these questions, or whether Gally simply brings to his master whatever scraps he can scavenge, I don't know. Gally is not above doing a little dirty work on his own account, for example stirring up the apprentices so as to drive down our trade. So I say, watch out for this man, don't trust him. Don't share a tavern bench with him. We in the Chamberlain's are free and easy fellows, we don't watch our tongues or guard our secrets very close. We must not allow our generous natures to be abused."

There was still something about Burbage's words that puzzled me. That the Chamberlain's had rivals who might stoop to underhand methods wasn't exactly news. Yes, we players might be relatively trusting, or careless in what we said and who we said it to, but we weren't exactly born yesterday. And I couldn't understand either the link which Burbage had made between Richard Milford and Tom Gally. Was he trying to blacken Richard's memory? I'd already suspected that Richard, most probably spurned by our seniors over his new play, was being courted by Henslowe through Gally. If so, good fortune to him. Or rather – if he hadn't been so shockingly murdered – it might have been his good fortune. The half question which had formed in my mind was put in full by my friend and co-player Laurence Savage.

"Dick, two men connected to our Company have lately and violently died, first a friend of Nicholas here and then Richard Milford. And now you warn us against loose talk and dirty dealing. Are you saying that there are worse things in store? Are you saying that Tom Gally, who is indeed known to most of us, is involved with what has happened?"

"I'm saying nothing of the kind," said Burbage. "I will not slander any man so. But we have enemies, there is danger abroad, and two people have died violently – as you say, Laurence. Every man should be on his guard."

This warning concluded our Globe meeting, which broke up even more sober than it had begun. If Dick Burbage had intended to bring us together and imbue us with a spirit of one-ness, his closing words had the opposite effect. What were we supposed to be on our guard against – each other? We cast watchful glances around. There was a forced quality to our jokes, and the tire-house was not, for once, a place to loiter in. Fortunately we had no performance scheduled for that afternoon.

Sitting by myself in the Goat & Monkey that evening, I continued to puzzle over Dick's words. He'd made everyone feel apprehensive, or rather had heightened the unease which already existed. And without giving us anything specific to look out for. Did he really consider that Tom

Gally – the 'playhouse moth', even if beetle would have been a more apt description – had taken a hand in the deaths of Peter Agate and Richard Milford? If so, it wasn't surprising that Burbage had spoken cautiously. A mere whisper of such a suspicion could lead to charges of slander. If Gally's aim was to disturb the well-being of the Chamberlain's Company, then he'd certainly succeeded. Possibly, by upsetting us, he had benefited Henslowe and the Admiral's Men too, although it was a bit simple-minded to consider that the fortunes of the two theatre companies were like a pair of buckets in a well: that is, if one was up the other must be down. It was more the case that, when the sun shone for one company, then it shone to a degree for all. And the same was true in the rain. Nevertheless, Tom Gally might be operating on his own. Pricked on by a petty spirit of rivalry, he might be one of those men who take pleasure in small, underhand victories. But to resort to murder . . .? There's a world of difference between stirring up a handful of apprentices to be rude to a couple of foreigners and stabbing men in cold blood in the lobbies of their lodgings.

I remembered that I'd glimpsed Gally and that superannuated old player Chesser conversing together in the Devil Tavern after our performance of *Troilus and Cressida*. Or at least I thought I'd seen them. But so befuddled was I during the evening that I could hardly distinguish between the real and the imagined. Anyway, what did it signify if they had been there?

Simply this, perhaps. That they had been on the scene (if my memory was accurate). And if they were on the scene, then they had a part to play in the story. It was like a drama. Characters don't just wander on, they all have function and purpose . . .

So what was Chesser's part in all of this? He hated the playhouse and feared it as a nest of devils, even if he couldn't keep himself away from the players' haunts. He appeared to be engaged on a lone mission to 'save' young men like Peter

Agate from being infected by the play-sickness. Chesser was not the absurd figure I'd first taken him for. But if he was no longer the clown that didn't mean that he was necessarily the villain. Would he go so far as to kill a man in order to preserve that man's immortal soul from damnation? Perhaps. There are individuals, plenty of them good men, who would consider the sacrifice of the body a small price to pay for the salvation of the soul. I remembered the fierce eye, the iron grip on my arm in Paul's Yard, as he told me to avoid the fate of my friend.

This was only speculation, impure speculation. None of it really got me any closer to the mystery of who'd been responsible for Peter's and Richard's deaths, their foul murders.

Murder most foul . . . I mused . . . murder most foul, strange and unnatural, as in the best it is. As WS describes it in *Hamlet*.

Best, worst, foulest.

And then this word 'foul' set off a train of ideas in my head.

The early draught of a play is called the 'foul papers', because of its blotchy and disorganized state. Richard Milford had trusted me enough to want me to read *The World's Diseas'd* in this early form, since he valued my opinion. Despite the compliment, I didn't much like the play. When the subject had been raised in the private box at the Globe where I had met Richard's rustic patrons, Lady Vinny Venner had seized on the phrase 'foul papers'. "Is it horrid?" she'd said hopefully. "Is it dirty?"

Neither she nor her brother had then read the play, although it was already at the printer's. I wondered whether in the interim one or both had bent themselves to the task of reading it, even if Lord Bumpkin claimed to have better things to attend to. But if and when they came to open up the book – and on the assumption that they'd get past Richard's flowery dedication – what would they find? A lurid tale of lopped limbs, lust and double-dealing, a tale in which an incestuous sister, named Virginia, ultimately dies in the arms of her bloodstained brother Vindice. Would it not strike even a couple as slow-witted as this pair that their own poet-playwright had made an unfortunate choice of name for his lascivious heroine? Would they laugh it off or treat it as a mortal insult? Wouldn't it appear as though Richard Milford – clever, citified Richard – was laughing up his sleeve at his rustic benefactors? Which was exactly what he was doing, with his 'subtle messages'.

There was an even more serious implication in all of this. Had Richard been hinting that young Lord and Lady Venner were actually incestuously attached? Perhaps he was. I didn't know them well, and didn't want to know them at all, but Robbie and Vinnie did appear to be close as brother and sister. Unnaturally close? Perhaps. Or maybe it was merely that they were both cut from the same coarse cloth.

Like the imputation that Tom Gally might have stooped to murder, this imputation of incest would be a dangerous slander if it got abroad. And get abroad it certainly would when *The World's Diseas'd* was published and – even if it was never intended for open sale – distributed among the Venners' private circle. If Richard Milford had lived he might well have been looking about for a fresh patron. And if he'd lived he might well have found it hard to land another patron, considering his propensity to stab the patron in the back, using his pen rather than a dagger. If he'd lived . . .

Brother and sister had been the last people to see Richard alive, apart from the murderer. The Bumpkins had left the Milfords at the door of the couple's lodgings in Thames Street around one o'clock in the morning. What if . . . if the noble lord and lady, outraged by the contents of the play, by the way Richard had poked fun at them, by the slanderous implications of a name . . . what if the lord and lady had waited for a few minutes so as to give the young couple time to prepare for bed, then returned to the front door, rapped loudly and, when Richard opened up, fallen on him? It didn't have to be both of them, of course. It ought to be the man (those powerful, meaty hands; the little porcine eyes). It was a man's job. On the other hand, I could visualize Virginia Venner wielding a dagger as readily as any tragic heroine. She possessed enough of her brother's fleshy strength.

I cast my mind back to the previous night.

So much had happened in twenty-four hours, and I had not been in my right mind for most of that time! I tried to remember the attitude of Richard Milford in the Middle Temple hall, his posture, his expressions, while he was standing between his patrons. He'd looked at me and I'd registered defensiveness, even hostility in his glance. He knew that I couldn't take Robbie and his sister seriously. But perhaps Richard's guarded look had nothing to do with me and was rather a response to an accusation, a verbal attack from his patrons. Had *they* suddenly understood that they were being held up to ridicule in *The World's Diseas'd*? Had *he* suddenly understood that they weren't as stupid and thick-skinned as he'd imagined? That you cannot accept patronage and then snigger at your patron behind his back? Certainly the Venners had looked red, redder than usual. From anger? From heat and drink?

There were far too many 'maybes' and 'perhapses' in this account, too much iffing speculation. At least, the Bumpkins would be questioned by the coroner because they were the witnesses who'd left Richard and his wife shortly before the former's death. But I didn't believe that the brother and sister would be as hard pressed as I had been by Alan Talbot, who'd almost assumed my guilt over Peter Agate's murder. The Venners were coarse sprigs of the nobility but they remained noble. Once a lordling always a lordling. In the absence of any firm evidence linking them to Richard's demise, a certain deference would be paid to them. They'd be taken at their word.

What did link this pair to Richard Milford was their patronage and his grateful, if hypocritical, acceptance of it.

He had dedicated his poetic *Garland* to R.V. THE ONLY BEGETTER and also *The World's Diseas'd*. The play, at present with Nicholson the bookseller, might hold more clues which could be somehow communicated to the authorities. I'd read the piece, but with an impatient, critical eye, and without any suspicion at the time that the playwright might have drawn his characters from life. Now I needed to examine more carefully a tragic piece which had turned out, tragically, to be Richard's last work. The problem was getting hold of a copy of *The World's Diseas'd*, since they were doubtless intended for private distribution only – if that was still going to happen after the demise of the author. The most I could do was to call by on Benjamin Nicholson tomorrow and request him to show me the play. I could claim, quite truthfully, to be a friend of Richard, someone concerned for his legacy as a writer. And I really should go and see Nicholson anyway about that debt, perhaps give him something on account.

So, while sitting solitary in a dim corner of the Goat & Monkey – although all the corners of the Goat & Monkey were dim – I pursued my thoughts. Mere speculation, at the moment. But an advantage of private speculation is that you don't have to justify it to anyone.

It was the mystery of Peter Agate's death which affected me more deeply than Richard's. Not only because I was implicated in his murder and was still waiting for Coroner Talbot's decision (*His blood was on you . . . I may recall you later*), but because Peter's arrival in London lay partly at my door. Like me, the squire's son had come to find his fortune in the capital. And when he'd had doubts soon afterwards about whether a player's life was really for him, I'd encouraged him to stay on. Would that he had returned home to our village, to his father and sisters! He'd still be alive and his blood – literally and metaphorically – would not have been on my hands. If I was to exonerate myself and obtain justice for my dead friend, then it was my duty to search out his killer. Even if I might find myself as his next victim.

And despite the snugness of the dim ale-house corner a chill spread over me, because I suddenly saw the whole affair in a different light. I breathed deep and attempted to think slow.

Like everyone else, I'd supposed that the person the murderer of Peter had intended to get rid of was Peter himself. But my friend was killed in the lobby of my lodgings in the uncertain light of a foggy afternoon. We were about the same height, the same age, Peter and I.

You can see where I'm headed. Nevertheless I tried not to jump to conclusions (as you've perhaps just done) but to take the matter one step at a time. You can understand my reluctance to jump to conclusions.

One question was whether the murderer had followed his victim back to Dead Man's Place – or whether Peter was, like Richard Milford, already inside the house and had been summoned by a rap at the door.

In my mind, I put myself in the murderer's shoes. They are a surprisingly comfortable fit.

I follow my friend through the fog, trailing his tall dark shape down the street. I wait until he nears the front door in Dead Man's Place and then put on speed to enter just behind him. He feels the brush of wind as a second person comes into the lobby. Peter turns round. He must turn round since he is due to receive his wounds in the front. Before that happens he opens his mouth in doubt or surprise. He says something like "Who are . . .?" or "What do you . . .?" but I cannot hear clearly for the blood pounding in my ears. And then I plunge the knife into Peter's chest. I am shocked by the resistance the blade meets. I have never done this before. But I am a strong young man. He is a strong young man too and, even though he has been given a fatal wound, he will not die straightaway. He begins to flail about, to strike out at his assailant. He batters me with his arms, and I am compelled to strike at him several times over. Probably unawares, I make noises. Grunts, shouts. He also makes noises as he breathes his last. Then – finally! – he falls back against the door and I can see that this man will never rise again even though he is still bubbling and breathing and bleeding.

It is time for me to leave before company comes. I force back the front door against the weight of his falling frame and flee into the street. The fog is thick. I run through the streets. When I have got a little way off, I realize that I am still holding the murderer's knife. Do I throw it into one of the ditches that criss-cross this part of Southwark or even into the mighty river itself? I can sense rather than hear the slurp of water within a few yards of where I'm standing while my breath adds thicker plumes to the white air. Why discard a serviceable knife though? There is no one here to see me. What is thrown away can be retrieved and used against me, however deep it's buried. And the knife might come in handy once more. So instead of throwing it away, I tuck it inside my clothing. I notice that there is blood on my ungloved hands. On my face too probably. And on my clothing, though I'm wearing something dark which seems to have already absorbed the stains. I didn't deliberately choose those dark clothes this morning. It must have been providence that I put them on.

Never mind all that. Hands can be washed. Clothes can be burnt. Consciences can be ignored.

I breathe deeply, surprised at how winded I am. This killing is a tiring business. And then, I return to . . . where do I return to? . . . to wherever it is that I have come from.

Another scene comes into my mind, different in its details but the same in essence. I am still wearing the murderer's shoes and they don't pinch me at all. In this scene, I go boldly up to the front door in Dead Man's Place, rap loudly and wait. If the landlord answers I have some excuse at hand. But the landlord doesn't answer. Instead it is the man I am looking for. A tall dark shape opens the door and says something like "Yes . . .?" or "What do you . . .?" but I can't hear clearly because of the blood which is already pounding in my ears and therefore, knowing my target, I plunge the knife into this man's chest. He staggers back into the dimly lit lobby. I spring inside after him. And the rest you know.

Now let's change parts. Handy-dandy. I will step out of the murderer's shoes and back into those of N. Revill but only for a moment. Now I will put myself in Peter's place, take up his role on that afternoon, walking home down the fog-bound street, as I might actually have been walking home myself. I sense someone slip through the door behind me, I spin round to confront him, I say "What . . .?" etc . . . or, in the alternative scene, I will go downstairs, summoned by a rap at that same door, and, opening it, experience a terrible blow in the chest.

For some reason it was easier for me to envisage myself in the former role, that of the murderer, than as his victim. It is more satisfying to play the villain than the victim.

Now I have arrived, reluctantly, at the conclusion which I was so reluctant to leap at before. There's no escape.

What if Peter had been killed in mistake for me?

Suppose that *Revill* was always the intended victim.

We looked alike. At least we had looked quite alike as boys. I remembered Peter's father confusing me with his son on several occasions. True, we'd grown unalike, just as we'd grown up and grown apart. But a stranger – if he'd been watching from a distance, in the fog, down a street, or if he'd come to the door of a dimly lit lobby – a stranger might well have taken me for Peter Agate. Or taken Agate for Revill. Especially since Peter's lodgings were actually mine. Master Revill the player lives in Dead Man's Place. A tallish, darkish-haired young man is seen turning in there, or he comes to the door in answer to a summons. What is more reasonable than to suppose that that man is the player?

Let's kill him then . . .

My hands were shaking. I put my tankard slowly down on the table in the Goat & Monkey, and took several deep breaths. I was convinced that the scene had unrolled as I'd played it out in my head. One of the scenes, anyway. It didn't much matter whether Peter had been trailed in the street or whether he was already inside the house. The end was the same. The surprise, the sudden attack, the bloody murder.

But whereas before I'd been unable to come up with a motive for Peter's murder, things made a little more sense if *I* was the intended victim. This wasn't self-importance, the swollen belief that I was big enough to have earned myself many enemies. I'd lived in London for more than three years and Peter for just a few days. I had not set out to cultivate enemies, although I'd inevitably incurred the displeasure of a few and the hatred of one or two. I thought of a certain steward in a house on the north bank of the Thames – but as far as I knew he was safely dead.* I thought of that dangerous band which had surrounded the Earl of Essex.** But, once again, they were mostly dead or imprisoned. And my role in that affair was not widely known.

No, if I was looking for a solution now, it must lie within the confines of this story. And since I had already fingered young Lord and Lady Venner for the murder of Richard Milford, could I now attach them for my murder – or rather for Peter Agate's (but in mistake for me)?

But my brain was weary with so much thinking and speculating. It was enough for one evening. I drained the last few drops from my tankard, and left the Goat. The fog hung in tatters. Useless threads of light could be discerned through the odd window. I groped my way through the streets to Dead Man's Place as fast as possible. My feet slid over slick, dirty cobbles. I scarcely bothered to keep to one side, away from the kennel in the centre where the muck slithered or

*see *Sleep of Death*
** see *Death of Kings*

stuck. I had more pressing concerns than filthy feet. Since I'd come to the conclusion – the provisional conclusion – that someone wanted to kill me, my senses were sharpened, however dulled my brain was. In the open air, on the streets, that conclusion didn't feel provisional at all. Here was I, a victim, the prey-in-waiting. Out there was the villain, the hunter. And how many hunters! What a strange pack had run through my mind this evening – Tom Gally, that old player Chesser, the rude brother and sister called Venner. I had accused them all.

The world was a dangerous place, full of murderers and would-be murderers. If the fog was a blanket concealing me from any attacker, it was also a cloak hiding him or her from me.

But I reached my house safely. I climbed the stairs, shut my door fast, crept into bed, pulled my fusty blanket up about my ears and fell asleep immediately.

Habeas Corpus

Two odd things happened the next day before I managed to visit Paul's Yard in the hope of requesting from the bookseller a copy of Richard Milford's *The World's Diseas'd*. The first thing was quite minor or appeared so at the time.

My fears of the previous night hadn't gone away but they were diminished in the foggy daylight and I set off for the playhouse in calmer spirits.

I'd no sooner arrived at the Globe – another rehearsal, life goes on, the show never stops – than I was pounced on by the tire-man.

"Your sleeve, Nicholas, what happened to it?"

For answer I held up my arm.

"Looks all right to me."

"I mean your Troilus sleeve. The brocade one with the gold figures."

Bartholomew Ridd, the tire-man, was a fussy, irritating little individual. Like all those who have charge of costumes for stage plays he behaved as though the real function of the playhouse was to show off his fine gear. Players were merely the frames from which clothes were hung. Now, it was true that a player would have to play for many weeks, even for months in the case of a 'king' or a 'queen', to earn the cost of the costume he wore. It was also true that some of our audience – and not just the women – paid more attention to what we were wearing than to what we were saying or doing. Costumes count.

None of this, however, made any difference to the fact that Bartholomew Ridd was a fussy, irritating little individual. He would have been fussy, & cetera, if he'd been a vagrant – or the Queen of England. Sometimes Ridd behaved like the Queen of England. Imperious and snappish. And I should know. I met her once.

"You mean the sleeve I gave to Cressida as a love-token?"

"Of course that's what I mean. What's happened to it?"

"Have you asked Peter Pearce? I gave it to the boy-player. I had to give it to him. It's in the play."

The memory of that painful moment in the Middle Temple banqueting-hall returned. *Wear this sleeve.* There I had stood, as if turned to stone, while Peter waited for me to hand over the rich gold token in exchange for a glove.

"Of course I've asked him," said Batholomew Ridd.

"You've asked him, and what does Peter say?" I said carefully.

"He doesn't know what happened to it."

"You searched the tire-house at Middle Temple?"

"Call that a tire-house! It was no more than a poky little space behind the hall-screen. No one appreciates the worth of my costumes. They require proper housing."

"Well then."

"Well then, Nicholas. It's all very well for you to say 'Well then'. You are aware that the sleeve was part of your costume . . ."

"My responsibility, you mean."

"Of course that's what I mean."

Ridd was in the right, and not only from a tire-man's limited point of view. From the instant we put the costumes on to the instant we put them off – donning and doffing, as it was called – they were our responsibility. It didn't matter that we might be required by the script to give away bits of clothing. It was up to us to get those bits back afterwards and return them unscathed to the tire-house. I suppose that I'd got a bit distracted in the unusual circumstances of the *Troilus and Cressida* performance. A different venue, the makeshift tire-house, the strange fit of forgetfulness which had overcome me during the play when I was meant to hand over the sleeve to Cressida, the heat and the drinking and talking afterwards. But none of this was really an excuse, and I knew it. I should have looked after my costume better. Nevertheless I felt I should also defend myself against Ridd's niggling.

"I am sorry that I had to unfasten the sleeve and give it away. It's in the play."

"Oh the play, the play! That's an excuse for anything these days. I must have a word with Master William Shakespeare and get him to stop his characters dismantling their costumes in this fashion. Costumes are not playthings."

"I thought that's exactly what they were – play things."

"Very funny, Nicholas. You'll cut yourself with that tongue of yours one of these days."

"I'm beginning to wish now that I'd cut my arm off rather than lose the sleeve."

"The trouble with you players," said Ridd, "is that you can't see beyond the ends of your own noses."

"I am truly sorry, Bartholomew."

"You will be sorry when I've had a word with Richard Burbage. That was a valuable costume and it's not much good with one arm, is it? You may find your wages docked to pay for a new sleeve."

And Bartholmew Ridd stalked off. I couldn't be that angry with Ridd, although he was a fussy little & cetera, because the fault lay with me. I'd have a word with Peter Pearce about the sleeve but it was I who should have retrieved the wretched thing after the performance. If Burbage decided to dock my pay until I'd earned enough sleeve-money, well then, I'd just have to grin and bear it. How costly was a gold-figured brocade sleeve anyway?

Never mind that. I had more pressing considerations on my mind. Such as: was I about to be indicted for murder by Alan Talbot, the Middlesex coroner? Such as: was Nicholas Revill the real, intended target of Peter Agate's killer?

By the middle of the day I'd more or less argued myself out of the second consideration, and gone back to the idea that the intended target of Peter's killer had been, all along, Peter himself. In truth, all this thinking and speculation tended to show one thing only: that I had no idea what was going on.

On a different track, investigating a different mystery, that of Richard Milford's murder, I crossed the river to Paul's Wharf. I chose the ferry. Alan Talbot's suggestion that I, a mere player, didn't have the money to pay for a water crossing still rankled slightly. I'd show him. I'd take the ferry whenever I wanted to. But I ought to have walked across. The day, which had begun not too badly (considering the murders which were springing up around my heels), now showed what it really had in store for me. That little altercation with Bartholomew Ridd had merely been the first course.

The ferryman took me for an out-of-towner who could easily be rooked, which I wasn't, and I took him for a cheating bastard, which he was, and we exchanged words. After the words we nearly came to blows at the foot of the steps on the far side, regardless of the arrival of two or three other ferries. The disembarking passengers hardly gave us a glance. Our quarrel may have had entertainment value but it was too cold and misty and miserable to stop and stare. We were squaring up opposite each other and I had half an eye out for the boatman's fellows pitching in to help him out. Then, luckily, several potential customers materialized through the fog on the top of the wharf. My bellicose friend had to choose between the pleasure of beating up a player or allowing the others to snatch all the fares. It wasn't easy for him. Punches or pennies? Taking advantage of his indecision,

I tossed my single penny – and not the two which he'd demanded – on to the slimy stone at his feet and quickly ascended the steps.

I set off in the direction of Paul's Yard and Nicholson the printer and bookseller. The ground rises quite sharply from the river bank at this point. There is a large open area to the east of Burleigh House and a path leading across it, or rather a wide indentation worn in the ground by the comings and goings of countless feet. Then you must pass through a narrow alley between buildings before coming out into Thames Street, the very thoroughfare where Richard and Lucy Milford lodged and where Richard had been so treacherously surprised two nights before. I knew their house, had visited there once or twice. It crossed my mind to call on the new widow but prudence prevailed. I was already implicated in one unlawful killing. I did not want to get involved with another, however distantly. *Then why are you setting off to see Benjamin Nicholson about Milford's play?* a voice in my head whispered. I had no answer to that.

I was wrapped up in these thoughts but even so I heard someone calling out some words. After a time I became aware that these words were "Look out!" And then again "Look out!" I had the leisure to wonder who the warning was directed at. I peered towards the mouth of the passage which leads to Thames Street. I couldn't see the entrance, hardly surprising since everything was obscured and mist-wrapped. But I did see a darker shape take sudden definition in front of me. And grow darker and larger. Like a great door opening up in the fog. There was a confused rattling and rumbling and then that repeated shout riding over the noise.

"Look out below!"

I flung myself sideways to the ground, and felt the wind of the cart – horseless but heavily freighted – as it rushed past my heels. Another couple of feet to the left and the iron rims of the wheels would have crushed my leg. A couple more feet and my earthly term would have been over. I lay hugging the sloping ground, safe for the instant. Somewhere over my shoulder the loaded cart proceeded on its downward path. I prayed that no one else was in the way. The rumbling and grinding seemed to last for a little eternity and then, abruptly, ceased. Seconds later there were a couple of resonant thumps.

"Man, are you well?"

I felt the warm breath of my rescuer on my face as he bent over me. He was panting. The voice was familiar. I twisted around and sat up, ready with a thousand thanks for his warnings. Then my mouth must have fallen open. Looking at me through his old rheumy eyes was Chesser, the chalk-coloured face even paler than the surrounding air. The aged player looked as surprised as I felt.

"Why, Master Revill, it's you. I didn't know it was you."

"I – thank you, Master Chesser. If you hadn't shouted out . . . what happened?"

By this time I was on my feet, shaky and uncertain.

"I do not know, master. The cart swept past me in the mist and I called out a warning in case there were any Christian souls between it and the river."

"We'd better go and find out whether there's anybody down there apart from me."

We discovered the whereabouts of the cart by smell. It wasn't so far off. A sweetish, vinous scent hung in the vicinity, more agreeable than the usual river odours or the brassy fog. By chance, the cart had slewed to one side and on to a relatively level patch of cobbled ground near the waterfront. Then, thankfully without running down any passers-by, it had fetched up against a pair of stubby stone stumps used for securing ropes or boat cables. The sturdily made cart was undamaged. But a couple of wine barrels had slipped under the straps which fastened them and tumbled off the back. One had shattered. Its contents pooled like spilt blood across the cobbles, running into the crevices and mingling with the scum and dirt. If this had occurred on our side of the river, the Southwark side, the householders would already have been out with their cups and spoons, even with their rags and clouts, to scoop and sponge up the dregs, mud and all. But here, on this respectable shore, the inhabitants were more restrained. In fact there was nobody at all on the scene apart from Chesser and me, no passengers embarking or disembarking.

I still felt light-headed and unsteady from my near escape. The scent of the red wine was in my nostrils. But I could work out what had happened. It wasn't difficult. This open area next to Burleigh House and at the top of Paul's Wharf was used by carters and carriers as a convenient space to leave their conveyances for a time. This wasn't because they were waiting to ferry their goods across the water – London Bridge was near enough and free as well – but because carters whose business lay on the north side were amusing themselves on our southern shores with diversions like brothels, plays and bear-baiting. Empty carts were sometimes abandoned here for hours, often with a hobbled horse standing patiently between the shafts. Given the slant of the ground down towards the river, the wise carrier made sure that the wheels of his cart were securely blocked. Anyway it was usually empty conveyances which you saw here rather than the laden ones. To leave a load of wine barrels unattended for even a quarter of an hour was unwise – or would have been unwise in certain quarters on the Southwark side. Then I told myself to stop judging everything by the lower, more lax standards of my own neighbourhood. Over on this northern shore, folk were different. They were restrained, they were law-abiding. (But a murder had occurred in a street near here two nights ago.)

Even so it was odd, this incident of the abandoned cart. The second odd incident of the morning, after the Troilus sleeve.

The more I considered it the more odd and troubling it seemed. The carter must have left his conveyance for a few moments, unhitched his horse perhaps. Was it lamed?

Perhaps he was waiting for a fresh horse. Perhaps the carter had gone off for a quick pot in a tavern or a piss in a corner, carelessly leaving his cart without blocks wedged under the wheels. Then it had begun to roll downhill of its own accord. It would naturally tend towards the wide indentation in the slope, the foot-worn channel. It had started to roll. Or been given a little shove by someone . . .

When he returned from his piss or his pot, the carter would be surprised not to find his cart where he had left it. He'd be angry, he'd be worried, wouldn't he? In his position I would have been. He'd start searching for his conveyance. So where was he then, this irate or anxious carter? I scanned the mist in an uphill direction but no one emerged. The only sound was Chesser's steady breathing. He had recovered fast from the excitement of the past few minutes. He was in good condition, for an old man. His senses were sharp too. Sharp eyes and big ears. Players are tough creatures, even superannuated players. He was saying something.

"What, Master Chesser?"

"A miracle, Master Revill."

"Oh yes, and thank you again."

"Thank God rather."

"I do. I have."

Seeing that there was nothing we could do about the cart or its contents and since there was no one harmed, I remembered my original mission and began to make my way up the slope again. Master Chesser kept pace beside me and I was glad of his company, to be honest. Not only because he'd almost certainly preserved me from injury, even from death, but because his presence, almost anybody's presence, would have been welcome in this white solitude.

"It was not my doing but God's," he said.

"You were the one who was here to help though, Master Chesser."

"But who directed my footsteps to this place?"

Who indeed?

A suspicion that I'd been trying to keep down was growing in my mind. It wasn't that Chesser himself had been responsible for the runaway cart – if so, why should he call out a warning? – but that *someone* had been. To my active brain what ought to have been a street accident became a murder attempt.

"Did you see – anything?"

"No more than I have already said I saw, Master Revill. The cart flew past me as if it had wings."

"Strange that it should have been left unattended."

For answer, Chesser shrugged and indicated two or three other carts which almost blocked the neck of the alley we were trying to pass through. There were no drivers. However, these conveyances were empty, apart from a few pieces of dirty sacking and staves of wood in the bottom.

"The question you should be asking, Master Revill, is why you have been preserved by God."

As we emerged into Thames Street, I refrained from saying that there were more immediate considerations on my mind, considerations such as: who was trying to kill me? But it would be churlish and ungrateful not to let Chesser have his say. Which he proceeded to have. Forgetting that he'd told me once already, he again recounted how the devil had appeared to the players during the Derby production of *Faustus*, a terrifying occasion for which he now thanked God, for was it not a warning to him and to his company to abandon their sinful ways? And now I, Revill the player, should treat this runaway cart as a warning from God. I too must depart from the paths of vice. Specifically, I must quit the Chamberlain's and resolve to live a purer life.

I might have pointed out that I did live a (relatively) pure life. Meant harm to no man, unless he meant harm to me. Kept my hand out of others' pockets. Kept it, by and large, out of women's plackets. Enjoyed or suffered from thoughts that were no more outrageous or unlawful than the next person's. Had not visited a whore-house for weeks – and even then my visit had not been in the way of trade but, rather, in the course of friendship. To my own ears I sounded a dull fellow. But all this abstinence from sin would have meant nothing to Chesser, not as long as I stayed on the stage.

"What does Thomas Gally say in this affair, he who works for Philip Henslowe?" I said, adding, "I've seen the two of you together."

"Master Gally encourages me in my work," said Chesser.

I bet he does, I thought. The work of sowing doubt and uncertainty among Henslowe's rivals.

"What is your work?"

"God's work."

"A species of preaching?"

"As you say."

"But you don't preach among the members of Master Henslowe's company, the Admiral's?"

"A man can only do as much as God gives him strength for. I consider your Chamberlain's to be more deeply mired in sin."

"This preaching is new work for you, Master Chesser. I have not seen you at it with the Chamberlain's before."

"A man may be a little brain-sick, sir. I spent some time in Beth'lem Hospital. I was cured with rods until I grew weary of them."

There was something dignified but also curiously matter-of-fact in Chesser's tone. He'd gone mad for a spell and been committed to Bedlam asylum, no doubt because he'd been worrying other people elsewhere in this town by his 'preaching'. As for his claim to be cured, who knew?

"I see," I said.

"If you fear for the Admiral's Company, Master Gally tells me that he is doing his best to redeem them."

"I don't fear for them. They can look after themselves. What does Gally do? Perhaps he leads them in prayer."

"You are not serious, Master Revill. It is you that I fear for. I fear for your eternal soul."

This rebuke was a bit reminiscent, in tone if not in substance, of Bartholomew Ridd telling me off for not caring enough about the Troilus sleeve. On the one hand, I hadn't taken sufficient care of a detachable sleeve; on the other hand, I was neglecting my immortal part. The rebuke was more acceptable coming from Chesser, however, if only because he had so recently saved me from losing something between a sleeve and a soul. To wit (as WS would have said): my life.

However, Chesser hadn't finished. He wanted to impress on me the wickedness of my acting crew.

"Why, man, your shareholders are not content just to take pennies from honest citizens, or to distract apprentices when they should be at work, or to encourage licentious encounters between men and women in the audience. Although they do these things too."

"Master Chesser, while I am greatly in your debt for what happened back there on the wharf I cannot lie down while you attack my Company. We do not 'take pennies' like thieves. We are given the pennies by those honest citizens in return for diverting them."

"Oh, but you are thieves, sir. None more than your shareholders."

"How so?"

"They stole an entire playhouse once."

This was not a madman's remark, although it might appear like that. Rather it was an allusion to the dismantling of the old playhouse known as the Theatre in Finsbury and its resurrection across the water as the Southwark Globe back in the winter of '98. Not much good pointing out that the shareholders owned all the timber and fittings of the Theatre (even if not the ground on which it stood). If Burbage and the rest wanted to take a playhouse with them when they moved they were quite entitled to do so. In Chesser's eyes, though, this was a most notorious theft. No wonder we were mired in sin.

There really was no answer to this accusation of playhouse-theft, and indeed I wondered whether the theft of an entire building was covered by any statute. I would have to ask my friends in Middle Temple. Chesser followed this up with a reference to the stealing of souls. My patience with the old man and my sense of obligation to him were wearing thin. It hadn't taken long. Time for a parting of the ways.

"I am going on to Paul's Yard, sir, about my private business now."

Chesser took the hint, or it may have been that he was heading in a different direction anyway. Commending my soul to God and with a reminder that I should quit the stage forthwith, he disappeared to the right towards Old Fish Street and into the fog. Immediately he'd gone I felt guilty. He was a harmless old man, a little addled but harmless, wasn't he? He was entitled to respect as an ex-player, and now he had a much deeper claim on me. I thought, with some shame, of the way in which the boatmen had briskly bundled him out of the Goat & Monkey. Well, next time I saw Master Chesser I would speak soft and considerate. I'd even buy him a drink, as long as he wasn't in the company of Tom Gally.

But the association between those two was seemingly explained. Henslowe's agent was making use – unscrupulous use – of poor Chesser to distract and unsettle the opposition. I wondered how many of my fellow players had been accosted by the Bedlam man and informed of the extra devil in *Faustus* and enjoined to leave the stage straightaway. Yet, if Gally was resorting to such threadbare means of undermining a rival company, that surely argued desperation on his part. Not so much a murderer as a petty intriguer.

As I paced out the last few hundred yards to Paul's Yard, my thoughts turned back to the runaway cart and my near escape from its iron-rimmed wheels. I discerned a plot. Perhaps it was this perpetual fog. Unable to see anything clearly, one fancied that one saw anything and everything.

It couldn't have been planned in advance, this 'accident'. Nobody knew that I intended to cross the river at all, let alone at that point and at that time. If the cart had been deliberately set on its downhill course in my direction – the hand of man, as it were, rather than the hand of God – then it must have been done on the spur of the moment by someone who'd come over the river at the same time as me. I'd been alone in the boat with the disagreeable ferryman, the one who'd tried to overcharge me. But there were other ferries on the water. Two or three at least had offloaded their passengers while I was arguing with the ferryman.

Wasn't it possible that I had been followed across the river in another boat, that my 'opponent' (for want of a better term) had run up the steps in order to get ahead of me in the fog? That, coming by chance across an unattended but heavily laden cart, he had seized on the opportunity to dispose of Revill in a single, clean 'accident'? Perhaps he'd been waiting behind the cart, crouching by the board at the hinder end, ready to leap out at me, before he realized that a simpler means was at hand. He could hear me coming up the slope now, my argument with the boatman over and done with. Quick! Angle the cart slightly so that it runs down the slanting path. A task which would call for a bit of strength but could be done with stout shoulders and desperate hands. Quicker now. He's coming! Remove the wedges holding the wheels. Jump back as the cart begins to roll.

It was only my good fortune that Chesser had been lurking somewhere on the scene; that, seeing and hearing the cart trundle past, he'd had the presence of mind to shout a warning.

Was this how it had happened?

Yes, said fear.

Don't be absurd, said common sense.

What do you know? said fear. Believe me, that was no accident.

I'll think about it, said common sense.

At last I emerged into Paul's Yard. The place was full of noise and hubbub, even though no one could see more than a dozen yards in front of their noses. Whatever the season, whatever the weather, it was always like this, a crackling witch's cauldron of indiscriminate ingredients, all bubbling and jostling against each other. Nicholson's was on the far side with the rest of the booksellers and I bent my steps in that direction. The noise was loudest over here and I soon realized why.

What I'd at first taken for a patch of dense low fog was actually smoke, shot through with little leaping flames. The continuous crackling and snapping which, from a distance, sounded like the buzz and flurry of human traffic was the noise the flames were making as they ate up timber and lath and plaster. The scurrying figures, the random shouting, the urgent commands, these were not the ordinary activity of Paul's Yard but the frantic efforts of shopkeepers and passers-by to control the fire. I felt that little illicit thrill which a fire in a public place always gives.

The gust from the flames brought a warmth to the winter air. Perhaps this was the reason why so many other citizens were clustering round, ready to help but more ready to watch, their enjoyment of the scene dependent on whether they had a stake or not in what was being destroyed by the fire. Someone had put himself in charge, possibly a head-borough, and a chain of individuals was passing slopping buckets to the point where the fire seemed most active. A couple of water bearers had been pressed into service and the empty buckets were being filled from the bearers' wooden churns. I guessed that in turn they were filling the churns direct from the Little Conduit nearby. Flakes of paper floated down through the air like black snow. One large fragment landed near my feet. It was not badly burnt and, without bending down, I could make out the words 'Being the true history of' but no more than that. It was a title page.

The fire had taken hold in the booksellers' quarter of the Yard. Some of the stalls usually positioned in front of the shops had been shoved to one side so that the chain of men and women relaying the water-buckets could get at the flames more easily. Books and pamphlets were strewn across the cobbles. I recognized two or three of the men in the chain as booksellers. I couldn't see Master Nicholson. Perhaps he was at the head of the line since it was his shop that was being ravaged by fire. Why didn't this surprise me, that it was his shop? It seemed all of a piece with this increasingly fraught day. The stalls were close-packed but they could be shifted. The shops, of which Nicholson's was one of the largest, weren't movable of course, and the risk of the blaze spreading sideways from one to another was considerable. Fortunately there was no wind. The stone wall (part of the Paul's precinct) which backed the bookshops would hinder the flames from going up in that direction while the open ground which lay to the front offered little in the way of opportunity for the flames.

There was nothing to do but watch. The heat from the blaze had driven off the fog in the immediate vicinty. Well, I'd come to see Master Nicholson or rather to get another glimpse of Milford's play *The World's Diseas'd* and here I was watching his stock go up to smoky oblivion. I owed him money. I could feel part of the debt weighing down my purse. I'd thought that Nicholson might be more receptive to selling or loaning me a copy of *The World*, if I came to pay for a few of the poetry books I'd bought. And now I remembered an occasion when I'd been drawn down a street in Pimlico by a delicious scent of roasting, only to find that it was emanating from a pie-stall on fire. By contrast, burning books give off a somewhat unappetizing, acrid smell. The water-buckets slopped from hand to hand, the human figures holding those buckets swayed from side to side as if they were engaged in a queer kind of dance, the flames jumped up and down (but a little less eagerly now). A mixture of steam and smudgy smoke rose from those places where the fire had been quenched.

All at once a cry went up from those closest to the blaze. There was a hurried retreat. I couldn't see straightaway why they'd stopped battling with the fire, but then a section of the brick side-wall of the shop seemed to quiver in the warm air before it lost its balance altogether and toppled down with a subdued sigh. Anybody next to it would have been crushed or injured by flying fragments. But the collapse had a useful effect. The seat of the fire lay underneath the wall. Now it was stifled as the flames disappeared beneath a pile of bricks and dust and mortar and plaster. I wasn't surprised that the wall had fallen so rapidly. Probably the timber supports had been chewed away by the fire. These bookshops were more permanent than the book-stalls but they were not like churches or mansions, not edifices built to last.

When the dust had settled, it became apparent that the fire had largely been extinguished, apart from a handful of scattered outposts which were even now being doused with water or soaking rags. It did not seem as though much of Master Nicholson's stock could have survived.

The crowd, realizing that no death or injury was in prospect, gave a kind of communal shrug preparatory to drifting off. Still, we counted ourselves lucky. One fire in a day, even one without serious harm, is enough to keep us all going.

"How did this happen?" I asked the man nearest to me. He didn't know and nor did three or four other male bystanders, although the question was passed down the line like the bucket of water going from hand to hand. Eventually I came across a gaggle of women. Since they are always better informed than men, I was confident of getting the story from them.

"How did this happen?" I repeated. I was told by one that the fire was no accident. In an authoritative tone she informed me that the conflagration had been started deliberately, that a 'naughty person' had walked up to the bookshop entrance with a bucket of smoking coals and tossed them into the interior where, given the combustibleness of the shop's contents, the flames had quickly seized control. A second woman supported this account, adding the detail that the 'naughty person' had been a lady, as could be seen by her dress. But this version was straightaway contradicted by a third woman who said, with even more certainty than the first two, that the bookseller himself had been responsible for the destruction of his premises and his stock. He'd accidentally overturned a chimney, one of those portable fires used for heating open areas like shops. The three women began to quarrel over which of their versions was correct, and so I left them to it.

My aim in coming to Paul's Yard was frustrated. I wouldn't get a glimpse of *The World's Diseas'd* now. I saw no sign of Benjamin Nicholson either. I would have commiserated with the bookseller if I had seen him. I regretted not settling a portion of my small debt with him beforehand. Of no use to offer it at this moment; it would be a drop to fill an empty bucket.

Instead I made my way towards Paul's and inside to the Walk, the middle aisle of the cathedral. I was searching for some peace and quiet to think in. Paul's Walk itself was no good for this purpose. It must be one of the noisiest and most irreligious places in town, with its peacocking gallants and sneaking thieves. But a great palace has many corners and so has a great church. I knew that I'd be undisturbed by Duke Humphrey's tomb since this is the spot where, for some reason, the truly hopeless congregate. To dine with Duke Humphrey is to go without one's supper. I found myself a bench to sit on close to the tomb. And I thought.

It may have been the accident with the runaway cart which put the idea in my head that the fire at Master Nicholson's was an accident of a similar stamp. They were 'accidents'. If the first two women were right, then a 'naughty person' had deliberately fired the shop just as – if my darker imaginings were correct – an equally naughty individual had pushed a cart downhill into my path. Hardly the same person since, although it was physically possible for one man to have created both 'accidents', the fire-raiser couldn't have known that I was about to arrive on the northern shore of the river. Couldn't have arranged for me to be run down by a cart while he was simultaneously firing a bookshop. There was also that strange detail, insisted on by one of the women, that the individual who'd thrown a bucket of fire into the bookseller was a lady 'as could be seen by her dress'.

As I'd expected, this corner of Paul's by Humphrey's tomb was quiet. A few vagrants paced silently up and down or sat slumped in angles. The truly desperate are mute. In this place of shadowy silence I constructed a plot which explained everything which had happened so far.

You can probably see where I'm going.

I started by travelling over some old ground.

Take Lord and Lady Venner now. Robert and Virginia. Robbie and Vinnie. The Bumpkins (even though this mocking title no longer amused me). Suppose that, opening up the pages of *The World's Diseas'd*, they had discovered that 'their' poet and playwright, Richard Milford, was holding them up to ridicule or worse by insinuating that they were not simply brother and sister, but lover and lover. Their reaction would have been outrage and horror. I'd already considered that they might have disposed of Richard Milford. But what if their ambition reached beyond one victim?

They knew that I'd read the play. Thought perhaps that I was keeping a copy of it – the 'foul papers' – in my lodgings. They knew that I knew their dirty, incestuous secrets. A different picture began to emerge. A shadowy picture in which a desperate man, or man and woman, set out to retrieve a damaging playscript, which would, if its contents became known, drive them out of the city in humiliation. Or, since incest is a crime, expose them to the more extreme rigours of the law. My supposition of the previous night returned. That

Peter Agate had been stabbed in mistake for me. Seeking to recover the playscript, Robert Venner had blundered into my friend instead. In the subsequent confusion he had run him through, either because he took Agate for Revill or in order to silence a potential witness.

I recalled the wary way in which Venner had looked at me after the *Troilus and Cressida* performance in Middle Temple. That piggy gaze. I was not dead but still there to be got rid of. So, once he had disposed of Richard Milford, he'd decided to finish the job by disposing of Nicholas Revill, only in a more subtle and spontaneous fashion. Not run through with a knife but run over by the iron wheels of a cart. While his sister, the lady, resorted to her own form of action by heaving a bucket of burning coals into the bookseller's where that dangerous play, that slanderous play, *The World's Diseas'd*, was being prepared for publication. What was the destruction of a shop and a load of books after all, when they'd already killed one man in error and another one quite deliberately?

My hands clenched tight. Now I held the Venners to account as villains-in-chief. They had killed two friends of mine, they had made one or more attempts on my life, they had fired a bookshop.

I must have disliked them very much to have thought so ill of them. I did dislike them very much. I wanted them to be guilty.

This was my plot then, the one conceived in the shelter of Duke Humphrey's tomb. It was that Lord and Lady Bumpkin had done all of these terrible things in order to protect their good names.

I might not have been altogether convinced by my own story but it would do to be going on with.

I quit Duke Humphrey's tomb, leaving it to its shadows and vagrants. But it may be that the gloomy air of that corner of Paul's infected me because I felt very low in spirits as I made my way through the Walk and out into the open air. Not even the sight of the gallants in the aisle, either flashing their new satins or covering up the holes in their old ones as they vied for each other's attention, gave me as much amusement as it usually did. The fire in the bookshop was thoroughly extinguished and a handful of people were picking through the charred remains. If my notions were correct then that conflagration could be laid at the door of Vinnie Venner, even as her brother had launched a loaded cart at me. It is a lowering experience to believe that someone is in pursuit of your life. Doubly so, when guilt is added to this, because I held myself responsible in some way for Peter Agate's death. I was still impelled by the desire to expose his killer or killers, and not only to save myself from a capital charge.

But every man must have rest from his conscience, relief from his woes.

And so my thoughts now turned towards Nell, the fair lady of Holland's Leaguer. I remembered that I had earlier determined to see her once more, perhaps for the last time. To see a friendly face. At this moment, as my other friends were being brutally snatched away from me, Nell stood out in my mind as my original London associate. However much our paths had diverged since, we had started out at the same point in this city as ignorant, unfledged country creatures.

From Paul's Yard I decided to make a last pilgrimage to Holland's Leaguer. If Nell was occupied then so be it. I'd wait until she was finished, or finished with. You may judge how eager, even desperate, I was to glimpse a friendly face when I say that I checked my purse to see whether I had sufficient to pay her. Four half-crowns was more than enough for the more exorbitant charges of Holland's Leaguer. I had all this money in my purse because I'd been intending to settle part of my debt with Nicholson. Now it might go to a whore instead. I'd never paid (her) before, and had vowed I never would. But if that was the price of seeing her again – and even though it represented a fortnight's pay to me – so be it.

I could of course present it to her as a gift rather than as a fee. That way, both our faces would be saved and our other parts satisfied.

It was about mid-afternoon on this fateful day when I came within misty sight of Holland's Leaguer. This great building had originally been a manor house and, in the general view, it had come down in the world by permitting itself to be turned into a house of ill-fame. Whatever indoor trade it served, though, the place was outwardly much more respectable than many of its Southwark neighbours. It had the appearance of a pretty urban fort, with diminutive battlements and a moat hardly wider than a gutter. On either side of the wide doors lounged a couple of women in red silk gowns, like painted posts giving notice of the delights within. (A truer sign would have been a board depicting a man with a decayed nose and a bald pate, advertising the delights of the pox.) The gate-women didn't seem to feel the afternoon chill despite the quantity of flesh on display. I couldn't help being reminded of Vinnie Venner although these women were much more fetching.

This Holland's Leaguer is a world unto itself or, less grandly, a little village, with many small groups and dependencies. Nell used to tell me how some of its occupants stayed inside the mansion for weeks on end. Whores were not the half of it. Like an army laid up in camp, the whores had to be adequately supplied. They had to be watered and provendered, and this required a baggage-train of sutlers and sumpters. The girls also had to be protected from customers who were disagreeable or wouldn't pay or who otherwise failed to keep to their side of the bargain, and *this* required a whole band of bullies and creepers, the captain of which was a one-eyed gentleman known as the Cyclops. He wore a red silken patch that enhanced his fearsomeness, and I'd heard it said that he wore the patch simply for effect and could see perfectly well with the concealed eye. No one dared to check, however.

Every army has its generals and for Holland's Leaguer there was an entire benchful of madams presided over by a madam-in-chief. Her name was Bess Barton. She was reputed to have been a great beauty in her youth and well worth the charge. But she had grown old, stout and ferocious and was now much more alarming than any male inhabitant of the place, the Cyclops included.

And, just as there would be in any village, there were odd folk hanging about Holland's Leaguer whose origins or presence couldn't be altogether accounted for. There was the simple-minded old woman who was supposed to be the offspring of one of old Lord Hunsdon's mistresses. Of no use now for trade, if she ever had been, she was maintained out of charity. Then there was a strange young man – actually called Orpheus, I believe – who had no gift in poetry or singing and no interest in the whores *qua* whores but who possessed an infallible nose for what the weather was going to do the next day or the next week. The brothel-business isn't as dependent as playhouse or bear-pit on the vagaries of the weather but trade is still affected by it, so Orpheus was indulged as forecaster-of-the-closet by the girls. There were other oddities and dependants about the place but not one of them is material to this story. I describe all this only to give you some picture of the brothel where I had spent some of my more pleasant hours in London . . . and to delay arriving at that part of the story which, now, can be delayed no longer.

I passed between the half-naked doorposts, who recognized me as Nell's paramour and did not trouble themselves with any extra nods and winks. There was an ugly male doorkeeper seated beyond this pair, and just out of sight from the public highway, but he too let me pass unquestioned. There was no objection to the occupants of the house having their own friends as long as it didn't interfere with trade. Indeed, no regulation was really necessary in this respect since the girls themselves were aware, to the last halfpenny, of the value of their time and of their wares. They had to pass over half of their earnings to the bench of madams. Therefore they had to be very much in love with – or besotted by – their paramours to give up their hours or their wares without getting anything in return.

I walked along the first-floor passage that led to Nell's crib. From the closed doors on either side came sounds expressive of delight, real or feigned. Or those were the sounds that probably came from behind doors. Absorbed in my thoughts I was only half conscious of my surroundings. So well-trodden was this path to pleasure that I could have found my way there blindfold. Likewise its sounds and smells I took for granted. When a figure banged into me before blundering off down the passage, I hardly registered it although some mild admonition may have escaped my lips.

I paused outside the door of Nell's crib and listened for sounds of activity, or rather of that one specific activity. Not a whisper, not a moan or a groan. Good. She could not complain that I was interfering with business. And now I observed that the door was not completely closed. I pushed at it slightly and it swung open. I had some cheerful remark to hand but it wasn't required because the room was empty. I strode in and took possession, as I had done so often. She would have a surprise, an agreeable one I hoped, when she returned from gossiping with Jenny or from her visit to the jakes.

It took some moments before my eyes grew accustomed to the gloom. Nell kept her curtains drawn whatever the hour of day or night – not so much to hide her activities from the eye of God or man but to reassure her customers that all was safe and private for them. Only one little candle burned, neglected, in a corner. By its indifferent light I saw what I hadn't noticed at first, that Nell was here after all. She was snugged up in bed with her taffeta quilt drawn over her. Strands of her hair were straggling above the cover. I made to pull back the quilt, to expose (perhaps) her nakedness, but thought better of it and instead cleared my throat. No response. I coughed more loudly then said her name. There was still no reaction from the sleeping figure.

Suddenly fearing the worst, I pulled back the covers. Nell was indeed lying there, on her back and naked. Her face was contorted and suffused and her tongue was stuck out at me. Her hands were raised so as to secure a sash or piece of thick ribbon round her neck. *Why does she want to hold the ribbon in place like that?* I thought. *See how it is buried in the soft flesh of her neck. It would be better for her health if it was loosened.* And, knowing in one part of my mind that this was useless, I tried to loosen her hold on the ribbon. But she refused to give it up to me even though I said her name several times over and pleaded with her to give it up. Eventually I prised her fingers from the sash or ribbon and, gently lifting up her head (how heavy it seemed!), I unwound the rich material from round her neck.

Then, clasping the ribbon, I sank on my knees to the floor.

That was how, many minutes afterwards, the two of them found me – Nell's friend Jenny and the Cyclops, the leader of the bully boys who kept order in the brothel – found me kneeling on the floor, holding the ribbon which had taken away my Nell's life and breath at one stroke and for ever.

Mea Culpa

"Did you kill her?"

"I did not."

"Do you know who did?"

"No."

"All you know is that you did not kill her."

"Yes."

"Did you want to kill her?"

"She was my friend."

And then Master Talbot said . . .

And then I said . . .

I was reminded of a play rehearsal, the same lines repeated but delivered with a slightly different intonation or emphasis. Or I was reminded of a nightmare in which events are helplessly duplicated but can't be avoided on that account. In other circumstances I might have laughed or cried. But I couldn't bring myself to laugh or, strangely, to cry.

This was truly dangerous, I told myself without conviction. I was as good as done for and yet I felt less troubled by this occasion than when I'd previously sat in this chair facing this inquisitor. I was once again in Coroner Alan Talbot's chambers in Long Southwark near the Bridge but this time I had not stepped in, albeit summoned, from the street but had been escorted from my prison cell to face questions about the murder of Nell. My gaolers stood outside the door but within earshot, in case I should suddenly turn desperate. I was not so much desperate, however, as despairing.

These questions were surely a formality. At any moment Talbot would organize an arraignment and trial. I could already feel the noose about my neck. In my present state of mind, the noose would not have been entirely unwelcome. At least I could share with Nell the manner of her death, a slow squeezing out of life and breath. In this fatalistic mood, I could barely rouse myself to listen to Coroner Talbot's questions let alone answer them. My main motive in dragging out this interview was to delay a return to the gaol and its stench. I never knew that ordinary streets, ordinary chambers could smell so, well, ordinary. I also wanted to delay that shameful walk back through the common streets between two hulking gaolers, a walk in which I imagined I could feel every passer-by's eyes boring into me like an auger. My giant escorts might as well have hung a sign about my neck reading 'Revill, the parson's son and player – and murderer'. The only consolation was that the gaolers were so large that people were more likely to look at them rather than the unfortunate wrong-doer in between.

"What?" I said.

"Part of your story again, Nicholas. The details concerning this sleeve."

"I have told you once already, Master Talbot."

"No, you have said nothing except to link the sleeve to your play at Middle Temple."

"I'm tired, Master Talbot."

"Your life is at stake."

"I hardly care."

"So we may as well hang you straightaway."

I grinned at him. A grin of gloom and despair, but a doomed man may still surprise himself. For some reason Talbot's remark seemed jocular rather than threatening.

"Well, it's what's going to happen, isn't it?" I said.

"That is not yet determined. All that is determined is that

justice will be done. But there are some preliminaries to be got through first. That is my task. So tell me about your *Troilus*."

I noted that Talbot's manner was less severe than when he'd questioned me about Peter Agate's death. His gaze was still hard and cold and he had the habit of pressing his palms flat on the table to affirm a point, but he called me Nicholas in an almost paternal way and was altogether less peremptory in his demands. I took this for a bad sign. To him, I was already dead.

"In my character as Troilus I have a sleeve which I detach from my doublet," I said mechanically. "This I pass over to my Cressida as a love-token. She, or rather he, gives me a token in return. But it was my token which vanished after the performance."

"And which was later used for a quite different purpose."

"Yes."

I could hardly look Master Talbot in the eye, as if I was indeed guilty of the crime with which I was charged.

For it was the sleeve – that token of love – which had been wrapped around Nell's young neck and then pulled tight until the life was choked out of her. In my distraction at finding her in her crib I had mistaken the sleeve for a sash or even a gaudy ribbon, and not recognized that piece of costume which I'd been wearing only a few days earlier. It was evident that the murderer had stolen it after the production of *Troilus and Cressida*, had filched it presumably from behind the scenes at Middle Temple. If it *was* the murderer who'd taken it . . . perhaps he (since I never doubted that the murderer was a he) had obtained it through someone else's good offices. It was the kind of thing that might happen *in* a play rather than at a play. If so, who – and why? In case the sleeve came in handy as a means of murder? Not an obvious choice to snuff someone's life out with. As a bitter joke, the badge of affection being turned into a fatal cord? In order to implicate Revill?

"What's that, Nicholas?"

"What?"

"You were saying something under your breath."

"Thinking aloud."

"So you never saw the sleeve again after you'd passed it over to – what is the name of your boy-player?"

"Peter Pearce."

There was no reason to give Master Talbot a false name, unlike with that boy-loving law student called Miller.

"You gave the sleeve to Peter Pearce," repeated Talbot, "who gave you a glove in exchange. What did you do with that glove by the way?"

Something about the question troubled me but I couldn't put my finger on it – or, seeing as we were talking about a glove, couldn't put my finger in it.

"Well," Talbot said. "What did you do with it?"

"I can't remember but it must have been returned to the tire-man in the usual way. If it hadn't been, either Peter or I would have heard about it from Master Ridd. He is a demon for clothes."

A sudden thought occurred to me.

"You could ask Ridd the tire-man about the sleeve which belonged to the Troilus costume. He knows I didn't have it because he threatened to tell Burbage and get the cost of the thing deducted from my salary. He taxed me about it on the morning of the day of – of – "

"The murder of your friend."

"Yes."

"Well, Nicholas," said Talbot, "you told this man Ridd that you didn't have the sleeve. That you'd lost it."

"I had lost it."

"But what would you have said to him if you had retained it in your possession, and were intending to use it for . . . some nefarious purpose?"

"Just the same. That I didn't know what had become of it," I said, crestfallen.

"Let us move back to the question of your friend, the harlot Nell of Holland's Leaguer."

"If we must."

"I regret that we must. You said that you hadn't seen this woman for many weeks before you visited her on the day of her death. Why had you kept away from her?"

"I was not one of her regular customers."

"Nevertheless you saw her often?"

"What I meant was that I never paid her. We were friends."

"But you hadn't seen her for a long time?"

"If what you're trying to establish, Master Talbot, is that we had a falling-out, then I'll save you the trouble. Yes, we had a disagreement of sorts."

"Over your other friend Peter Agate, your dead friend?"

"No, not him."

"Someone else?"

"Possibly."

"Who?"

"I don't know."

"Last time we met, Nicholas, you said that being jealous over a whore was like being resentful of the wind for brushing your enemy's face as well as your own."

In other circumstances I might have been flattered that Master Talbot had remembered my words so clearly. Now it gave me no pleasure.

"A speech which you called poetical," I said. "I am embarrassed to recall it."

"Because it wasn't true?"

"Nell was more than a whore, to me. I should not have spoken of her so. I *was* jealous, I was resentful. A little resentful."

Just as I'd earlier surprised myself by grinning at Talbot's comment about being hanged straightaway, so I was taken aback to hear myself utter words about jealousy and resentment. It might perhaps have been politic to pretend that Nell had meant nothing to me, and so diminished my motive for killing her. But, in the face of Talbot's cold penetrating gaze, I fell back on honesty. As well, something inside me urged openness – not only with the coroner but with myself. I had parted from Nell, the last time I'd seen her, in a bad mood. I wished we'd at least had the chance to make up before her death. We hadn't, and I would not now pay off her memory by suggesting that I had ever been indifferent towards her.

I wiped away some water which had gathered in the corner of an eye. Talbot looked steadily at me. I knew what he was thinking, *A murderer may weep too over what he has done*. Or perhaps, more cynically, he thought that I was a good actor. (I was a good actor.)

"This figure which you say you passed in the passage at Holland's Leaguer, tell me more about him."

Ever since that terrible afternoon, I had rehearsed the moments leading up to my discovery of her body. Passing between the twin gateposts of the flesh and the ugly male doorkeeper beyond, climbing the stairs to Nell's floor, walking along the approach to her crib. The trouble was that I'd been so preoccupied with my thoughts that I'd hardly noticed my surroundings.

"Someone brushed past me, that's all. Knocked against me."

"Man or woman?"

"A man by his bulk and tread. Yes, definitely a man."

"You did not look directly at him?"

"No. He seemed to be all muffled up. I was thinking of other things. And he was gone before I'd got my wits about me."

"He must have come from one of the other whores."

"Perhaps. Yet I don't remember hearing any words spoken or any door closing."

"You've just said that you were thinking of other things."

"Even so . . . "

I paused. Something was hovering at the edge of my

memory. I hadn't seen what the man looked like or what he was wearing, I hadn't heard him say anything, but . . .

"What is it, Nicholas?"

"This man had a – a smell."

"Smell?"

"A rank smell. Like a fox's."

"Then we shall have to set the hounds on him," said Talbot jocularly. "Let us return to more material considerations."

"Have you questioned the gateposts, the doorkeepers I mean?" I said. "Those women could testify about the time I arrived at Holland's Leaguer."

"They have been questioned. They do not tell the time by the clock but by the number of customers entering between them."

"Did they see any men leave?"

"They see men leave constantly."

"I'm sorry, Master Talbot. It was a foolish question."

"Besides," said the coroner, "do you not know that such a place must have many irregular exits, you with all your knowledge of stews?"

I thought of all the floor-traps, sliding windows and counterfeit panels which dotted Holland's Leaguer. Nell had shown me a few and I guessed at the existence of dozens of others. A gentleman needs to be able to make a quick disappearance from a brothel.

"Another point, Master Revill. Do you suppose that the occupants of a house of ill-repute would make good witnesses – about anything?"

"You'd be surprised what they know about humankind."

"No doubt,"said Talbot. "But they're not usually given much credit in a court of law. You will have to look for help elsewhere."

"I am indifferent to my fate," I said.

"There is still the question of Peter Agate's death unresolved."

"I have it hanging over me," I said.

"Is that an admission?"

"No, but I cannot forget finding his body. The blood everywhere."

"You are making a habit of finding bodies."

"Call it a vice rather."

"Call it what you like," said the coroner, "justice will still be done."

I shrugged.

"Would you still be so indifferent," persisted Talbot, "if I said that you have also come under suspicion in the matter of Richard Milford, the murdered playwright?"

"What!"

"It is reported that you were seen in close converse with his wife in Middle Temple on the night of his death . . ."

I thought of Pye and Jute and those other fledgling lawyers. No doubt they'd been happy enough to go sneaking to Talbot.

"That doesn't make me his killer!"

" . . . and that there was talk between you and Mistress Milford, talk about a murdered man."

I was dumbfounded. I could hardly speak. Or rather there was so much to say, I hardly knew where to begin. Talbot looked pleased to have finally roused me.

"Talk to her, go on," I said, "I ask you to talk to her. Or let her talk to you, at you. Maybe you can make sense of her maunderings. I didn't know what she was talking about."

"Your outrage is less plausible than your regret," said Talbot. His earlier, almost paternal manner had disappeared. In the midst of my distraction I wondered if it had been a device to draw me out.

"Anyway," I said, "on the night of Richard Milford's death I had drunk myself into insensibility."

"So the story goes."

"It's a true story."

"Drunkenness is easy to feign, especially for a player."

"I may not be able to contradict you in much else, Master

Talbot, but at least I can in that regard. No, drunkenness is not easy to play. Only the laity, I mean untheatrical persons, would think so."

I spoke with more force than I'd intended. It was a footling point but it was the only area in which I could counter anything he'd said.

"I defer to your experience of drunkenness, both real and feigned, Master Revill. But you are accused, or likely to be accused, of rather more than drunkenness. Three unlawful killings to be precise."

"Come one, come all," I said, sinking my head in my hands and fearing now that everything was lost, well and truly lost. My earlier state, when I'd believed myself to be accused of one or (at most) two murders, had almost been happiness compared to this. If before I'd been numb, now I didn't know whether to laugh, cry or rage.

Here sat or slumped Revill. Nicholas Revill, the parson's son and player – and monster. Yes, monster; mere murderer wasn't bad enough any longer. Three violent deaths were being laid at my door. Give me the noose now. Fling it over that timber up there. I will clamber up on the chair, hook the rope about my neck and hurl myself into space. What does it matter that I risk eternal damnation by self-slaughter? Eternal damnation is no more than I deserve.

"Well now," said Talbot, in an apparent return to his more conciliatory manner. "Look up, Nicholas. You do not have three necks. One charge would suffice."

I did look up. Was he trying to comfort me? Or rub salt into my wounds? I could not tell.

"Why gild the lily then?" I said. "If one charge will take me to Tyburn."

"Justice must be served. The truth will out, all of it."

His cold stare fixed me and his palms pressed down on the table between us. There was a kind of fervour in him now. I judged that Talbot must be very confident of himself for, in his eyes, he was alone with a man who had despatched three other human beings, yet he had been happy to leave the gaolers outside the door while he interviewed me. Perhaps it was simply that he knew his man. I wasn't going to spring up and attack him. The only person I might have attacked was myself.

The coroner now called for the gaolers and those hulking fellows entered the room. There is a pair of giant wooden figures set up at the London Guildhall and brought out for processions from time to time. Going by the names of Gog and Magog, they are among the tutelary deities of the city. Perhaps they are meant to scare off our enemies by the ugliness of their expressions as well as by their size for I've never seen more displeasing faces in effigy. But real life is always able to outstrip art, and my two gaolers were more than a match for the Guildhall giants both in point of size and ugliness. So, in my mind, I had baptized the pair Gog and Magog. I'd been pleased that my feeble spirits could rally to even this shallow show of wit. But there was nothing really amusing about them – or about my situation. I was still dumbfounded by Talbot's multiple accusations.

Now the giant gaolers came to stand on either side of my chair.

"Return Master Revill to the Counter prison," said Talbot. "Look to him carefully or you will answer to me."

These men didn't talk. Rather they made gurgling sounds like boggy water disappearing down a hole in the ground. In time one could doubtless have learnt their tongue, but life is short (mine seemed especially likely to be short at this moment) and a man ought to devote his leisure to pleasure or, failing that, to some worthwhile activity. Learning how to interpret the gurgles made by a gaoler did not seem to me a good use of my remaining days on this earth.

In response to the coroner's instructions, Gog gurgled and Magog gargled, but in a deferential fashion. And Talbot appeared to understand them.

"You will be recalled for more questions, Nicholas Revill. I shall see you again."

I nodded, having run out of words.

Talbot nodded back at me, then at the gaolers. Obediently, I took my place between them and, together, we left the coroner's house. Once out on the street, it might have occurred to me to make a run for it. Or it might have occurred to you perhaps. A couple of considerations held me back. One was the cold amazement which I was suffering under and which weighed me down more effectively than any shackles would have done. To be unjustly accused of murder – and of not one, not two, but three killings – may cause any man to question the workings of providence. But before that happens it turns him almost to stone. I was barely able to put one foot in front of the other, let alone to run. The second consideration was the size and strength of my escort. The giants would be on me in a trice. They carried staffs as a badge of office and these were no trumpery wands but long and heavy enough to inflict damage.

I might have paid for my escape in a different sense, a monetary sense. Even in my brief time in gaol I'd discovered how money counted inside. But I had almost nothing left now – so rapacious were my gaolers – certainly not enough to bribe Gog and his brother. And besides I judged that the giant pair, instructed by Talbot to take good care of their charge, were likely to be more in awe of the coroner than they were interested in pecuniary gain.

So we traversed the familiar streets of Southwark until we reached our goal, which was my gaol. I mostly kept my head down and don't know whether anyone recognized me, but it's likely they did. I say 'my gaol' advisedly for this Southwark borough has almost enough prisons, wards and confines to accommodate each of its citizens separately, so wicked are we south Londoners. There's the Clink, there's the Marshalsea, there's the King's Bench and White Lion, & cetera . . . and then there's the Counter. There are other

Counters on the other side of the river but this is the Southwark prison of that name.

I had been taken here after being apprehended at Holland's Leaguer in the room where Nell's body lay. The Cyclops stood guard while Nell's friend Jenny ran to get assistance. But in truth I was not in a mind to run anywhere. I continued to kneel on the floor, clutching at the Troilus sleeve which had been the death of my friend.

Eventually Jenny returned with the headborough, Doggett, the one who'd been summoned in the aftermath of Peter Agate's murder. She looked at me in horror – for she had been the friend of my good friend, and knew me – and I shook my head but could not tell whether she understood my denial. As for the constable, if he was surprised to find me once more in the presence of a corpse he didn't show it. He pronounced the scene unwholesome, foul and villainous, and this time made a formal arrest. Doggett and the Cyclops and a couple more of the brothel bully-boys then ushered me off. I moved as if in a dream. The Cyclops enjoyed manhandling me. The red silken patch over his eye seemed to glisten. I might have forgiven him if he was doing it because of what had happened with Nell. But he was doing it because he liked it.

We were headed for the Counter. It is a formidable edifice, this prison, although not for the obvious reasons. The building was once St Margaret's church but many years ago it was given over, or rather sold and defaced, to temporal purposes. I'd walked past it many times (it is near the Tabard Inn) without giving it a second thought. There's an odd appropriateness to a church being turned into a prison, at least in one aspect. In a place where men were once exhorted to leave their sins they are now punished for not doing so.

Doggett the headborough rapped on the double doors which had formerly admitted worshippers. After some time, we were let in by a lantern-jawed, red-eyed fellow who was plainly irritated at having to quit, even for an instant, the card game he was enjoying with a fellow gaoler. While he cast his eyes over the five of us – Doggett, Revill, the silken-patched Cyclops and his two companion brothel-creepers – the guard's bloodshot gaze kept flicking back towards his associate, as if *he* was the real wrong-doer and was sure to cheat him at the cards. Then, without a word, Lantern-jaw jerked his head towards a stout inner door and returned to his game. Both guards were sitting on stools either side of a chimney which filled the little room (probably the former church porch) with heat and fug, augmented by pipe smoke. Between them was a chest, on top of which their greasy cards were laid together with two neat piles of coin. They showed no curiosity about any of us.

Doggett knocked at the inner door. Waited. Knocked again. Waited shorter. Knocked for longer. I am the law, the knock said, pay attention to me. The lantern-jawed gaoler looked up and gestured impatiently with his pipe stem. Go through, the pipe stem said, and leave us in peace. The door wasn't locked or bolted (and this surprised me). Doggett, conscious of the dignity of his office and perhaps feeling a bit of a fool, undid the door and led the way in. Pushed by the Cyclops, I followed. Beyond the porch was a lobby. Here sat another gaoler. He too was busy after a fashion, since he was scraping the dirt from under his fingernails with a knife and then examining the abundant material deposited on the tip of the blade before wiping it on his buff jerkin. This must have been a very engrossing occupation because it was at least a minute before he looked up at our group, despite Doggett's frequent coughing, hemming and throat-clearing. This gaoler said nothing at first but, like the previous one, cast his eyes across our group. Then sighting down the blade of his little knife, in a style that reminded me of Tom Gally sighting down his index finger, he indicated me.

"He's the one."

Given that I was accompanied by a couple of brothel-bullies, a foolish-looking constable and a villainous individual wearing a red patch over one eye, it took some perspicuity on the part of this gaoler to single out the man the rest of them intended to lock up. If I'd been in his place I would have clapped up any one of my companions before myself.

"He is a most notorious malefactor," said Doggett proudly.

"He looks it."

"Has done terrible things."

"They all have."

"Monstrous deeds."

The fingernail-picker was silent. He was not going to satisfy my escort by asking what those monstrous deeds were. I stood abashed. My heart and mind were almost numb. I could see the absurdity of what was happening but could not feel it.

"He has performed murders a-plenty," said Doggett finally, "and should be watched."

"Oh, he'll be watched," said the gaoler, bending his attention once more to his nails. "Take him to Wagman. In there."

We passed through yet another door. The entrance to this prison was as elaborate as the entrance to a palace – or a brothel. By now I knew the form. In a corner of a further room, slightly larger, were two more gaolers (the ones I later christened Gog and Magog). They were not diverting themselves with a deck of cards or fingernail-scraping. They were not doing anything except, perhaps, remembering to breathe from time to time. In the opposite corner, behind a delicately gilded table, there was a coffer-seat chair and on this was enthroned an outsized individual. On the table was a whole goose-wing's-worth of quill pens and a stack of finely bound ledgers. This fat man was Wagman, the principal turnkey, as I soon learned. He ran the business of justice, kept the books, charged for accommodation, took movables like the gilded table or the quill pens in lieu of cash, & cetera.

I was enrolled by this chief turnkey into the prison's Black Book. When I gave the name of my lodgings, in Dead Man's

Place, Wagman laughed. Then we turned to business and after that I was left to myself. Constable Doggett seemed reluctant to abandon me since I was evidently such a catch, but he was eventually told to shog off by Wagman. The Cyclops departed with his brace of bully-boys from Holland's Leaguer, each of them giving me a farewell cuff about the head. Wagman looked on without objection. Gog and Magog gurgled in their corner before shoving me through yet another door and showing me my lodgings for the night.

Once on the inside of the Counter, beyond all the porches, lobbies and ante-rooms, there was little sign that the place had been a church, except for a certain complacent solidity about the walls. Luckily, I still had my money, in the purse which had first been intended to pay off part of my debt to the bookseller Nicholson and then, when that scheme failed due to his shop burning down, had been intended for Nell (as gift rather than fee).

One of the four half-crowns in my purse was enough to buy a better house for the night than I would have enjoyed without the garnish, which is the gaolers' quaint term for extortion-money. By 'better' I mean a stenchy, cold, dank room little larger than a coffin, with straw for bedding, a couple of dirty sheets, and a candle-stub to illuminate all this misery. There were rows of these cave-like residences on either side of a central passage, with a second floor reached by a rickety stairway. I was reminded of a honeycomb, but one built out of harsh limestone. My cell was full of cobwebs. When I pushed the light into a corner it provoked much frantic, long-legged activity. There was a warped, battered door to the cell but it had no lock. The door was for form's sake only, without purpose. It wasn't to keep me in – or to keep anyone else out, either. A prisoner with enough cash can walk out of almost any gaol in London, unless he is much in demand by the authorities, as I was.

On the one hand, the cell wasn't so much worse than my Dead Man's Place crib, although smaller. On the other hand,

I was paying much more to the turnkey for a single night here than I had to my landlord Benwell for a whole week. It was an abuse. The turnkey Wagman should be locked up. In fact, the whole crew of gaolers looked – and behaved – as though they should have been locked up. I believe many of them had been once, including Gog and Magog. Well, this cobwebbed, filthy chamber was my lodging until my money ran out – which it would do in about three days' time or even sooner (since I had to feed myself out of those three remaining half-crowns as well).

Shivering, I lay down to sleep on the thin pallet. I tried to put an end to this day. This terrible day which had begun with Bartholomew Ridd berating me over the missing sleeve from a costume doublet and had ended with the discovery of the fatal purpose to which that sleeve had been put. In between, I had almost come to blows with a boatman, nearly been crippled or even killed by a runaway cart, and witnessed a bookshop deliberately destroyed by fire. In the silence of Paul's church by Duke Humphrey's tomb I'd attempted to link these events together and believed that I'd found the thread in the shape of those noble siblings, Robert and Virginia Venner. But I could not fit the latest and most terrible turn of events, the murder of Nell, into any pattern at all.

Nothing made sense. Or did not make sense in my present state. I simply wanted to draw a curtain between myself and consciousness. But, even though it was night by the clock, the day refused to crawl into a corner and die. I slept very fitfully. In the morning I woke to consider my situation. It didn't take much consideration. My situation was bad. In fact, it could hardly have been worse.

These prisons are like the world beyond the walls. That is, they are divided and subdivided into petty sections where the few lord it over the many. The few are the sergeants, turnkeys and tipstaffs. The many are the miserable occupants. The former strut. The latter suffer, and try to make the time pass faster or slower, depending on whether they are comfortable or in pain. Mostly they are in pain. Money counts even more on the inside than it does on the outside. Without the garnish you get banished to the Hole. Underground in the old church crypt huddled those wretches whose purses were empty or never full in the first place or whose friends were penniless and unable to buy them their daily requisites. These, literally the lowest of the low, were condemned to a perpetual twilight where they slept unblanketed on a bare floor and fed off charity scraps. The Southwark Counter wasn't the worst for neglect and cruelty – I believe that the palm goes to Newgate or the Fleet – but it was no laggard in this respect either. During the first night I slept very little, as I've said, partly because of my miserable state of mind and partly because of the wails and moans coming up from beneath the ground, like the sounds of the damned in hell. For some reason the noise diminished during the day. By the second night I'd almost got used to the din.

In any case I had my own troubles to attend to. There was not only my imminent danger, for it was obvious that I was going to be held to account for the murder of Nell, but also my great grief at her death, and at the violent manner of it. All the little irritations and jealousies of our friendship subsided, and I remembered – or chose to remember – only the golden times we'd enjoyed together. I thought not just of her body and its sweets, but of her self. Her good nature and her cheerful spirits. Her laughter and her quick wits. More than once, one of us had tumbled out of bed, the narrow beds in my various lodgings or the wider one in her crib, convulsed with laughter at something the other had said or done. I recalled the time she'd tipped a loaded chamber-pot out of the window straight on to the head of my landlady, Mistress Ransom. I'd forfeited my lodgings as a result but could not hold it against her. No more than she had held against me my brief amour with the wife of a fellow member of the Chamberlain's. She hadn't held it against me when all was said and done. When all was sad and done . . .

Nell was an expert in what she called the sacking law and full of tales about it – for all that she'd only been at the game for three years or so. I couldn't vouch for her earlier time in the country though. In fact I had my suspicions of her activities before she arrived in London and we'd met. She'd told me once of how a penance had been imposed on some country whore which required the said whore to stand at the church door, bare-legged and barefoot, wearing a white sheet and with a candle in her hand. Well, of course, she'd said, it just offered the naughty woman a better chance to show off her wares. Plenty of men came by to ensure that she was keeping her penance and to get a good ogle. That was you, was it? I asked. She would not answer except teasingly, but the story provided us with enough diversion for that day and, thinking of it again now in my little prison room, I laughed once more and then began to weep.

The tears – a drop in the bucket of misery in this church turned prison – were for myself as well as for her. Nell and I had arrived in this great city more or less at the same time and now it seemed as though both of us had reached our term together. She, though, had died like the innocent she was while I would die a despised death on the scaffold. Blameworthy in the eyes of the world (and this was before I had been interviewed for the second time by Coroner Talbot), I was to blame in my own eyes too. Guilt is contagious, spreading quickly from accuser to accused. And who could deny that I carried the plague? All who knew me were bound to die, and die suddenly, by violent murder. Peter Agate, Richard Milford, and now Nell. It was just as well that Revill had been taken off the streets and would shortly be hoist on to a scaffold, there to end his wretched existence before he could do more harm to innocent people.

I tried to console myself. First, with the knowledge of my own innocence. In this I had only a limited success for the reason I've already suggested. Second, I told myself that being in prison was no great disgrace. Why, the playwright Ben

Jonson had been incarcerated on a capital charge (but he had killed a man honourably in a duel). Others that I knew had been clapped up for debt, for assault, for slander. Any man may swear out a warrant against another and, if he has the cash to secure a couple of arresting sergeants, will see his opponent brought behind bars for a time. None of the Chamberlain's Company would have thought the worse of me for being in clink if I'd been involved in a tavern brawl or defaulted on a debt. It was almost seen as a badge of honour to fall foul of the law at least once. But to be accused of three killings . . . there was no way to wash this off.

So, when my friend Jack Wilson came to visit me not long after my interview with Talbot, I almost cried with gratitude. He'd had to pay to get in. This is the truth about prisons: you pay to get in, you pay to stay in, you pay to get out. But the chief turnkey, the portly Wagman, had extorted only threepence from Jack, a little more than the groundlings paid at the Globe although for an infinitely less cheerful spectacle.

"Oh Jack," I said. "You don't know how good it is to see a friendly face in this place."

We were walking like sentries up and down a wide passage, which must have been the church aisle in earlier days, holy days. On either side were the coffin-sized rooms. A watery light filtered in from the plain high windows at both ends. At the top end of the 'aisle' was a larger area – it was probably where the altar had once stood – in which those who could afford to purchase food were permitted to sit at a table and consume whatever their purses stretched to. So far I had maintained my place at the table, eating and conversing fitfully with my fellow prisoners. But my money was about to run out. Then, unless I could obtain credit, it would be down into the Hole, the hard floor and charity scraps.

This aisle was a place of communal activity, particularly during the reception of visitors. Urgent conversations, desperate bouts of laughter, whispered asides, elaborate negotiations, occasional scuffles, all were staged on this little strip of flagged ground. From beneath our feet came the continual susurration of the people imprisoned in the crypt. Cellar rats.

"I am sorry to see you here, Nick, in this foul place."

I noticed Jack surreptitiously pinching his nose from time to time. I'd already accustomed myself to the stench.

"How is our Company?" I said.

"Oh, we carry on, you know. We are preparing for two fresh pieces next week."

"I remember. I was due to appear in both of them."

"I am taking your part in one."

"That's *Fortune's Eyes*?"

"Yes. Forgive me."

For answer, I clapped him on the shoulder.

"While Michael Donegrace is taking your part in the other, in *The Law's Delay*."

"A wonderful title," I said.

I couldn't prevent the bitterness, the irony, entering into my voice. In this new play I'd been due to play the part of an advocate, a corrupt and eloquent pleader who may be bought by the highest bidder. How apt that I now found myself subject to the law's delay in reality – although I feared that all too soon I would be subjected to the law's rigour.

"Dick Burbage says though that you may resume the part – if – "

"I am not going to be released in time, Jack."

"Stranger things have happened."

"I am not going to be released at all."

"And Master Shakespeare asked me to convey his greetings – and condolences on – on the death of your friend."

This affected me more than anything that Jack had said so far. Without troubling to conceal it, I brushed away the water from my eyes. Slowly we threaded our way past the other knots of people in the aisle. Turned round, marched back again like sad sentries. Two individuals were squatting on the floor playing draughts. There was an animated trio of merchants, in here for their own protection and waiting to come to composition with their creditors (so they'd told me, quite proudly). A well-dressed man, more of a gallant than a tradesman, was in close consultation with the chief turnkey, fat Wagman. A red-faced woman and a couple of small children were visiting a man who habitually wore a long, mournful face. His expression hadn't changed. He did not look pleased to see her or the children and stood there, stroking his face. The urgent conversations, the whispered asides.

"I didn't do it," I said.

"I know," said my friend. "All those who know Nicholas Revill know that."

"Not quite all. Coroner Talbot is determined to find me guilty."

"He is a hard man, he has that reputation."

"He says that justice must be done."

"I have brought you some money," said Jack Wilson. "Is it safe to hand it over?"

"Do you think this place is full of thieves?"

Jack laughed.

"There is a kind of twisted honour among these people," I said. "I mean among the gaolers. They will sell anything but they will not take money by force, except as a last resort. They can get more by extortion."

Glancing round, Jack handed me a purse. I did not forget myself so far as to examine its contents like a hungry creditor but it felt weighty enough. It was just as well that Jack went on to speak because I was suddenly too full to say anything. Anyway he guessed my question.

"No, it's not mine, though I've added my share. This is the gift of the Company, Nick. It is bad enough being in a place like this without having to go through the additional misery of being deprived of food or drink or a bed. I once had to endure a few days in the Clink."

"Did you? Why?"

I was inexplicably pleased to hear this.

"A small misunderstanding over an affray in my younger, wilder days. So I know a little of what it's like."

"That group are clapped up for debt," I whispered as we skirted the trio of merchants. I was eager to move the conversation away from my own woes.

"They don't look too unhappy about it."

"It's an odd fact that some of the inhabitants of this place are here by choice. Those merchants are waiting until their creditors get desperate enough to settle on any terms. They will still come out at a profit."

"I would rather be free and poor," said Jack.

"But it's that gentleman over there, the well-dressed one talking to Wagman, who has pulled the neatest trick when it comes to a debt. He's made a profession of it."

"How so?"

"This is the third or fourth time he's been inside. He has boasted to me of how he gets himself arrested on a trumped-up charge of owing a few pounds, and waits for his friends to get the money together to free him. Then he gives Wagman his commission and walks out whistling, a free man. It gives him enough to live well on for a month, he says."

"What about his generous friends?"

"Oh, they can go whistle too while they're waiting for their cash."

"One day they will run out of cash or patience," said Jack. "And he will run out of friends."

"I rather think that day might have come," I said, looking at the earnestness of the dialogue between Wagman and the gallant.

"And what crime has that individual committed, the one who is being pawed by that woman?"

"He is called Topcourt and an unhappy man. He's mild and soft-spoken, and guilty of already having a wife."

"That woman?"

"That woman might be the wife. On the other hand, she might be the other woman, if you see what I mean."

Even as I said this, the red-faced woman's pawing turned to blows. Topcourt stood there, long-nosed and passive as a donkey, while the woman's fists thudded into him. She varied this with a few open-handed slaps to his face. Following their mother's lead, the children also started to flail at him. Fortunately he was well protected by a thick woollen coat. This domestic tussle was hardly remarked on by anyone else in the aisle.The other prisoners were apparently used to seeing Topcourt beaten up. It wasn't even amusing.

"In fact, he may already have a *couple* of wives apart from her," I said. "I think he cannot say no. He would agree to anything."

"I can see why he's unhappy."

"Not for the obvious reason. He's says he's unhappy because he's being released tomorrow. His women have clubbed together to pay for his release."

"Why do they want him out and free if he's deceived them by marrying several times?"

"I don't know. Perhaps they think that prison is not a sufficient punishment. They can do better themselves."

"And perhaps he'd rather stay here in the Counter than face the wives outside."

"You have probably hit it."

"No, I think she is hitting it," said Jack as the rain of blows continued. We watched. It was as good as a play. Then, abruptly the woman turned on her heel and left, with her children clinging to her skirts. Topcourt still stood there, stroking his face, as patient and silly-looking as a donkey.

"You have made friends quickly in this place, Nick. Or got their confidences at any rate."

"Much of the table-talk is about crime. A few of us deny everything but the majority are pleased to boast about what they've done."

"So what have you said?"

"That I'm in here for debt, like most of the rest of them. I don't want to lay claim to three murders."

"You could say you were innocent."

"No one would believe it if I did. Strange. You can claim the most gross crimes in here and everyone believes you. But innocence is the one thing that nobody credits."

"Then it is a little world in here, like the stage-play world."

"It's one I'd just as soon not be a part of."

"All experience is useful."

"I used to think so, but am revising that opinion."

"Well," said Jack, "don't become like your other friends over there and make a practice out of going to gaol. We could not afford another subscription."

"I will save you the trouble," I said. "A noose comes cheap. If we were doing Kyd's *Spanish Tragedy* now I could actually be hanged up on the stage. Do you think Burbage would approve?"

"No."

"Just think of the audience we'd get. You could double the prices at the door."

"Don't be ridiculous, Nick."

"I promise to make a good end. I will kick and struggle with the best of them."

My tongue was running away with me and I could not entirely control my voice. For a moment I took the idea seriously. After all, in Thomas Kyd's *Tragedy* there's a villain who goes to the scaffold convinced that it's all in play and that he will be pardoned at the last moment. He isn't. He dies, his laughter choked off. Well, why should not Revill be truly hanged for the delectation of our audiences? It was only a play, wasn't it? The audience would all go home afterwards.

"I will give my last performance gratis," I added.

Jack stopped in our pacing up and down the church aisle. He turned about and put his hands on my shoulders and looked me straight in the eye.

"Nick, you shall not talk so. Do not abandon hope. Do not sink to the level of this place."

"I thought it was a good joke," I said.

"It was. But there are some jokes that are worse than despair. And, believe me, if you were really about to be turned off you would not be convincing in the part."

This was reminiscent of the little discussion which Coroner Talbot and I had had about playing the drunkard. I brought myself to a smile.

"I thank you for this," I said, patting the place where I'd secreted the purse of money from my Company. "You are to convey my love and gratitude to my friends. God willing, I shall see them all again."

"God willing, you will, and soon," said Jack Wilson.

And with that he left me.

I was cheered by his visit and for a time indulged myself in notions of acquittal and release. But soon I sank into the glooms once more. My fellow prisoners, whose predicaments had seemed amusing or interesting while I'd described them to Jack, now wearied me. So I retreated to my cobwebby box. I fingered the purse which Jack had given me. At least I was guaranteed a few more days and nights in here through the generosity of my friends, the players. I could buy more candle-stubs. What was the point though? I lamented that I had nothing to read, nothing to distract me. I watched a spider going about his horrid business, scuttling backwards and forwards between the centre of his web and a fly which was trapped in the suburbs of his kingdom. Well, this little room was my kingdom. Like WS's imprisoned King Richard the Second I strove to draw parallels between my cell and the great world outside. But it was too easy to see myself as the fly with Coroner Talbot as the energetic spider, and I soon abandoned the effort.

If this was a story I would have been looking about for ways to escape from my captivity. There would have been a hidden floor-trap under the straw, or a whole section of the wall capable of being removed at a single stroke or by dint of scrabbling with hands and nails. (But the stonework, although powdery in places, was solid. There wasn't even a finger's width of a crevice to burrow into.)

In a story the purse which Jack had given me would contain a scrawled map illustrating a secret route out of my cell. A map sketched in invisible ink, made with onion juice or urine, which would emerge when held over the flickering flame of a candle. (But the purse contained nothing more than coins. I opened it and checked.)

In a story, Wagman the turnkey would have a beautiful daughter who, falling for the charms of the handsome young player-prisoner, comes to him in the middle of the night and, after a hasty embrace and whispered endearments, leads him out past the slumbering guards and turnkeys. *It is quite safe, my darling*, she breathes in my ear, *they are dead to the world. I slipped a draught into their possets. Remember me in your dreams*. (But, if Wagman possessed a daughter, it was most unlikely that she was beautiful. And, anyway, she would know better than to spend her time hanging around prisons in the hope of meeting handsome young players.)

Soothing myself with these stories I fell into an uneasy slumber. I didn't dream of tearing down the prison walls to emerge into the sunlight or of the gaoler's beautiful daughter ushering me past the drugged guards. Instead I dreamed a grotesque scene in which I was indeed being executed on the stage of the Globe playhouse, more or less as I'd described it to Jack Wilson.

Dick Burbage approached me in the middle of the performance – although this was not Kyd's *Spanish Tragedy* but some other play as yet unwritten – while I was actually standing on the scaffold. Except that it was not a scaffold but a chair. I remember being irritated at this. If I was prepared to go to the trouble of being hanged for the Chamberlain's, they might have provided something more colourful, more dramatic than a humble chair. Then, as if sensing my displeasure, Burbage insisted on paying me at a double rate, telling me it was the least he could do considering the size of the audience that afternoon. I kept on protesting that this was unprofessional – couldn't he see that we were in the middle of a play, for God's sake? I was doing it for the good of the Company and, besides, what use would the money be to me after I was dead? But Burbage talked about keeping the books straight and at last, to shut him up, I wrapped my hand round the coins he was holding out.

Then it all happened very quickly. Even as I felt the warm money in my grasp, someone tugged the chair from beneath my feet. The noose tightened about my neck. The rope was rough and it burned. A sea of faces looked up at me. Burbage was right, we had a full house. Some gazed in excitement, some in horror, but all with interest. I didn't blame them. In their position I'd have done the same. I was glad that, with my dying breaths, I was conferring a benefit on my Company. Then I concentrated on fighting for those breaths. But the noose was tougher than my windpipe and I could hear wheezing. In my mind's eye I now saw the noose as a closing circle towards which I was running. If I could only get through it before it closed altogether . . . I urged myself forward but my legs could find no purchase on the ground and my lungs would only drag in spoonfuls of air and the circle of rope was fast shrinking to a zero, to a pinprick, to a nothing . . .

I woke up, sweaty and shivering. A grimy sheet had knotted itself around my neck. In my slick palm lay a mound of coins from Jack's purse. I was doubled up as if to shield myself from an assault. I stretched out at full length on the straw pallet, panting and shaking and wondering whether I was really so very glad to be recalled to life. I feared that the scene which I'd just dreamed about would soon be enacted in reality, and that the last faces I'd see would be not the Globe spectators but the howling mob at Tyburn. I saw myself at the bottom of the ladder with the gibbet and the slack, hungry noose standing out against the blue sky. The light was dazzling. I wanted to shade my eyes but my hands were shackled behind my back. It was a beautiful day, though . . . the sun sat snug in his heaven . . . not a day to die . . .

I must have fallen asleep again because the next thing was that someone was pulling at me by the shoulder. It was William Topcourt, the gentleman with more than one wife. He was holding a lighted candle-stub. What was he doing in my room? There was barely space for one.

"Master Revill, Master Revill!"

Topcourt's worried face hung over me, elongated in the flickering light.

"You must go now," he said.

"What?"

"It is time for you to leave."

I sat up on my pallet. Was this part of some continuing dream?

"What are you talking about?"

"I have a paper."

Stooping down, he waved something white in front of my eyes. I took it from him. With his other hand he held the candle so close to the sheet that the paper almost scorched.

"Be careful!" I said.

Topcourt withdrew the candle to a safe distance. I screwed up my eyes and tried to make out the writing. There was an imposing signature at the bottom together with a red seal. After a moment I dropped the paper in exasperation. Why was he bothering to show me this? Had he woken me just so that I could share in his good fortune?

"You're a lucky man," I said, hardly striving to keep the irritation out of my voice.

"A lucky man?" said Topcourt, as if amazed anyone might see him in that perspective. He squatted down beside me on his long haunches. "Oh, I see, you mean because my name is . . ."

"Yes, because your name is on this paper. Or, to put it another way, this is a ticket of leave with your name entered on it."

For an instant I wondered whether he could read but I knew already from his voice and demeanour – long-faced and donkey-nosed as he was – that he was a gentleman. Therefore he could read.

"It's your passport out of this place, man," I said. "It gives you your liberty, liberty under licence. So you'd better keep it away from the candle flame."

"But *you* are to take it. Those are the instructions."

"*Instructions?* Master Topcourt, if I'm to understand you you'll have to talk slow and take things in order."

For some reason this was the style that one fell into when talking to the bigamous – maybe the trigamous – Topcourt. A weary and slightly patronizing style. Maybe this was the tone which his wives had adopted when they made him marry them.

"I shall do my best to explain, Master Revill. This – this ticket of leave I have had for a few days. But this note has just been given to me."

From somewhere within the folds of his voluminous coat Topcourt extracted a second sheet of paper with writing on it. He made to hand it to me but I brushed it aside.

"Just tell me in your own words."

"I – I am given – in short – my freedom has been bought."

"Yes, I know. Bought by your, ah, friends. I am happy for you," I said.

"But I don't want that freedom out there. I am more free in here. I prefer the freedom of prison."

What had Jack Wilson said about Topcourt? *Perhaps he'd rather stay here in the Counter than face the wives outside.* Remembering the way I'd seen him being berated and struck by one of them, and of the similar attentions he'd received from the children, this probably wasn't so far from the truth. In this topsy-turvy world it seemed as though most of the occupants of the Counter prison had actually sought their incarceration or, once inside, preferred to stay here.

"Well," I said, "*de gustibus non est disputandum*."

"No indeed," said Topcourt, "you cannot argue with a man over – over his tastes and preferences."

And, whereas before I'd thought of this individual as a gentleman and an ass, I now saw him in a new light as a scholar and a gentleman – but still a bit of an ass.

"How can you be more free in a prison, Master Topcourt?" I said, to lead him on.

"Master Revill, it will not have escaped you that – my relations with women are – not of the happiest."

"An inkling, I had an inkling," I said.

"I am afraid that if I left this place, I would be compelled to face the wrath of – of various individuals."

His long face took on an even longer cast in the candle's uncertain gleam. He spoke with resignation.

"And I have another fear. Once outside these walls I fear that I will be made to marry again."

"Made to marry?"

"Some demon urges me to put my head in the yoke of matrimony – again and again."

"I know that you are already married."

"Yes. Triply so." He sighed. "That is why I am here."

You can't help but admire a man with three wives even though you may at the same time doubt his sanity. I spoke with a new respect.

"Just think, though, sir. If you were free of the Counter prison you would have a choice of three bolt-holes to rest your, er, head in."

"I cannot house with my wives. I am not friends with them. They are wild horses."

He seemed to shiver.

"You could have refused your wives in the past," I said, interested despite myself. "Refused all but one of them anyway, and saved yourself some trouble. Just as you could refuse all future offers."

"But they are all so persuasive beforehand. So winning.

And my demon is always urging me to bow my head beneath the yoke of matrimony once more."

"I can see it might be safer for you to stay in prison. Or safer for the women of London. But there are females here in the Counter too."

"I know," he sighed. "Temptation is everywhere."

"Show me that note," I said, realizing that we would get no further in this direction.

I read the note and then read it again. Matters became a little clearer, or rather became less obscure. I was jolted, though, by the initials on the bottom.

"Did this individual – " I indicated the initials – "give you this in person?"

"Through an intermediary," said Topcourt. "A friend of yours. They are both waiting."

"Waiting where?"

"Near this place."

"Aren't you afraid of what might happen to you if you stay, Master Topcourt?"

With my hand I mimed a rope tightening round my neck.

Topcourt looked baffled and then said, "No. But anything would be better than – than to face the wrath of my wives or to run my head into the noose of marriage again."

"You don't mean it," I said. "Anyway I can't let you do it."

"They'll discover their mistake soon enough," he said.

I wasn't sure who was going to discover their mistake. His wives? Our gaolers? But I allowed it to pass.

"I can't let you do it," I said again.

I could let him do it, of course. I was simply testing the waters, seeing how far he would go. And it seemed somehow improper to take advantage of a madman. For Topcourt must be mad. A man who is three times married, a man who talks of being compelled to marry again by his inner demon, a man who prefers to stay in gaol. If he hadn't already been in a prison, he ought to have been locked up in a madhouse.

And there was no guarantee that the substitution scheme would work. Every chance it wouldn't work, in fact. But what alternative was there . . .?

"Very well," I said. "Give me your coat."

Topcourt hesitated a moment then, standing up, shrugged himself out of his woollen coat. I took off my doublet and gave it to him in exchange. We were about the same size or, if anything, he was slightly taller than me. The coat, more of a cloak, enveloped me. I hunched up my shoulders and pulled it about my ears. I probably looked truly villainous now, like one of the conspirators in WS's *Julius Caesar*.

Topcourt stooped and ran his hand over the floor of my cell, smearing it with grime. Then he rubbed his bony fingers over my cheeks and forehead. I flinched at first but soon realized his purpose.

"I have been here longer than you, Master Revill – "

"Nicholas, please, seeing as we are so familiar."

" – and I wear a prison-smudge."

Topcourt spoke of this as though it was a kind of mark or badge to be proud of. He stood back to admire his handiwork. My face felt as though it had been painted for a performance on stage.

"Wagman is no fool, he will not be fooled," I said.

"It is night. The turnkey should be elsewhere."

"So I'm just to walk out of here – with this?"

I held up the ticket of leave. The seal looked like a blotch of fresh blood.

Topcourt nodded, stroking his long face.

"It is simple, Master – Nicholas. You want to go while I want to stay. We can both be satisfied."

"And your wives?"

"Keep away from them."

That wasn't what I meant but I didn't pursue the matter. That vision of a hanging which I'd had earlier – the gibbet and the hungry noose against the blue sky, the dazzling light – flashed before my inward eye. It was worth going out of one's way to avoid such a fate. As for Topcourt's fate . . .? Well, what harm could come to Topcourt that he wouldn't welcome in preference to his trio of wives? I had a quick tussle with my conscience and won easily.

I grasped him by the hand and walked out of my cell. I decided to get as far as I could before I was stopped or before Topcourt returned to his senses. It was late evening and the main passage of the prison, the 'aisle' where the inmates wandered during the day, was empty, as far as I was able to tell in the dimness. From down below, from the subterranean Hole, came nocturnal moans and wails.

I walked steadily down the aisle and towards the first of the various lobbies and chambers which lay between Revill (or rather Topcourt) and the outside world. I knew that these rooms would be guarded, for however lax and corrupt the gaolers, two or three of those gentlemen were always in attendance looking for the chance to levy some payment. I had in my hand the 'ticket of leave' signed and sealed by a magistrate and purchased by the wives of another man. It gave formal permission to a prisoner by the name of William Topcourt to depart from the precincts of the Counter prison in the Liberty of Southwark. It granted him freedom under licence.

I put to one side all the problems which lay in the future, even though that future might be only a few minutes away – problems such as what would happen once I was outside the walls of the Counter (but I very much doubted I'd get so far), or what would happen to Topcourt or to me if I was stopped, unmasked and returned to my cell. Instead I concentrated entirely on the present moment. My mind raced. A dozen thoughts passed through it in half a dozen seconds.

I was walking out of the Counter in the guise of William Topcourt, a man three times married. It was all quite simple, wasn't it? Where was the obstacle? All I had to do was present the ticket, signed and sealed, to the gaoler or gaolers and wait for them to wave me through. If challenged, what should

I do? What would Topcourt do? He would withstand indignity in a dignified way, be wearily patient. I imagined myself as Topcourt, poor harassed Topcourt. Although he carried something of a hang-dog look which caused him to stoop, he was taller than me. So possibly the two factors cancelled each other out. He had a bigger, longer nose. I tugged mine in the hope of making it larger. His face was thinner. I sucked in my cheeks. I needed a gesture, and found it straightaway in Topcourt's reflective habit of stroking his face.

But none of this mattered a great deal. I didn't really look like William Topcourt, I'm glad to say. (It's funny how tough vanity is. It will survive almost anywhere.) In the first guard-room, which I was approaching at a steady, stealthy pace, there shouldn't be much light. Candles aren't cheap. My collar was pulled well up. I was wearing the smudge of prison. On the playhouse stage, it's not only the sceptre or the crown which marks out the king, any more than the distracted lover is signified by disordered clothes and folded arms. These props and gestures do signify but they're not enough by themselves. Rather, it is *attitude*. The player is a king because he looks like a king, and he looks like a king because he knows he *is* a king, at least for one afternoon in his life. And the player is a lover because he looks like a lover . . . & cetera.

Not just playing the part of William Topcourt therefore, but *as* William Topcourt, I quietly opened the inner door of the first guardroom. This was the chamber where the chief turnkey was accustomed to sit during the day behind his fine gilt table, toying with his quill pens and balancing his books. I paused on the threshold and breathed deep. The table and the throne-like chair were unoccupied. I'd been dreading the possibility that Wagman might still be here. I wouldn't have got past his sharp eyes, not unless they'd been blinded with gold scales. On my induction into this place, only four days earlier, the two gaolers whom I'd christened Gog and Magog had also been in attendance. Now there was only one guard, a fellow I didn't think I'd seen before. I heard him before I spotted him. He was noisily asleep on a bench in the corner. A candle guttered by his feet. It gave off just enough light to catch the pewter rim of a pint pot lying on its side nearby. The room reeked of small ale. The gaoler's snores ruffled the gloom. Obviously he had not dared to make himself more comfortable on the chief turnkey's throne – or had simply fallen asleep where he sprawled on the bench.

This individual could have sat, or slumped, for a proverbial picture entitled *The Price of Indolence* or *The Perils of Inebriation* or similar. In the said picture an escaping captive (me) would have been sneaking past him. Such is the odd working of the human mind that I almost resented his neglect of duty. Such is the even odder working of my mind that I considered waking him up to show him my ticket of leave. After all I was William Topcourt, the thrice married man, fully entitled to quit this place. Had not my wives paid good money so as to get their hands on me? But common sense prevailed. There were still two more chambers to pass through after this one. I tiptoed across the room, alert for any change in the sound of snoring. None came, although my friend did blend a rippling fart together with the noise coming from his nose-horn as if he were trying out different bass notes at once.

I paused at the second door. This was the entrance to the middle lobby, where sat the guard who'd been so mightily impressed by Constable Doggett's recitation of my crimes that, for an instant, he had ceased scraping the dirt from under his fingernails. I made to ease open the door. It didn't move. Gently at first, then with increasing desperation, I pushed and pulled at the handle. The door, which was a solid one, stayed shut. I tried to remember whether the door had been locked when I'd been escorted this way a few days ago. I thought of knocking on it and waiting for someone to open it up from the other side. I thought of waking the snoring guard and demanding that he release me. I thought of creeping up on him and detaching the key from the ring which he wore on his belt – true, I couldn't see a key or a ring or a belt but I was sure that he wearing them. After all, he was a gaoler. A gaoler on the playhouse stage would have been equipped with a very large set of keys to jangle and flourish.

Then I thought that I should examine the door more carefully. In the very feeble candlelight I noticed what hadn't been obvious before, that the door was bolted top and bottom. An odd prison, this place, where the entrances were secured on the wrong side, as if to stop people getting *in*. Then I thought of the Counter's previous incarnation as St Margaret's church. In a church you sometimes have to keep people out, but you very rarely need to keep them in, much as some parsons might like to. Anyway this was more to do with the sexton than the parson since it would have been one of the sexton's tasks to ensure that the pyx and plate and other valuables were protected from thieves and he'd naturally bolt and lock up from inside before leaving the church, probably by an unobtrusive door in the crypt or vestry. I remembered as a boy accompanying John, my father's sexton, while he made his rounds, locking, bolting, fastening. 'Fast bind, fast find' was the proverb that governed in this case, as it did for Master Benwell in my old lodgings. Therefore the church doors had to be secured on the inside.

All this crossed my mind in a few instants. I don't suppose that I'd been in this chamber with the snoring, farting guard for more than half a minute.

Swiftly I slid back the bolts, top and bottom. My luck held. The bolts, well greased, moved without a scrape or a squeak. The guard rumbled on, heedless, untroubled. I pulled at the door and it swung inwards. The room beyond was dark – and empty. There was no guard excavating the dirt from under his nails at knife-point. There was no one there at all.

Now one more room remained to pass through, the outer porch. This chamber was occupied. A thin line of light was visible under the far door. A sudden bark of laughter from beyond it made me jump. In the person of Master Topcourt I strode forward. I breathed a quick prayer to the patron saint of players (St Genesius, if you're interested). With my heart thudding in my chest, I knocked on the door and opened it.

Two guards were present, the same two in fact who'd been sitting in the porch on the day I was inducted into the Counter prison. They were still smoking their long-stemmed pipes, still perched on stools either side of a chest on which lay a scatter of greasy cards and little piles of coin. For all I knew they hadn't stirred for the last four days, except to answer the calls of nature. This room was better lit but there was an obscuring, eye-itching fug of pipe-smoke and chimney smoke.

The lantern-jawed guard eventually glanced up.

Pronouncing the word 'Topcourt', I held out the precious piece of paper, the 'ticket of leave'. My hand shook slightly.

The guard was evidently used to such documents for he gave it a fairly cursory glance with his bloodshot eyes before passing it across to his gaming partner. I doubted that either of them could read, although they recognized the stamp of officialdom when they saw it. This other man laid his cards face down, screwed up his eyes and held the portion of the document containing the magistrate's signature and seal under his bulbous, spongy nose. He sniffed deeply at the wax seal, as if he might thus inhale the majesty of the law. So far not a word had been spoken apart from my giving a false name.

Then the second gaoler grunted and handed the paper back to the first fellow and returned his attention to his hand. I licked my lips and attempted a smile – because a prisoner departing from a gaol should surely be glad – but it was only a grimace that came out.

"How do you call yourself, master?" said Lantern-jaw.

"William Topcourt."

"Well, what have *you* done?"

Done? What had I done? For a moment I couldn't remember.

"Women," I said.

The gaoler with the spongy nose flicked his eyes in my direction with interest. I stroked my grimy cheek, seeing how my uneasiness could be turned to advantage.

"What's your offence, man?" said Lantern-jaw, still holding tight to my ticket of leave with one hand and using the other to point me out with the stem of his pipe.

"Women are my offence, I say. Three times over. I am married three times over. William Topcourt is my name."

"Oh, we have heard of you," said the other gaoler. "You are a most notorious adulterer."

"A limb-lifter and an arch fornicator."

"They'll be making a ballad out of you next."

I looked abashed, as if the prospect of fame was unpleasing. The room grew hotter. The folds of my coat or cloak hung heavy about me.

"So cheer yourself . . . Topcourt. Leave those long faces behind."

"You do not have three wives waiting for you outside, sir," I said, trying to imitate Topcourt's resigned intonation.

"Are they outside?"

"Round a dark corner, I expect," I said.

"You'd be better off locked up, wouldn't you then," said Sponge-nose.

I gestured helplessly towards the signed and sealed paper as if to say, it's out of my hands now.

"My wives, they think otherwise and have purchased my liberty."

"It's not you should be locked up anyway, Master Topcourt," said the first gaoler.

"I am mostly of your mind, sir," I said mournfully.

"Not you but your pintle should be locked up, out of women's reach."

"That one is truly a case for a prick-case," said the other.

Now I smiled, smiled weakly, as Topcourt would have done. There are some men – most men perhaps – who'd be glad enough to have their hardihood with three wives celebrated and even laughed over but I judged that William Topcourt wasn't among them.

"One thing, master," said Lantern-jaw. "Enlighten me now. Which of your three wives is going to couch with you tonight? Or is it more than one that you'll be having?"

I saw the glint of envy, of prurient curiosity, in his bloated eyes. And the other one's nose would have been all a-quiver if it hadn't already been so swollen up and spongy. Be careful, I told myself, don't overplay this. These men are quite capable of keeping you inside out of spite, in order to stop you couching with anyone at all.

"That depends," I said, "on which of my wives has the biggest – "

"Thingy?"

"Nonny-no?"

"The biggest stick," I said. "I'm sorry to disappoint you, gentlemen, but I won't be 'having' anyone tonight. You wouldn't credit the brutal treatment I will receive at the hands of my wives. You would not think that the ladies could be so barbarous."

I shivered, despite the heat and the enveloping cloak. I stroked furiously at my cheek and then tugged at my nose.

"Like I said, you're safer in here," said the second gaoler.

"I must take my punishment like a man," I said. "I am a sinner. I have done wrong and cannot avoid retribution. It is my fate. Though my wives beat me with rods and canes I will not cry out. I am a changed man and walk with God now."

As I'd half hoped, all this talk of punishment and sinning appeared to make them lose interest. They would be receiving no bedchamber titbits from me. They reached for their cards again and I cleared my throat and indicated the ticket of leave. Lantern-jaw handed it to me. I shuffled, but shuffled purposefully, in the direction of the double church doors which were the final barrier between me and the street.

Lantern-jaw waited until Sponge-nose had played his hand and then he played one of his own and only after that did he deposit the remainder of his cards alongside his pipe on the chest. Wearily he raised himself to his feet. I now saw that a pendulous iron key hung from his waist. He stroked it lasciviously and then waggled it up and down.

"Maybe your wives would like a touch of this, eh, Master Topcourt? Can you speak for them?"

I leaned forward and pretended to inspect his instrument.

"I fear they could not accommodate such a massy engine, sir, and one with so many intricate wards too. I could not hope to compete with it."

This piece of complimentary filth seemed to do the trick. The gaoler inserted the key – it was large, almost requiring two hands to manoeuvre it – and, rolling his bloodshot eyes at me, twisted it in the keyhole. Then he seized a great iron ring and pulled back one of the double oak doors, which creaked on its hinges.

I had a glimpse of the outside or, more accurately, a whiff of it. It must have been raining because the sound of pattering drops and the fresh smell of a shower slipped through the half-open door together with a draught of cold air. It's odd, but until that moment I hadn't thought much about getting out of the Counter, only about negotiating the various ante-chambers to it. Now – with the world only a few feet away from where I was standing – a violent desire to quit this miserable place suddenly overcame me. I only just stopped myself from bolting through the narrow gap. Instead, pulling my cloak tight about my person and clutching my precious ticket of leave, I went to ease through the space.

And then the lantern-jawed gaoler put his shoulder to the door and closed it once more. Somehow I wasn't surprised. It had been too easy so far, too straightforward. The door shut with a thud. Laboriously he retwisted the key in the keyhole.

"Not so quick . . ."

Folding his arms, he leaned against the door. He looked pleased at whatever confusion of expressions I was wearing on my face. Despair – pleading – anger. No acting now. The prize had been dangled before my face then whisked away.

"Who are you?" said this gaoler.

My stomach lurched. They'd known all the time who I was, these two. They'd been toying with me. For an instant I was on the edge of admitting the truth but I checked myself.

"You know that – that I am William Topcourt."

"*What* are you, though?" said the other gaoler, who was still occupied with his cards. I took a tiny grain of comfort from the fact that he hadn't shifted from his perch. I calculated my chances of springing at the insolent fellow by the entrance, twisting round the great key, tugging the door open and making my escape into the street. No chance. The two of them would be on me in a trice.

"What am I?" I echoed.

"Describe yourself, William Topcourt," said Lantern-jaw.

I began to suspect that there was some game going on here, a game to whose rules I wasn't privy.

"Well, a fornicator, yes, I freely admit it," I gabbled. "A sinner and a malefactor. A prisoner for my crimes."

"And who are *we*?" said the man with the cards in his hand.

"You gentlemen are my gaolers," I said, adding the right note of deference.

"Entitled to . . . ?"

Ah! I had it now. The fact that I understood them must have shown on my face but the gaolers, tired of beating about the bush, now grew more direct and fired off their requirements like bullets.

"Peck."

"Shot."

"Brass."

"Coin."

Of course, it *was* a game that we were playing. An extremely old one, the oldest one in the book. I could have kicked myself for my slowness, for my failure to grasp the single rule of the game, the single and simple rule. The rule is: you pay. Win or lose, you pay.

"Forgive me, sirs," I said, fumbling under the cloak for my purse.

Fortunately I hadn't spent much of the money which Jack Wilson and the rest of the Company had so generously supplied – or rather not all of it had yet been extorted from me. I drew out a pair of half-crowns, which seemed to be the standard rate in this gaol, and solemnly presented one to the spongy-nosed gentleman sitting on a stool and the other to the lantern-jawed gentleman leaning against the church doors. A swift glance, then the coins were palmed and disappeared.

"You have no angels about you," said the man by the door, pointing to the region of my waist where he'd spotted my purse. He was referring to those old coins, the ones that were often counterfeited and that Master Shakespeare was so fond of making puns about.

"No angel but only a little devil down there," I said.

And – at long last! – this salacious answer seemed to meet requirements. Without another bawdy remark, without another word, Lantern-jaw turned the key of the door for a second time, swung it back on its creaky hinges and then, with mock ceremony, bowed me out into the street.

I slid past him, expecting at every moment another summons, a further demand for cash. None came. I walked, slowly at first then at an increasing pace, away from the building that had once been St Margaret's church. Behind me I heard the door of the Counter prison thud shut.

Despite Master Topcourt's topcoat I was soon damp from the drizzling rain which seemed to insinuate its way underneath, but I didn't care about this. I halted, breathed deep several times to clear my lungs of the prison air and turned my face up to the night sky. It was cloudy but I didn't care about that either. At some point while I'd been inside, the fog which seemed have been clinging to London for weeks – tighter than a miser to his money-bags, closer than a new bride to her groom, more desperately than a condemned man to his life (take your pick) – had decided to let go of the city. Free! Free!

Although the outlook was very bleak – since I was, essentially, a fugitive from justice – nothing could take away from this brief sense of liberation. Yes, it was true that I had lost everything. I could never rejoin the Chamberlain's Company and would surely have to flee from the city and resign myself to a runaway's life. But even the prospect of living wild and unprovided for didn't seem so awful at this moment. Or not so awful as a long period cooped up in the Counter . . . or the much worse prospect of dangling from the hempen rope of Tyburn tree. Near where I stood, gulping down these heady draughts of freedom, was the Tabard Inn. I even considered having a celebratory ale to mark my release from captivity. I think that I was not entirely in my right mind at this moment.

"Master Topcourt!"

I jumped.

"Nick!

A man's voice.

"Master Revill!"

A woman's voice.

From round the corner of Kent Street came two shapes. It was too dark to recognize them but I already knew who they were.

Jack Wilson came up and peered into my face until he was quite satisfied.

"It *is* you, Nick. We've been waiting. I thought they might have let out the wrong man."

"They did let out the wrong man."

"The wrong wrong man, then."

The second shape drew near.

"Master Revill," she said, resting a hand on my arm.

"Mrs Milford," I said. "I – I have not had the chance to condole with you on your loss."

"My husband is dead," she said simply. "But not at your hands."

I experienced that prickling on the back of my neck which I'd had after the *Troilus and Cressida* performance. But at the same time I felt a little burst of gratitude because she was so confident of my innocence.

"You know who did it?" I said.

"No," she said. "But you shall find out."

We must have made an odd trio, standing there in the middle of the street on a drizzly night, having a whispered discussion about murder. As my eyes got used to the dark I was able to pick out features, Jack's nervous smile, Lucy Milford's fixed gaze.

"It was Lucy's wish to get you released, Nick," Jack said.

I turned towards Lucy.

"I know. Thank you. I read your note. You have both put yourselves at risk to preserve my worthless corpse."

"When you told me about William Topcourt," said Jack, "and how he didn't want to leave the prison and when I saw the way one of his wives was treating him – well, it wasn't difficult to slip back again afterwards even if I had to oil a few palms on the way. And then I had a talk with Topcourt. You were right about him. He is a good fellow and readily agreed. *He* didn't want any payment. He would have paid to stay inside, I think. He already had his ticket of leave and hadn't dared to tell his wife about it. One of his wives."

"Even so, I don't understand why Topcourt was willing to stay behind . . ."

"Why not?" said Jack.

"Well, you know . . . "

In Lucy Milford's presence I was curiously unwilling to

refer to the hempen noose or Tyburn tree. All the same, Jack got my drift.

"Master Topcourt believes that you were locked up in the Counter for debt. That's what you told everyone, wasn't it?"

"Oh Jesus. You didn't enlighten him? You must have told him surely?"

"Why should I? You said yourself that you were reluctant to lay claim to three murders. Especially as you're innocent."

"Oh God."

I thought of the baffled way in which Topcourt had looked at me when I'd performed the neck-stretching mime. He'd thought that he was merely substituting for a man who'd been imprisoned for debt, not one up on a capital charge. He'd thought that taking my place would give him a few extra days or weeks out of the clutches of his wives. Not offer him a short cut to the gallows. What were his words? "They'll discover their mistake soon enough." It looked as though it was Topcourt who'd made a mistake, a grave mistake. Or been grotesquely imposed upon.

The honourable action would have been to march straight back to the Counter and resume my place in the cell, to await Coroner Talbot's final summons . . . and the arraignment, trial and sentence which must follow. But I didn't move.

"Don't worry, Nick," said Jack, blunter than I was able to be. "They'll hardly hang the man."

"They will if they think they're hanging me."

"They'll find out their mistake soon enough," he said, echoing Topcourt's own words in the cell.

"I suppose so," I said.

"And then they'll hardly top Topcourt for being three times married."

"I suppose not," I said.

"You must go, Master Revill," said Lucy Milford, again touching me lightly on the arm.

"You may call me Nicholas, seeing as you have saved my life. Both of you have saved my life."

"Still you must go. It isn't safe here."

"Not safe for you either. You're aiding a fugitive."

"We are safe enough," she said, speaking with queer inwardness.

"But where shall I go to?" I said.

"You know where to go when you are in trouble," she said.

But I couldn't return to my lodgings in Dead Man's Place, couldn't resume my place in the Chamberlain's Company, couldn't resort to Holland's Leaguer and my friend Nell, couldn't go to any place . . . except . . .

. . . except . . .

And then I knew where I could go, where I had to go.

Incognito

I walked all night, keeping the river to my right, skirting Lambeth marsh and then heading southwards towards Putney. By first light I was well away from Southwark, away from the Globe playhouse, the Counter prison, Holland's Leaguer, Dead Man's Place, and all the rest of it. The day dawned wet and ragged, with clouds scudding freely across the sky and the rain coming down hard. William Topcourt's great coat kept off the worst of it but I too must have looked wet and ragged. Gusts of wind buffeted against me and water ran down my face, all of it delightful to someone who had spent several days incarcerated in a stinky prison. It was still so early in the morning that few people were about and those I did encounter were mostly heading towards the city rather than away from it.

At Putney I took a ferry across the river, knowing that the shorter route for the moment lay on the north bank of the Thames. Luckily I still had money in my purse. Sitting in the ferryman's boat I felt for the first time like a fugitive but I took good care to play the part of a lawful traveller, looking confident and decisive as though I had business somewhere instead of being a mere runaway. Then on the far side I bought some brown bread and set off once more at a brisk pace, tearing myself great mouthfuls as I went. Despite having been awake now for more than twenty-four hours – and the comforts of gaol had not been so great that I'd slept quietly there, to say nothing of my troubling dreams – I was curiously refreshed. The brisk air blew away the fogs and fusts of London.

From time to time on the route I glanced round but, although the way was busier now, I could not see any single figure who – even to my straining eyes – appeared to be in pursuit. Common sense suggested that if I was going to be followed and apprehended it would have happened before this point. The danger now lay in a chance encounter, an unexpected challenge. The track was muddy and miry but not so bad as it would have been later in the winter and I was able to make fairly good progress, even to overtake the odd lumbering cart. I considered hiring a post-horse but the expense deterred me almost as much as the thought of spending hours on horseback. Saddles are hard and horses unpredictable in my experience. I'd sooner trust to my own legs than rented ones. Besides I was not in such a great hurry to arrive.

Towards midday the rain slackened off and I bought some more bread as well as milk and cheese from a good housewife and made a quick meal of them by the roadside, reserving a little of the food for later. It tasted much better than prison fare. Freedom is almost as good a sauce as hunger. So far I'd been walking mostly in open country with clear prospects on either side. There was comfort in being able to see some distance in every direction. I drank down the cold, gusty air. The bare trees shivered on the edges of fallow fields and pasture but I sang to myself as I swung along, to the undoubted benefit of the occasional herd of pigs rooting about beneath the trees or among clumps of gorse.

Near the more wooded country south-east of Buckingham, the afternoon began to fade, the number of passengers on the road thinned out and suddenly I grew conscious of my isolation. It's not wise to be travelling alone when the light starts to leave the sky. The traveller on horseback digs in his spurs to reach the nearest inn. The one on foot lengthens his stride. There are plenty of rogues who will rob you on the road after dark – yes, and think nothing either of plunging the knife in after they've relieved you of your goods, since the price of murder is the same as the price of robbery. The gallows waits for both offences. And it would be an ironic enough fate if I was stabbed to death on the road out of London even while I was escaping from a capital charge.

But I wasn't altogether willing to commit myself to the shelter of an inn for the night. I passed one with a large, brightly painted sign swinging outside. Rain was starting to drip from the sky again. The inn was called the Night Owl. A prosperous-looking rider was alighting from his horse in the yard while an ostler slipped his bag from the saddle-bow. I visualized this gentleman entering the inn-chamber, where a fine fire would already be burning, and calling for sack and a servant to pull off his riding-boots. I could easily have followed him in, made myself comfortable by the fire and mulled over a drink too. My feet and calves were aching from the journey. I was beginning to feel the accumulated damp and cold of the day. Topcourt's woollen coat was starting to weigh heavy.

I checked my pace and half turned towards the entrance to the Night Owl. Then, almost without thinking, I turned back and resumed my progress. The way ahead wasn't particularly inviting since it soon lost itself among dense clusters of trees under whose branches dusk had already gathered. But the idea of mingling with other travellers in an inn or at the least exchanging words with a curious landlord and his tapsters daunted me, even though I'd managed to put a good few miles between myself and my enemies in London. What if word had somehow got out that a notorious murderer was on the loose? What if Coroner Talbot had sent out agents to track me down? Perhaps that fine-looking gentleman who'd been dismounting in the yard was looking for me. Not very likely, not likely at all – but he could have been.

An acute awareness of my plight suddenly rushed in on me. I was an escaped prisoner, a wretch with three killings to his name. No one in the world was my friend, apart from Jack and Lucy back in London. Everyone would shrink from me in horror if they knew what I'd done. What I was supposed to have done. Surely the substitution of William Topcourt for Nicholas Revill in the Counter prison had been discovered by now? Part of me hoped that it had, for Master Topcourt's sake. (But a larger, selfish part hoped that it hadn't.)

I paced slowly among the dank trees for a little while longer, not knowing what to do, whether to go on walking – but this seemed foolish since it would be easy to wander off the path and besides I was growing too tired to go on much further – or whether to search out some mossy nook or leaf-strewn corner of the forest to rest my head in. I wasn't much in love with the second idea either. Sleeping in a forest may be good enough for fairies and eloping lovers in a play but even they had the wit to choose a dry night in midsummer. In this dithering mood I was about to turn round and retrace my steps to the Night Owl when I spotted a low square shape through the trees off to my left. I made my way towards it and discovered a broken-down hovel, roofed more with holes than with beams and straw. I don't know who it once housed, whether a charcoal-burner or a swineherd or even a hermit, but there were no signs of occupation now, no sticks of furniture, no pile of warm ash, no primitive bed. This was good enough for me. I thanked Providence for throwing a house into my path, in case Providence felt like dispensing any more substantial favours in my direction.

I found the angle of the hovel which was the least wet and cold and, slumping against the corner post, chewed at my last chunk of bread and sliver of cheese. Whereas before I'd wolfed them down with appetite, now they seemed to stick in my throat. Rain dribbled through a gap in the roof and then through a matching gap between my neck and the collar of Topcourt's coat and I did not have the will to shift and avoid it. All the vigour of the morning seemed to belong to another life, and not mine either. Eventually, I huddled down inside the coat and lay in my corner, half curled up as I have seen dogs lie when they have been banished from the fire and are feeling aggrieved.

The night was endless. Once I woke up and thought I was back in prison. Then I thought, almost fondly, of my old lodgings in Dead Man's Place, my little room with its bed and its roof and and its walls and its floor and other bare necessaries. And I struggled to turn my mind away from the woman who had sometimes shared the bed in that room, for the memory of her was still very raw. I compared what I had had then with what I endured now and, like the dog kept from the fire, felt extremely sorry for myself. I fell asleep again and woke convinced that it was dawn. But it was still pitch dark. All around me was the patter of rain from the bare branches and the drip of water through the holes in the roof. From time to time there would be a rustle or a sliding sound from the forest, as some night creature went about its business. I huddled further down inside Master Topcourt's coat and attempted to sleep. At another point during that endless night I dreamed that some oafish animal had invaded my hovel, snuffling and panting in search of food or shelter. If I keep very still and quiet, I thought, perhaps it'll take me for a bundle of rags and leave me alone.

When I awoke properly, a weak and watery light filled the hut. I saw that the oafish beast was no dream. In another corner of my tumbledown shelter another unfortunate individual was sleeping. All I could see of him was a shag of hair and beard, framing an unpleasing set of features. He was lying, snoring and spluttering, under a weather-stained mantle that was much less adequate than mine. There were holes in the boots that protruded from the other end. I made a silent exit before he too woke up. However dire my predicament I was still in possession of a whole coat and sound boots, to say nothing of a purse with a bit of coin in it. I did not want to put advantage or temptation in anyone's way.

Even lying down he looked bigger than me. For certain he must be more desperate, difficult though that was to believe.

I blundered off through the woods. Hunger clawed at my guts. I marvelled at the hardiness of those who spend their lives in the wild as beggars and vagrants. All that stands between us and them is a stout pair of shoes and a little coin. For an instant I contemplated turning right round and going back to Southwark, to the streets and buildings of the city rather than the bare paths of the wood. But in among those streets were coroners, prisons and gallows . . . So I shook off my self-pity and started to stride out as I'd done on the previous morning and eventually walked myself into more cheerful spirits. The sun showed dimly to one side, as if in approval.

Once again I was able to buy some provisions from a housewife. She invited me to come in – her man was away across the fields, she told me several times, and he would be away all day – and then she made me sit at her table and take some porridge. She would have provided more than simple sustenance, I think, particularly when she glimpsed the contents of my purse. But there was a baby swaddled up in a corner and another one on the way, to judge by her belly, and an older child crawling around in the dirt and she had a wall-eye as well as a notable absence of teeth and I had better things to do with my money. Besides I was not in the mood. At the moment I didn't think I'd ever be in the mood for it again. So I warded off her questions, complimented her on her porridge (which was indeed very filling), exchanged some of her bread for cash and set off once more.

It was a wearisome journey and it would be wearisome to recount it all in detail. Day succeeded night succeeded day. Eventually I reached the great plain north of Salisbury across which I'd walked with the Chamberlain's Men in the summer of the previous year, on the way to Instede House.* I couldn't

* see *The Pale Companion*

help thinking of how different things had been then, of how blithely I'd kept company with my fellows, despite all the adventures which had overtaken us. In the summer the skies were open, the larks sang and the path curled dustily across the plain. Now clouds tumbled low overhead and the chalky track was sogged and rutted. There were very few travellers. It was the afternoon and I wondered whether the players would be performing at the Globe and, if so, what play they were presenting. What pieces had Jack told me were in prospect when he visited me in the Counter? *Fortune's Eyes* and *The Law's Delay*, weren't they? I'd been due to appear in both. Well, my space would have been filled – rather as when a soldier falls in battle another one steps up to take his place, and no man spares a thought for the fallen, at least in the heat of battle. Now, I noted, I was inclined to think of the Chamberlain's Company as 'they' rather than 'we', and this was not the least of my losses.

After three or four nights on the road, sleeping in whatever shelter I could find and buying food by the wayside or in the villages, I decided to risk staying in an inn well beyond the western edge of the plain. The Green Dragon was warm and welcoming. I snugged down in front of the fire with a glass of ale and ate the largest meal I'd had for several days. Giving the name of William Topcourt – after all I'd already taken his coat (but, please God, wouldn't be responsible for taking his life as well, a little voice whispered) – I spun a tale to the landlord and to an inquisitive chambermaid of how I was returning home because my father had died. Bereavement is a good way of encouraging sympathy without provoking too many further questions. My haste to get back would account for my travel-stained, distracted manner. I slept well, sharing the bed with only one other traveller, to whom I told the same tale of mourning, and set off the next dawn, well breakfasted and renewed.

And the next night I did the same, lodging at an inn on the Bath road, at a place whose name I forget. Ate well, slept sound, started fresh. My store of money had carried me a long way – but then it was not being extorted by a pack of turnkeys but was gladly surrendered to hospitable landlords and good-hearted housewives. By now I had fallen into a rhythm of walking. My legs seemed to move of their own accord and, even though I was blistered and footsore, I was sure that they would take me, slowly but steadily, to the other side of the earth if they had to.

As I got nearer my destination, however, I felt less sure of what I was doing. When we were standing in the Southwark street, Lucy Milford had told me that I knew where I should go and the realization of what she'd meant had struck home a few moments later. Literally struck home. But now I was by no means confident of the reception I'd get or – assuming that I was at all gladly received – what I would do afterwards.

Even so it was a pleasure to be entering my own country now. No doubt my eyes and nose were partial but the Somerset air smelled fresher and sweeter, the pastures looked better tended, the sheep-cots were neater and the sheep themselves less bedraggled, despite the wind and the rain. I could smell the sea or imagined I could smell it from the higher places I walked across. And it was a pleasure to hear familiar accents in the hamlets I passed through.

I was not so far from my home village of Miching when an odd thing happened. For some time I'd been watching a figure making his way towards me on the road. By now I'd passed a good few travellers both on foot and on horseback and we usually contented ourselves with a greeting, although some averted their eyes as if they had as much reason to be secretive about their journey as I did. But when this individual drew closer he suddenly tumbled down in the roadway. Once on the ground he jerked about like a fallen puppet being tugged upright by its strings. Then he seemed to give up the struggle and to lie still on his back, giving an occasional twitch.

I observed all this as I walked towards this man. I didn't walk any quicker but neither did I slow my pace, although I did turn round to ascertain that there was no one else behind me. We were in open country, with a few windswept trees. As I approached the figure I heard a subdued groaning and noticed that he was moving his head from side to side. There was something strange about the lower part of his face and, as I drew nearer still, I saw that he was frothing at the mouth. When I'd got within a couple of yards of him I stopped, folded my arms and watched.

This gentleman was slightly built, with a tapering nose and a high forehead across which were smears of dried blood. It was difficult to tell his age, he was perhaps about my own years or a little older, but his face was all brown and weather-worn indicating the outdoor life. He was bubbling at the mouth and uttering sounds that were without meaning. Most disconcertingly, his eyes were open but the pupils had almost rolled up into his head and nothing except a yellowy white was visible.

I would have stepped around the figure and moved on down the road but something about him made me hesitate. So, without going any closer, I stood and waited. The wind whipped at my hair and I shrugged myself further in Topcourt's coat. The man on the ground writhed a little more before going calm and quiet. His eyes closed and the foaming ceased. I coughed to let him know that I was still there and, sure enough, after a minute or so, he opened his eyes, normal now, and looked around with a vacant expression.

I clapped a few leisurely claps, in that mocking fashion of which we are all master, like an unimpressed spectator in the theatre. His gaze flickered towards me and apparently took me in for the first time. He seemed to consider. Then, with sudden agility, he sprung to his feet. He wiped at his sudsy mouth.

"I knew it wasn't going to work," he said.

"Why?" I said, genuinely curious.

"I can tell in moments if it's going to. If the cony comes close and leans over or gets down on one knee, then it'll work."

"Gets down on one knee so that he can be beaten over the head?" I said.

A pained expression crossed the man's mobile face.

"Gets down in order to help a fellow human being."

"Who's about to rob him."

"Not rob him."

"What then?"

To be honest, I didn't know why I was engaging this gentleman in conversation. Perhaps I'd been so starved of dialogue on the road that I was happy with any company, even that of a cony-catcher – or to be more specific a counterfeit crank. These gentlemen travel about our kingdom and when they see a likely prospect in their way they tumble down all in a heap, frothing at the mouth and making moan. After a period they come to themselves again, all ignorant of their surroundings but grateful to the kind lady or gentleman who has stopped to assist them. They claim to be victims of a falling-sickness which may strike them down at any moment, and they present a most piteous spectacle, with their faces all bloody and muddy from where they have fallen in previous fits. But the real victim or cony in this situation is the innocent passer-by who delves into his purse to relieve the unfortunate.

"What is it then if it's not robbery?" I said.

"I give good Christian men and good Christian women the chance to show charity and offer alms," said this impudent fellow.

"By trickery."

"No one suffers. They go on their way with their hearts warmer."

"And their pockets lighter."

"A small price to pay for a good deed."

"I am pleased to meet a philosopher on the road," I said.

The man gave an ironic little bow. He saw me looking curiously at his mouth, still whitened and sticky-looking.

"Soap. When I see someone in the distance I slip a small piece into my mouth and suck – suck judiciously."

"And what about that?" I said, indicating the bloody smears on his forehead.

"Paint."

"You should try sheep's blood instead."

"You speak like an expert, Master – ?"

"Topcourt. I should do, because I'm a player. A tragedian."

Saying these words gave me a curious sense of relief. Even though they contained a minor untruth – a false name – they contained a larger and truthful fact. I *was* a player. I was still a player.

"Where do you play?"

"Oh, in London, with the Chamberlain's Company, the finest company in the land," I said, then added in case he was wondering what I was doing so far away from such a fine group, "I am out of the city because – because my father has recently died and I am on my way home."

"I should have known better than to try and trick a Londoner," he said.

"You weren't to know it," I said, almost as if it was I who had tried to trick him.

"My name is Abel Glaze," said this man. I wondered whether it was his real name. He almost stretched out his hand to grasp mine but restrained himself at the last moment. Perhaps he considered that both of us were in the same line of business, playing parts, deceiving people.

"How much can you expect to make?" I said.

"I once earned fourteen and threepence halfpenny *in a day*."

He spoke proudly. I wasn't surprised. It was more than I earned at the Globe in a couple of weeks.

"That was up near Reading way," said the counterfeit crank called Abel Glaze. "Folk are more generous in those parts than they are down here."

"More gullible, you mean."

He shrugged. I grinned – grinned for the first time in many days. Who was I to look down on this individual, I who was on the run from the law for much more serious offences than feigning sickness?

"Like you, Master Topcourt, I play more than one part," said Glaze.

"I suppose you couldn't spend your whole life falling down. It would be tedious."

"You should see my old soldier," he said, unburdening himself. "With the wounds I received in the Low Countries. Unslaked lime and a dab of iron rust excite the pity of the ladies and the admiration of the men. I have a limp that I can call upon and many tales of the battle of Zutphen."

"You are a resourceful fellow," I said, not altogether mockingly.

"No lie, I was there at the battle when I was no more than a boy," said Glaze, "but I came off unscathed through the shot and smoke. Not a scratch. And now the wars provide me with a living in peace, the wars and the falling-sickness."

There was something engaging about Abel Glaze. I was reluctant to part company with him while, for his part, he seemed eager to spill out the secrets of his trade. Perhaps he too was hungry for company. The wind blew in our faces. His eyes widened. I looked behind me and saw two figures travelling down the route I'd come on, and the sight prompted me to get going again. But first I rummaged in my purse and found a twopence piece. Glaze's sharp nose quivered but he made a don't-trouble-yourself gesture – after all, weren't we fellow players? And he was certainly more prosperous than me. Nevertheless, grateful for the diversion he'd provided, I tossed the coin to him and he caught the glinting silver, threw it up in the air and caught it once more overhand. Then giving another little bow, not so ironic this time, he said, "I shall remember you kindly, Master Topcourt," and set off in the direction of the two advancing figures, a man and a woman.

I wondered whether he would try his tricks on them. I didn't stop to see but put on speed to leave the scene.

Within a couple of hours I was within sight of my old village. I came over the brow of the hill and – heart beating fast, and not just from the uphill climb – glanced down almost fearfully. When I'd last seen Miching on a fine spring morning my vision had been clouded by terror and pity. The doors to the houses were daubed with red crosses and pleas for God's mercy. Some of my father's parishioners were being forked into a burial pit. Of my father and mother there was no sign (of course they were dead). The chief thing I remember is the absolute silence of the place, as if a great hand had pressed down on the village and stifled all the life out of it. I think that, unknowingly, I'd been expecting everything to be unchanged from my last terrible visit – that is, I expected the same absence of sound, the same deathly stillness.

But, on this gusty afternoon in late autumn, there were signs of renewed life. Smoke was being hustled away from cottage chimneys by the wind. A dog barked down below. Screwing up my eyes, I could make out an individual coming through the lych-gate of the church. The activity surprised me. But the surprise was misplaced. It was now several years since the plague had struck Miching and, although most of the villagers had died, a few survived. Peter Agate had told me as much. Houses and other places can be fumigated and made fit for human habitation once more. Eventually the disease seems to grow tired and run its course. All is not lost. Why, in the years that I'd been absent in London, a little troop of children had probably been born to replenish some of the old stock. For some reason, I felt my eyes prickling and dabbed at them. I stood a long time gazing at the scene which lay spread out down below.

Then I neatened my clothing, tugging Topcourt's coat about me. I hoped I didn't look as though I'd passed the best part of a week on the road. Fortunately the couple of nights which I'd spent in the inns had enabled me to get rid of some of the smudge of travel.

I set off at a downhill march, not to the heart of the village but towards the great house which lay at a little distance, a life-preserving distance, from it. This was Quint House, the residence of the Agates. I walked steadily, afraid that if I checked my steps now my resolution might falter. For what had seemed a good idea as I fled from Southwark – that I should return to the place of my birth and seek shelter with the family of my old childhood friend, while I took stock of my predicament – now looked a less certain thing with every step I made towards their front door.

What claim did I have on them? I was Peter's friend, but Peter was dead. I'd written to the family a heartfelt letter, explaining something of the brutal circumstances of his death but without suggesting that I myself had fallen under suspicion for it. I'd supposed, in a careless kind of way, that the Agates might be glad to hear more details of his death from the friend Peter had sought out in London - or, if not his death, then of his last days, and quite happy days they had been too.

If Mistress Margaret, Peter's mother, had been alive, I know she would have welcomed me with open arms. But she was dead. In her place was Gertrude, the harpy-like stepmother whose claws and flapping dugs Peter told me he'd run away from. As for father Agate, old Anthony, the one who had bitterly opposed his son's plans to go on stage, what would he say when he clapped eyes on a member of the disgraced tribe of players on his doorstep? Even though I'd been unaware of Peter's intentions before he'd arrived, wouldn't I somehow be blamed for luring Peter to London and so bringing about his death? That was assuming Anthony Agate even remembered me. Then there were Peter's sisters . . . but what was I to them? Only one, Anne, had been there for Peter and me to shoo away and trip over. The others had been little children, inconsequential and out of sight. And Anne I'd most likely tweaked and teased horridly. If she remembered me at all it would probably be with indifference or distaste.

So, all in all, my plan seemed not just ill thought out but futile.

Half a dozen crazed notions ran through my head as I covered the final furlongs to the Agate mansion.

Why should I stop here in my old village? Almost everyone I knew was dead. I could just keep going, letting my legs carry me where they would. Why not simply plunge on into the wilds of the West Country and there make do with what I could grab and grub? After all, Abel Glaze made a good living out of tumbling down in the public highway or exhibiting his fake wounds to interested viewers. I was no less of an actor than him.

Or I might head for a seaport, to Bristol or Plymouth, and there take ship to . . . to a new life in another land. But I was no great lover of boats. The widest strip of water I knew was the Bristol Channel. And the only foreign country I'd ever had a glimpse of was the wild mountains of Wales, and they were quite enough to be going on with.

So I continued in my progress towards Quint House and entered by the front gate, passing between pillars surmounted by great stone balls. As a child I'd thought they looked as big as the globe. The house, built of a stone that even on this overcast day looked warm to the touch, stood four-square and solid before me. To one side was the small chapel which had been erected by old Peter Agate, the pious grandfather of the family. I traversed familiar gardens and walked up the flagged path. A gardener was raking the fallen leaves. He looked up incuriously.

I contemplated going round to one of the side entrances but, in the event, knocked at the main door. When no answer came, I rapped more loudly. I heard footsteps inside. My mouth was dry. I had no idea what I was going to say.

A pale-faced woman opened the door. She was wearing mourning but wasn't dressed like a servant. She looked too young to be the new lady of the house, Peter's stepmother, Gertrude. Too young and too attractive for a harpy. There were shadows under her eyes. She regarded me almost in bafflement and didn't seem inclined to speak.

"Is the master of the house at home?"

"The master?" she echoed.

"The mistress then?"

"She is with Ralph Verney of Miching."

"Ah," I said, not recognizing the name.

"They are talking of monuments."

"Monuments, of course," I said. Then, realizing that I needed to make matters clear, if only for my own sake, I started again.

"I – I am an old friend of the Agate family. Or, to be more precise, an old friend of Peter Agate."

As if the name was a cue on stage, the face of the woman in front of me suddenly crumpled like a screwed-up cloth. She clung to the doorpost for support and looked down at the floor of the porch.

"I'm sorry," I said, beginning to have an inkling of what this might be about. "Are you – you are Anne, yes, you must be Anne Agate."

As I said the words I saw that this was indeed Peter's oldest sister. When I'd left Miching – when I'd run away from the village – she'd been a girl. Now she was a young woman.

"Who are you?" she said, between choked-back tears.

For an instant I considered calling myself Topcourt – my incognito, the name that I'd doled out occasionally on my journey – but what would be the point of that? If I couldn't play myself in my own village there was no hope left for me.

"Revill, Nicholas Revill."

"Is it?" she said, glancing up with brimming eyes, and as if doubting my own identity.

"Yes."

"He that was the parson's son from Miching?"

I nodded.

"I remember you now. You are changed, a little."

"You are greatly changed . . . Anne."

"You wrote a letter to us from London."

"With bad news in it. I am very sorry I had to write it."

She brushed at her eyes and, through the tears, came a watery half-smile.

"You said kind things. In among the – the horrors you said kind things."

"Peter was a good friend."

"You were a good friend to my brother."

"Not good enough."

"You saw him at the end."

"Almost," I said, not wanting to enlarge on that final scene in Dead Man's Place.

"Now you have come from London to see us?"

"I have been on the road these many days."

"Then you are welcome," she said, standing to one side.

As I entered through the front door of Quint House, Anne Agate almost fell against me and we embraced without thought, in shared grief for her brother. My own eyes were full by now. We were standing in the lobby, which opened into a large panelled hall such as you often find in these old-fashioned country houses. Abruptly Anne pulled away from me. Standing in a doorway on the far side of the great hall were a man and a woman, watching us.

I was able to identify the woman straightaway from Peter's description. She was dressed in showy black and her cheeks were a hectic red. This must be Gertrude Agate. The man standing in the shadows behind her was a serious-looking fellow, not Anthony Agate but seemingly many years younger. Presumably this was Ralph Verney, whoever he might be.

"Who is your friend, Anne?" said the woman. "Tell me now please."

"Not mine but a friend of Peter's," said the girl.

"Nicholas Revill, madam," I said, making a little dip with my head. "I used to live in this village. I am a player from London."

"Revill?" said Mrs Agate, squinting towards me. She came closer, inspecting. Looked me up and down. "It was you that wrote us about my stepson."

"I profoundly regret that I had to be the one to convey the news," I said.

I felt awkward.

"What are you doing here?" she said.

"I have come to pay my condolences in person. I am only passing through."

Not altogether true, but not altogether untrue either. Mrs Gertrude Agate, however, didn't look impressed or pleased and, after another glance up and down, she stepped back.

Fortunately, the man in the doorway chose this moment to come forward. He was also wearing black, set off by a small white ruff. It was then that I put two or three things together – this gentleman's grave demeanour and sober dress, his presence in this house of mourning, the talk of a monument (presumably a church monument for Peter). I realized that I was looking at my father's replacement. Life had indeed returned to Miching: smoke rose from its chimneys, dogs barked in its streets, and there was a priest back in the pulpit. It was probably he who I'd seen coming through the lych-gate of the church.

"I believe I am the son of your – your predecessor," I said, moving forward with my hand extended.

"I hope that you know who you are, sir," said this clerical gentleman.

His innocent joke was a little too near the truth, but he meant nothing by it. Ralph Verney introduced himself. We shook hands. He had an open, candid gaze. Anne Agate watched with approval. Close to, Verney looked youthful enough, even though I don't suppose he was more than a year or two older than I was. But when I thought of the minister of Miching, of course I thought of my father, earnest, reverend, a little frightening. Essentially an old man – to a boy or a young man's eyes. So anybody else would be a mere youth in comparison.

"I have heard of you, Master Revill – but I have heard rather more of your father."

"Much more, I hope," I said.

"He had a proper care of this parish."

Thinking of the way my father had returned to tend to its dying members, and so exposed himself to pestilence and death, I could only bow my head in agreement.

At this point, there was a loud coughing from Mistress Gertrude.

"We have not yet finished our discussion, Ralph, over the best way to commemorate the dear departed," she said.

I seemed to hear a kind of sneer in her words. I thought it was an unfeeling way to refer to a stepson, even if one who had, no doubt, displeased her by rejecting her advances. I remembered Peter's description of her, the shudder of horror he'd given. I noted also the familiarity with which Gertrude Agate addressed Verney, her use of his first name – well, parson or no parson, she was old enough to be his mother, I suppose. He was quite handsome too, and so might be at risk. From the very slight frown that crossed Parson Verney's face, I judged that he'd noted the familiarity too but was sufficiently in control of his features not to let it show much.

"Excuse me, madam," I said. "I did not mean to interrupt you."

Ralph Verney turned towards Gertrude Agate. Before she could draw him back into the room off the great hall, I said, "I ask your pardon again, Mrs Agate, but I would like to see your husband."

To my surprise, Gertrude Agate stopped in her tracks, turned round and almost seemed to smirk.

"Why?"

"To pay my respects to him."

"You will have a task in hand," she said.

"I will not detain him for more than a few minutes."

Then I shall be on my way, I thought, there's nothing more for me in this house.

"He'll wait," said Mrs Agate. She seemed to be enjoying my uncertainty.

I noticed Anne Agate looking distressed, her face beginning to crumple up once more. As for Ralph Verney, he wore an expression of discomfort which he wasn't bothering to hide.

"Anthony Agate is dead," the parson said finally.

"My husband has been dead this long month," said the ungrieving widow.

"My father is dead," said Anne Agate.

Exeunt

So the story that I'd spun when travelling westwards in the guise of William Topcourt – that I was hurrying back home because of my father's death – contained a kind of truth, after all. Only it was the father of Peter Agate who had died, rather than Topcourt's supposed sire. The monument which Anthony's widow and the parson were discussing was to the father and not – as I'd thought – to the son. For old Anthony Agate had perished not long after my friend quit his home for London. When Peter turned up on my doorstep, and as far as he was concerned, the old man was still alive and still breathing fire and brimstone over his son's intention to become a stage-player. I wondered that no one had thought to inform Peter of his bereavement and then remembered that no one knew where to find him. The first news that the Agate family received about their son and brother was in my letter, the one telling them of his brutal murder. It was a double blow, the mysterious death of the only son coming hard on the heels of the father's demise.

There was no mystery about Anthony's departure from this world. He had caught a fever in October. At first they'd thought he'd recover. The moment of crisis had come and gone. He had dined on rabbit stew. He was sitting up in bed in his chamber on the last day of the month. The autumn fruit from the orchard had been carried up by the gardeners for his inspection. Trays of quince (after which Quint House was named, I think). Baskets of crab apples and peaches and medlars, that fruit which grosser folk call 'open-arse' on account of its appearance. But Anthony Agate had no appetite for any of this produce of his garden and merely picked at a bunch of grapes. The grapes were the last thing he ate. He had an unexpected relapse as the sun went down and expired at the low hour of three in the morning. Ralph Verney had been summoned at the end. The parson was newly arrived in Miching. After my father's death the requirement had fallen once more on the lord of the manor to bestow the living of Miching. But, since most of the village was dead, it was no very urgent requirement. The pulpit stayed empty like the church. Eventually Anthony Agate had settled on Ralph Verney. Neither man could have known that what was only their second or third meeting would take place at the death-bed of one of them.

I got these details and others besides from Anne Agate. Whatever the discomfort, even the fear which she and her sisters might have felt in the presence of their father, everything was swallowed up in genuine grief for him. Within the space of a couple of years, the three sisters – Anne and Margaret and little Katie – had lost their mother, their father and their brother. The plague has often commissioned his twin, that rascal death, to cut wide swathes through a single family. Indeed the pair take a delight in cutting down every human stalk in a bunch except one, so that the survivor's ragged solitude looks like mockery. But there seemed an especial cruelty to the fact that the Agates had been spared the fate of the rest of Miching village only for some of them to fall under the rascal's scythe shortly afterwards.

What must have made life more difficult for the surviving sisters was their new mother. Their parents had both been whisked away by death, and so had their brother. In their place was this . . . this harpy. I'd seen something of Mistress Agate at our first encounter in Quint House and saw a little bit more of her a little later in the story. She had a round red face, gappy teeth (yes, I know what that signifies), a wandering eye and a moist palm (and what that signifies too). Instinctively, instantly, I believed what Peter had said about her. She was hot-livered, loose in the hilts. Yet it couldn't be denied that – for all her harpiness – there was a certain attraction to the idea of Mistress Agate getting her claws into you. You might enjoy being gripped by her, having her hot breath panting on your face, her reddened cheek rubbing against yours. And she left you in no doubt that she would grip, pant and rub. And you would enjoy it, probably, and be shame-faced about it afterwards, probably.

Anyway, that was the bed-trick she'd played with Anthony Agate, and had tried to play with Peter.

But now her husband and her stepson were dead. If Gertrude Agate had ever been prepared to shed tears for her husband's death they were all dried up now. I doubted she did shed any except for form's sake on the way to the churchyard. Erecting a monument was a different matter. That was a reflection of her importance in Miching. As for her attitude towards her stepdaughters, that could be described as – what had Peter's word been again? – *attentive*, but without any real warmth to it. The warmth that Mistress Agate gave off was a different kettle of fish. Well, why should she care for three young women? They weren't hers. But the odd thing was that she did seem to mind about them. Or at least to want to keep them close and in sight, particularly Anne. Perhaps she saw the oldest daughter as a rival. I remembered the way she had demanded, sharply, who I was while we were standing in the great hall. But again, why shouldn't she? She was the mistress of the house now.

Although I had considered moving on from Miching almost as soon as I'd arrived at Quint House, I was induced to stay by the kindness of Ralph Verney. He invited me to spend some time in the parsonage. It was my old home. It's difficult to convey how strange and unsettling I found it to enter those old, dark rooms once more. Rooms where my father had read and studied and written his sermons, where he'd held court, settled disputes, dispensed advice and delivered admonitions, while in the kingdom of the kitchen my mother kept just as tight a rein over the household accounts and the single slattern called Susan who worked under her. Despite being larger than any of the other dwellings in the village, the parsonage was not a grand house, certainly not in comparison to the Agate residence. Yet when I dwelt there with my father and mother, it had seemed the centre of the world. Or rather one of the poles of that world, the other being Quint House.

As I've said, Ralph Verney was new to the parish. Indeed, the parish of Miching was in some sense new to itself, since the village had almost tumbled wholesale into the pit and had only lately started to drag itself out again. Even so, I was surprised by how *normal* daily life seemed to be. Towards the end of November things were bound to be quiet and a touch dreary, and there was that sense of shutting up shop for winter. But there was also hay in the barn, just as there were sheep in the pen and cheese in the loft and ale in the tub and bacon hanging from the rafters. The surviving villagers had clothes on their backs and thatches over their heads.

There were many gaps in the neighbourhood but some of them had been filled – with incomers who were related to those families which had perished, and with other incomers who had no prior connection at all with Miching but who knew how cheap land and property could be in the aftermath of the plague. And there seemed to be a lot of little children and babies about the place. The parson told me he'd baptized three in the previous month alone.

Ralph Verney himself was unmarried. The slattern – whom (I regret to say) my mother had somewhat tyrannized over in the kitchen – had shared in the general fate. To attend to his domestic needs, Verney kept an ageing widow woman who originated from a village over the next hill or two. Mrs

Hobbs presented no danger to him, marital or otherwise, in my opinion. She was a decent woman, clucking and motherly. She spoke a broad Mummerset that wouldn't have been believed on stage, and was inclined to make oracular but meaningless pronouncements like, "An chud ha' bin zwaggered out of my life, 'twould not ha' bin zo long as 'tis by a vortnight." Most of the time I could follow her – this was my own country after all. The rest of the time I nodded in agreement at whatever she said. I think Mrs Hobbs rather enjoyed having two young men to fuss over in the parsonage.

Among the survivors was John, my father's sexton. A tall, bony man, he'd always looked to my child's eyes like a walking skeleton. He was a kind man, no death's-head. But his daily proximity to death – among his other duties as sexton, he dug the graves in the churchyard and tolled the mourning bell in the belfry – seemed to have inoculated him against the old rascal. He'd survived the plague. He was as taken aback to see me as I was to see him. My last glimpse of him had been as he was sitting above the village, instructed by my father to stop any traveller going down into that plague-stricken place. I'd ignored his strenuous warnings of course, but it was typical of John that he should have been so determined to carry out my father's final commands. And now John was as devoted to Ralph Verney as he had been to my father.

I'd also taken to Parson Verney from the moment I'd clapped eyes on him at Quint House. He had a dry manner which concealed a certain shyness. He didn't ride around on a high horse – literally or metaphorically – but on a modest cob. He talked easily to the villagers, without condescending and without showing a pride or consciousness that he wasn't condescending to them. And he was more considerate towards Mrs Hobbs than my mother would ever have been. I wondered how long he'd stay in Miching and whether he'd seek out another living, particularly after the unexpected death of his patron. My father had passed his whole life in the one village, but he was an old-style parson and Ralph was young and probably ambitious. Maybe I saw a little of myself in him. My one-time self, that is.

It was generous of him to invite me to stay in the parsonage, when I might have been about as welcome as the cuckoo in the nest. For one thing, this enabled me to put off a decision on what to do – or rather where to go – next. I'd come back to Miching because it seemed as though the solution might lie here. The idea had jumped into my head as I stood talking to Lucy Milford in the Southwark street. But what solution? Or the solution to what? In reality I was simply running away from my troubles. Returning to the only place I knew, like a wounded dog crawling back to its kennel. Now it seemed as though I had no choice but to run on.

My old life, my old self, was well and truly dead. In fact, when they found out who I was, the handful of villagers who'd survived from my father's time, including John the sexton, were as surprised to see me as if I'd returned from the dead like Lazarus. But my state was not so healthy or hopeful as Lazarus's. I was a fugitive from justice, an escaper from the Counter prison, a man with the suspicion of three murders hanging over his head. Running away in the first place was an admission of guilt.

Several times I woke in the night, woke several times every night, and waited for the bleakness, the hopelessness of my situation to rush over me like a black wave. Then I would tell myself that at least I was still alive and free, not dangling from Tyburn tree to be pecked at by the kites. I would tell myself that I was back in my home village, for the time being among friendly people. And that would make me think of the true friends I had lost, like Peter Agate, like Nell . . . and so the black wave would sweep over me once more.

Several times I almost confessed everything to Ralph Verney, told him of my predicament, threw myself on his mercy. If he wanted to send for the nearest magistrate once he'd heard my story, well, perhaps that would be for the best. But I held my tongue. Oddly, I thought that he might not believe me, and would consider me mad rather than judging me guilty or innocent. And if Verney was wondering about my absence from London, he didn't show it. Maybe he knew better than to wonder. Anyone who is at all familiar with the life of a player knows that it is about as secure as quicksand. No, less secure than quicksand. Prolonged absences from work, enforced resting between engagements – for the player this is business as usual.

The other person who seemed to welcome my arrival in Miching was Anne Agate. I saw now what I hadn't noticed at that first encounter on the doorstep of Quint House, her resemblance to Peter. Not so much in looks – although she had his handsomeness in a female form – but in her good-hearted seriousness. Yet she wasn't altogether earnest. Sometimes she'd smile and laugh, and then she'd remember that she had lately lost a father and a brother and look sad again. I saw a little of her and liked her a lot. But no more than that . . . if that's the direction your thoughts are tending in.

From Mistress Gertrude Agate, formerly Potts, the grieving widow, I had a different kind of reception after the comparative frostiness of our first meeting. I'd encountered her a couple of times since and come to those personal conclusions about her which you've already been treated to. I felt her moist palm close over my hand more than once. Sensed her roving eye linger awhile on my fine form. Picked up more than a compliment or two directed at me through those gappy teeth. She was forward in compliment. I couldn't quite work out the reason for the change in her from suspicion to warmth. Perhaps she was merely struck by the appearance of a handsome young player – her words, not mine. But my pulse didn't race faster, or not much faster anyway, although she did make me feel uneasy. But even though she retained certain qualities, she was old enough to be my mother, old enough to be everybody's mother. (And I remembered that she had been Peter's mother or stepmother, briefly, and had attempted to seduce him.) It would have been a mistake, however, to dismiss her as a ramping widow, all hot and lonesome in her bed even while her husband was scarcely cold below ground. There was more to her than that.

One afternoon a little more than ten days or so after my arrival in Miching I was up at Quint House for the last time. I had decided to leave the village the next morning. There was nothing more for me here. To leave and go on the road and let it lead me where it would. To become a counterfeit crank like Abel Glaze and earn fourteen and threepence halfpenny during a single day in Reading . . . to lose myself in the wilds of Wales . . . to take ship from Bristol or Plymouth . . . There were many shapes to the future, none of them very enticing.

The afternoon was fine and calm, a moment such as you sometimes enjoy just before winter's onset. Anne Agate had given me a prayer-book which belonged to her brother, in memory of him. It was small and portable. I would carry it on my travels. We kissed chastely and I left her, having already said goodbye to her younger sisters. I was making my way along a border which was interrupted by stone urns and sombre yews. Round the corner was a raised, gently curving walk which overlooked the orchard. Here grew peaches, apples, medlars, and other fruit besides, as well as the quinces which gave to the Agate house its name. Now the branches were all bare and the ground muddy and unkempt. But the sky was blue while the air was unexpectedly soft. At the end of the walk I paused to admire the scene.

"Master Revill."

I recognized Gertrude Agate's voice. She must have seen me coming when I was at the far end of the curved walk. Partly hidden from sight, she was sitting inside a stone pavilion which gave a view across the orchard and then further over the fields and hills to the west. A deep red creeper clambered its withered way over the stonework of the pavilion. All I could see of the lady of the house were her silk-stockinged legs stretched out in the autumn sun and her hands languidly cradling a pear. I moved round and stood in her light. She was sitting on a cushion on a stone bench. There was a table beside her and a pewter plate loaded with pears, together with a little paring-knife which glinted in the sun. Also on the table was a hat with a veil attached and a pair of embroidered gloves of dark velvet. A jug of wine and a nearly drained glass stood nearby.

"Mrs Agate. I have come to say farewell."

I hadn't intended to say farewell to her. Hadn't thought to see her again, in fact. But the courtesy cost nothing. An unfathomable look passed over her face.

"You catch me enjoying my fruit," she said, looking at me with an expression I couldn't decipher. Since her hat and veil were on the table, her hair was free and exposed. It was still a coppery colour, and in its day must have been a fiery sight.

"A fine crop," I said, glancing at the loaded platter.

"You wish to share my crop?"

I smiled awkwardly. Mrs Agate made me feel awkward, and she knew it.

"So you are returning to London?" she said.

"No, not London. My fortunes don't lie there any longer."

"A pity. London is a fine place for a young man, full of opportunities."

Not if you're a fugitive from the law, it isn't, I thought.

"I dare say you're right, Mrs Agate."

"Where are you going then?"

I glanced over my shoulder in the direction of the declining sun. Was that where I was going? I didn't know.

"I – I don't know," I said.

"A handsome young man like you will make his own fortune. Or take his fortune where he finds it."

As she said this she leaned forward. She was wearing mourning, of course, but it was mourning cut to her advantage. That is, low-cut. Between her breasts she clutched the pear.

"As to my fortune, I'm about to find out," I said.

"Perhaps you are going off to preach?"

"Preach? Oh no, not me."

She was looking at the prayer-book which Anne had given me and which I was still holding. I moved to one side and put the prayer-book on the table near her gloves. Sacred and profane.

"It belonged to Peter."

She squinted against the sun.

"Was my stepson a pious boy? He seemed so to me. You were his friend."

"Pious enough," I said.

"Some say that religion is a toy," she said.

I was taken aback to hear such a – well, a masculine – sentiment in the mouth of a woman.

"Ralph Verney would be surprised and sorry to hear you say so," I said.

"But the parson is not here to hear it. And it is *you* who are surprised and sorry."

I shrugged and she patted the space next to her on the bench as a sign that I should sit. I sat, half reluctantly. The seat was warm from the sun. Accidentally or otherwise (I am sure it was otherwise), her flank snugged against mine after a moment.

"I only said that, Nicholas Revill, to see its effect on you."

"Are you satisfied now?"

"We shall see. You would like some wine?"

"I – no, I do not have a strong head."

She looked amused. She neatly quartered the pear, licked her fingers and, spitting a segment on the paring-knife, held it up before me. I plucked the fruit from the tip of the knife and put it in my mouth. The taste was a small, sweet shock. Mrs Agate put another quarter between her own lips.

"You forbid yourself wine but not fruit," she said. "No forbidden fruit."

I smiled, almost despite myself. She was a quick-witted woman, no doubt about it.

"Will you not stay another day or two?"

Now she laid a hand on my thigh. I felt the warmth of it through my leggings. I concentrated on savouring the last shreds of the fruit.

"Is it good?"

She meant the pear (although of course she also meant the other thing).

"Ripe," I said.

"Ripest is best," said this middle-aged widow.

"Provided it is not too long stored."

"There is someone I should like you to meet," she said, ignoring my last remark. She licked pear juice from her lips and caught a little dribble with the other hand as it made its way down her large chin. Then she reached out and slurped the dregs from the wine glass.

Her resting hand advanced slightly up my thigh. I stayed still. It was not – absolutely unpleasant.

"Who do you want me to meet?"

"My son."

"Peter? But he is – "

"Not him. I have a proper son."

I remembered that Peter had mentioned this, that she already had a son.

"Where is he? Is he here?"

"He is not come yet but he will be here soon. Won't you stay?"

"I cannot stay, Mrs Agate."

"Don't you usually obey a lady's requests?"

Now the hand squeezed. In promise, in warning. I said nothing.

"Why are you leaving, Nicholas? Are you in trouble, Nicholas? You are, aren't you? Tell me."

I was within an inch of spilling out my story. But instead I got abruptly to my feet. I grabbed the prayer-book from the table and in doing so dislodged the pewter plate with the fruit and the gloves. The wine jug swayed precariously but stayed upright. The pewter fell with a clatter, the pears rolled across the stone floor of the pavilion. Confused and red in the face, I scrabbled to pick them up from the ground. Gertrude Agate looked on in amusement. I restored the objects to the table. I brushed at the dark velvet gloves to clean them of dust. The gloves gave off a musky odour. The nap on them was like the nap on a peach. I handed the gloves back to their owner.

She let the gloves dangle from her juice-sticky fingers and made as if to give them back to me.

"You should really consider staying."

"No, I am decided. I shall leave at first light tomorrow."

"Then take your prayer-book if you like, Nicholas, but won't you also take one of these gloves? They are perfumed. Smell it and think of me. You could keep it under your pillow."

"Thank you – I – no – "

And I backed away from the pavilion and almost ran down the path that curved round the late Anthony Agate's orchard.

It took me some time to recover from my meeting with the late Anthony Agate's widow. Like Hamlet's mother, this Gertrude was still fresh in mourning and fresh in other ways too. I wasn't sure whether she had been trying to seduce me or tease me, or both. Was this how she had approached Peter? Probably. He'd said it was one of the reasons why he'd hastily departed from Quint House. Not only disgust but also fear that he might succumb to his stepmother.

I wondered why she wanted me to meet her son.

I wondered lots of things.

For the widow's gesture, in attempting to get me to take one of her musky velvet gloves as a keepsake, sparked off a train of ideas, although not ones directly connected with that loose lady. I thought back to the Chamberlain's performance of *Troilus and Cressida* in Middle Temple, and of how I had exchanged a doublet sleeve for a glove. Of how I'd frozen at that moment so that young Peter Pearce had been left exposed in the full glare of candlelight with hundreds of spectators waiting for our next moves, my next move. I thought of how the doublet sleeve had vanished from Bartholomew Ridd's stock, or had never been returned to it, in order that it might be wickedly used to stifle the life out of Nell. And I remembered the glove, Cressida's glove.

After that I moved on to consider that second and final interview with Coroner Talbot, the time when I'd been escorted by Gog and Magog from the Counter prison to the coroner's house in Long Southwark and questioned over Nell's death. He'd asked me about the sleeve – *and the glove*. We'd gone through the scene when the lovers parted, almost as if he were Burbage instructing the players. What had Talbot said exactly? I struggled to fasten down his words. Something like – no, very like – "You give the sleeve to Peter Pearce, who gives you a glove in return." And then adding casually, "What did you do with that glove by the way?"

I'd known that there was something odd about the question at the time but hadn't quite been able to put my finger on it. Now I could. It wasn't that Talbot was curious about the stage transaction. That was just part of his investigation into the murder of Nell, the effort to trace the 'progress' of the Troilus sleeve. No, it was a different question which occurred to me now: how had Talbot known about the glove in the first place? How had he known that I (or Troilus) had taken a glove in exchange for Cressida's taking a sleeve?

Either I had told him – or he had been watching the play.

Once more I struggled to recall the detail of that fraught interview. *Had* I told him? I didn't think so. I've a good memory – always useful in cases like this. And, anyway, why should I inform him of some piece of stage business? He'd been the one who was interested, not me. While he was questioning me, I'd been sunk in despondency, dejected and indifferent about detail.

And so it followed, almost certainly, that he *had* seen the play, had been present at the one and only performance of *Troilus and Cressida*. Well, why not? There was a bunch of legal high-ups sitting at the back of the Middle Temple banqueting-hall, comfortably installed underneath the great bank of portraits. The crown of the legal profession was there. Justices, benchers, serjeants-at-law – and coroners. Hadn't I been aware of that at the time? Perhaps, at some level, I'd even noticed that Talbot himself was there.

Steady, steady, I told myself. Think clearly.

So what if the coroner had been present at the performance? Why not? There was nothing odd or sinister in his presence in Middle Temple. I hoped that he'd enjoyed the performance. The only strange aspect to the matter was why he hadn't told me he'd been there. Why, when he was questioning me in Long Southwark, he hadn't saved time and trouble by simply saying, "I was there. I saw you exchange sleeve and glove with the boy-player." Perhaps he wanted to hear my version of the story. After all, justice was important to him. He'd said so often enough. And justice depends on facts.

Facts, Nicholas, facts.

Well. What did I know for a fact about Alan Talbot? That he was hostile enough towards us players. He'd made some disparaging comments about our frivolous treatment of some subjects. When he'd shown me the daily view from his staircase window, the severed heads of traitors displayed at the end of London Bridge, he seemed to be drawing a contrast between the authentic penalties of the law and the sensational, make-believe retribution which often takes place on a stage. And through my mind had flashed the ludicrous antics which occurred in Richard Milford's *The World's Diseas'd*. But you would not claim there was anything unusual in Coroner Talbot's attitude, not for someone in his position of authority.

Nothing unusual either in his coldness towards the other habits of Londoners. "Do you players often visit whores?" he'd asked me, well knowing the answer. He'd called it a vice. If it was a vice it was a general one. Many people practised it, both as buyers and providers. But that's no defence of whoring, he'd no doubt say. Sin shared is not sin halved.

What if it was *his* vice as well, his sin? The righteous man, or the one who makes a show of his righteousness, often has something to hide. It may be so in life. It certainly is on stage. The upright judge, the wealthy merchant, the proud king, all of them have secrets to hide in the playhouse – if they didn't have secrets there would be no future for them, no disaster in the wings, no disgrace crouching underfoot.

At this point I naturally thought of Nell and of her hidden admirer, her secret paramour. This unnamed being was a lawyer. She'd as good as told me that he was a lawyer. I'd been assuming that he must be one of the students from the Inns of Court, someone young and energetic like cocky Michael Pye. In fact, I'd pretty well settled on Pye as my rival. But a coroner may also be called a lawyer. Nell could well have put herself under the protection of an older man. The more I thought about it the more convinced I became that that was what she would do, would have done. Why go with youth? They have energy but they lack almost everything else that matters, like money. And I knew that Nell was growing dissatisfied with her situation at Holland's Leaguer. A mere player was no longer good enough for her. What better than a man like Talbot, powerful, established, well-to-do.

Coroner Alan Talbot lived close enough to Holland's Leaguer. That was no proof of anything. Most of Southwark was close to one stew or another. And anyway you'd be unlikely to uncover him as a regular customer, even if he was one. The establishment was discreet, under the direction of Bess Barton. And, besides, Talbot had said himself that its occupants made unreliable witnesses. Just as he'd said that a brothel must have many irregular exits. Well, I suppose that you didn't have to know the inside of a brothel to know that. Still, it was all . . . highly suggestive.

Talbot's house in Long Southwark was convenient not merely for the brothel, where Nell had been surprised and strangled. It was also close to my own lodgings in Dead Man's Place, where Peter Agate had been surprised and stabbed. And close to the Bridge which offered the quickest route to the other side of the river. To Thames Street, for example, where Richard Milford had been surprised and stabbed.

So – beginning with a glove and ending with three murders – I built up my own indictment against Coroner Talbot, just as he had tried to indict me for those same murders. And his persecution of me made sense too, because if I could be held to account for them then Talbot would not only have diverted suspicion from himself, he would also have disposed of a troublesome player. One less of the frivolous tribe to corrupt and distract the world.

There remained the little matter of motive.

And a little more thinking provided one.

Evidently justice had gone to Talbot's head and infected his brain. He was embarked on a crusade to clean up London by ridding it of players and playwrights and whores. One of each: Agate, Milford, and Nell. I remembered the fervour in his eyes. A hard, impatient man. Justice took too long. It demanded the wearisome fact of a crime before the offender could be hanged. Why not skip the tedious process and go straight to the gallows? It was like jumping over the first four acts of a play, so that you get straight to the good bits, the fights and the punishment and retribution.

These thoughts and suppositions occupied me during my final night in Miching. I'd told Ralph Verney that I was leaving and he had generously pressed me to stay, although in a different style to Gertrude Agate. But no, I said, I must get back. And as soon as I'd said this, I realized that I was not going to travel westwards in the direction of the setting sun, not going to take ship at Bristol or Plymouth, or lose myself in the Welsh marches. No, I was returning to London, returning to face Coroner Alan Talbot, returning to obtain justice once and for all.

I'd no idea how I was going to accomplish any of this. But during that last night I lay sleepless in my bed in the parsonage, imagining myself confronting Coroner Talbot with the evidence of his wrongdoing. Or – since the evidence was rather thin – I would confront him with my conviction that he was the villain of the piece. Then he would start, like a guilty thing surprised. He was bound to start. Murder will out, they say. Truth will out. Those were his own words.

I rose early, before first light, and hastily made preparations for my departure. Not much preparation was required since all the baggage I carried was, essentially, myself. My purse still had a little money in it. Probably not enough to get me back to London. Well, I'd have to trust to providence for that. And I still had William Topcourt's woollen topcoat. I made a vow to restore it to him, travel-stained as it was. I hoped the poor fellow was safe in the Counter prison, safe from his wives, safe from being strung up under the name of Revill.

Mrs Hobbs, Verney's housekeeper, provided me with porridge and concerned words – most of which I could follow – and generally clucked about in her motherly way. Ralph himself was at the church. The seven o'clock service would be almost over by now. I took one final glance around the place where I had lived for so many years then opened the front door

And slammed it shut again.

It wasn't yet fully light but I had seen, clearly enough, a man in a hat, a feathered hat, a man coming up the path towards the door of the parsonage. It was the very man who had been occupying so many of my thoughts: Coroner Alan Talbot!

I didn't stop to consider what he was doing here in a Somerset village, many miles distant from Southwark. (Although if I had, the answer would have been obvious enough. He was looking for me.) I didn't stop to confront the man whom I'd been convicting, in my head, of a string of murders and from whom I had dreamed of extracting a confession.

Instead, instinct took over. I ran.

I ran past a startled Mrs Hobbs and exited the house by a door which opened off the kitchen. Even as I scrambled to get out of the back door I heard a thunderous knocking at the front.

There was a muddy track which led directly from the rear of the parsonage to the church, and which was out of sight of the front of the house. I hared along the track, wrenched open the rusted gate which gave on to the graveyard and took shelter behind the nearest headstone. Mindlessly I took note of the name on the stone – it was Thomas Wilkins, from one of the village families – while I tried to regain some control over myself.

I had thought myself safe from pursuit. But not so. Here was Coroner Talbot, like an avenging angel in a feathered hat, striding up the front path of my old home in order to seize hold of the fugitive from justice. How had he discovered my hiding place? For a moment I credited him with some supernatural powers. From over the churchyard wall I heard voices. I recognized Talbot's voice and the local tones of Mrs Hobbs. I couldn't hear what they were saying and it may be that he was having some difficulty grasping her Mummerset. But there could only be one topic of conversation. The coroner would be enquiring after the whereabouts of N. Revill while the housekeeper, once she'd understood who he was looking for, would surely explain that I'd just rushed through the back door. "Chid niver zeen anythin' like 'ee, zur." Or she could simply point to the direction I'd gone in. I couldn't rely on their mutual incomprehension lasting long.

From inside the church came the thin sound of singing. Not many people there, judging by the muted noise. The day was dawning in full colour but dull and bleary for all that. Some ancient idea of sanctuary came to me. I rose from my crouching position behind T. Wilkins's headstone and made for the west end of the church which was graced with a tower, the highest structure in Miching. The west door was ajar as was the inner door leading off from the porch. Now the whisper of the litany had replaced the ragged singing at the far end. I recognized Ralph Verney's voice. Immediately inside the porch was a small postern-like door which, I knew, opened on to a spiral staircase. The staircase ran up inside a turret that clung to the tower like a thumb. There were two exit-points from the staircase. One gave on to the belfry and then, on the upper level, the second exit emerged on to the roof of the tower.

I'd spent a lot of time at the top of the tower as a boy. There was a flat roof, guarded by little battlements, which had served as my castle on summer afternoons. A very satisfactory castle, almost a kingdom. I doubted any king ever felt prouder or more secure and powerful. The lead of the roof was warm on bare legs, too. Now, many years later, I tugged at the little door to the turret. It wasn't locked, as I knew it wouldn't be. It creaked in the way that I remembered, like a snatch from a reedy old tune. The stone stairs spiralled up into the dimness. Quickly I eased through the door, pulling it fast behind me and shutting out the faint sounds of worship. For an instant I stood in almost total darkness, breathing in the familiar smell of dank stone.

Then I began to climb, sliding my hands over the ashlar walls. Every now and then the outer wall was interrupted by narrow apertures like loop-holes. I passed the entry to the belfry, where hung the great bells which summoned the village to mourn and celebrate and pray. At the top of the stairs was the second door. Recalling that it opened inwards I groped for the handle and tugged at it. No movement.

I pulled harder, without success. For a moment I thought I'd have to creep back down the spiral staircase and find myself another hiding-place, and then I pushed at the door instead of pulling and it opened straightaway. Our memories are strange, slippery things. I'd used that entrance on innumerable occasions. How could I have remembered the creak of the door at the base of the tower yet have forgotten which way the one at the top opened?

I came out on the lead-lined roof of the tower. This morning the lead looked cold and massy. It was slick with dew. The wind – there was always a wind up here even though it might be still as death down in the churchyard – blew a few flecks of rain in my face. There was no shelter on the roof, only the little box-like place in the corner where the stairs emerged and which you had to crouch to come through. I walked across to the parapet and surveyed the scene.

Everything seemed to come to a pause. What now?

The neatly disposed headstones down below were like the pieces in a board game. A game whose rules I didn't understand. As a boy, though, they hadn't troubled me, those headstones. I was more interested in the long view. From the highpoint of the church tower I had kept watch for my enemies while they were massing on the Somerset hills. The wind rustled through the churchyard trees and it was the breath of approaching armies. As long as I stayed on the top of the tower I was safe. Sometimes Peter Agate and I had hidden up here together.

Now I saw a man below advancing towards the base of the tower at the same side I'd come in by. He stopped by the west door. He was all small, reduced to his hat and his shoulders. He looked like a beetle. It was Talbot, I recognized him by the feather in his hat. I could have dropped a stone on him, if there'd been a large stone to hand and if he hadn't looked up while I was doing it (I don't think I could have dropped a stone on to his bare, upturned face). I would have watched him writhe his way to death. But there was no handy stone and he disappeared into the tower, through the west door. I waited, hoping I'd firmly closed the postern-door at the base of the turret. I'd left the top one half open, so that I might hear any mounting footsteps.

I visualized Talbot checking the small congregation in the church. No, there was no Revill there in among the good housewives and honest labourers. I imagined Talbot poking his nose into the side-chapels and behind the grander monuments. Shaking his head. Perhaps by now John the sexton had come up to ask what he wanted. A visitor at the early morning service was almost unprecedented. Particularly someone like Talbot, whose dress and bearing carried the stamp of authority. A legal gentleman from London. They would whisper urgently together. The sexton might be surprised to hear that the son of the old parson was a fugitive from justice, even more so to discover that I was a multiple murderer. Then John might recall that I'd been fond of hiding away at the top of the tower when I was a lad.

At that very instant I heard, from the roof of the tower, the creak of the door at the bottom of the turret. I don't know why it sounded so clear. Perhaps the circular stairwell magnified any noises. Then I heard the tread of feet mounting the steps, two sets of feet. I wondered if Jack was accompanying him. To me all the footsteps, no matter who they belonged to, were as inexorable as fate. There was no way out. I was trapped on the roof. If I hadn't been so foolish as to take refuge in a childish sanctuary I might have been halfway to the next village by now. But what would have been the point of that? Coroner Talbot, the nemesis with the feather in his cap, would pursue me to the ends of the earth – and certainly as far as the next village.

I gulped down my last draught of Somerset air. It was mild and gentle, or seemed so to me, for all that we were on the lip of winter and there was rain in the air. I turned about and stood with my back to the door that opened on to the roof, hands grasping the rough stone of the battlements, and gazed for the final time over the scenes of my boyhood. I heard two men moving faster as they reached the top of the stairs, heard them pause as they registered the presence of a figure leaning over the parapet, heard one of them step out on to the lead-lined tower roof. It cost me an effort not to look round.

Then came that familiar, cold voice.

The coroner's voice.

"This is the man I seek."

My mind in a whirl, I followed Alan Talbot up the sloping track which led to Quint House. There'd hardly been the time for him to explain things or, more accurately perhaps, hardly time for me to grasp them, or the great changes which had taken place over the last half-hour. Changes in my perception, that is.

It had indeed been John the sexton who'd suggested to Talbot that I might have taken refuge up in the church tower. Talbot had told him that it was most urgent that I should be found before I harmed myself. The coroner must have seen the panic on my face as I opened the door of the parsonage. I no longer felt panic-stricken. Just deeply confused.

But there was no opportunity for explanations at this stage. We had already reached the gate to Quint House and were striding up the flagged path to the front door. Talbot rapped loudly, with the force if not the majesty of the law. The door was opened by Anne Agate. I guessed, from what Talbot had told me, that she knew who he was. Scarcely troubling to greet her, he shouldered his way into the house. As he passed Anne I saw her gaze fasten on mine, and her eyes flick sideways.

Taking the hint, I didn't follow Talbot inside but took off around the flank of the house, retracing my steps of yesterday afternoon when I'd surprised Gertrude Agate in her little pavilion. Then it had been warm, the sun hanging like a coppery apple in the sky. Now it was overcast. Too late

I remembered that, because of the way the orchard path curved round, anyone sitting in the pavilion could see a visitor advancing from a distance.

As I drew closer to the pavilion I heard voices. A man and a woman's. A cautious instinct made me slow down, almost walk on tiptoe. They sounded preoccupied, too busy to notice anyone approaching. Within seconds I was standing by the withered red creeper which covered the pavilion. The conversation inside continued uninterrupted.

Something about the way I was standing – or rather stooping (because when you eavesdrop you crouch slightly) – reminded me of my part of Troilus in WS's play. The love-sick Troilus who, in the last act, goes on a delegation to the Greek camp, and there discovers the faithlessness of his lover Cressida. He eavesdrops on her when the Greek Diomedes whispers soft words of love in the night air. He sees her when Diomedes wheedles from her the gift – the sleeve of the doublet – which is not Cressida's to give, because Troilus has entrusted it to her together with his heart. Well, what I was overhearing now, standing outside the pavilion, was apparently a scene of love and devotion. It merely happened to be between a mother and her son, as I soon discovered. And it involved a sleeve – the Troilus sleeve – as I also soon discovered.

"Where did you get it?" said Gertrude Agate. And then before the other person could answer she said, "Is it . . . the one?"

There was no response except a little laugh or snort.

"Let me see it," said Gertrude. "Let me feel it. It is good cloth."

"Players have expensive clothes," said the other.

"Look at this gold work. How did you do it now?"

"One twist and a squeeze," said a voice I recognized but couldn't immediately put a face to. "Or a little more."

"A little more for a little whore," said Mrs Agate.

"A *quicumque vult*."

It took me a moment to realize that they were talking about Nell. And then I knew the identity of the man. I fitted the voice to a face. A round, red-headed face. I remembered that occasion in Middle Temple hall, when I'd first encountered the gaggle of law students, and when they'd exchanged humorous Latinisms describing whores.

"Is that one of your legal terms, dear?"

There was a slurping sound. Mrs Agate was drinking. I fervently hoped she would choke.

"Only a London term for a whore," said Edmund Jute. "She would never have done . . . "

"Done what, my dear?"

"Done for a gentleman. She was beginning to have ideas that she *would* do, but she wouldn't."

"Did you have her before . . . you know?"

"During," said Jute.

Mrs Agate sniggered. My fists clenched and I felt sick. A kind of red mist descended over my eyes for an instant.

"You didn't bring it away with you?"

What was 'it'?

Ah, of course, the sleeve.

The Troilus sleeve, which Jute had taken after the performance in Middle Temple hall and which he had used to strangle Nell.

"Coroner Talbot gave it to me," said Jute. "It was evidence in the case against the player but, since he is plainly guilty, it is no longer required."

"The coroner *gave* it you?" said Gertrude.

"Not 'gave' exactly. It would be better to say that I borrowed it from his cap-case at one of the inns."

"Naughty boy," she said, but full of admiration. "What if he had found out . . .?"

"Then it would easily be blamed on an ostler. They are dishonest, paltry fellows."

"You take risks, my darling."

"No risk when the coroner has it so firmly fixed in his

head that Revill is a murderer. A murderer several times over."

"He looks like a murderer," said Mrs Agate. "Haggard and shifty. But handsome in his way."

"Master Talbot talked of nothing else all the journey down," said Jute. "Revill's guilt, that is, not his handsomeness. He is consumed with fury at the way the player slipped through his fingers in London and determined that justice shall be done."

If a smirk was ever audible I reckoned that Gertrude Agate's was then.

"It is fortunate that I wrote to my boy to tell him of the wicked player's arrival," she said.

"Talbot already had an idea that Master Nicholas would return to his home village. But he was grateful when I informed him. And even more grateful when I offered to accompany him."

"To visit your mother?"

"And see my estate."

"Not yet."

"One day."

"May it be long in coming," she said.

"You should not wish yourself long life, mother."

"Why not?"

"You are tempting fate."

No reply, except a slurp from the wine glass.

"It is bad luck to wish yourself long life, I say," said Jute again.

I wondered at his insistence.

And then there was a long silence in this loving dialogue. When Gertrude Agate next spoke her tone was quite different. It was like the chill which descends after the sun goes behind a cloud. A glass shattered on the ground.

"What have you done?"

"It is rather what you have done. You taught me the way when you poisoned the old man. That was the beginning."

"It was for your sake, Edmund."

"So is this, for my sake."

"You could have waited."

The voice was growing weaker, wheezier.

"Oh wicked son," she wailed. It was like a line from a play.

"I could have waited," said Edmund Jute. His voice was remarkably even and untroubled. "But I have acquired a taste for it now. I have not yet told you about the playwright . . . "

No need to enquire what this particular 'it' was, the activity for which he had acquired a taste. And no reply from Gertrude Agate either – she was beyond enquiry – except a strangled cry and a strange noise as if she was tapping her feet.

"Spiced wine will hide a multitude of sins, mother."

There was a thump and a series of terrible retchings and groans, as if the damned had been permitted to speak. I stood round the corner, among the withered creeper, until the sounds became unbearable. Then I moved out into the open.

How can I describe the scene before me? How can I convey its horror? I did not sleep easy for many nights afterwards.

Edmund Jute – the red-haired law student, with the round innocent face – stood over the body of his mother as she writhed and flailed her last. She was on her back, purple and mottled in the face. Her eyes were wide and stary. She looked but did not see. Her clothing was disordered and vomit-stained, and one of her breasts was exposed. Her state was horrible enough. But more horrible, much more horrible, was the behaviour of her son. Having done his worst, he was now doing nothing. He was watching her, standing quite unmoved a little to one side. It flashed through my mind that he had probably watched the dying agonies of Peter Agate – and Richard Milford – and Nell – in the same detached spirit.

So absorbed was he in this dreadful scene of his own making that he did not become aware of my presence for an instant. Perhaps I cried out. Then Edmund Jute turned round and saw who it was, and saw that I knew his cold wickedness. We looked each other in the face and – this is most strange – I was ashamed for him, since he belonged to some distant branch of humanity and could not be ashamed for himself. And I was angry. And I don't know what else besides. Then Jute reached for the little paring-knife which still lay beside the platter of fruit on the table and swept through the air towards me.

Without thought, I raised my arm up to deflect him, and caught him a swinging blow on the side of the head. He must have already been off balance because the blow, not strong in itself, was sufficient to knock him to the ground. As he lay there, close to his dying mother, a red mist descended again in front of my eyes. It was blood, my own blood. His knife must have caught me after all, somewhere on the forehead. I wiped at the blood to clear it from my sight and fell on him and we tussled on the ground. I smelled on him that feral smell which I had smelled in the wake of the headless figure which had swept past me in Middle Temple and which I'd afterwards glimpsed in the corridors of Holland's Leaguer. It was a rank, vulpine scent. Ever afterwards when I smelled it – smelled it naturally, that is, in the open air – it made me think not of a fox, but of Jute and the scent he exuded when death and murder were in question.

We were down there on the flagged stonework of the pavilion for hours. It seemed hours. Yet in reality, it can only have been seconds. Jute kept trying to reach around with the little knife and gouge me in the back. Once again Master Topcourt's coat helped to protect me, and Jute was unable to gain a real purchase on me. And I kept batting his hand away and trying to catch hold of his stabbing wrist. His breath was hot in my face and his rank scent high in my nostrils. Then his mother, Gertrude, intervened. In her dying throes she made a rattling noise in her throat and her own arm swept out and knocked the knife from his grasp. There was more strength in that final blow than there was in both our hands.

The paring-knife fell on the stone and in an instant I had it in my grip and in another instant was burrowing away at the chest of the man who lay beneath me, like a dreadful lover.

It was a sharp-pointed, sharp-edged knife, for all that it was little.

Even so, it wasn't easy. I was shocked by the resistance which met the blade. Jute battered at me with his arms, and I was compelled to withdraw the blade and strike at him many times over. The knife seemed to tangle in his garments, and sometimes the blade skidded on some inner obstacle. But I suddenly knew that I would win. By main force and determination and cold anger, I knew that I would win. I grunted. I thought of Nell – no, I didn't think of her but felt her presence. I shouted. I remembered Peter Agate, my friend from Miching. I spoke. Doubtless I spoke. Spoke incomprehensible things. Edmund Jute made noises too as he breathed his last, with his mother beside him.

But he did breathe his last at last, and I rolled off him, exhausted.

Finis

"Did you kill him?"

"Yes."

"Are you sure, Nicholas?"

"Yes, I think so."

"But he might have fallen on his knife, his own knife?"

"I – it is possible, I suppose."

Only it hadn't happened like that.

I had no more than a blurred memory of those last few moments of my mortal engagement with Edmund Jute. But I was sure of one thing. That he had died at my hands, not his own. I would not have had it any other way. This wicked young lawyer had slaughtered my friends because they were in his way. And if anyone was justified in despatching him with a perfect conscience it was I. My conscience may have been clear – I tried to argue with myself that it was clear, I had killed Edmund Jute in self-defence – but that didn't prevent a single dream from pursuing me for a long time afterwards. In my dream I was struggling with Jute in a lead-lined cistern that was slowly filling with blood. I had to dispose of him before the blood rose over our heads, and put an end to both of us. I had a knife but so did he, and his knife was bigger than mine. In addition there was a cord dangling from his waist with which he could strangle me. We were both slick with blood and panting hard, and I was terrified of losing my footing and slipping beneath the rising tide of red. On every occasion I woke up, sweating and breathless, before this fight was concluded.

Jute might not have been on my conscience but he was still lodged in my head and it was many months before the dream faded. Alan Talbot, however, was determined to exonerate me of any blame in the death of Edmund Jute. I couldn't help reflecting on the irony of this, that after all the coroner's work in trying to pin on me the guilt for murders which I hadn't committed, he was now attempting to leave me free and clear.

By the time Talbot arrived on the scene in the pavilion the main action was finished. Gertrude Agate (or Jute, as she was by the first of her three husbands) was dead, poisoned by her own son. That same son was stretched out beside her on the ground, holed and stabbed. At a little distance lay Nicholas Revill, covered with blood. A shambles. At first sight, Talbot told me, he thought we were all dead. Then I groaned and stirred, and he was glad to see that something might be recovered from this ruin.

The coroner's attitude towards me had undergone a sea-change, even when he was still in London. He had ridden down to Miching not in pursuit of an escaped felon but in pursuit of the truth. When Jute – who had learned of my whereabouts in a letter from his mother – went to the coroner to inform against me and proposed that the two of them should travel to Somerset together, Talbot had seized the opportunity of keeping an eye on the man he had begun to suspect of the Southwark murders.

"How did you know?" I asked. "Why did you suspect Jute?"

We were travelling back to London, after matters had been sorted out in Miching – or sorted out so far as they could be after such a shocking tragedy (of which more in a moment). We travelled fast by horse, Talbot and I. The roads were stickier than when I'd walked this way about a fortnight earlier but they were still passable. I wasn't comfortable in the saddle but wanted to get back to London as quickly as possible.

Talbot already had his rented horse from the outward journey and I hired a sturdy hack from a stable in Wells, at the rate of a shilling for the first day and eightpence per day thereafter. Talbot loaned me the money, telling me that I could repay him when I resumed my position with the Chamberlain's Company. I didn't say that I wasn't certain I still had a position with the Chamberlain's. He also paid for my share of our lodgings. One of the places we stopped at was the Night Owl near Buckingham, the very inn which I had been too fearful to stay at during the early stages of my trudge out of London.

We kept company, Talbot and I, but it was an uneasy journey for me. I couldn't rid myself of my old image of the man as a cold-eyed questioner, with the power to cast me into gaol and worse. For his part, Talbot seemed easy enough, almost genial and expansive. As we travelled or stopped and ate, it was my turn to ask questions. (I've condensed the conversations we had for the sake of easy reading here.) I was naturally curious about the chain of circumstance, the thread of suspicion, which had led him from Southwark to Miching.

"How did you know?" I repeated. "What made you suspect Edmund Jute?"

"He was too hot for justice."

"He was a lawyer."

"That was what made me suspicious."

"I thought that justice was the supreme good," I said, remembering how Talbot had always insisted on it.

"So it is. But Jute was eager, over-eager, to have you hunted down for the sake of justice. And that made me to turn the matter upside down, and to ask myself whether he wasn't really more interested in hunting you down than in the justice."

"To make sure that I was finally silenced for *his* crimes."

"When Jute came to see me," said Talbot, "bearing a letter

from his mother which said that Nicholas Revill had turned up unexpectedly in Miching, I asked myself why he was so concerned with an escaped felon."

"I was a murderer. Perhaps he was worried about his mother's safety."

"If he was he didn't mention it. In any case Gertrude Agate said that you were just passing through. And so Jute was insistent that we should boot and saddle up immediately before you could get away. But I delayed, and set myself a question or two to answer."

"Do you often ask yourself questions, Master Talbot?"

"If I do, I'm at least sure of an honest answer. Or at least, honest uncertainty. Sometimes the right question will take you a long way. For instance, when your friend Peter Agate died I asked myself what should always be the first question in such cases."

I said nothing. Talbot was enjoying this, in his legalistic fashion. Let him have his hour or two in the sun.

"It was, who benefited from his death? Now, it was plain that you didn't benefit from it. In fact, it was plain that your friend was so newly arrived in London that his death was more likely to be connected with where he'd come *from* rather than where he'd arrived *at*. You said yourself, Nicholas, that he was an inoffensive fellow, one without enemies. So who would want to kill him?"

"You thought that I would, for one."

"It looked as though you had, or might have done. But then you protested your innocence."

"You believed me?"

If I sounded surprised it was because I was surprised.

"I didn't *disbelieve* you," said Talbot.

"I wondered why you made no move against me. I was expecting to be arrested at any moment."

"You didn't seem guilty. One gets a nose for guilt after a time, although it's not an infallible nose. The problem was that murder seemed to be dogging your heels, Nicholas.

There was the death of Richard Milford, and just before that your interest in his wife and all that talk of a dead man – "

"I'm not interested in Lucy Milford."

Talbot looked at me.

"Oh yes, all right, I am."

"Be careful, Nicholas, I may know more than you think. I saw you talking together after the play."

"So you *were* at the performance of *Troilus and Cressida*. In Middle Temple?"

"Yes. I enjoyed the play, to an extent."

"You didn't mention that you were there when you were questioning me about it."

"It wasn't material, to use your expression."

"I thought you didn't approve of plays – or players."

"I don't as a rule," said Talbot. "But this was a little different. A dry piece. It wouldn't appeal to the public. Too intelligent for them."

"Don't underestimate the public," I said, thinking that William Shakespeare would have been proud of me for such a liberal sentiment. "Even so, with this Trojan play, I rather think the shareholders are of your opinion."

"I defer to you in the question of plays and public taste, Nicholas. Just as you must defer to me when it comes to crime and punishment."

"I do," I said, feeling rebuked. I could not be comfortable in this man's company, for all that he had helped to save me.

"Then, after Richard Milford's death," Talbot continued, "there was the murder of the woman in the brothel. That was when things began to look really bleak for you. You were intimately linked to Nell of Holland's Leaguer, you were in the stew moments after she died. You were almost begging to be arrested, tried and hanged."

"I thought . . . "

"Yes?"

"Nothing."

I stopped myself from saying that at one stage recently I'd

thought that *he*, Alan Talbot, was the murderer of Nell. Instead I reverted to something he'd mentioned earlier.

"Hers wasn't a – a death which benefited me though, was it? To go back to your question. Who benefits?"

"Ah," said Talbot in his legalistic, hair-splitting way, "I didn't say that that was the *only* question, merely that it was the *first* question. True, you wouldn't have benefited from your friend Nell's death, you wouldn't have gained advantage from it – but it might have satisfied your jealousy – or someone else's jealousy – or their anger – or their pride – "

" – or their need for advancement," I added, thinking of the fragment of dialogue I'd overheard between Edmund Jute and his mother, about the murder of Nell. That she had had to be discarded because of her ambitions and Jute's sense of his place. 'She was beginning to have ideas that she *would* do,' Jute had said, and my gut tightened at the memory.

"You see," said Talbot, "there are plenty of motives for murder. But it never hurts to begin with the most obvious one. Who benefits? So after the first murder, after Peter Agate's death, I set myself to find out a little about him. I discovered that he came from a distinguished old family, which probably wouldn't have been happy with the idea of his going on stage – "

"They weren't."

"That he was the only male child in a family of girls. That he came from a large estate just outside your own village."

"You didn't know that his father had died, though?"

"Not at the time. And 'been murdered' would be more accurate."

"Gertrude killed her husband?"

"Yes, even though it will never be known for certain. But a letter was discovered in Jute's lodgings which – hinted at that possibility. She was too cautious to commit herself outright to paper."

"You searched his lodgings?"

"I had them searched, after he had come to see me with his

mother's letter, and while I was delaying and asking myself questions. He roused my suspicions, as I've said. There were other letters from her besides the one reporting your arrival in Miching. They corresponded frequently. Among them was one describing the manner of old Anthony Agate's death. She had underlined the words 'rabbit stew'. Twice."

"Perhaps she was sending him a recipe."

"Only if the rabbit had been fed belladonna first."

I must have looked baffled because Talbot explained.

"The nightshade isn't only deadly on its own account. If you eat a bird or a rabbit which has eaten one of the berries, then you may be just as easily poisoned. I understand that Anthony Agate was making a slow recovery from a fever. His daughter Anne tells me that the last things he ate were rabbit stew and a few grapes. After that he suffered a relapse."

"She poisoned him for his estate."

"Or if it wasn't done that way with the rabbit stew, then it was done another way. I doubt that the fever was genuine. Anne Agate said that her father was always as strong as a horse. Yes, she poisoned him for the sake of the estate, or for the sake of her son."

"Much good it did her. But there was another son who would have inherited. I mean, Peter Agate."

"And who'd disappeared," said Talbot. "To make his fortune as a player, although no one knew that."

"What if he had returned to Miching? To claim his inheritance."

"No doubt she would have dealt with him in the same way that she dealt with Anthony Agate. But she didn't have to. Because Edmund took over now."

"When Peter arrived in London and got to know my Company and so got introduced to the law students at Middle Temple . . . "

"Yes. By pure chance. And Edmund Jute saw his opportunity. Here was the heir to Quint House and all its lands, fallen into his lap. All he had to do was to ensure that young Agate never returned home."

"I rather think I might have prompted Jute to make his move," I said. "I told him that Peter was thinking of going back to Miching. My friend was not altogether, ah, happy in London. He thought of it as a place which brought out his worser self. I am sorry for it."

"Sorry for London?"

"Sorry that I should have given Jute his cue to act."

"Do not reproach yourself, Nicholas. Jute was a man who had murder in his blood. Think of his mother. He must have imbibed it with her milk. He would have done it, with or without your prompting. After the first occasion, he enjoyed killing. I have met the type before."

I'd already told Talbot of that chilling exchange between mother and son, of how he'd acquired a taste for 'it'. Now I said, "And that is why he went on to murder Richard – and Nell?"

"There your guess is as good as mine. It may have been that he was covering his tracks."

"By committing even more murders?"

"The best place to hide a fallen leaf is on the forest floor," said Talbot in riddling mode. "I mean, that if he wanted to cover up the motive for killing Peter Agate then an opportune way to do it was to kill others, and confuse the issue. That you would be blamed for it was an unexpected blessing."

"Blessing!"

I almost choked on my drink.

"Any motive might have done," pursued Talbot. "For example, there was some altercation between the law students and Richard Milford after the play in Middle Temple. I noticed that myself. Perhaps Jute was so swollen with arrogance that he determined to pay the playwright back there and then. Or rather, somewhere else and a little later."

"And with my friend Nell," I said, "I think it was the belief that he was better than her and that he did not want her company when he became a gentleman with a fine house and lands. He had been visiting her for some time, I believe. And she must have got ideas from things that he said or promised . . . For she had – she had ambitions, you know, and was not content to be a whore all her life – and she was – "

Here I embarrassed myself by breaking down into tears. We were in the inn-chamber of the Night Owl, sitting side by side on a settle. I turned my head aside from Master Talbot and stuck my face into my tankard, not wishing him to see my grief, while he, like a true English gentleman, pretended that there was nothing wrong with me.

" – she was a thousand times better than him," I finally got out through clenched teeth.

Our journey to London was nearly over. It took four days and, by the end of it, I could hardly walk. Still, the hard ride, in the teeth of the worsening weather, and the discomfort of keeping my place in the saddle as well as keeping up with Alan Talbot, helped to steer my mind away from the dire events of the autumn.

As we rode Talbot revealed other things. While he and Edmund Jute had been riding down to Miching together, on their hired horses, the young man had let things slip, perhaps more things than he was aware of. Talbot finished the journey convinced he was keeping company with a murderer. It was a family concern too, handed down through the generations. Talbot believed that Gertrude Agate had done away with her first two husbands – one Thomas Jute of Sutton Valence and one Randolph Potts of Peckham – respectively, some thirteen and six years previously. There had been a similar history of a prolonged fever and an apparent recovery, followed by a rabbit pie and an abrupt demise.

I vowed never to eat rabbit pie again. And a thought occurred to me (though I didn't pass it on to Talbot). It was what Edmund Jute had said to his mother after she'd drunk the poisoned wine: "*You taught me the way when you poisoned the old man. That was the beginning.*" I'd assumed he was referring to Anthony Agate, his stepfather. But it might have been his natural father, Thomas Jute, that he meant. Perhaps killing his mother was a cold, delayed revenge for her killing of his father, if that was something that concerned him. Or perhaps it was simply that he was impatient to come into possession of Quint House, and had set himself to finish off Gertrude almost as soon as he'd arrived in Miching, assuming in his arrogance that I was taken care of, as good as dead, and that his mother's sudden departure could be passed off as a sudden fit. Or perhaps it was, even more simply, that he had acquired a taste for killing and could not be weaned from it. Whatever the reason, we would never know now. They were all gone from us now into oblivion.

Talbot also thought that Jute had instructed his mother to keep me in Miching as long as possible, or at least until the coroner should arrive and I could be apprehended. That would explain Gertrude Agate's amorousness on the afternoon before her death. I remembered the pear juice dribbling down her chin, the warm hand on my thigh, the questions about where I was going. Equally, Mrs Agate could have been serving her own appetites here. A young man, almost any man in fact, was to her like a hare to a hound. She couldn't help herself.

Talbot and I parted in Southwark. We arrived on a late afternoon in early December. I signed a formal deposition in his chambers in Long Southwark to the effect that Edmund Jute had died as a result of wounds which were self-inflicted. That wicked young man had killed himself in a fit of remorse after he was surprised in the act of poisoning his mother. He had also confessed to the murders of three other people, two of them from the borough of Southwark and one from over the water in Thames Street. The charges which had resulted in my being clapped up in the Counter prison were annulled. I was a free man again. There was a strange mixture of truth and untruth in this version of events. But Talbot was insistent on it. It seemed to serve some higher notion of justice and truth – and who is to say that he was wrong?

I returned, unutterably weary and saddle-sore, to Dead Man's Place. Samuel Benwell had not found anyone to take my place. I don't think he'd been looking for another tenant. I wasn't surprised. Who'd take a hole of a room like mine? And the landlord didn't seem surprised to see me. He didn't even mention murders, or anything like that.

"Been touring, Nicholas?"

"Something like that, Master Benwell. Can I have my old room back?"

"Are you still with the Chamberlain's?"

"Yes," I said, although the truth was that I didn't know.

"Any titbits?"

"There is a great scandal in the offing."

He licked his thin lips.

"But I am tired now. I'll tell you tomorrow – or the next day – or the one after . . . "

Muttering, I plodded up the stairs and opened my door and threw myself on my low bed. The room wasn't much – it was hardly anything – but it was home.

At the end of a story there's a certain satisfaction in settling the characters into their appointed stations. It must be rather like the satisfaction which the tire-man Bartholomew Ridd feels when all his costumes come back at the end of a play, and are put away, neat and folded in their resting places. So it is with some of the remaining figures in this story.

I can't speak for the spirit in which Coroner Talbot quit the village of Miching but I was heartily glad to see the back of my birthplace, and hoped never to have to return to it. Two people had died there, violently and within minutes of each other. I had escaped murder by a hair's-breadth. It was as if that old rascal death, angry that the occupants of Quint House had been spared the pestilence, was determined that they should nonetheless suffer extensively. In this case, though, you could not say that the son and mother should have been spared. If anyone ever deserved to die . . .

My feelings – and, I think, Alan Talbot's – were chiefly for the three Agate sisters, Anne, Margaret and Katie. They had witnessed their mother's and father's deaths within little more than a year, and lost a loved brother. Now those murderous intruders into the family, Gertrude and Edmund Jute, had perished on their doorstep. They couldn't be expected to feel grief for the pair but they did feel the shock, the horror of what had occurred.

It took several days to deal with the aftermath of the event. Talbot's authority did not, of course, extend to the wilds of Somerset but he still carried weight – both in his office and his person – with the local coroner (who had to come from Wells, some miles distant). The two men were closeted together for a long time. No doubt Talbot described his investigations into the murder of Peter Agate, as well as his suspicions about the death of Anthony Agate and Gertrude Jute's first husbands. I was called on to add my twopenny-worth. Talbot had already questioned me about what had happened and we had agreed a version of events. I couldn't help reflecting that this was the *third* occasion on which he'd interrogated me about a violent death. This time, however, as I've said, he was determined to exonerate me of any blame.

Mother and son were buried without much ceremony on the north side of Miching churchyard. The parson Ralph Verney, good Christian that he was, prayed for the repose of their immortal souls. I don't think he knew – or perhaps he didn't choose to know – the full wickedness of the pair.

The full extent of it was kept from the Agate sisters too. They were consoled by me, to a degree, but much more by Ralph Verney. Mrs Hobbs, clucking, maternal Mrs Hobbs, suggested that the young sisters should move into the parsonage for a time – "Chill look a'ter the poor volk, poor parentless volk" – but Anne Agate, who was now the head of the family, said that none of them were going to shift out of the house where they'd been born. Even so they were without a protector, and there was an estate to superintend.

The parson was a constant visitor at Quint House. He was a true Christian in his devotion to all his parishioners, prosperous and poor. Although he and Anne Agate were soon betrothed, I don't believe that he planned this at the outset. But a parson needs a wife. Anne was guileless too, I think, and did not aim to ensnare Ralph Verney. But it's also the case that a young, single parson in a parish is like a mark for all the young ladies (and often their mothers) to aim at.

This happened some time afterwards of course – but not too long afterwards. Ralph wrote to me with news of the betrothal, and I was glad to know that some good had come out of the terrible events which had unfolded at Quint House.

My return to the Chamberlain's and the Globe was oddly like my return to Dead Man's Place. It was as if I'd never been away.

Dick Burbage said, "Out of prison, Nicholas?"

"It was all a mistake," I said. "Someone else committed all those murders."

"We knew that," he said. "You're not the first person to be locked up for something you haven't done."

"Not just locked up," I said, feeling that he wasn't taking this seriously enough.

"What then?"

"I might have hanged."

"You wouldn't be the first innocent on the gallows either."

This was a bit more robust than I cared for.

We were standing in the tire-room. A performance was in the offing, although not (alas) as far as I was concerned. Fortunately at this point WS came up and greeted me more warmly than Burbage had done. I remembered that he had also sent me greetings, via Jack Wilson, when I was in the Counter prison.

"What news?" I said.

"Our patron is no better and the Queen is no worse," said WS.

"I meant in our fortunes."

"People need diversion in these gloomy times," said WS. "We've had a good few weeks, in your absence."

"But not on account of my absence, I hope," I said.

"We have a new man," said Burbage.

And my heart sank. You keep your place in a company of players by keeping your place. If you falter or give way, then everyone behind you sweeps past, trampling you underfoot in the process. All the good deeds you've done in the past don't count for much. They are alms for oblivion (as WS says in *Troilus and Cressida*).

"A new man," pursued Burbage. "I would say that he is very dextrous, wouldn't you, William? Very able . . . "

A grin passed between Burbage and Shakespeare, and I felt more uncomfortable still. One man more meant one space less. I was unwilling to broach the subject of my future directly, though, for fear I might be told that my services were no longer required.

"Seeing that he was a friend of yours, Nick, you'll be pleased to know that we have decided to put on Richard Milford's last thing," said WS now.

"*The World's Diseas'd*?"

"It is our tribute to a dead author," said WS.

"More to the point," said Burbage, "the tragic violence of Milford's death has aroused a certain, ahm, interest in our congregation."

'Congregation' was Burbage's individual way of referring to our audiences at the Globe.

"Good for business," said WS.

"I believe," said Burbage, "that we'd have full houses for a week if we presented Milford's laundry lists. And it was very important to keep *The World's Diseas'd* out of the hands of the Admiral's. They were interested in it, you know. Henslowe never misses a trick, Henslowe and his creature

Gally. But we have an obligation to Richard Milford, he was our man."

I thought Burbage and Shakespeare were explaining themselves too much. They were ever so slightly shamefaced and I remembered the shareholders' humming and ha-ing beforehand over *The World's Diseas'd*. Well, if Richard Milford was looking down on us from the great tire-house in the sky – that place where we shall all go to put on new costumes – then he would have been gratified to see two rival theatre companies fighting to present his last work.

"Gentlemen," I said, "there's something you should know in relation to *The World's Diseas'd*."

The two shareholders looked politely attentive.

"It contains much violence – and incest."

"Oh Nicholas, we know," said Burbage. "Is this meat too strong for your stomach?"

"I could tell you a darker tale and a true one too," I said. "But that's not what I wanted to say. You may know that Richard Milford picked up a couple of patrons recently. A brother and a sister. Rustic but nobs, you might say. Or you might say, nobs but rustic. The trouble is that they could have served as models for the incestuous brother and sister in the play."

WS and Burbage again exchanged glances.

"You mean Lord Venner and his sister?" said WS.

I nodded.

"In fact, I think they have already recognized themselves and taken drastic steps to ensure that the play would never see the light of day."

I'd hoped that Burbage and WS wouldn't press me to give details. I knew now, of course, that Robert and Vinnie Venner were not guilty of Milford's murder. Nevertheless, they might have been sufficiently incensed by their 'portraits' in *The World's Diseas'd* to have set fire to Nicholson's bookshop. I didn't want them throwing a bucket of coals on to the playhouse thatch.

The seniors looked baffled and in the end I had to explain matters, to reveal my suspicions to them. To tell how I'd witnessed the literary conflagration in Paul's Yard, and come to the conclusion that it had been started deliberately. (I said nothing about the runaway cart which had almost killed me on the quayside, having come to the conclusion that it was indeed an accident. One can be too suspicious, seeking out plots everywhere.)

"Oh no," said WS, trying hard to keep a smile off his face.

"No?"

I was glad – in an irritated sort of way – that he was finding everything so amusing.

"That fire wasn't deliberate. I have dealings with Nicholson. I know him quite well. He is a man of infinite amiability. But very careless, over debts and so on. And very careless with his pipe too. He's inclined to put it down all smouldering, on the nearest item to hand. He told me that that was how the fire started, with him laying his pipe down on a pile of paper."

"Well," I said, slightly deflated. "But it doesn't affect my main point, about *The World's Diseas'd.* That the brother and sister may think that they have been slanderously traduced in it."

"We were aware of that and I have already taken it into account," said WS with an odd formality.

Now it was my turn to wait for an explanation.

"What William means," said Dick Burbage, "is that one of the reasons we hesitated over *The World's Diseas'd* was precisely because of the way Richard Milford might – only *might*, I say – have represented his patrons in a less than flattering light."

So much for my belief that I'd been the only one to detect this!

"But now of course there is this tremendous demand for Richard's work, and it is our duty to meet that demand."

"So I have made some small changes in *The World's Diseas'd*," said William Shakespeare. "Turned the incestuous brother and sister into mother and son, for example. Small changes, mere nothings. Now no one can think that Richard ever intended to slander his patrons."

"But the play was also being printed," I said. "By Master Nicholson."

"Alas, the whole printed stock was destroyed in the fire," said WS. "All that remained for me to work from was the foul paper copy."

Well, if Richard Milford was still listening to our conversation from the great tiring-house in the sky, he mightn't be so gratified now. To have his words tampered with by Master Shakespeare, of whom he had no very high opinion. Anyway, gratified or not, he was out of it now. *The World's Diseas'd* would be performed posthumously, and the public would flock to see it because of the violent circumstances in which its author had died. In fact, the manner of Richard's death wouldn't have been out of place in one of his own plays. Perhaps he should have stuck to comedy.

"What?" I said.

Lost in my own reflections, I hadn't heard what WS was saying.

"I was saying," said WS, "that we'd like you to take the part of Vindice, the revenger."

"In *The World's Diseas'd*?"

"Well yes. If the violence and incest aren't too much for your delicate spirit, Nicholas."

"I am a player, gentlemen," I said. "I will speak the lines as they are written, speak them to the best of my ability."

WS clapped me on the shoulder, and my heart overflowed to know that I still had a place, that I was restored to the Chamberlain's and scheduled to play a leading part in a piece by my late friend Richard Milford. Any doubts I'd had about *The World's Diseas'd* disappeared. It was unquestionably the author's posthumous masterpiece.

My heart lifted further to hear what Dick Burbage said when he called over to someone who'd just come into the tire-house.

"Hey, new man, come and met one of our old stagers."

Revill: the old stager!

And then my heart – or guts – did a little dip to see who it was coming towards us.

"We termed him dextrous," said WS, "dextrous and able. Well, able by nature, Abel by name."

There in front of me stood the individual whom I'd encountered on the road west. The counterfeit crank who'd tumbled down with an attack of the falling-sickness. The man who'd proudly informed me that he'd once made a great deal of money near Reading. I recognized the tapering nose and lofty forehead underneath his face paint. He was no longer smeared with bloody marks or stuffing his mouth with soap, but was about to go on stage dressed as a clown or zany. That fitted, I suppose.

Abel Glaze started slightly to see me. Then, collecting himself, he did that queer, half-ironic little bow which I remembered from the road. Dick Burbage introduced us, once again referring to me as an old stager (which was naturally very pleasing).

I noticed WS looking at us curiously.

"You've already met, you gentlemen?"

Very quickly, before I could think of an answer, Glaze said, "Master Revill reminds me strongly of a friend I once had."

"Oh yes?" I said, wondering if he was going to give me away. If he did I might just hint at one or two things I knew about *him*.

"William Topcourt by name. You're as alike as two pictures. Do you know him?"

"The name's familiar," I said. "Well, every man has his double, they say. How did you come to join our Company?"

"I met a man on the road, Master Revill. He told me that the Chamberlain's Company was the finest company in the land. So I determined to come to London and join them."

"He spoke no more than the truth, that man on the road," I said.

"I owe him something," said Glaze.

"No more than twopence," I said to the bafflement of Burbage and Shakespeare.

Mention of William Topcourt reminded me that I hadn't returned his coat to him. I was aware that he was no longer confined in the Counter. The imposture whereby I'd been released from gaol in 'error' for the much-married man had become known to Coroner Talbot. He'd mentioned it to me on the journey up from Somerset. Mentioned it by-the-by. To my surprise he had not been angry at the prison exchange, even though his authority had been flouted, since by the time he discovered it he'd almost concluded that I was not responsible for the Southwark murders. I was relieved too. If my sleep was disturbed by many things, at least it was not disturbed by the appalling thought that an innocent man had gone to the gallows in my stead.

I eventually tracked Topcourt down to lodgings in a winding lane near St George's church. My friend Jack Wilson had befriended Topcourt and knew where he lived, although he was under strict instructions not to reveal that gentleman's whereabouts to his several wives. I was admitted by a slatternly landlady, who visibly brightened when I said who I was looking for. Topcourt's room was inferior even to mine in Dead Man's Place, but he had to lodge somewhere and – as he pointed out – he could no longer afford what it cost to stay in the prison. It was cheaper to live in freedom.

He was grateful for the coat, although it was no more than he was entitled to. I had done my best to clean it, for it had been extensively bloodied after my fatal tussle with Edmund Jute, to say nothing of all the marks and stains of travel. Topcourt didn't hold it against me that he had exchanged places in prison with a supposed murderer rather than a debtor. Indeed, I'm not sure that he ever discovered precisely what I was alleged to have done. I enquired after Topcourt's marital status, thinking to hear that he was still living in fear of his three wives. He was still in fear of them, he told me, and then he announced, with a shake of his long head, that he was due to marry again soon. The prospect didn't seem to cheer him. But temptation was everywhere and his demon was hard at work. When I enquired who the lucky woman was, he gestured in a downstairs direction and said that it was his landlady.

"She think I'm a good match," he said gloomily. "She doesn't know the half of it."

Well, at least he got his coat back.

Of course I also visited Lucy Milford, Richard's widow. She was still living in Thames Street in the apartment she'd shared with her husband. With the Chamberlain's presentation of *The World's Diseas'd* in prospect, his posthumous fame seemed likely to be larger and more profitable than his living reputation.

"So you are playing Vindice?" she said.

She had by now overcome her shyness with me and was able to look me in the face, and more besides. She was wearing mourning, which became her.

"Yes. They have given me Vindice."

"The avenger."

"A strong part. I murder my mother, for example."

This was one of the changes which Shakespeare had introduced into the play, diverting the stream of incest so that it flowed in a different direction. Now the character of Virginia was mother to Vindice while Sostituta became his . . . oh, who cares? It would be tedious to recount all the little alterations which WS had introduced into the plot of *The World's Diseas'd*, tedious and pointless because I doubt you'll ever hear of this play again. But Shakespeare's changes had improved the play, in my opinion. Even so, *The World's Diseas'd* would go down to posterity – in the unlikely event that it went down at all – as the work of Richard Milford, and perhaps WS was happier that way.

I didn't have to point out to Lucy Milford how uncomfortably close art had come to life, as a result of these little changes in the play. For what had Edmund Jute done after all but poison his mother and then stand coldly by to watch her in her death throes. Whether Edmund Jute and Gertrude had also been amorously – and unnaturally – atttracted to each other, I didn't know and didn't want to find out. The advantage was that mother and son were both dead and, unlike the living Venners, were in no position to find fault with the play.

I outlined what had happened in Miching and at Quint House to Lucy Milford, since she was more than entitled to know the identity of her husband's murderer and to be assured that justice, of a sort, had been done. I didn't go into too much detail. She was a sensitive woman, readily given to seeing horror in her mind's eye.

But there was one thing I had to discover, if I could. It was what Richard Milford had said to Edmund Jute after the *Troilus and Cressida* performance. I recalled how that murderous man, with some of his fellow students, had been ogling Vinnie Venner's tits in a mocking rather than a lascivious way, and how Milford had shooed them off with a few choice words. If that comment had been sufficient to prompt Jute to stab the playwright then they must have been harsh words indeed.

I asked Lucy Milford whether she'd overheard her husband's rebuke to the students, but she hadn't.

"Except," she said, "he made some reference to nasty little boys when we were returning home. Or it was silly little students. He said he'd told them that they were all nasty boys."

This hardly seemed enough to provoke one man to stab another. But then, I reflected, the slightest insult may cause a man to pick up his knife, especially when that man's senses are inflamed by drink. Kit Marlowe had been stabbed through the eye during a quarrel in a tavern, and died straightaway. What one man can laugh off, another takes to heart. There was besides, in Jute's case, his newly acquired 'taste' for killing. He'd discovered how easy it was to perform with Peter Agate, and how easy to shift the blame as well. Now he moved on to rid himself of an irritating playwright who'd called him a nasty little boy. And after that he turned his attention to a troublesome whore who had deluded herself into the belief that he might rescue her from Holland's Leaguer.

"How did you know that it wasn't me?" I said to Lucy. "When you got me out of gaol, you said that, whoever it was that had killed Richard, you knew it wasn't me."

"I do not know how I knew," said the widow. "It was a certainty, but I don't know where that certainty came from. No more than I know where that vision of a bleeding man came from. It was Richard, but it was not him too."

I recalled the shudder she'd given in the Middle Temple hall, the wide-eyed stare over my shoulder.

"You have the gift too," she said.

"Gift?"

"Of seeing things."

I thought of all my speculations in these Southwark murders, of how I'd blamed in my mind first one person then another, from harmless old Chesser to the less harmless Tom Gally, from the rustic Venners to Coroner Talbot. Just about everybody, in short, except the person who'd actually committed the crimes. I thought too of how I had woven plots involving these individuals, and had also turned accidents – runaway carts, blazing shops – into malicious acts. Far from seeing into the future, as Lucy Milford perhaps could in some sense, I wasn't even able to understand what was happening around me in the present.

"No, I don't see things," I said. "In this whole business I have seen almost nothing right. I have not got the gift."

But if I didn't have the gift of second sight – more of a curse than a blessing, in my view – I had other things.

I had my freedom.

I had my place in the Chamberlain's Company once again.

And I had some comforts too.

For, as the end of this dire year of 1602 approached, I found myself consoling and being consoled by a soft-voiced woman.

You see, I cheered a dead man's widow. All in the interest of a happy ending, you understand.